INDEPENDENCE

a novel

Ryan Allen

Cover design and artwork by Lee Guile

This is a work of fiction. The characters, names, incidents, places, and dialogues are products of the author's imagination, and are not to be construed as real. The story takes place in the future, for crying out loud.

First printing: November 2014

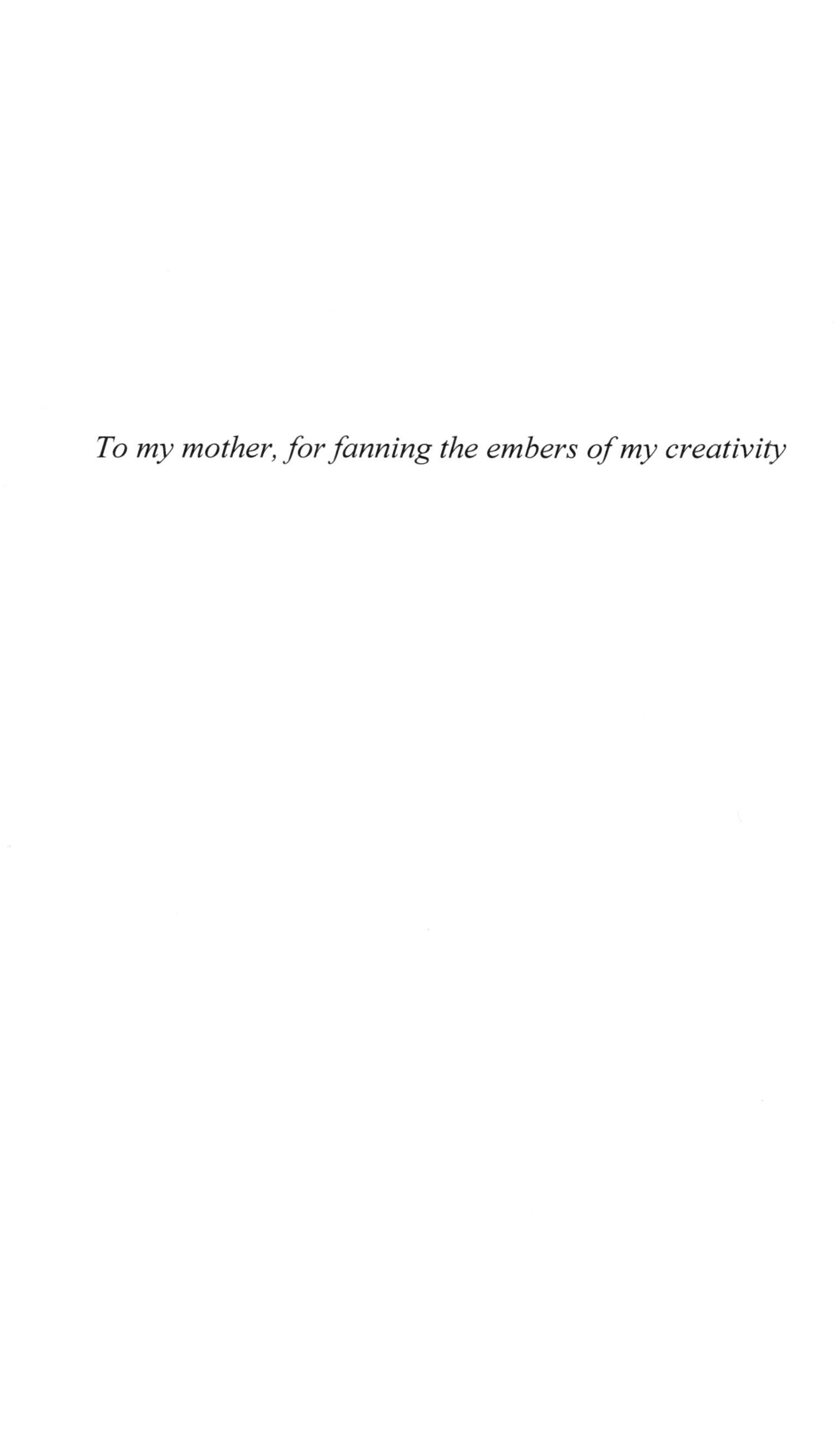

To my mother, for fanning the embers of my creativity

Chapter 1

The intermittent dripping of an unknown liquid onto the concrete floor might just as easily have been a bass drum beating in Adam Winter's ear. His right eye twitched, opened a sliver and then closed shut. The room was filled with intense, unnaturally brilliant light. He moved his tongue against the back of his front teeth and pursed his lips together. His mouth felt like a leather pouch with an oversized prune inside of it. The taste of bile he detected turned his stomach. He made an effort to groan, but only a wheeze was audible.

Keeping his eyes shut tightly, Adam peeled his cheek off of the cold concrete and pushed himself from a prone position up onto an elbow. Every part of his body ached as if he had just run a marathon and then immediately jumped into a stone tumbler. It took thirty seconds for him to build up the courage to try and move to a sitting position. Once there, however, he was sorry he had. The throbbing in his head matched his racing heart beat for beat. He reached his hand to his forehead to try and massage away the pounding. As he did, he detected something warm and sticky on his fingers. His fingers went higher, through matted hair, until they reached the source of the blood. The hair over several inches of his scalp was shaved off and stitches ran like a zipper through the center of the area. He pressed his fingers down lightly and felt the skin give way. It felt like a small piece of his skull was missing and his scalp had been stretched together and sewn over the top of the void.

Still conscious of the bright light, Adam grabbed the collar of his black t-shirt, pulled it over his face and forced one eye open a sliver. The light was still nearly blinding, but he could make out a few shapes. There was an overturned metal folding chair a few feet from where he sat. Beyond the chair there was a sofa and an end table with a lamp on it. The lamp seemed to be the source of the overpowering light. He thought it odd that such a small, ordinary-looking lamp could emit such a brilliant glow. Turning his head away from the light, he crawled to the end table and found the switch on the lamp's base and turned it off. Slowly, he lowered the shirt from his face and opened his eyes. He surveyed the room. It appeared to be an apartment. The furnishings were meager, but there was a kitchen with a small table and two chairs.

Strangely, he noticed he could still make out all of the objects in the apartment, though the single window in the room was dark. Though mostly void of color, aside from a slightly green tint, objects in the room appeared with incredible clarity and depth. He began to notice that the apartment was alive with a variety of sounds as well—the hum of something mechanical, a scratching noise and the dripping he had noticed when he first woke up.

For several minutes, Adam strained to recall the events that had brought him to this place, but his memories seemed abstract and fuzzy. A small steel tray lay upside down on the floor. Various surgical instruments littered the vicinity. An IV bag secured by gray duct tape dangled from a coat rack. The hose had been ripped from the bottom and what little fluid remained was dripping onto the floor.

Adam seemed to recall a meeting with someone and some sort of conflict arising from the meeting. Images of faces with surgical masks looking down at him flashed through his mind.

The hum of an engine and tires moving over a littered street in the distance brought Adam out of his thoughts. For about sixty seconds, he listened to the vehicle drawing nearer and nearer until it sounded like it should be right on top of him.

He heard three vehicle doors open and then slam shut. He counted eight pairs of boots outside on the pavement moving at a steady pace, growing louder and louder. Suddenly, the front door burst open. Simultaneously, the thunderous crash of the door slamming into the interior wall, the angry voices shouting orders and the incredibly bright beams from several flashlights hit Adam like a train. He threw his hands over his ears and shut his eyes tight as he retreated to the floor. Something sharp pierced the side of his neck, and the muscles throughout his body almost instantly relaxed. The chaotic noise faded, and everything went dark.

Chapter 2

Adam slowly willed his eyelids open. The windowless box he was in was void of a light source, but he could clearly see the walls around him. They were bare, with just a single metal door directly in front of him. The floor where he sat seemed unusually cold. He glanced down at himself and saw that he was naked aside from a pair of briefs, which did not look familiar to him. His wrists and ankles were cuffed and chained together.

He took a quick inventory of the various ailments he remembered having previously. His headache seemed to have subsided, and the soreness throughout his body that he had felt earlier was also gone. He reached up and checked the stitches in his scalp. The skin had grown tight around them, and there was no pain. Altogether, Adam actually felt quite strong, despite being slightly groggy.

From somewhere beyond the room where Adam was being held, he heard a heavy door open and shut. Three sets of footsteps began clicking and clapping down what sounded like a long hallway. A pair of women's heels, a pair of men's dress shoes and a pair of rubber-soled boots, Adam guessed.

"Why is he alive?" Adam heard a deep voice demand.

"He didn't run. He was captured in the apartment," a hoarse male voice answered.

"I believe he may be a Trident, sir," a female voice added.

"What makes you think that, Scion?" the deep-voiced man asked.

"Sir, there've been rumors of a Trident who was to meet with a Rugby cell of The Response," the male voice responded for the female. “Our intelligence led us to the apartment where the man was extracted. As you are aware, the six Responders who fled were each gunned down within a two kilometer radius of the apartment.”

“You didn’t answer my question, Scion,” the deep voice grumbled.

“Well, sir, in addition to the intelligence we received, we have been unable to identify him. His biological signature is not in the Central,” the female replied.

“I’m sure it’s in the Central, Marshal. Your people should have run it again before bringing me all the way here.”

“Sir, you wouldn’t have been notified unless we were positive. We received clearance to run his biological sample through multiple historical layers in the Central, and each came up negative for ID,” the hoarse voice rebutted.

By this time, the voices and footsteps sounded as clear to Adam as if they were right there inside the cell with him.

“Has anyone asked him?” inquired the man the others kept referring to as “sir.” “Has this traitor been interrogated?”

“No, sir,” the female replied. “Our attempts to bring him to full consciousness were unsuccessful.”

“All right, let’s see if we can rouse him and have a little visit. Open it.”

Adam anticipated that light would flood into the cell once the door opened, so he closed his eyes tightly. He heard a number of electronic beeps as the security devices were disarmed.

The door slid open, and the three sets of footsteps entered the cell. “Looks like he’s come around,” the hoarse-voiced man observed.

Adam covered his ears with his hands and whispered. “Could you please keep your voices down?”

“What was that?” asked the deep voice.

"If you wouldn't mind, I would appreciate it if you could whisper," Adam requested in a barely audible voice. "My ears are just a little sensitive today."

"I am Senator Jaxon of the Social Order of Unions Great Plains Dominion. You are in government custody," the deep-voiced man declared—his voice still at full strength. "Identify yourself."

"That wasn't a whisper," Adam muttered as he increased the pressure of his hands over his ears.

Multiple scents seemed to attack Adam's nostrils all at once. There was a hint of underarm odor and someone's fishy breath. Mingled with these were some pleasant smells as well. He detected lady's deodorant, some sort of lotion or perfume and minty toothpaste.

"Let's get right to it, shall we? Who are you working for?" the Senator inquired, only lowering his voice slightly.

"Well, Senator Jaxon, I wasn't really working at all," Adam whispered. "I was just sitting here alone in the dark wondering why no one had come to visit. And now, here you are. I consider it a real treat. I'm just sorry I don't have anything to offer you in the way of a drink or a place to sit. Frankly, I'm a little embarrassed."

"I prefer it if a man looks me in the eye when he speaks to me," the Senator informed his prisoner, apparently annoyed that Adam's eyes were still shut tight.

"I absolutely agree and would be more than willing to lock eyes with you, Senator Jaxon, but the light from the hall is a little too bright for my comfort. Perhaps you could adjust the dimmer switch. Is there a dimmer switch out there? Why don't you all come in closer and shut the door behind you?"

"Our friend here seems to be a little hung over, Marshal. Might he borrow your glasses for a few minutes while we talk?" Senator Jaxon asked.

The other man stepped forward and placed a pair of tinted glasses over Adam's eyes. Adam inhaled and decided he could safely pin the B.O. smell on this man. He assumed the Senator was the oyster bar patron.

"Actually, liquor isn't the culprit today, sir," Adam explained as he cracked one eye open. "I don't partake."

The intensity of the light seemed to lessen as Adam focused on a single object at a time. He zeroed in on the pair of expensive-looking black leather shoes on the ground in front of him. Slowly, he raised his head, trying to focus on one object at a time; first, a belt buckle, then a tie, then a nose. The Senator was a tall man in his fifties, Adam guessed, based on the deep lines in his forehead and under his eyes. His hair was salt and pepper with the salt overpowering the pepper above his ears. Adam's eyes moved to the right and focused on the trigger of the weapon the other man held and then up to the nametag on the gray and white military-style fatigues he wore—*Mar. Sinclair Marbury*. Marshal Marbury's face was hard, with a square jawline and a round nose. He was a few inches shorter than the Senator, but was athletically built. Adam focused on his eyes momentarily. They were dark and menacing and gave nothing away.

Adam's eyes moved back past the Senator to his left and focused on a silver-colored ring on the right hand ring finger of the figure standing there. The ring was polished with a large baguette-cut sapphire mounted on it. Moving up, he focused on the woman's neck for a moment. Though each pore was defined to his eyes, her skin appeared soft and young. Lavender shaded lipstick on ample, well-formed lips held his attention.

"Why were you found in an apartment known to house members of The Response?" the Senator's voice boomed, startling Adam and bringing his attention back. "Are you one of them?"

Adam ignored the question and pretended to shiver. "Do you think you could find me something warmer to wear?"

"We can make you much more comfortable after you tell us what we want to know." The Senator sounded as if he was losing patience. "You may begin by telling us your name."

Adam fixed his eyes on the Senator's. His periphery was slowly taking shape, and he was finding it more bearable to have his eyes open. "You've introduced yourself, but you haven't introduced your companions." He was still whispering, though he was beginning to notice that the painful sensitivity in his hearing was gradually improving.

"You may consider being a little more cooperative, or you're going to get to know the Marshal here much better," the Senator threatened.

"The Marshal? I'm not really sure he and I would have a lot to talk about. He was kind enough to lend me his glasses, but to be honest, he smells like he needs to hit the showers. You know what I mean?" Adam replied as the Marshall stiffened. "And who might the *Scion* be?"

"I'm Melena Jax—" the female began.

"We are not here to answer *your* questions!" Senator Jaxon interrupted. "Who told you she was the Scion?" he demanded. "Who told you she was my daughter?"

"You did," Adam responded.

Senator Jaxon took a deep breath and then exhaled. "Federal law prohibits enhanced interrogation techniques being used on private citizens."

"Well, that seems fair," Adam whispered.

"But I'm not sure you can prove that you're a citizen."

Adam looked down as if to search himself. "I can't seem to reach my wallet with these cuffs on. Ms. Jaxon, maybe you could …"

Senator Jaxon glanced over at the Marshal. Taking his cue, the Marshal moved toward Adam and raised the butt of his weapon. It appeared to Adam as if the Marshal was moving in slow motion. Adam lifted his hands and caught the stock of the weapon just as it was about to crash into the side of his head.

"Whoa, Sinclair!" Adam raised his voice for the first time. "Man, you just about smashed your own glasses."

The Marshal looked stunned by how quickly Adam had reacted.

"Marshal, wait." The Senator's daughter put her hand on his arm. "We don't really need to play this man's games, and perhaps this isn't the ideal setting for an important interview like this anyway. I think we may have something in our lab that will help loosen our friend's tongue a little." She turned to her father. "I'd like to request he be transferred there. I've been anxious to find a test subject for the new project."

Adam's eyes slowly went from the Marshal's to the young woman's as she turned her face back toward him. He locked on her eyes. They were round with long, dark lashes framing them. Strands of every shade of blue seemed to explode from the small black center. Adam was momentarily speechless, but soon found his voice. "Yeah, yeah, we can go check out your lab, you know, if that's better for you."

"Sir, will you approve this change in venue?" the young woman who had identified herself as *Melena Jax*— inquired. "I believe we'll find him much more cooperative with a little scientific assistance."

To Adam, the prospect was beginning to sound less desirable. "Actually, I probably need to get going."

Adam started to get to his feet, but Marshal Marbury grabbed him by the shoulders and shoved him back to the ground. "You will not move until ordered to do so!" he shouted, looking like he was itching to inflict some type of physical pain on his resistant prisoner.

"Calm down, Sinclair. I'm not gonna …" Adam trailed off, noticing the Senator giving his daughter a nod. She stepped forward and produced a small syringe which she proceeded to plunge into Adam's shoulder.

"Hey!" Adam objected. "Take it easy! I really take issue with people stabbing needles into me without my permission." He drew a deep breath. "If you were to politely ask me to go to your lab … well, I still probably wouldn't want to go. I'm not gonna lie to you. But it would have been more appropriate to at least have the invitation extended. Don't just assume that because you have nice skin and pretty amazing eyes that I would want to go there with you. Frankly, if you treat people you've just met like that—like, just walking up to them and sticking needles in them—I don't see your circle of friends expanding very far. I'm not telling you that to be rude, I'm just not all that impressed with you so far. That's all I'm saying."

Senator Jaxon sighed. "How long will the sedative take to shut him up?"

"It should have been instantaneous," Melena Jaxon answered, looking annoyed and slightly bewildered.

"Oh, am I supposed to be getting sleepy now? Because I'm really not," Adam lied. His body was beginning to feel heavy. "You know what I think is part of the problem with our interaction so far—I mean why it's been relatively unpleasant? Well, I think you are all really over-dressed. Now, I think this is a good idea so don't just dismiss it right off the bat. Why don't the three of you strip down to your skivvies as well and sit down here on the floor with me? I think that will level the playing field a little—improve our communication, you know?"

Adam tried to continue talking to keep from drifting off, but the sedative was starting to have the desired effect. "What do you guys have going on later? I could go for some nachos right now if you have any. I haven't seen anything I would consider—" Adam could resist the drug no more. His vision blurred and, once again, everything went dark.

Chapter 3

Adam sauntered down Main Street in the city of Rugby in what was once North Dakota. His parents had told him that Rugby had once been a very small town until the oil boom brought people to the area in droves. Within a few years, it was a thriving community and eventually became home to several million people.

Adam's mother and father were with him now. The three of them were on their way to the theatre. Rugby had become a hub for culture and the arts, and Adam and his parents were on a special outing. His brothers and sister were at home while he and his parents spent a little time together. As they approached the box office, it abruptly morphed into the entrance of a high school gymnasium. The sound of a basketball bouncing on a hardwood floor confused Adam. He looked down at himself. He was not dressed in his uniform. He panicked. The referee blew his whistle signaling the jump ball to begin the game. The game was starting and not only was Adam not on the floor, he wasn't even in his uniform! The sudden change in location and scenario triggered reality in Adam's mind. He realized he was dreaming, and as soon as he did, the dream evaporated.

"How close are we now?"

"About thirty more minutes, according to my itinerary."

Adam became aware of several female voices nearby.

"I didn't realize the lab was so far from civilization."

"Everything we're going to be working on at the lab is classified," a familiar voice explained. "Most of the staff there are chemists or pharmaceutical researchers, but they're all working on government projects. Our subject will be just the second person to undergo a new chemical therapy, designed by Dr. McArthur and Dr. Janekowski, which allows us to access memories from the subject's mind without their awareness."

"We boarded and were off before I could be briefed, so I don't have any background on this program. Tell me how the therapy works."

"Sure. A series of drugs combine to essentially transport the subject back to specific points in their memory, and they re-live them in their own mind. The drugs make them just conscious enough of their actual surroundings that they will answer questions and describe the events they are recalling." Adam recognized this as Melena Jaxon's voice. The other was not familiar.

"Were you involved in the original therapy?"

"No, but I studied under Dr. McArthur at Columbia, and we've done some virtual training. I'm proficient in the drug application part of the therapy. Actually, this is my first visit to the lab as well. Only a few of us have been given security clearance to even have knowledge of the lab's existence, so, I guess, congratulations to us." Melena remarked, smugly.

"It's obviously pretty highly classified." The unidentified woman let out a long sigh. "I bet you're going to miss your personal page, huh?"

Melena laughed. "Yeah, I can't remember being without it for more than a few hours, but communication to and from the lab is limited due to the classified nature of our work there. I was told we'll be supplied with pages, but they're police issue and are to remain at the lab. Electronic communications from the lab are transmitted with encryption through the Central so they can't be intercepted by Responders or foreign intelligence or even other government departments." Melena sounded eager to share what knowledge she had of the lab and the project.

Adam was fully conscious now, but continued to lay still with his eyes closed. He could hear two hearts beating and two sets of lungs breathing nearby. He assumed they were an armed escort. He could feel restraints on his arms, legs and head and realized he was strapped to a gurney. There wasn't much hope of escape in his current state, so he concentrated on the two female voices. The more information he could glean from their conversation, the better. He could hear wheels moving rhythmically over tracks as the vehicle they were traveling in vibrated. He concluded that it must be a train, but the ride was not as smooth as city transit.

The Federal Government had spent hundreds of billions of Euros on public transportation. The transit cars were state-of-the-art twenty years ago when they were first installed. They were filthy and full of vagrants now, but the ride was still as smooth as ever. The train Adam was now riding in was noisy and rough. He determined it must be an old Amtrak train.

"Wow. It's been a long time since I've seen real mountains. This is really beautiful," Melena observed, apparently gazing out of a window. "Honestly, I've spent so much time studying in New York and Rugby that I almost forgot what nature looked like."

Adam considered the train's destination. From Rugby, they would have to be traveling west to encounter any mountain ranges within a reasonable distance. Somewhere in the Rocky Mountains, he guessed. There was no telling how long they had been traveling. He was surprised that he would be allowed to leave the Great Plains Dominion and Senator Jaxon's jurisdiction. He worried that if this chemical therapy that Melena had described was administered to him, that it could compromise his errand and put a lot of lives in danger. He wondered if he would be able to resist the drugs or manipulate any intelligence that he may be forced to reveal. At length, he determined that he could not afford the risk. He would have to escape before submitting to the interrogation.

"Be on your toes once we stop." It was one of the guards, and he sounded much closer to Adam than Melena and her companion. "From what I've heard, this prisoner was ordered here by Senator Jaxon himself."

"I wonder why they're bringing him clear out here," the other guard remarked.

"No idea. Shouldn't be too bad for you and me, though. We just need to keep him strapped on the gurney until he's processed, then he's out of our hands. The tranquilizer will last for at least another hour, so he'll still be out when we transition him."

"You ever been to the Mountain Dominion before?"

"Yeah, as a kid. There's a place beyond Helena called Yellowstone that used to be open to the public. I went there with a school class once a long time ago. I remember there was this hole in the ground that was filled with water, and the water would get really hot, and every once in a while it would shoot straight up in the air about fifty meters."

"Really? You sure it wasn't fairy dust shooting outta the ground?"

"No, I swear! It shot steaming water straight up! It was amazing! It's untouchable now, though. This entire area is a federal park, but it was a huge tourist attraction way back. It can't be more than six or seven hundred kilometers south of here."

"Okay. Whatever you say, Old-timer."

Adam fought the urge to smile. He had a pretty good idea of where he was now. For three summers as a teenager, he had spent two weeks in the mountains of what used to be Montana and Idaho. His Boy Scout troop had traveled to the region for camping and survival training. When the United States of America was dissolved, the Social Order of Unions closed all National and State Parks to the public. Adam's unit had entered the area using cold-engine gliders to avoid government detection. Adam remembered loving the mountains. He loved the time he'd spent learning to find food and make shelter to escape the elements and just being in nature. For most young people these days, experiencing nature was merely a simulation on a gaming console.

Adam was still lost in his memories when the train began to slow. The sound of the train's wheels on the track began to echo as if in a chamber. He decided that they must have entered some sort of tunnel. After seven or eight minutes in the tunnel, the train finally came to a halt. Adam kept as still as he could. If he was going to make an escape, he needed his captors to believe he was still unconscious.

A hydraulic door hissed open and Adam could hear several voices shouting out orders to various personnel. The two guards moved to the gurney and began to push it toward the door. Adam remembered that one of the guards had mentioned that they would transition him. This would likely be his best shot to make a run.

The gurney was lifted off of the train and set down. Adam heard footsteps coming closer and picked up a familiar scent—Melena. He was beginning to feel a bit like a dog, being able to identify people this way. He felt her reach behind his neck and fasten something around it.

"All right, go ahead and move him to the elevator," Melena directed.

The guards, Melena, and her associate from the train all stepped into the elevator alongside the gurney, and Adam heard the door close. He felt a rapid descent for nearly a minute before the elevator slowed and came to a stop. When they exited the elevator, he heard a short "beep" come from whatever Melena had placed around his neck. He opened one eye just a sliver to get a glimpse of his surroundings. The lighting was not particularly bright, and he was finding the sensitivity that he had experienced before was becoming less intense. It was still uncomfortable, but he was learning to deal with it. The room was obviously a laboratory. There were hoses and wires running along the floor and desks with large monitors displaying data, graphs and the like. A number of different chemical smells mingled together reminded Adam of the odor of a hospital. There was a coffin-sized glass tank filled with what appeared to be water in the middle of the room, surrounded by wires and monitoring equipment.

Adam heard a group of footsteps coming closer. There was a slight echo, which led him to believe the group was walking down a hallway.

"Thank you, gentlemen. Our unit will take it from here," a pleasant-sounding male voice ordered.

Adam waited for the owner of this voice to come into view. The two guards from the train marched back into the elevator, and the door shut. Adam could hear the elevator rise into the shaft.

"Dr. McArthur!" Melena called out.

"Ms. Jaxon! How wonderful to see you!" the man replied.

"Thank you so much for accepting us on such short notice."

"I am not likely to refuse a request from the great Senator Jaxon or his lovely Scion," Dr. McArthur admitted. "In all honesty, I have been looking forward to having you here to see the project."

Melena offered her hand, and Dr. McArthur stepped forward and shook it. He was a tall, thin man with receding grey hair and a closely-trimmed, white goatee. He was flanked by a total of four Federal Police agents in full gear.

"Well, shall we prep our subject?" Dr. McArthur signaled for the police agents to come forward.

Adam had not seen an exit from the lab so far. There was the elevator, however, and the hallway Dr. McArthur and his security team had come from. He would have to disable the four agents quickly if he was going to run.

The police agents each took one of Adam's limbs and began un-strapping them. As soon as the strap across his forehead was loose, Adam sprang to life. He drew both of his legs back toward his chest and kicked forward, slamming his heels into the noses of the of the police agents who were near his feet. He then grabbed an arm of each of the other two agents and pulled them together across the gurney—one agent's face ramming into the other's shoulder. In one fluid motion, he rolled off of the gurney, picked it up and threw it into the two agents who were both clutching broken, bleeding noses. He whirled to face the other two agents. Their eyes widened, observing the speed with which Adam was able to move. Before they could reach for their weapons, he landed a side kick into the forehead of one agent and a crushing gut punch into the other.

Once all four agents were on the floor, Adam darted toward the hallway where Dr. McArthur and his entourage had entered the lab. As he reached the threshold, he felt a sharp pinch in the back of his neck. His entire body became tense and then relaxed completely. His legs crumpled beneath him, and he slid to the floor with a loud thud. He wanted to get up and run, but his body was completely unresponsive. He was paralyzed. The device Melena had fastened around his neck had accessed his nervous system via remote control.

"Well, Ms. Jaxon, what a lively subject you've brought us," Dr. McArthur casually remarked, apparently not surprised by Adam's inability to flee.

The four police agents rushed over to recover Adam. They lifted him up and carried him toward the glass tank. Dr. McArthur removed the hospital-style gown Adam was wearing, and the agents lowered him into the tank. His body was completely submerged with the exception of his head. Melena and the woman from the train began attaching cables to receptacles on the sides of the tank. Adam's skin began to tingle as though thousands of tiny fish were swimming around him in the tank. The tingling was soon replaced by warmth, and then the warmth was replaced with a prickling sensation.

Melena stood up once she was satisfied with her work. "Thank you all for your assistance. This prisoner may possess sensitive information. My orders are to interrogate him with only the assistance of Ms. Sorbent here. However, I will appreciate having security available should the situation call for it."

"Of course, Ms. Jaxon," Dr. McArthur replied. "Do you feel comfortable with the equipment?"

"Thank you. Yes. Your training was thorough, and I've reviewed the specifications at length. I think we should be able to proceed without issue," Melena answered confidently.

"Excellent. Dr. Janekowski is currently in New York, but I am assigned to the facility through the duration of your stay. Please contact me through my page if you need assistance." Dr. McArthur smiled and turned, signaling the four police agents to fall in behind him.

Chapter 4

Once the lab was clear, Melena's attention turned to her anonymous prisoner and test subject. She hoped that she had come across as confident to Dr. McArthur. As an instructor in her studies at Columbia University, he had become somewhat of a mentor to her, and she didn't want to disappoint him. She felt competent using the equipment, but criminal interrogation was not something in her current repertoire. That is why Hava Sorbent had been assigned to assist her. Hava worked in Melena's father's administration as his top advisor and liaison to the Federal Police. Melena did not know her well, but Hava worked closely with the Senator, and he obviously trusted her.

Hava's reputation was that of an ambitious, if not cutthroat, climber of the ranks. Melena had insisted to her father that she was capable of fulfilling this assignment alone, but he felt that she needed someone with her who would be willing to press their prisoner a little harder should Melena waiver. Melena wanted to impress her father as much as she wanted to impress Dr. McArthur, so she was glad to have Hava there to make sure the memory therapy was a success.

"That was quite a display a minute ago," Melena complimented the partially submerged prisoner. "You've obviously had some training. Where did you receive it?"

He only stared back at her. She wasn't sure what it was about him—and she tried to convince herself that it wasn't just the sarcastic wit and cute smile she had witnessed back in Rugby—but she somehow felt empathy for the treatment he had received since being in custody. His light brown eyes seemed innocent and almost trustworthy. She had been assured, however, that this man was dangerous to the security of the

Union, and her own investigation into his identity led her to believe that he may be Trident. The religious remnant, nicknamed *Tridents*, were a real mystery to Melena. Their clinging to a belief that a god, or three gods, not only existed, but took an interest in mortals' lives just seemed simple-minded to her. Historically, religion was at the root of so many wars and conflicts and only served as a means of getting people riled up against one another. Her own opinion aside, practicing religion was illegal in the S.O.U.

"Have I been charged with a crime?" the prisoner finally spoke up.

"Your biological signature is not the S.O.U.'s database. Why is that?" Melena inquired.

"Melena—do you prefer Melena over Your Majesty?" the prisoner asked.

Melena suppressed a smile. "Why would you call me that?"

"I just don't remember ever addressing a Scion before, so I wasn't sure of the protocol. *Your Majesty*, I really think we're wasting our time here. After all of the sleeping I've been doing over the past—what? Days? Weeks?—I don't even know how long you people have been holding me. Anyway, I'm not sure I can distinguish between my dreams and reality. So, before you get all crazy with your magic potions and your little bath tub here, I'll tell you what I think you want to know." The prisoner sighed and went on. "I've been searching high and low to find a certain wizard. Not the kind wearing a robe with a long gray beard or anything like that. This wizard is really more of a floating head. From what I've heard, he's cranky and yells a lot, but I was told he could send me back to Kansas. If you're trying to get to him through me, you're out of luck. You'll have to earn the trust of some winged monkeys before—"

"That won't really be a problem," Melena cut him off, suppressing a grin. "We're prepared to assist you in retrieving some memories that we're interested in." She tried to sound threatening. "Would you like to tell me your name or should I find out on my own?"

The prisoner looked unimpressed. "Melena, what kind of mascara do you use?" He narrowed his eyes, studying hers. "It's understated, but really makes those lashes pop. Personally, I think you are in the wrong line of work. If you get tired of being a Scion and ruling over the masses, you should really consider—"

"All right!" Hava shouted, "That's enough of this. Ms. Jaxon, may we please begin the session?"

The prisoner's eyes shifted over to Hava. "Now, don't get jealous. You have very lovely … uh … ears. Honestly, it's kind of hard to tell what's under all that ink. But hey, it's what's on the inside that counts, am I right? How are your insides? How would you rate your insides on a scale of one to ten?—ten being the highest—no, ten being the lowest."

Melena made a great effort not to laugh. She had also found it difficult to look directly at Hava's face as it was completely covered in tattoos. Facial tattoos had become quite popular, but Melena was unable to understand the appeal.

Hava reached into the tank and grabbed one of the prisoner's thumbs. She slowly bent it back, palm up, toward his forearm until he began to wince.

"Okay, Hava," Melena broke in, "let's get started. I don't think standard methods will be necessary at all."

Hava released the prisoner's thumb and nodded to Melena.

"Seriously? Good cop/bad cop?" The prisoner smiled. "You ladies really are pros. I didn't realize who I was dealing with."

Hava looked as though she might go for the prisoner's thumb again.

"Hava, is it? Hava, I didn't mean to upset you," the prisoner explained. "That was actually quite painful. I was this close to telling you where the wizard is."

Melena reached onto the chemical tray that had been prepped. She carefully measured the appropriate dose of the first drug into a vial and then poured it into the tank where the prisoner lay. The brown liquid swirled through the tank, turning the solution an amber color. The prisoner's demeanor almost instantly changed. His eyes partially closed and rolled back into his head. Melena measured out the second component and poured it into the tank.

"How far back are you taking him?" Hava asked.

"Should be about a week."

The prisoner's mouth was moving, but he was not speaking.

Melena began the interrogation. "Where are you?" she asked. She waited a few seconds, but there was no reply. "Where are you?" she repeated.

The prisoner hesitated for a moment and then answered. "Aunt Esther's. We're out in the yard. The sun is out."

"What are you doing there?"

"Saying goodbye. They're all here."

"Who is there?"

"Aunt Esther, Uncle Paul, my cousins, friends."

"Where is Aunt Esther's?"

"Independence."

"Why are you saying goodbye? Where are you going?"

"I'm going to Rugby."

"Why are you going to Rugby?"

"To begin my errand."

"And what is your errand?"

"I haven't received it yet. I have to go to Rugby to get it."

Melena tried not to be overly-excited, but it was working! He was definitely Trident if he was from Independence. She had taken a huge risk asking her father to allow her to bring his prisoner to the lab, but it was going to pay off.

"What's your name?

"Adam Winter."

"Who are you meeting with in Rugby, Adam?"

"I don't know."

"What's your overall agenda?"

"To serve God and my country."

"And what is it that your *god* wants you to do?"

"He wants me to help reestablish a free people and restore the United States of America."

Although this is what Melena expected to hear, it still sounded shocking to hear it said aloud. The guy was attractive and somewhat charming, but what he had confessed was just absurd. For him to actually think that a government with power over all of North America, Europe, Australia and South Africa could be overthrown and a relic of a nation carved out right in the middle in its stead was ludicrous. And believing that some ridiculous deity wanted it done was just plain silly. He seemed quite serious about his errand, however, and that did make him a threat to the government.

"Do your aunt and uncle and friends support this effort?" Melena continued.

"Of course they do."

"Treason!" Hava spat. "He'll die for his words. I promise you that."

Melena turned and delivered a stern look to Hava. The last thing she needed was for Hava to confuse the prisoner and disrupt their session. Hava backed down, but continued glaring at the unconscious prisoner in contempt.

Melena went back to the chemical tray and prepared another dose. "I'm going to move forward a few days." She explained to Hava. She finished mixing and poured the liquid into the tank. The solution in the tank took on a dark green hue as the drugs made their way through it.

"Where are you now, Adam?" Melena asked. The prisoner began to tremble and convulse mildly, but settled down after a moment. "Adam, where are you?" Melena repeated more softly in an effort to sooth him.

"I … I … I … I'm in Rrrrugby. Rugby at the train station."

"Who else is there?"

"I don't know anybody."

"What are you doing there?"

"Waiting. Waiting. Wait … wait …"

The prisoner began to convulse, causing the chemicals in the tank to slosh over the edges.

Melena turned to Hava. "This shouldn't be happening. We need to get him out of there." She felt concerned as she bent down to remove the wires from the tank.

"No!" Hava shouted, grabbing Melena's hand. "He's about to tell us what he was doing in Rugby!"

"He shouldn't be reacting this way!" Melena shot back, pulling her hand out of Hava's grip. "I'm not going to lose him before we get anything."

"Give him another few minutes," Hava argued. "He's already incriminated himself. If he doesn't pull through, justice will have been done."

Melena gave her an icy glare. "I said he's had enough for today," she annunciated through gritted teeth. "We'll pick it back up in the morning."

Hava looked as though she would continue to protest, but then thought better of it. She nodded and stepped away from Melena.

Melena removed the page and stylus she had been given when she arrived from her jacket pocket and unfolded the device. She quickly penned a message to Dr. McArthur requesting that the police agents return to remove the prisoner. Within moments, the security team arrived back in the lab. The prisoner continued to convulse. Melena leaned over the tank and placed her hand on the side of his head to steady him. Upon being touched, his eyes flew open and locked onto Melena's. They were wide with fear and confusion. He stared, pleadingly, into her eyes for a long moment before fading back into unconsciousness.

Chapter 5

Melena sat, page in hand, reviewing her notes at the bedside of the prisoner, whom she had discovered through her interrogation was named Adam. She was amused at his name. It was the name of the character in Trident mythology who was supposed to have been the first man on the earth. Woman was created from his rib. She smiled to herself at the thought.

Her gaze rose to the bed where this strange man lay. When she first entered his cell back in Rugby, she had noticed that he was attractive, but he was an enemy of the state so she hadn't thought much of it. He looked so peaceful now. His wavy, dark hair was disheveled, but it suited him. He had been without a shirt plenty since being in custody and even beneath the hospital gown he wore, it was difficult for her to ignore his muscular build. She thought that perhaps he had been trained by The Response or some other organization where he would have undergone rigorous exercise. Whatever he had done, it worked for him. As she studied his face, she couldn't shake the impression that he was an innocent, if misguided person. His religious ideology and desire to restore the good ole U.S. of A. to its former glory was disturbing to her, but he just didn't seem like a dangerous person.

Melena wondered what life must have been like for Adam in Independence. The city of Independence, in what was formerly Missouri, was a mystery to her. She marveled that one city, right in the middle of the North American continent, could maintain immunity from the S.O.U. She had seen the tall walls of the city in images, but that was all. Somehow, images of the city from above taken by aircraft or satellite were always obscured, and the city's defenses had yet to be penetrated by

Federal Police siege attempts. Independence was completely self-sufficient, not receiving any food or medical supplies from the government. Police intelligence had so far been unsuccessful at intercepting any substantial electronic communications. The city leadership and the defense strategies of Independence both remained mysteries. Most of the S.O.U. leaders had accepted Independence as a lost cause, but Melena's father, Senator Cai Jaxon, had not—especially since Independence was located within the Great Plains Dominion, which was his to govern. He had made it his mission to bring down Independence and force its citizens to submit to the S.O.U.'s rule.

One day, Melena would inherit her father's seat in the Senate over the Great Plains Dominion as his Scion—his heir. She was curious about Independence and believed that the people there should accept S.O.U. rule, but she wasn't nearly as passionate about bringing it down as her father was. When she had heard that a man who had been captured in a raid on a Response cell was unidentifiable by the Central—the S.O.U.'s vast citizen database and government communications hub—she knew her father would be interested. The Central contained biological signatures and files on each individual residing within the borders of the S.O.U. The only exceptions were some of those living in Independence. The government's older records contained files on many who were suspected of living in Independence, but a good portion of its population was unaccounted for. Without a file or access to their banks, these individuals could not be taxed.

Melena knew that information her prisoner, Adam Winter, possessed could be extremely valuable to her father's efforts to identify Independence's leadership, infiltrate it and learn the city's weaknesses.

Adam began to stir. His eyes fluttered open, and he turned toward Melena. He stared for a moment and then suddenly jerked his arms and legs in an effort to flee. He was, however, chained to the bed so his efforts were futile. After a few moments, he stopped thrashing. He stared up at the ceiling and then yawned.

"What's for breakfast, Your Highness?" Adam breathed out in the midst of his yawn.

Melena smiled. "How about you stop calling me that?"

"I'm sorry. I told you how inexperienced I am at addressing royalty. Let me try again. What's for breakfast, Lady Jaxon?"

Melena smiled in amusement, but tried to ignore his jab. "What do you remember from our interview yesterday?" she asked.

"Well, I remember relaxing in your luxurious hot tub while wearing your favorite little red briefs," Adam recalled. "It felt so nice, I must have drifted off. Thank you for finding me a suitable bed and getting me all tucked in. How did you sleep? I hope you didn't sit up in here all night worrying about me."

"No. I slept fine, thank you," Melena lied. She had been sitting up most of the night before finally dozing off for a few hours. "Do you recall our conversation while you were in the lab?"

"I'm so sorry, Your Majesty; I probably nodded and said 'uh huh' a lot, but I have to confess that I wasn't really listening. I promise to work on it, though. I know women sometimes just want to be heard."

Melena rolled her eyes at him and shook her head. "We do have some breakfast for you." She summoned one of the police agents standing guard outside the door. He came forward with a triangular-shaped silver pouch and ripped the top off of it. Holding the opening of the pouch to Adam's mouth, he squeezed the contents out, nearly gagging Adam. Reluctantly, Adam finished off the food in the pouch.

“Wow.” Adam grimaced. “That was delicious. Honestly, I’m a little nervous about the bill for my stay here. The superb food and amenities, the unparalleled hospitality … I’m not sure I can afford this place.”

“You can’t.” Melena smiled. “You are my special guest.”

He smiled back at her. “Oh, I appreciate that. I think that one night is sufficient, though. I don’t want to be a burden on you any longer.”

“You’ve been a pleasure.” Melena matched his sarcasm. “I think we’ll have you stick around for a little while longer.”

“Okay, but if you want me back in the hot tub, I have to insist that you join me. Did you pack a bathing suit?”

Melena smiled widely. She had to give the guy some credit for his resiliency. He wasn’t breaking down. She wondered if he really didn’t remember what he had experienced during yesterday’s interrogation. Dr. McArthur had explained to her that subjects were in a dream-like state during the treatment and would likely not recall the experience as anything more than a dream, if they remembered anything at all.

“Well, since you brought it up,” Melena began, “I thought we would head back to the lab. But unfortunately, the tank is too small for the both of us.”

“Oh, I think we’d manage.” The corner of Adam’s mouth curled up in a sly grin.

Melena smiled back. Then utilizing her handy remote, she activated Adam’s collar rendering him paralyzed once again. She motioned for the police agents to retrieve him and return him to the lab.

Hava was waiting in the lab as Adam was positioned into the tank. “I’ve been in communication with Senator Jaxon,” Hava informed Melena. “He received my report on our interrogation yesterday and requested I contact him through my page. He expressed his concerns about you either being manipulated by the prisoner or simply unable to stomach the process of gleaning information from him."

Melena glared at Hava. If her father had felt this way, why couldn't he tell her directly? Melena was sure that Hava had reported a very one-sided account of the interrogation, making Melena sound incompetent.

"He expects results today," Hava continued.

"And that's what he'll get," Melena replied with a curt smile.

Melena had always had a desire to impress her father, although he had never expressed significant interest in her. He worked and travelled so often that Melena had rarely seen him while she was growing up. She had attended prep school in New York City at a school for ruling-class children, so the distance between them had really begun back then. She didn't have any siblings, and her mother had always been anonymous to her, so her father was really the only family she had. Once she finished with her University studies, she was able to return to Rugby and work for her father's administration. She still didn't see much of him, however, and he treated her more like a subordinate than a daughter when they did interact.

Melena noticed Adam observing Hava closely. "Tu es ravissante ce matin, Hava," he announced. "Parlez-vous français?"

"Oui," replied Hava, "être tranquille."

"I told her she looks lovely this morning," Adam informed Melena. "She told me I looked well also."

Melena guffawed. "I'm pretty sure she told you to shut up."

Adam's expression looked both surprised and impressed. "Melena also speaks French, Hava," he relayed.

Melena prepared the chemicals for the tank. She wanted to resume right where they left off. She took the first vial in her hand and was about to pour it into the tank.

"Melena," Adam began, his expression turning serious, "don't do this. You don't have to do this."

Melena hesitated at the look on Adam's face until she felt Hava's eyes boring into the back of her head. She broke his gaze and poured the contents of the vial into the tank and once again it turned amber. Adam immediately responded to the drugs in the same way he had the previous day.

"Adam, are you at the train station?" Melena asked. There was no response. "Adam, where are you?" After a few seconds, his mouth began to move. "Tell me what you see."

He finally spoke up. "I can't see anything. It's dark."

"What do you hear?"

"I hear people talking."

"What are they saying?"

"They're talking about the key."

"What key?"

"It's a stamp."

"Like a data-stamp?"

"Yes."

"What kind of data is on the stamp?"

"I'm not sure."

"Do you know where you are?"

"I'm in a vehicle. There's a hood over my head."

"Where are they taking you?"

"I'm not sure—somewhere safe to transfer the stamp to me. We're stopping now."

"Tell me when you can see something." Melena waited for thirty seconds to try and let the memory play out. She wondered what kind of information the stamp might contain. She figured that the people transporting Adam must have been the Responders who were killed near the apartment where Adam was found.

"I'm indoors now. They took the hood off of my head, but the room is pretty dark. There's a woman sitting across from me."

"Did she tell you anything about the stamp?"

"She says that the best way to get the stamp to Independence is to implant it in me. She wants me to get onto a table. There's a man with a mask and latex gloves by the table."

"Where are they going to implant it in you?"

"I don't want them to do it!"

"What's happening?"

"Men are holding me down. Stop! Get off of me!" Adam was clearly distressed. He went for several seconds without saying anything.

"Where is the stamp?" Hava broke in. "What did they do with the stamp?" She turned to Melena. "Get him to talk!"

"Adam," Melena spoke gently, "are you all right?"

Adam remained unresponsive.

"He's holding out!" Hava shouted as she moved closer to Melena and the chemical tray. "What's on the stamp? What else do you know?"

"Hava, give him a second," Melena directed calmly, trying to quell Hava's impatience.

Hava took a step closer and her hip bumped into the chemical tray. Several of the glass vials crashed onto the floor. One broke on the tank's edge, spilling about half of its contents inside. The drug swirled through the tank, turning the solution black.

"Hey!" Melena shouted. "What are you doing?" She tried to shove Hava out of the way.

Adam began to convulse as he had the day before. The drugs were a delicate mixture, and Melena wasn't sure what would happen to Adam if the wrong combinations were administered. He continued to shake for a few moments and then settled down and became still.

"Adam?" Melena leaned over the tank. "Are you okay?"

He was still for several seconds before muttering, "Mom? Dad?"

"Adam, are you with your parents?"

"My whole family."

Melena worried that enough of the drug had spilled into the tank to take Adam years back into his memory. "How old are you?"

"I'm ten."

"Are you at home?"

"No, we're in Chicago."

"What are you doing there?"

"The trial."

"What trial."

"Ours."

"Whose? Your family's? Your family is on trial?"

"Yes, but it's not really a trial. We're being sentenced."

"What are you accused of?"

"They say we are guilty of preaching God and spreading discontentment."

"Are you going to a re-education camp?"

There was no response.

"Adam?"

"No! Leave her alone!" he shouted, frantically.

"What's happening?"

"They're taking my mom."

Adam's head began shaking from side to side. "Dad! Jacob! No!" he yelled. "No! Anna!" His eyes shut tightly and tears welled up until they spilled over, ran past his ears and into the tank.

"Adam?" Melena spoke, hesitantly. "Adam, what happened?"

"They're gone." He was sobbing.

"Were they taken away?"

"No, they were injected in the arm. They killed them!"

"Who did they kill?"

"Mom, Dad, Jacob, Joseph, Anna. All of them."

"What's happening to *you*?"

Adam's breathing started to become shallow and frequent. Perspiration began running from his hairline down into his face.

"Hava, get Dr. McArthur!" Melena ordered.

Hava ignored her. "I'll bet they implanted it right there," she observed, calmly. "Look, where his hair is shorter." She reached over and put her fingers on a section of hair that had been shaved.

"We can figure that out later!" Melena shouted. "Get Dr. McArthur in here before this man goes into cardiac arrest!"

"We need to get in there and get that stamp," Hava replied, obviously unconcerned with the health of their subject.

Melena quickly pulled her page from her pocket and sent her request for help to Dr. McArthur. She turned back to the tank and began trying to lift Adam out. "Help me!"

Hava shook her head in disgust. "The Senator will be disappointed when I tell him about your sympathy for this traitor."

Melena almost had Adam out of the tank when the police agents arrived and took him from her. Once completely out of the tank, his eyes flew open, and he looked wildly around the room trying to get oriented. He began to struggle with the police agents. Melena reluctantly took the remote from her jacket pocket and activated his collar once again. His body instantly went limp.

Chapter 6

Adam found himself back in the bed where he had spent the previous night. His wrists and ankles were once again chained to the bedframe. The paralysis from the collar was wearing off and feeling began to return to his extremities. He wasn't sure exactly what had happened in the lab. He had been awakened suddenly and was only now getting over his disorientation. Whatever had happened in there, it had created a lively discussion between Hava, Melena and Dr. McArthur. There were several walls separating them, but Adam could hear their debate clearly.

"We found out what we needed to know," Hava explained to Dr. McArthur. "The prisoner has sensitive data stored on a stamp that has been surgically implanted in his head. We need you to extract the stamp immediately."

"We don't know for sure where the stamp was implanted," Melena argued. "He didn't tell us whether or not that even occurred—only that it was the intention of the Responder agents to do it. He was resisting. The transfer may not have even taken place."

"He has it," Hava insisted. "There is a section of his hair that has been shaved. Why would that be?"

"Yes, but there's no evidence of an incision. The incident was only a few days ago. Don't you think there would be stitches or an open wound?" Melena's voice escalated. "You're so anxious to get into this man's skull that you haven't bothered to consider any other possibilities. It's because of your interference that we didn't find out what happened with the transfer of the stamp in the first place!"

“Ladies …” Dr. McArthur tried to manage the situation. “Why don’t you contact Senator Jaxon and see how he would like to proceed?”

“Senator Jaxon has given me full authority over this interrogation. It’s my call to make,” Hava stated.

“*I* am in charge of this interrogation. You were brought along to assist me should I request it,” Melena countered.

“It’s cute that you think that, Ms. Jaxon. Your father wanted to give you an opportunity, but I’m here to clean up the mess he figured you’d make.” Hava didn’t sound like she was even trying to disguise her disdain for Melena now. “Dr. McArthur, you will retrieve the stamp from the prisoner. Can you do that from his room or do you need more space?”

“This isn’t a surgical facility, Ms. Sorbent,” Dr. McArthur explained. “I’m not prepared to perform a procedure like that.”

“It’ll be simple,” Hava directed. “Cut into his head where the hair is shaved and dig until you find the stamp.”

“I don’t have the proper monitoring equipment to keep him alive during surgery,” Dr. McArthur protested. “It should be done at a medical facility. This facility is equipped for research only.”

“That’s not my concern, Dr. McArthur.” Hava’s voice rose. “Just remove the stamp intact, and we’ll return to Rugby with it!”

“What?” Melena shouted. “Are you insane? We’re not going to kill this guy by digging around in his brain looking for something that may not even be there!”

“Ms. Jaxon, your services are no longer required. Return to your quarters, and remain there until we are ready to board the train back to Rugby,” Hava ordered. “Dr. McArthur, prep the lab. I will have the prisoner brought to you there.”

There were no more voices, just footsteps headed off in several directions. Adam began searching the room for something to help him escape his bonds. He knew that if he didn't find a way out, he wouldn't survive. One set of footsteps approached his room. They were women's heels—Melena.

"I'm transferring the prisoner," Melena informed the police agents outside Adam's door. "I need the key to his shackles. The prisoner and I will proceed on foot. I can activate his collar at any moment should he attempt to flee. You are not to accompany us. You are to stay here and await further orders"

The door opened, and Melena entered the room. Adam said nothing. Melena hurried to his bed and began unlocking the shackles on his ankles.

"I've been ordered to transfer you back to Rugby for further interrogation," Melena lied. "Do not attempt to resist. I won't hesitate to activate your collar and have the security team escort you."

"Okay." Adam complied as she loosed the shackles on his wrists.

Melena's hands trembled, slightly as she pulled open the cuffs. "We're on a tight schedule so move quickly and do as I say."

Adam nodded. Melena took his arm and pushed him toward the door. They exited the room and moved past the security team. Melena led Adam down a long hallway, through the lab and to the elevator door. She placed her palm on the call screen and waited for the elevator to descend down the long shaft.

"Where's the prisoner?" Adam recognized Hava's deep, menacing voice from somewhere in the distance. Melena didn't hear.

The elevator arrived, and Adam and Melena entered. They ascended for ten seconds before the elevator slowed and came to a stop. Melena went to the controls and tried to get the elevator moving again. Adam could hear the blaring of an alarm coming up through the elevator shaft.

Melena turned to face Adam, a look of panic on her face. “They’re going to kill you.”

“I know,” he replied, calmly. “Thank you.” He stepped to the door and began to pry it open. He worked his fingers into the crack and pulled hard. The doors separated a few inches and Adam began wedging his body in between the doors. Suddenly, the elevator jerked. “It’s gonna drop!” Adam pushed the doors open a little wider. “Jump down. There’s a drop of about three feet. Go!”

Melena squeezed past Adam through the doors and hopped down onto a concrete floor in a dimly lit hallway. The elevator began descending. Adam leapt out of the elevator cab just as it began dropping down the shaft. He got to his feet, and Melena immediately grabbed him by the arm and pushed him forward, taking control.

“We need to get to the train. I’ll take you back to Rugby and make sure that you are treated humanely,” Melena promised. “We just need to get there before Hava does.”

They ran down a long hallway with solid rock walls. There were no doors along the walls, just a service light every twenty feet or so. At the end of the hall, there was a large metal door. Upon reaching it, they searched for a knob or handle but there was nothing there. Melena tried to pry it open with her fingers, but it seemed to be locked from the other side.

“Come on.” Adam turned and ran back to the elevator opening with Melena following close behind. He got near the edge and looked out into the shaft. “There’s a ladder on the other side of the shaft.”

Melena peered out into darkness. “How do you know? I can’t see anything.”

“Trust me. The shaft is wide enough for two cabs, so there must be another cab that accesses the other side.” Adam looked down. "The other cab is only a few floors down. If we can get on top of it, we'll be able to reach the ladder."

Melena strained her eyes trying to see what Adam was seeing. "How could you possibly know that? It's pitch black in there."

"I can see just fine. There's a steel structure between the two cabs. It's like a track that they both ride up and down. We'll have to jump out onto it."

"No. We're going back this way. We'll find a way to open that door at the end of the—"

Adam didn't wait for her approval. He leaped from the edge out into the shaft.

"Adam!" Melena screamed.

"I'm fine," he called back to her from the darkness. "It's not that far."

"I said we were going back down this way! Don't think I won't activate the collar if you can't follow my instructions," Melena threatened.

"If you do that now, you'll find me in a mushy puddle at the bottom of this thing. Come on. Jump as far as you can. I'll catch you."

"Catch me? With what? What are you holding on with?"

"My legs and feet are secure between two poles. My hands are free. I promise I'll catch you," Adam assured her.

"I'm not going risk my life jumping out into a black hole because some freaky Trident promises he'll catch me," Melena snapped. "You jump back over here right now!"

"Freaky? Well, maybe a little, but I promise I wouldn't let you get hurt trying to help me. If you jump straight out as far as you can, you'll land right in my arms."

"Not a chance."

"Melena … please trust me." Adam's voice echoed, softly through the shaft. "We can do this." He smiled to himself as he watched her pacing back and forth across the opening, debating the options in her mind.

Finally, she inched her feet toward the edge of the opening. "Adam," she called out into the dark shaft, "you swear you can catch me?"

"I swear."

"Crap," she muttered as her feet left the floor, and she hurled herself toward Adam's voice. A scream escaped her lungs, but was cut short as she slammed into Adam's chest. He wrapped his arms around her and pulled her in tight. Her fingers dug into his shoulders trying to secure herself as her feet dangled.

"Grab onto the poles," Adam instructed. He held on as her right hand groped in the darkness searching for the track. Once she found her grip, Adam swung her around so she could get her footing.

Melena sounded like she was going to hyperventilate. "This was such a bad idea. Oh, we're dead."

"Hey, relax. We're gonna be fine. We just need to climb down a few feet to the other cab."

"You're insane! How can you see anything?"

"I'm not really sure how, it's just been kind of a recent thing, but I can see pretty well in the dark." Adam moved out behind Melena and reached an arm around her waist. "We'll do this together. Just take it slow, and I'll be right here to help you if you have any trouble."

They slowly climbed down the track—Adam keeping a hold on Melena. "You're doing great," he assured her.

"Shut up."

Soon, Adam's toes reached the cab's roof. Taking Melena by the hips, he lifted her off of the track and onto the roof of the cab.

"Do you want to go up the ladder first?" Adam asked.

"I don't want to go up the ladder at all. Ground level is probably 200 meters up," Melena complained. "You go first in case there are any unexpected obstacles."

"I think you're just trying to look up my gown," Adam teased.

"I can't see anything in here, you moron."

Adam moved to the ladder to begin his ascent. "There's a gap in between the cab and the ladder—enough space to fall down. Be careful." He gripped the ladder and climbed several rungs before stopping. He could hear voices inside the cab below.

"Get to ground level, and wait for them there." It was Hava's voice through a police transmitter.

"Ten-four," a voice inside the elevator responded.

"What's the matter?" Melena asked. "Why are you stopping?"

"Grab onto the ladder!" Adam shouted. "The elevator's about to go up."

"How do you—" Before Melena could finish, the elevator began moving upward with her still on top. "Adam!" she cried out.

As the elevator began moving up the shaft, Adam reached across the gap and caught hold of the top edge of the cab and held on, his legs swinging back and forth between the cab and the ladder. As the cab sped up the shaft, Adam held on for all he was worth. As it approached the top, it began to slow. Looking up, Adam could see the end of the track attach to the ceiling of the shaft.

"Lay flat, Melena!" Adam shouted.

"Adam?" Melena sounded bewildered at the sound of his voice.

"Get down!" he yelled.

The cab slowed to a stop. Adam reached his foot across to the ladder and hoisted himself up to look up onto the top of the cab. Melena's face lay flat against the cab roof, her eyes wide. The ceiling of the shaft was only inches away from crushing her.

"Are you okay?" Adam whispered. "Don't try and stand up."

"How did you get here so fast?"

Taking her hand, he pulled Melena toward him, sliding her toward the edge of the elevator. He grabbed her under the arms and began pulling her off of the cab. Abruptly, the cab jerked and began falling back down into the shaft. Adam held on tight as Melena's legs came swinging down into his side. She wrapped both arms around his neck and hung on. "I've got you," Adam assured her. "Grab onto the ladder."

Her hand located a rung, and she secured herself.

"What now?" she asked, clearly exasperated.

"There's a ledge at the base of the doors over there," Adam replied. "I'll step over to it and see if I can get the doors open." He held onto the ladder with one hand and stretched his free foot over to the ledge. This time, the doors separated easily and light flooded into the elevator shaft. He pulled the door closest to him all the way open and reached his foot into the opening. Melena let out a little chuckle.

Adam turned his head back to look at her. "What?"

She shook her head. "Nothing. It's just your gown is gaping open in the back," she admitted. "It's quite a sight."

"I knew you were trying to peek. You do like my little briefs." Adam reached around the door frame and pulled himself inside. "Give me your hand." Melena reached her foot out onto the ledge and took Adam's hand. He pulled her up into the opening, and they both looked from side to side. "Do you know where we are?"

"No," Melena answered. "This doesn't look familiar.

Adam and Melena turned a corner and nearly bumped into a man in a white lab coat. Three additional lab-coated men followed behind him. They all stopped and stared at their visitors. Beyond the four men were dozens of glass cells with people inside.

Adam turned to Melena. "This isn't the cafeteria. This is the place with all the … the people in glass … uh, sorry, fellas, I think we made a wrong turn."

There was an unoccupied lab coat hanging from a hook on the wall next to where Adam was standing. He pulled it off of the hook, and then took Melena's hand and spun her around, heading in the opposite direction.

"Wait!" one of the men yelled.

Adam pulled Melena down a hallway until he spotted a large set of double doors. Once through the doors, they found themselves outside of the facility and inside one of the rail tunnels.

"Where's the train?" Melena wondered aloud.

Adam's head snapped up. "Someone's coming," he warned. He led Melena out onto the tracks.

"Stop right there!" a voice shouted. Adam turned to see five armed police agents emerging from the double doors, with Hava right behind them.

Adam quickly selected the tunnel to the right, and he and Melena raced into it.

"Melena," Hava shouted after them, "you're assisting in the escape of an enemy combatant! Now you're a traitor too!"

Melena slowed her pace momentarily.

"Take them out—both of them," Adam heard Hava instruct the police agents. He felt a jolt of adrenaline and grabbed Melena by the hand, yanking her toward the tunnel wall. Gunshots rang through the tunnel as the agents opened fire. Adam could hear each round ricochet off of the floor and walls. His pace accelerated quickly until he was nearly pulling Melena off of her feet. He slowed just enough so that she could keep up. The heels she was wearing were making it difficult for her to run in the loose gravel. Shots continued to ring through the cavern and sparks lit up the darkness each time a bullet struck stone or the steel tracks. The tunnel continued to grow darker the deeper they fled.

"This way." Adam pulled Melena to the right into a branching tunnel as the tracks forked. After running for several more minutes, Adam stopped to let Melena catch her breath. The sound of gunfire had ceased.

"What … am I doing?" Melena managed to ask herself between great intakes of breath. "We have … to go back. I'll … talk to them."

"Melena, I'm sorry you're involved in this, but you did the right thing," Adam reassured her. "I don't think it's safe even for *you* to go back."

"I don't … know what … to do," she gasped. "Maybe, I could—"

"Hang on," Adam interrupted. "I hear something."

"You hear everything. What's with that, by the way?"

"A train's coming," he announced.

A tiny light appeared in the distance. Adam could feel the vibration on the tracks below. He helped Melena to her feet, and they started running deeper into the tunnel. The headlamp of the train grew brighter, and the rumble of the tracks grew more intense. Adam spotted a branching tunnel to their left up ahead. He tried to calculate in his mind whether or not he and Melena could make it there before the train reached them. He grabbed Melena's hand and pulled her to the left side of the tracks. Her heel caught in the gravel, and she went down onto her knees. Adam reached down and pulled her up. The train was bearing down on them now. Automatic weapon fire blasted the tunnel wall behind them. Melena screamed. Just as the train was about to overtake them, Adam pulled Melena around the bend and into the branching tunnel. The train sped past as bullets sent gravel spraying into the air just behind

Melena's feet. She screamed again, but the sound was drowned out by the deafening clatter of the passing train.

After deviating at two additional forks, Adam thought it best that they stick with one tunnel and either make it back to the lab or out of the facility.

"This is so unnerving—trudging through complete darkness," Melena complained after walking in silence for ten minutes. "I still don't understand how you can see."

Adam sighed. "I don't either. I also don't understand why I smell a skunk."

"What?" She sniffed the air. "I don't smell anything. What does a skunk smell like?"

"Uh, kind of … bitter, I guess." Adam struggled to think of the right words to describe the scent. "I don't know … like a skunk. Haven't you ever smelled a skunk before?"

"I don't know. Not that I remember." Melena squinted her eyes. "Wait. I *can* see something. I think I can make out the tracks way up ahead."

"What do you know, there's a light at the end of this tunnel." Adam smiled even though he knew Melena couldn't see his face.

"You're pretty pleased with yourself for that, aren't you?"

"Naw." Adam shrugged. "I mean … it was all right."

"You want an award?"

"I do have better material, but yeah, I'll take an award."

"It's the 'You're Obnoxious Trophy.'" Melena tried not to smile herself.

"I don't know what to say. I just … what an honor. Is it big? If it is, I'll have to expand my trophy case."

Melena just shook her head.

As the end of the tunnel grew near, Adam could see that it was evening outside. It looked like they only had about an hour or so before the sun went down.

"I need to contact my father." Melena took her page and stylus out of her pocket. "I'll explain what happened and arrange transportation back to Rugby."

Adam snatched it from her hands. "If you activate this page, you'll broadcast our location." He turned away from her and began writing on the page with the stylus.

"What are you doing?" Melena tried to look around his back to see what he was up to.

"I'm rerouting the power to circumvent the system." He scrawled with the stylus for another ten seconds. "Okay then." He folded up the page as small as he could and then placed it on the train track. Then, picking up a large stone, he slammed it down onto the device.

"What are you doing?" Melena reached down and retrieved the page. It hung limp in her hand—just a thin plastic rectangle now. "You broke it!"

"How long do you think it would take Hava to track us once a signal emerged from that page? Do you think if you contacted *His Majesty,* he could beat her to us?"

A black and white creature scurried across the tracks ahead of them. "What was that?" Melena gasped, grabbing hold of Adam's arm.

"I think it was a wild wombat." Adam made a concerned face. "Do you think it saw us?"

"Why?" Melena panicked. "Are they dangerous?"

"That was the skunk I smelled earlier," Adam admitted, letting her off the hook. "It's harmless as long as you stay out of its way."

She let go of his arm. "Jerk."

Adam chuckled under his breath. "All right, let's find you a five-star hotel before the sun goes down." He thought it best that they keep their distance from the tracks. Fortunately, the pine forest they entered was thick enough to hide them quite well. He slipped on the lab coat he had been carrying.

"We must look like quite the outdoorsy couple—me in my rugged hospital gown and lab coat combo and you in a durable pant suit and heels."

"I doubt we'll run into anybody out here. This area's restricted to the public. It's a Federal Park," Melena informed him.

"What a great place to raise lab rats." Adam eyed her. "Out here in the restricted Federal Park."

Melena didn't respond.

"What month is it?" Adam asked.

"It's August 17th. Don't be so dramatic," Melena chided. "You've only been in government custody for a few days."

"Well then, you're in luck. It shouldn't dip any lower than forty to forty-five degrees tonight."

"What are you talking about? It's not even forty degrees now." Melena looked confused.

"Fahrenheit," Adam clarified.

"Oh. Well, what's that in Celsius?"

"Oh, seven or eight degrees." Adam replied.

After hiking for fifteen more minutes, Adam decided they ought to use the remaining daylight to make a bed to sleep in. They came to a small lake and then backtracked a ways up the stream that fed into it and found a concealed spot.

Adam began searching the ground. "Help me gather up some logs."

"For a fire?"

"For a bed," Adam answered. "We'll want to be off the ground." The two of them gathered fallen logs and sticks and shaped them into a canoe-sized rectangle. "Now, we need to gather up as many pine needles and leaves as we can find and put them inside."

Melena stopped gathering and put her hands on her hips. "What about *your* bed?"

Adam grinned. “You’re not sharing?”

“Ha! You’re dreaming. Why don’t you get started on your own?” Melena smiled as though she had caught him trying to get away with something.

“As you wish.” Adam began the process again. After gathering a few logs, he glanced over at Melena just in time to see her leaning over the stream, putting cupped hands to her mouth. “No! Melena, don’t drink that!”

It was too late. “What?” she asked, innocently, wiping her mouth on her sleeve.

“Oh, boy,” Adam sighed. “At least you didn’t drink too much.”

“We’re in the mountains. Isn’t it like … spring water?”

Adam just shook his head.

“What’s wrong? Can it hurt me?”

“Let’s just say it may put a little spring in your step later on,” he chuckled.

“I don’t get it.” She eyed him a moment. “I think your just messing with me again.”

“I wouldn’t dream of it.”

Adam finished gathering the filling for his log bed just as the last light of day faded. “Okay, I guess I’ll hop into bed over here.” He climbed into the pine needles and leaves and nestled into the middle of the pile, scooping what he could over the top of him.

“I just get in the middle of all of this?” Melena verified, scooping up a handful of pine needles.

“Yep, just snuggle on in.”

Melena followed suit and climbed into her little nature-bed. There was silence for several minutes. It was a clear night, and the early stars were beginning to be visible as Adam gazed up at the sky.

“Adam,” Melena broke the silence. “I’m really sorry about what happened to your family.”

Adam was caught off guard. He wasn't sure what he had revealed during the interrogation. Apparently, more than he thought. "How did you discover that piece of information?"

"It was actually by accident," Melena admitted. "Hava knocked some of the drugs off the tray and into the tank and sent you back much further into your memories than I intended."

Adam remained silent.

"Anyway, I'm sorry," she repeated.

"Well, it turns out that the people who were so tolerant toward different lifestyles and sexual preferences and scientific ideas weren't very tolerant of people of faith." Adam's eyes burned as he recalled the horrific details of his family's murder.

"Can I ask you something?"

"Why not?" he relented.

"How did you survive?"

Adam sighed. "I *was* sentenced, you know. Their intent was to execute a ten-year-old boy. My dad was a medical doctor and a cancer researcher. He had developed a blood additive—actually, it's a modified virus that fuses itself onto blood cells and gives the body a greater capacity to heal, regenerate tissue and resist harmful substances that are introduced into the blood stream. I'd been receiving treatments of it since I was about eight years old. After the sentencing, I was injected with a lethal drug like the rest of my family, but my body rejected it. I did lose consciousness for a time while my body fought it off, but I woke up lying next to my family members who were not so fortunate. I waited until they left us alone and then fled."

"Hadn't your other family members been treated with the virus?" Melena asked.

"My siblings were, but it was more effective in younger children, and my body just seemed to accept it better than theirs," Adam explained. "It saved my life then and has several times since."

"I guess that explains why you were able to resist my sedatives," Melena reasoned. "It's probably why the memory therapy wasn't as effective as it should have been. What about your vision and hearing? Is that a result of the virus too?"

"No. That's something new. I'm still working that out." Adam reached up and rubbed his head where the Response's surgeon had opened his skull. The incision was healed completely, and the bone had grown over the void that had been left. "What about your family, Princess? Any siblings?"

"Nope, just me. I'm an only child. Actually, I've never even met my mother. She left when I was just a baby. I was pretty much raised by my nanny."

"The Senator didn't help you with your homework or tuck you into bed?" There was obvious distain in his voice.

Melena ignored it. "No, not really. He's a busy man. He's always been a busy man."

"Well, I'm sorry." Adam was actually sincere now. "We'd better get some rest. Who knows what adventures tomorrow will bring?"

Both fell silent for several more minutes.

"Adam?" Melena spoke up.

"Yeah?"

"I'm freezing!" She hissed through chattering teeth.

Adam chuckled. "You are?"

"Do you maybe want to come over here?"

"Oh, no, thanks. I'm pretty cozy, but I appreciate the offer." He was enjoying being right.

"Please?"

He let out a groan and then got up and shoveled all the leaves and pine needles that would fit from his bed into Melena's before climbing in next to her. She turned away from him so that he could spoon her and keep her warm.

“Don’t get any ideas,” Melena warned.

“Hmm,” Adam grunted. “I was about to say the same thing to you.”

Chapter 7

Something had been troubling Melena as she tried to remain asleep. Eventually, she willed her eyelids open. Adam's face was just centimeters from hers. She watched him sleep for a few moments. She was grateful he was beside her. It would have been a long, cold night with just leaves and pine needles to keep her warm. The sky was beginning to lighten, signaling that morning was near. Quite abruptly, Melena felt something stir inside of her. Her eyes went wide with panic. She began frantically trying to uncover herself and get up. Her elbow hit Adam in the shoulder, and he stirred.

"Hey, you okay?" he mumbled.

"I need to get out of here!" Melena finally got to her feet and scurried out of the makeshift bed and off into the trees. There was a great urgency inside of her. She couldn't remember ever feeling such intense pain in her abdomen. The cramping in her stomach made her wish she could just die and be done with it. She retreated into the woods as far as she could before relenting.

"Melena, are you okay?" Adam called out through the trees.

"Go away," Melena grumbled. "Don't come over here."

There was a pause before he spoke. "All right, I'll be over here if you need me."

Melena struggled for what seemed like an eternity before the cramping finally began to subside, and she felt like she might survive. "Adam?" she called out.

"Yeah?"

"What should I use to …" She closed her eyes and cringed. "Wipe with?" She was instantly humiliated by her question.

"Uh, are there any green leaves near you?"

Melena looked around, but didn't see any green leaves within reach. "No, only pine needles and sticks."

"I'll find some for you," Adam's voice trailed off as he apparently went in search of leaves.

Melena tried to think of what she had eaten recently that could have made her so sick, but she really hadn't eaten much of anything since arriving at the lab. Suddenly, it occurred to her what Adam had meant by his comment about the water she had consumed from the stream putting a *spring in her step*. If the stream water was the culprit, it had certainly done that.

She heard the sound of Adam's footsteps crunching sticks and pine needles nearby.

"Melena, I've got some leaves for you," he called to her.

"Don't look at me!" She was mortified. "Shut your eyes."

Adam walked toward her voice with his arm across his face, shielding his eyes and nose. When he thought he was close enough, he reached out the handful of leaves he had gathered to her. She took them from him. "Thank you. Now go away."

Melena struggled for a few minutes to get herself cleaned up. Unsatisfied, she determined that leaves would be inadequate. She remembered the lake they had come upon the previous day and determined that a quick bath would make her feel much better. "Adam, I'm going down to the lake. Stay here."

"Okay," he answered. "Holler if you need me." She thought she detected amusement in his voice.

"It's not funny!" she yelled after him.

"I know!" he called back, sounding even more amused.

When Melena arrived at the lake shore, the sun was just hitting the top of the mountain peak to the west. The lake was like a little bowl, catching the runoff from the snowmelt in the spring. Majestic evergreens lined the shore. She thought it could possibly be the most peaceful and beautiful sight she had ever seen.

Finally getting down to business, she undressed and hung her clothes on a pine bough that hung over the water. Since she hadn't bathed since leaving Rugby, she decided she might as well make the most of the opportunity. She gasped as her feet made contact with the ice-cold water. It was almost painful as she waded knee-deep into the lake. Summoning all of her bravery, she counted to three and sat down. The frigid water lapped up onto her back, taking her breath away.

After a few moments, a slight movement in her periphery caught her attention. On the opposite side of a large boulder down the shoreline, a curious creature was standing in the lake a few meters from shore looking right at her. It was an awkward looking thing. It had light brown fur and stood on four legs. It's rounded snout and large ears made Melena wonder if it could be some kind of deformed horse.

After staring at her little visitor for a few seconds, she heard a grunting sound. Strangely, it didn't sound like it had come from the little creature. She listened carefully until she heard it again. After a third time, the animal responsible for the grunts emerged from around the boulder. It was a much larger, darker version of the one she had been sharing a bath with. It continued grunting and started walking toward Melena, throwing its nose into the air as if to shoo her away. Melena stood and began slowly backing out of the water. "It's okay. I was just leaving." She tried to keep calm, but it continued moving toward her. As she backed up, her heel caught on a large rock, tripping her and sending her splashing into the icy water. Gasping, she quickly recovered her footing and continued her retreat, keeping an eye on her pursuer. As she reached the water's edge, she backed into the bough her clothes were draped on, knocking them off of the limb and into the water. The creature snorted loudly and started coming at her more aggressively. A scream escaped Melena's lungs as she turned to run back up the streambed toward camp. She looked over her shoulder and saw the creature increase its gait in pursuit.

"Adam!" Melena screamed. She looked over her shoulder again. The creature was closing in. She heard limbs crashing in front of her. Suddenly, Adam burst into her view. He flew through the brush and onto the streambed, heading directly for her. He was moving so quickly that she thought he might run her over. Instead, he reached out and shoved her aside as he sped past, knocking her to the ground. She fell beneath a large fir tree, landing in a relatively soft pile of brown needles. The dark creature's thundering hooves beat the ground as it galloped past her. Adam had run right past it. Confused, the beast stopped and turned around, trying to locate the intruders.

"Hey!" Adam yelled. The creature spotted him and took off after him. Adam darted down the streambed back toward the lake. Melena had never seen anyone move so quickly. In a flash, he was out of sight with the dark beast following behind.

Melena raised herself into a crouch. The forest had gone silent. She kept her gaze down the streambed, waiting for a sign of Adam or the huge creature that pursued him. After a minute or two, she heard a rustling in the trees. She poised to bolt if the strange creature came back into view. The crunching of pine needles and the sound of sticks cracking underfoot grew closer as she waited. Soon, Adam appeared from within the trees, Melena's dripping clothes in one hand and her shoes in the other. Upon spotting her, Adam turned his head away, averting his eyes. Melena used her arms to cover herself the best she could.

"Are you okay?" he asked.

"Yeah, I think so."

Adam cleared his throat. "I'm sorry for pushing you down. It was just that—"

"No, don't apologize," Melena insisted. "You probably saved my life."

He stopped and set her clothes and shoes down on the grass and then removed the lab coat he had been wearing. "Here, why don't you put this on?" Without turning his head, he tossed the coat in her direction. "You won't want to be wearing wet clothes all day. We'll need to get these dry."

"Thanks," she muttered.

"I know you've been hoping to get another glimpse of the back of these fancy red briefs anyway."

Melena failed to acknowledge his joke. Her heart was still beating rapidly. "What happened to the … thing?" She looked around, wondering if the creature would reappear.

"What thing?" Adam picked up her wet clothes, turned his back to her and began walking back to camp.

"The big thing that was chasing me, you idiot!"

"Oh. Its ship returned to earth and beamed it back up," Adam replied matter-of-factly.

"Adam! What was it?" She hurried to finish buttoning up the lab coat before taking off after him.

"It was a cow moose and a little calf. You must've gotten too close to her baby. She was not happy with you."

"Where are they now?" Melena asked, looking nervously over her shoulder.

"I just led her back to her calf and got out of sight. I don't think she'll leave her baby to come back again."

Melena scurried to catch up to him. "How are we going to dry my clothes?"

"Well, we need a little fire anyway to cook breakfast."

Melena suddenly noticed how hungry she had become. As they arrived back at camp, she was startled by two small balls of fur lying limp on a log. "What is that?"

"Well, one is the Easter Bunny and the other is Peter Cottontail."

"Gross!" Melena was disgusted. "What are you going to do with them?"

Adam didn't answer. He picked up a stick and knelt down beside a small log and a pile of bark and dried leaves that he must have gathered together prior to the moose attack. Placing one end of the stick onto the log, he began spinning it between his hands. His hands moved back and forth so quickly that the stick became a blur. After a few seconds, smoke began to rise from the log. He took some of the bark and leaves and placed them near the end of the stick and then continued spinning. More smoke rose from the log. He leaned over and gently blew on the source of the smoke. Even more smoke resulted, and then a small flame appeared on the bark. He continued to blow on the flame until it grew larger and spread to some of the twigs in the pile. Soon, a little fire was blazing.

"Look at you." Melena was impressed. "You're a regular little boy scout."

"I *am* a Boy Scout," Adam responded. "I'm actually an Eagle Scout."

"Nice try. The Boy Scouts of America was disbanded before you were born," Melena argued.

"Not where I come from." Adam smiled.

"Independence?"

He shook his head. "Sounds like you did learn a few things from our little interview."

"A few things," Melena confirmed.

Adam proceeded to gather up a dozen or so small, round stones from the streambed and placed them in the fire. He then picked up a fist-sized stone with a sharp edge and took it over to the dead rabbits. Picking one up, he began to saw at the fur above the shoulders with the stone. After getting through the fur, he worked his fingers under it and began pulling the skin off of the carcass. Melena turned her head, not wanting to see the rest.

"I'm a vegan," she informed him.

"Okay, great. I guess I'll eat these myself. You can just help yourself to whatever looks good." He made a sweeping gesture with his hand, indicating the grass and brush near the stream bed.

Melena found a large stone and rolled it near the fire. She took her wet pants, blouse and underclothes and spread them out on the stone, hoping the heat would begin to dry them. She located another stone and rolled it near the fire as well and placed her jacket on it. Then finding her heels, she decided she would wear them right away. She noticed Adam watching her.

"That really is a stunning outfit on you," He complimented.

"Thank you." She struck a pose and then pointed at him. "You know those are illegal, right?"

"What?" Adam asked, looking down to search himself.

She produced an impish grin. "Your sleeves are a little too short to conceal those guns you know."

Adam laughed. "What a line."

She walked to him, gripping one of his biceps with her hand. "You obviously work out."

"Yeah, I work out. It's a habit now after years of training for football, I guess."

"Really? I played futbol myself at Columbia University," Melena bragged.

"I can tell. You have very muscular legs. I played *football*, though. Not soccer."

"Like American football?"

"Exactly like American football."

"American football is illegal, Adam," Melena lectured. "It's dangerous."

"Oh, I agree. That's one of the things I like about it. You know what else I enjoyed that is illegal and dangerous? MMA."

"MMA?" She narrowed her eyes. "What's MMA?"

"Mixed martial arts," Adam explained. "It's a combination of kickboxing, wrestling and judo. I never competed professionally, but I liked it, and it was good exercise."

"Yes, that's also illegal," Melena confirmed, "and dangerous."

Adam chuckled. "Man, we peasant people are so fortunate that the government's there to protect us from making our own decisions."

Melena decided to change the subject. "So, what's Independence like? Did you go there after your escape in Chicago?"

"Not right away. I was too scared to try and go back to Rugby and didn't feel safe in Chicago, so I took a train to Kansas City. I lived on the streets for about six months before I decided to contact my aunt and uncle. They thought I was dead, so they were skeptical when they first heard from me. They thought the S.O.U. Government was trying to draw them out."

"How did you convince them?" Melena turned to look at Adam, but after noticing that he was still working on preparing the rabbits, she turned away again.

"I showed up on their doorstep."

"In Independence?"

"Yep."

"How did you get there? I mean, how did you get into the city?"

Adam laughed. "I teleported, of course."

"You teleported?" Melena was so mystified by Independence that she almost believed him.

"I'm kidding. Actually, my body was liquefied, and I was transported through a hole in the wall inside a garden hose—same as everybody else."

It took Melena two or three seconds to realize she was being played. "I'm serious."

"Well, *Princess Jaxon,* I believe you had your opportunity to ask me those kinds of questions already. If you neglected to extract that information from me, that's on you."

Adam walked over to Melena and offered her a skinned rabbit carcass on a stick.

"Oh, that looks super-yummy, but I'm going to pass." She was hungry, but the dark pink and white mess with a stick stabbed through it didn't exactly look appetizing to her.

"I'm gonna recommend that you don't pass," Adam advised. "I'm not sure when we'll have another opportunity to eat, and we have a lot of ground to cover today."

"Oh, do we?" Melena challenged. "Just where is it that we're headed?"

"Well, I thought we'd rendezvous with some friends in Rexburg."

"Rexburg? Do you have any idea where we are now?"

"Sure." Adam took both rabbits and propped up the sticks that went through them on a rock and proceeded to roast them over the fire. "We're somewhere between Glacier Federal Park and Flathead Federal Forest."

Melena was stunned. "How could you possibly know that? You were unconscious for the entire trip." A mischievous grin stole across Adam's lips. "You weren't unconscious, were you?"

"I was for some of the ride," He confessed.

The scent of roasting meat found its way to Melena's nostrils. Despite her recent conversion to Veganism, she was often tempted to return to her carnivorous ways. It wasn't as though there were a lot of options up here. She wasn't sure what plants, if any, were edible, and it had been a long time since she had last eaten.

"It's really amazing—to answer your first question."

"What?" Melena wasn't sure what he was referring to.

"You asked what Independence was like."

"Right. So, what's amazing about it?"

"It lives up to its name. People there are self-sufficient. They go to their jobs and put in an honest day's work. They take care of their families and look after those who need help."

"That doesn't sound so different from the rest of the Dominion."

"Doesn't it?" Adam scoffed. "A seventy percent unemployment rate among those not employed by the government throughout the Great Plains Dominion and the rest of the S.O.U.? Crippling taxes for anyone attempting to make a profit?" He shook his head. "People in Independence choose their education, pay for it, choose their trade or profession and work hard at it. They take care of the needs of their families and donate their excess money and time to those who are less fortunate. They're not forced to do that. They *choose* to do it. There's no poverty in Independence. Everywhere else you go, there's hardly anything *but* poverty. The only people with any means at all are high-level government employees."

"That's not true," Melena rebutted. "There are a lot of people in the private sector who make a good living."

"Well, I guess there are the exceptions of high-ranking officers in corporations that support certain government leaders. They do pretty well as long as they stay in line." Adam's eyes remained fixed on the slow-spinning rabbits he was roasting. "Actually, the best thing about Independence is the freedom to worship God as you see fit. You may be surprised to know that not everyone there believes the same. There are Christians, or *Tridents,* as you like to say, and Jews, Buddhists and Muslims, Hindus and Agnostics. All are allowed to follow their own conscience."

"Until it all blows up," Melena interjected. "Religion breeds conflict and division. One of these days, the people will rise up against each other, and the whole thing will fall apart."

"It's possible, I guess. Conflicts can arise. But that doesn't mean you stifle everyone's faith to try and avoid it." Adam's brow furrowed as he stared more intensely into the fire. "It's in our nature to want to know what lies beyond this world and how to make whatever comes next the best we can for ourselves and our families. We all want to know what the purpose of our life here is. Without faith, there's no hope. Without hope, what's the point in living? Demonizing religion and making it illegal has killed people's hope. You may as well have just killed the people."

Adam removed both rabbits from the fire and propped one up against the rock. He lifted the other, took an end of the stick in each hand and bit into the meat. The disgust Melena had felt earlier turned to envy. Hunger pains gnawed at her stomach.

"Wow," Adam remarked. "This is no silver pouch of mystery goop like back at the lab, but it's pretty good. I'm glad there are two. I feel like I could eat three or four."

"Maybe I'll just have a little taste." Melena moved closer to him, her mouth beginning to water.

"Sorry." Adam turned away from her. "My offer has expired. Weren't you gonna make a tossed salad or something?"

"Please, Adam?" Moving around to face Adam, she put her hand on his arm and gave him her best puppy-dog eyes.

"My goodness. You're going right to the goo-goo eyes to get what you want?"

"Hey, a girl's gotta do what a girl's gotta do, you know." Melena batted her eyelashes and flashed him a grin intended to shorten his breath a little. It appeared to be successful.

"That's pretty good. Instead of a taste of mine, I'm going to reward you with an entire rabbit." He bent down and picked up the stick with the other rabbit on it and presented it to her.

"Well, aren't you sweet?" She bit into the roasted flesh and thought it may have been the best thing she had ever tasted. "How did you catch these little guys anyway?"

"Well, they were curious, and I was hungry … and, apparently, pretty quick."

After enjoying several more bites of her rabbit, Melena decided the fire could use a little more fuel in order to dry her clothes more quickly. She found a large stick and tossed it into the flames. The stick catapulted several live coals into the air. The largest one landed on the sleeve of her jacket. The fabric ignited. Letting out a short scream, Melena dropped her rabbit kabob on the ground and rushed to recover her burning jacket. She took hold of the opposite sleeve and ran to the stream holding the flaming garment out in front of her. Then tossing the jacket into the stream, she proceeded to follow it as it floated along with the current. The flames were extinguished, but when she realized she was headed back in the direction of the moose, she opted to abandon the jacket in favor of returning to the safety of camp.

"What happened there?" Adam asked, clearly amused with her panic-driven actions. He had picked up the remains of her rabbit and was brushing off the dirt.

"It's fine. I don't really need the jacket anyway." She snatched the rabbit from him and proceeded to devour every last morsel without saying anything more about it.

After finishing off his meal, Adam took the rabbit skins and stretched them out across two sticks. He then held them near the flames.

"What are you doing?"

"I'm just preparing our drinking vessel."

"What do you mean?"

"I'll show you." After searing the inside of the skins, Adam dug a shallow hole in the ground with a stick and lined the hole with one of the rabbit pelts. He then took the other one and headed toward the stream.

"What are you doing with that?" Melena called after him.

Adam didn't answer. He sprinted downstream and out of sight. He returned after a minute with what remained of Melena's jacket and the pelt, cupped and filled with water. He took it to the hole he had dug and dumped the water into the other rabbit skin. He then took the jacket and ripped the remaining sleeve off of it.

"Hey!" Melena protested.

"You said you didn't need it."

Adam wrapped the wet sleeve around his hand and went over to the fire and removed several of the small stones he had placed there earlier from the coals and dropped them into the water. Steam rose into the air as the stones became submerged. He repeated the process.

"What does that do?" Melena inquired.

"It brings the water temperature up and kills the organisms in it."

"You're going to drink water out of that thing?"

Adam nodded. "You're welcome to go back to the stream for a swig, though, if you'd like."

Melena didn't need to be reminded of her experience with stream water. "I guess I could drink a little rabbit-water." Once the water had cooled to Adam's satisfaction, he lifted the pelt-bowl out of the hole and held it out to Melena. Holding back her dark hair with one hand, she leaned forward and took a sip. She pulled back and made a face to communicate to Adam her disapproval of the taste, but proceeded to drink. The entire process was then repeated until they both felt adequately hydrated.

Chapter 8

Once Melena's clothes had dried, she put them on under the lab coat and then returned it to Adam.

"We'd better get going." Adam started walking into the woods.

"How do you know which way to go?"

"We'll parallel the tracks at a distance. They should lead to a settlement eventually. We need to find some transportation."

"We're not going to Rexburg, Adam." Melena's tone turned serious. "We're going back to Rugby. You're still my prisoner, you know."

"Oh, I know. I just thought we might want to stay alive. Do you have a plan to get us back to Rugby safely?" He waited a few seconds for Melena to answer, and when she didn't, he turned and continued trudging through the trees.

After following the tracks around the lake for about three miles, Adam spotted a small cabin nestled in the pines. Cautiously, Adam and Melena approached it. It appeared to be abandoned. A few of the windows were broken, and the roof was in poor repair. Adam went to the back door and peered through the broken window in the door. The place was a mess with obvious signs that animals had inhabited it more recently than people. He gripped the door knob, and it fell off in his hand. He tossed it onto the porch and reached through the broken glass, turning the knob from the inside. The door creaked as he pushed it open and entered. Melena opted to remain outside.

Once inside, Adam entered one of the bedrooms and opened the closet door. Several pairs of jeans and a few shirts hung from a crooked rod, undisturbed. The jeans he decided on were three sizes larger than his waist, but after locating a brown leather belt, he was able to cinch them up for a decent fit. He selected a blue and black plaid button-up shirt and put it on. The pair of cowboy boots he spotted on the floor were also a few sizes too large, but were an improvement over bare feet, so he decided to go with them. On the shelf in the closet was an old, straw, western-style hat with a green feather sticking out of the band. He placed it on his head to complete the ensemble.

"Yee haw!" Melena remarked as Adam exited the cabin.

"Ma'am." He tipped his hat to her. "Whoever lived here had great taste. This is exactly how I dress back home."

Melena laughed. "I don't doubt it one bit." Suddenly, the smile on her face disappeared and was replaced by a look of panic.

"What's wrong?" Adam asked.

"Nothing." She clutched at her stomach. "Stay here." She half-walked, half-ran into the cabin, slamming the door behind her.

Adam smiled to himself and walked down to the lake. He skipped a few stones across the water as he waited for Melena. He felt guilty for taking pleasure from her pain, but he just couldn't help himself, considering her posh upbringing and cluelessness when it came to the outdoors.

Eventually, Melena emerged from the cabin door and walked briskly to him. "Let's go," she commanded, grabbing him by the arm and pulling him away from the cabin.

"Hold on," Adam protested. "I wanna go back inside and see if there's a bigger belt buckle in there."

Melena slapped him on the shoulder and pushed him forward. "No, you don't. Come on."

"I'm sorry." He cleared his throat. "Are you okay?"

Melena let out an exasperated sigh. “I will be once I’m home in Rugby and out of this stupid … nature!”

As the pair continued around the south end of the lake, they began to detect signs of civilization. Roads and old buildings grew more and more common the further south they travelled. *West Glacier* a weather-worn wooden sign read as they entered the small ghost town. The homes and cabins all appeared to be abandoned. There was no sign of human habitation anywhere.

“Looks like when this area was made a Federal Park everybody was evacuated,” Adam observed as they walked through a dilapidated old neighborhood. “How nice that they all had the opportunity to find new homes somewhere else.”

Melena had nothing to say.

Adam continued his sarcastic rant as they walked. “Well, at least there’s room up here for a secret lab where people can live in peace in their little glass cells, right?”

“I’m not really sure what that lab was all about. It was kind of creepy,” Melena admitted.

“And you know what they say about people who live in tiny glass houses?” Adam smirked.

“Yeah, I think your definition of *houses* is a little broad. I’m going to talk to my father about that. It doesn’t seem right to have people locked up like animals.”

Adam snorted. “They’re probably better off than a lot of other people living under this government. So, what’s your plan, Scion, when you become Senator of the Dominion? What changes will you make to better the peasant’s lives?”

“*When* I become Senator?” Melena shook her head. “I may have just put all of that in jeopardy.”

Adam stopped walking and turned to look at her. “Don’t take this too harshly, but I hope you’re right. The best thing that could happen to you, Melena, would be to get yourself out of this cycle of oppression. You really have no right to assume power over the people without being elected."

"I would be elected," Melena protested. "My father was elected. My grandfather was elected."

Adam rolled his eyes at her. "Come on. I mean a real election. Not by people whose paychecks are signed by your father. Not where the common people are threatened with starvation if they don't keep your family in power."

"It's not like that, Adam."

"Isn't it? Isn't it exactly like that?" Adam insisted, unrelenting.

"You think everything is so simple. It's a complicated system, but, yeah, I do have plans to improve the Dominion," Melena defended.

Adam turned and resumed a brisk pace, kicking a small stone across the street in front of him. "That's good. So do I."

Melena hurried to keep pace with him. "So, what, Robin Hood, you're going to swoop in and restore *America*, and everyone will kneel down and thank *God* for it, and it'll all be one big utopia?"

Adam stopped abruptly and turned on her. His jaw tightened, and his smoldering eyes bore into Melena's as she met his gaze. "You know what? I don't care what you think of me and my faith and ideology, but know this about me—I will never stop fighting until the principles of liberty and prosperity govern this country again. I won't relent until we no longer live under a government where families can be torn from their beds in the middle of the night, tried in a mock court and executed on the spot for the crime of believing in God and telling someone about it!" Adam felt his neck getting warm and the muscles in his back tightening as his voice began to rise. "You're absolutely right. I am going to help restore *America*! I frankly don't care if that sounds ridiculous to you. People everywhere are crying out for freedom and for the opportunity to prosper. They won't live under the thumb of the political elite any longer. They just need a voice. We're going to give them a voice." He turned around and stalked ahead, not bothering to look back at Melena as he continued shouting. "You can be part of it or be destroyed by it, but it's happening either way."

Silence prevailed as the search for life in the little town resumed. Eventually, the only modern-looking building in town came into view—a small train station. Keeping his distance, Adam listened carefully for signs of human occupation inside the station. All he could hear was the hum of the batteries that powered it. Upon entering, his eyes quickly swept the small area, confirming that the station was empty.

Melena walked up to the large monitor mounted on the wall. "According to the schedule, a westbound train is due to arrive tomorrow morning at six a.m."

Adam nodded. "Okay. We can probably just sleep here. We'll have to figure out a way to get on board without being detected." Adam searched the station for a restroom until he located one in the back corner. "I'm gonna use the restroom. Just stay right there."

Upon returning from the restroom, Adam found Melena standing in the middle of the room waiting for him, the remote to his collar in her hand. "An air conveyor from Rugby is on its way to extract us."

Looking over her shoulder, Adam noticed an emergency call pad built into the wall. "You gave Daddy a call, did you?"

"Adam, you're going to need my help if you're going to survive. I promise you'll be treated fairly when we get back to Rugby. If you cooperate, I can persuade my father to release you after the stamp is recovered."

Adam began walking slowly toward her. Melena backed up, holding the remote out in front of her. "Don't make me use this, Adam," she threatened. "I've been assured that you won't be harmed as long as you don't resist." Adam continued moving toward her. "I've done it before, Adam. Stop!"

Adam took two more steps toward her and then froze. "Someone's coming."

Melena hurried to the window and peered out, searching up and down the train tracks and adjacent street. "I don't see anything."

"I can hear them. Sounds like maybe two police transports and a solo-rider," Adam guessed.

Chapter 9

Melena continued to search the streets outside through the window. After a few seconds, the posse came into view. "Hava!" she gasped. "Adam, this has got to be Hava. I don't know how she could have—" She turned her head and scanned the station. "Adam?" she called out, but he was nowhere in sight. She went back to the window and watched as six armed police agents surrounded the station. Removing a sleek, black helmet, Hava dismounted her solo-rider and stood in front of the station door.

"Melena," Hava shouted at the door, "I'm here to offer you the opportunity to redeem yourself. You and the traitor can come out now, and I may allow you the chance to live to tell your side of the story to the Senator."

"Your services are no longer required, Hava," Melena shouted back. "An air conveyor is en route to take the prisoner and me back to Rugby. You can return to the lab, and I may allow *you* the opportunity to apologize for sabotaging the interrogation and trying to kill both of us."

Hava laughed out loud. "Oh, little Ms. Jaxon, you are a funny one." The station door burst open, and four police agents filed inside and surrounded Melena. Hava entered behind them and closed the door. "Where is he?" Her curly black hair whipped her face as her head swiveled from side to side searching the station for Adam.

"He's secure," Melena bluffed, "but he'll be long gone if you don't back down until our transport arrives."

Hava smiled at Melena, the tattoos on her cheeks changing shape with the curvature of her mouth. She stepped up to Melena and looked her in the eyes. Then, to Melena's surprise, she cocked back and then buried her fist into Melena's cheek, sending her sprawling onto the wooden floor. The remote to Adam's collar dislodged from Melena's hand and went tumbling across the room.

"I'm so sorry to be the bearer of bad news, Melena, but there is no air conveyor coming for you." Hava walked to the remote and picked it up. "When are you going to wake up and realize that I am an extension of Senator Jaxon's leadership? I am the true Scion. Do you honestly think that such a strong leader would turn the Dominion over to a spoiled, weak little girl?" She reached down and grabbed Melena by the throat and lifted her to her feet. "I suggest you learn some respect in a hurry because your life is literally in my hands."

Outside the station, there was shouting and several spurts of automatic weapon fire, then silence. Hava's attention turned to the door. "What's going on out there?"

The door opened, slowly. Adam's face peeked in around it. "Hava, I need to borrow your ride."

"Kill him!" Hava shouted to the police agents. The agents fired at the door, but Adam was no longer there. In a blur, he flew across the room and barreled into the nearest agent, causing him to slam into the agent next to him and sending both crashing to the floor. After receiving a swift roundhouse kick from Adam's boot to the side of the head, the third agent lost control of his weapon and it spat several rounds into the leg of the fourth agent. They both went down. Before the first two agents could recover, Adam spun back to them and delivered kicks into each of their faces, leaving all four either writhing on the ground or unconscious. Adam gathered their weapons and tossed them across the room.

"That really is amazing." Hava still had Melena by the throat. "I'd love to know how you did that, but I'm not curious enough to let you live to tell me." She smiled as she lifted the remote to Adam's collar and pointed it at him. She pushed the button and waited for him to collapse. Adam remained on his feet. Then, in a flash, he was in front of Hava landing a punishing right cross directly into her forehead. Upended, her feet flew into the air, and the first thing to hit the floor was the back of her head. She was out cold.

Adam stood over her. “That’s the first time I’ve ever hit a girl, but you’re so repulsive I don’t think it counts.”

Melena was stunned. She just stood gaping at him.

Adam gave her a mischievous grin. “You wanna stick around and wait for that air conveyer, or do you wanna go for a ride?” Without waiting for an answer, he turned and walked out the door.

Melena stood in the doorway and watched Adam mount the solo-rider. He looked up at her with a confident grin and waited for her decision. She lingered over the threshold for a moment considering her options. Finally, she tightened her lips together and shook her head. “Crap,” she muttered before running down the steps and climbing onto the vehicle behind him. He handed her Hava’s helmet. She tilted her head back, pulled the helmet on and wrapped her arms around Adam’s torso as the solo-rider’s front wheel left the ground and the vehicle leaped onto the road, leaving the train station in a cloud of dust.

Chapter 10

It had been dark for nearly three hours before the solo-rider arrived in Rexburg. Adam turned the headlamp off before turning onto a dirt driveway and stopping in front of a large barn. "Anybody home?" he called in the direction of the barn.

There was silence for a few moments then a voice called back from inside. "What do you stand for?"

"Truth and honor," Adam replied.

One side of the barn door rolled open, and Adam drove inside into darkness. As soon as the door shut, the lights came on inside the barn.

"Adam, where've you been, man?" It was the same voice that had requested the password.

"Camping, Droven. What've you been up to?" Adam answered.

Two young men and a young woman emerged from behind an old farming tractor. The guy Adam called *Droven* strode up to the solo-rider as Adam and Melena were dismounting and embraced Adam. "Oh, man, you *have* been camping. You stink like smoke, brother."

Droven was tall and handsome with dark brown skin, big brown eyes and a shaved head. Dimples formed in his cheeks as he grinned at his friend.

"Adam!" The young woman rushed to Adam, her long blond ponytail waving back and forth behind her as she ran. She also embraced him. "What happened?"

"Well, I told you we should've been more careful cooperating with The Response. Their idea of delivery was slightly different than mine." Adam smiled at the group and then turned and acknowledged Melena. "Guys, this is Melena

Jaxon. She helped me escape Federal Police custody and is now my prisoner."

Melena removed her helmet and gave Adam a fierce look. "I'm your *what*?" He didn't answer, but nodded in the direction of the group. Melena turned to the others. "Hi." She put her hand up and gave a quick wave.

"Melena Jaxon?" The other young man—a short, fiery-haired and freckle-faced guy—gave Adam a confused look. "As in the daughter of Senator Cai Jaxon?"

Adam raised his eyebrows and looked at Melena. "Wait, are you two related?"

Melena didn't know what to say. Her mouth opened and shut as she looked around the group and then back at Adam.

Adam smiled as he rescued her from the awkwardness. "Yes, she is the very Scion of the Great Plains Dominion."

The redhead looked even more confused. He stared at Melena, then back at Adam.

"Melena is in it pretty deep for helping me," Adam explained. "There's a very heavily tattooed, very jealous woman pursuing us who would like to do her in and take her place as Scion."

The blond-haired, green-eyed girl faced Melena. "It sounds like you were pretty brave to help Adam." Her gaze lingered as she studied Melena.

Melena gave her a quick grin back, not quite sure how to respond.

"What are you wearing?" Droven asked, obviously amused by Adam's outfit. "Are we headed to the rodeo?"

"What's the rodeo?" the blond asked.

"Rodeo was an exhibition where cowboys competed in various skills with livestock, Jivvy," the redheaded guy related. "It was outlawed about twenty years ago because the government thought it was unkind to the animals and dangerous to the cowboys. My dad used to ride mustangs in the rodeo when he was young. It was quite popular in this area."

"How did *you* know about rodeo, Droven," Adam laughed. "Have you ever been on a horse?"

"Oh, yeah, all the time. They used to roam the streets of K.C." Droven shook his head. "C'mon now. I just have knowledge of all sorts stored right here." He tapped his temple with his finger.

"I do need a change of clothes," Adam conceded. "I'm slightly conspicuous in this."

"Well, shall we head below?" the girl the redhead had called *Jivvy* asked.

"Are we … *all* going below?" The redheaded guy looked at Adam, then at Melena, then back at Adam.

"Of course, James." Adam smiled. "We could definitely use a warm shower and a good night's rest. Do you have room for Melena, Jivvy?"

"Sure. There's an extra bed, and I should be able to find something for her to wear."

Droven walked to the barn wall and arranged some hand tools that mounted to it. Once they were all in place, several wood planks on the floor slid back, revealing a metal staircase. Jivvy lead the way, motioning for Melena to follow. At the bottom of the staircase, Jivvy opened a door and walked into a large office. Melena surveyed the room and was instantly curious at some of the tech that was being utilized. It looked advanced beyond anything she had ever used or even seen. There was a three-dimensional virtual map stretching horizontally across a table, with bubbles of data hovering over certain points on it. Weather systems, tiny aircraft and land vehicles moved across the map as if in real time. Above three desks, there were large, transparent monitors covered in graphics and text that appeared to be floating in mid-air.

Adam came up behind Melena, took her by the shoulders and hurried her through the office and into another area, which appeared to be living quarters. There was a lounge area with two bedrooms branching off from it.

Jivvy motioned with her hand. “Melena, if you want to come with me, I’ll see if we can get you cleaned up a little and find you something to wear to bed.”

Melena gave Adam a quick glance, looking for reassurance, and then followed Jivvy into one of the rooms and shut the door behind her. “Thank you … *Jivvy*, is it?”

“It’s Jivvissa, but everybody calls me Jivvy”.

Jivvy seemed friendly. She was strikingly beautiful. She had clear, creamy skin and big green eyes. Melena found herself wondering what her relationship with Adam might be.

“The washroom is right through that door.”

“Great,” Melena sighed. “I really appreciate this.”

Melena entered the washroom and closed the door. She stood at the sink and stared at herself in the mirror. Her hair was dirty and matted from wearing Hava’s helmet for the past seven hours. What was left of her make-up was smudged and smeared. More concerning to her than her appearance, however, was her discomfort with the situation she was in. She was associating with apparent enemies of the S.O.U. The scenario seemed bizarre, yet she had been accepted into the safe house without question, excepting the redheaded guy who seemed quite uncomfortable with her presence. And what to think about Adam? She couldn’t deny that she was beginning to care for this strange, yet amazing guy who was responsible for causing her so much trouble. She wondered why he continued to trust her after she had betrayed him at the train station. Was it because he had feelings for her too? She shook her head to bring herself out of her thoughts. She went to the shower and turned the water on, then undressed and stepped inside. The warm water felt like a dream come true.

Jivvy was laying out clothing on the extra bed for Melena when she exited the washroom. “You look about my size, so hopefully this will fit.”

Melena smiled and quickly dressed. “This will be great. Thank you so much.” She slipped under the covers and was nearly asleep by the time her damp head hit the pillow. She thought she heard Jivvy say “good night,” but she was too exhausted to respond.

Chapter 11

A series of codes and algorithms flashed through Adam's mind—white characters on a black backdrop. He struggled to decipher the data that continually moved across the stage of his mind until he was pulled out of his dream by the sound of voices in another room.

"I'm sure it's not what a Scion would typically wear, but given the circumstances, that's probably best."

"It'll be perfect, Jivvy. Thanks for everything."

Adam sat up and looked around the room. Droven was already up and in the washroom.

"So, you and Adam are friends?" he heard Melena ask.

"Yeah, we've known each other for years. My mom and his aunt are close."

"Oh, that's great."

Adam felt a little guilty for eavesdropping, but it wasn't as though he had a choice. Somehow, his senses had been heightened to amazing levels. Whatever The Response's surgeon had done to him while inserting the stamp into his brain, it seemed to have caused some definite physiological changes. He determined to request an evaluation by the medical staff in Independence when the stamp was removed. Maybe they would have some answers. He wondered if extracting the stamp would reverse the changes in him. Aside from the initial discomfort and extreme sensitivity of his sight and hearing, it had become quite advantageous. In addition, the physical agility and speed he had acquired was simply incredible. It was as though the time gap between his mind willing his body to move and his body actually responding had been reduced to being virtually instantaneous. These new traits had proved quite useful and had saved his and Melena's lives a few times already.

"So, what made you decide to help Adam?" Adam was trying not to listen, but Jivvy's question caught his attention.

"Well, one of my colleagues wanted to perform a sort of crude surgery on Adam that probably would have killed him. I didn't think that was justified or necessary, so I decided to try and get him back to Rugby where he would be safe," Melena recounted.

"Well, I'm glad you did. I don't know what I would've done if we'd have lost Adam. He's a huge asset to us and just a really great guy." Adam had never heard Jivvy speak about him that way. She always tried to act tough around him and rarely expressed her feelings.

Droven appeared in the washroom doorway. "You about ready to get this thing started, or are you gonna sleep the whole day?"

"Yeah, I'm up." Adam got out of bed and headed to the washroom. "Get outta there so I can get ready."

Adam moved past Droven and was about to shut the door behind him. Droven caught the door. "Adam, I'm glad you're okay, man. The way that whole thing went down with The Response was a mess, and I can't believe you ended up in S.O.U. custody." He shook his head. "You know, I didn't mention it last night, but it's pretty impressive the way you and Jaxon's daughter busted outta that lab."

Adam smiled. "Thanks, man. If I impressed you, it was worth it." He shut the door and turned the water on in the shower. He sighed as he thought about how grateful he was to be reunited with people he trusted. Droven was his closest friend. Adam thought of their first encounter on the streets of Kansas City when Adam was eleven years old. Droven was also living alone on the streets and trying to survive. They had both discovered that the dumpster outside the mayor's mansion was a virtual goldmine for leftover food. One day, they arrived at the dumpster at the same time to claim a meal. A fistfight had broken out, and Droven had pummeled Adam pretty good. After leaving him on the ground with a bloody mouth and nose, Droven had taken pity on Adam and tossed him a few slices of bread as he made his exit. Thereafter, they began working together to find food and to keep each other out of trouble.

After Adam moved to Independence with his aunt and uncle, he arranged for another family to take Droven in. The rest was history. They had gone to school together, played football together and been nearly inseparable. When Adam had taken Melena's page from her after emerging from the rail tunnel, Droven was the first person he thought of to contact. He knew his friend would come through for him, so he used the device to send him a message to arrange their rendezvous in Rexburg.

Adam's thoughts returned to the present as he stepped into the shower. Fortunately, Melena had gone to sleep before the rest of the group the previous night, so he was able to collaborate with Droven, Jivvy and James to formulate a plan to get them all back to Independence. James had intercepted a communication to all Federal Police units that a fugitive called Adam Winter had kidnapped Senator Jaxon's daughter and was at large. Surveillance cameras from the lab had captured a number of images of the two of them so his face had now been broadcast to the entire Federal Police organization. It was nearly twelve hundred miles from Rexburg to Independence and every unit along the way would be looking for them.

Once everyone was dressed and had eaten breakfast, they convened in the lounge to discuss disguises and travel plans.

"Melena, how do you feel about facial tattoos?" Droven asked, walking into the room holding several colors of ink pens in his hand. "I'm thinking flames." He bobbed his head up and down while giving her a wide grin. "You too, Adam. How about a skeleton face for you?"

"I was thinking about getting one of those anyway," Adam replied without cracking a smile.

"Is that really necessary?" Melena asked, sounding slightly uncomfortable with the idea.

"It'll be harder for any Feds who see you to ID you. It'll make it a little harder for the visual scanners to recognize you, too. It won't help with the structural ones, but it's better than nothing," Droven explained.

"Will you excuse Melena and me for a second?" Adam asked, taking Melena by the arm. He led her into the kitchen and turned to face her. "Listen, I want to take you with me to Independence. Of course, you're not actually my prisoner so I'll give you the option. You can stay in Rexburg and wait to be extracted by your dad or …" he paused, "you can come with me. It might be dangerous getting there, but I would love for you to see it."

Melena didn't answer right away. She studied his eyes for a few moments. "I suppose Hava is still out there searching for us." She seemed to be considering this. "Maybe I'd better stick with you." She flashed him a soft grin. "You promise to protect me?"

There was no humor in Adam's eyes when he answered. "I'll protect you with my life."

Melena's heart warmed, and her smile grew wider at that.

"Before we go," Adam continued, "I need you to know that—because of everything that's happened—my life may be in your hands again at some point. I can't risk you threatening to paralyze me with your remote."

"I don't even have the remote anymore, you moron," Melena chuckled. "Anyway, you obviously managed to remove the collar."

Adam reached up and rubbed his neck where the collar had been.

A perplexed look crossed Melena's face. "I forgot to ask you what happened in the train station when Hava tried to activate it. Why didn't it paralyze you like it did before?"

Adam chuckled back at her. "Seriously? I disabled the collar and the remote that night in the woods. I just wore it around after that because I thought it was fashionable."

Melena burst out laughing. She leaned into him and gave him a little punch on the chest with her fist.

Adam picked up a lock of her long, milk-chocolate-colored hair from off of her shoulder. "We'll probably need to shave this off if we're gonna fool anyone." He tried to make his face look serious.

She didn't buy it for a second. "Well, if you think it will help …" She wasn't as good at looking serious. "C'mon, let's go get you a skeleton tat on your face." Her hand ran down his arm and stopped when her fingers reached his. They interlocked for a moment as she pulled him back into the lounge area and then let go.

"Droven, I would like blue flames, please, with orange tips," Melena announced.

Droven's dimples appeared as he smiled, broadly. "Well then, get over here and let me do my work." He found his blue pen and popped off the lid.

Chapter 12

Adam placed a pair of sleek, dark glasses over his eyes and examined himself in the washroom mirror. He wished he would have had Droven draw a skeleton face on him back when they were playing football. It looked quite intimidating. It also disguised his features really well. The dark glasses only enhanced the look, in addition to improving his vision even further. Melena appeared over his shoulder in the mirror to give herself a look as well. Jivvy had provided her with a grey beret-style cap with a small brim on one side. Her hair was gathered up into the cap. Droven's artwork on her face looked pretty impressive. Her deep blue eyes sparkled in the midst of the flames he had penned on. Adam decided that she would also need dark glasses. Her eyes were too recognizable, even surrounded by an elaborate fake tattoo.

The clothes Jivvy had given Melena—a grey top, black shorts and tall black leather boots—fit remarkably well. When Jivvy showed up in the doorway to take a look at the two of them, he couldn't help but notice that the two women were very close in height and body type.

"James is ready with the Vector," Jivvy informed them. "Let's get moving."

James was just unplugging an electrical cord from an old, small, government-produced, battery-powered vehicle called a *Vector* when the group emerged from the barn. "This thing can only hold a charge for about eighty kilometers, so we're going to have to stop more frequently than would be ideal."

Adam shook his head, disgusted. The technology to power road vehicles had surpassed that of the Vector decades ago, but the batteries the Vector used were cheap and the corporation contracted to produce them was nice and cozy with some government officials. Numerous political campaigns had been funded through their generous donations.

Droven walked a small, beat-up solo-rider out of the barn, then climbed on and fastened his helmet. He secured a long black bag behind the seat before starting the engine. He had volunteered to ride ahead of the Vector and scout for trouble. "I hope this piece-a-junk can make it to Independence." He shook his head. "I'll have to ditch it when we get there, though. Ain't nobody in town gonna see me on this thing."

Adam and Melena climbed into the back seat of the government vehicle while Jivvy slid into the front seat next to James, who was looking more than a little apprehensive. "You ready, James?" She smiled at him, attempting to calm his nerves.

"I really appreciate your help, James." Adam reached up and grabbed him by the shoulder. "We're gonna be just fine, man."

"Yep," James responded, trying to sound confident. "Let's do it." He picked a blue and white baseball cap up from off of the dash and pulled it on over his red hair, then pulled the vehicle out from behind the barn and turned out onto the street.

Jivvy turned to face Melena in the back seat. "Melena, have you ever done a long trip in a road vehicle before?"

"Um, no, I think this will be my first," Melena replied. "How long do you think it will take us?"

"In a legal land vehicle?" Jivvy rubbed her chin, looking thoughtful. "Probably twenty-four hours driving straight through, if we go the eighty-kilometer-per-hour speed limit. If we were in my C-twenty-six, it would probably take us ten," she bragged.

"Wow. Is a C-twenty-six an air vehicle?" Melena asked.

"No, it's a sports car. It has a combustion engine."

"A combustion engine?" Melena looked confused. "You mean like an old gasoline-fueled engine?"

"No, I mean like a *new* gasoline-fueled engine. It has quadruple the horse power of the piece of garbage we're riding in now."

"Hey," James protested. "Don't talk that way about my baby."

Jivvy gave him a quick smile to acknowledge him and then went on. "Could outrun a Federal Police Chaser without any trouble. It gets almost three hundred miles per gallon, but there's no place out here to fill it up.

"Of course there's nowhere out here to fill it up—it's illegal." Melena sounded only slightly condescending. "A road vehicle that can go that fast sounds pretty dangerous."

"Oh, it's not dangerous if you know how to handle it. It's not any more dangerous than what Adam drives back home." Jivvy turned to Adam and waited for him to enter the conversation.

"I'm just gonna grab a little nap." He leaned his head against the window, but left his eyes open behind the dark lenses. "You two continue getting to know each other."

"What do you drive, Melena?" Jivvy inquired.

"Actually, I don't do a lot of driving. I have a driver for short trips and usually take an air conveyer if I'm going a long distance."

"Wow. That sounds pretty convenient—makes me wonder how productive regular people would be if they could get around as easily." Jivvy grimaced. "Sorry, Melena, I didn't mean for it to come out that way. I just meant that it would be great if everyone had access to good transportation."

"What about you?" Melena asked, ignoring the jab. "How did you get to Rexburg so quickly?"

"Uh, I don't think I'm ready to share that information quite yet. I can tell you, however, that Droven and I could definitely get home quicker if we didn't have any extras." Jivvy turned forward and faced the windshield, indicating that the conversation was over.

"So, James …" Melena leaned forward. "Are you from Independence too?"

James seemed startled and sat up in his seat. "Um, no, no, I was actually born and raised here in Rexburg, and I live here now. That barn belonged to my family back when they used to farm potatoes."

"Oh. So, how did you get mixed up with a dangerous fugitive like Adam?" Melena asked, playfully.

"I'm not sure I want to incriminate myself." James was more serious about his comment than Melena was about hers, but he continued anyway. "My family makes regular trips to Independence to attend conferences. Adam's aunt and uncle have hosted us at their home for as long as I can remember. Adam's probably the most loyal and sincere friend I've ever had."

"Excuse me?" Jivvy broke in. "And what am I?"

James hesitated. "Jivvy's the prettiest friend I've ever had." He finally managed a smile.

Jivvy threw her head back and laughed, then punched him in the arm.

James' face suddenly turned serious. "Droven just came upon a police scanner less than two kilometers down the highway. It's a visual scanner."

"How are you two communicating?" Melena asked.

"Oh, I've got his eyes and ears," James answered.

"What does that mean?"

"Well, one of my lenses projects what he sees up here on the windshield." James tapped his finger on the glass high on the left side of the windshield. "And I can hear his voice in my ear."

Melena looked baffled. Neither the lens nor the projection was visible.

"Adam, what's the call? There isn't an exit between here and there." James' voice sounded tense.

"I think we'll draw attention to ourselves if we leave the highway. Might as well see if our disguises are any good."

The four of them sat in silence for a minute or two.

"All right, we're through," Jivvy informed them.

Adam sighed. "I guess we'll find out pretty soon whether or not that worked."

The mood inside the Vector became much more somber with the possibility of a police presence making itself known at any moment. The passengers fell mostly silent for the better part of an hour until a light on the dash began flashing.

"Looks like she's about spent," James announced just before they reached the outskirts of Blackfoot. "There's a charging station up ahead that we ought to use before we get into town."

"I agree," Adam spoke up. "Let's avoid a busier station."

James exited the highway and pulled into the government-run charging station.

"This is ridiculous," Jivvy complained. "We're going to have to stop every eighty kilometers to charge this stupid thing?"

"It may not be as convenient," Melena defended, "but it's much better for the environment than the carbon belcher you described earlier."

Jivvy rolled her eyes, but said nothing. A quiet tension seemed to be growing between the two women.

“I’m going to use the restroom,” Jivvy huffed as she exited the vehicle and headed for the small convenience store.

“Me too.” Adam opened his door and climbed out. He looked back at Melena. “You doing okay?”

“Yeah.” She smiled, but didn’t look at him.

Adam left his glasses on as he entered the store. He tried to avoid the gaze of the large, bearded cashier as he made his way to the restroom. When he emerged from the restroom, he made a beeline for the front door, but waited for Jivvy once he was outside. After a few seconds, Jivvy came out the door. Adam caught her by the arm and turned her to face him. “Jiv, take it easy on Melena. I really think that once she sees what Independence is like, she’ll come around.”

Jivvy sighed in the direction of the parked Vector. “I hope you know what you’re doing, Adam. I mean, taking a future S.O.U. Senator inside the walls is a bad idea if you ask me. I would think that would be obvious.”

“I know it seems that way, but we have to start winning the hearts of the people. Getting someone with influence to see what this nation could be like might be worth the risk. Besides that, I just somehow feel compelled to take her there.” Adam suddenly perked up. He could hear a vehicle approaching. “Someone’s coming.”

Jivvy looked over his shoulder. “Don’t turn around. We might have a problem.”

Adam concentrated on the low hum of the engines. “Sounds like two chasers. How many agents can you see?”

“Looks like three in one chaser and two in the other.”

Adam heard multiple chaser doors open and shut and boots walking through loose gravel.

“What’s this?” Adam heard one agent whisper to another.

"I don't know," the other agent answered. "They look like about the right age, but that girl's blond. The Jaxon girl's a brunette."

"They're coming toward us," Jivvy whispered, her lips as still as a ventriloquist.

"It's all right," Adam assured her with a grin. "There's only five of them."

Without warning, Jivvy leaned in and pressed her lips onto his. Adam's eyes widened. Jivvy's were closed. He felt as though he should pull away, but realized after a moment that she was trying to protect him by hiding his face from the police agents. The kiss became more passionate, however, as the officers drew closer. Her hair fell across his face, and Adam couldn't help but notice how good she smelled. She reached her hand up behind his neck and ran her fingers through the hair on the back of his head.

"Hey," one of the agents called out. Jivvy and Adam went on as if they didn't hear. "Hey!" he repeated, a little louder this time.

Finally, Jivvy broke the lip lock and looked up at the agent. "Yes, officer?" she sighed, giving him an annoyed look.

Adam kept his back to the agents, but turned his head slightly, revealing the dark tattoo on his face.

The agent held out a page with an image of Melena and Adam on the screen. "Have you seen either of these two around here?"

"No, sir." Jivvy shook her head. "The guy is cute, though. Who is he?"

The agent didn't acknowledge Jivvy's question. "What about you?" He tapped Adam on the back with the page.

Adam turned his body just enough to glance down at the image. "Don't think so."

The agent glared at the two of them for a moment and then walked back to his companions. "When was this image taken? Does our perp have a facial tattoo now?" Adam heard him ask the other agents.

"Negative. The image is only two days old."

Adam put his arm around Jivvy's waist and casually led her back to the Vector. The agents disappeared inside the store.

"Are we charged up?" Adam asked James as he opened Jivvy's door and helped her inside.

"Not quite. She needs about three more minutes."

Adam climbed into the back seat and set his eyes on the store's front door, hoping he had seen the last of the police agents.

Melena leaned forward. "That was quick thinking, Jivvy."

Jivvy turned around and smiled. "Thanks."

Melena sat back. "Very convincing."

Adam turned away from Melena and smiled to himself. She was trying to sound sincere, but the jealousy in her voice was evident. He thought about Jivvy's aggressive move. It had definitely taken him by surprise. It was unlike her. He wondered where *that* Jivvy had been back in high school when he had made multiple efforts to get her attention. Eventually, he had come to accept that she would never see him as anything other than a friend. Not that he thought the kiss meant anything. It was tactical. He had to agree with Melena, however—it was very convincing.

The police agents filed out of the store, each holding a cup of coffee, just as James was disconnecting the power cable from the Vector. James hurried back into the vehicle and started the engine. He was trying to keep an eye on the agents as he pulled out and had to slam on the brakes to avoid an oncoming vehicle. The sound of skidding on the gravel under the Vector's tires caught the attention of the agents. They stared for a moment, but made no move to pursue as the Vector pulled onto the street and headed back toward the highway.

Chapter 13

Once again, codes and data ran through Adam's mind. They moved so fast that he couldn't detect any patterns or recognizable information. Eventually, the symbols and numbers began to slow down.

"Adam."

Adam thought it was odd to hear his name. He didn't see anyone.

"Adam!"

After a second, he recognized James' voice and opened his eyes. Melena's head was lying on his shoulder. It looked like she had also nodded off at some point.

"What's the matter, James?" Adam yawned.

"I'm sorry, man. Droven was singing in my ear so I turned it off for a few minutes. I didn't see the scanner, and we went through it."

"Visual?"

"Structural. I'm sorry. He tried to warn me, but I couldn't hear him, and this highway's too dark to have seen it."

"It's okay, James. We'll just keep our eyes open. Where are we?" Adam looked out the window, but could see only gray rocks and brush in the darkness.

"We're about sixteen kilometers from Green River."

"We probably ought to get off the federal highway," Jivvy suggested. "We should get off at Green River and take another route."

"I agree." Adam rubbed his eyes as Melena began to stir.

"Where are we?" Melena sat up and tried to see out of the dark window.

"Just about to Green River." Jivvy looked over her shoulder and smiled at the groggy couple. "You two have a nice nap?"

"Yeah, how long have I been out?" Melena asked, straining to see the clock on the dash.

"Oh, about two hours, I'd say. We took the mountain highways to avoid scanners and this *environmentally-friendly* engine was a less-than-stellar climber, so we haven't gone as far as we'd hoped we would," Jivvy explained.

"Come on, Jivvy, it wasn't that—" James' attention turned to his rear view monitor where the flashing of red and blue lights had appeared. "Uh oh."

Adam turned and looked out the back window. Two chasers were coming up fast.

The Vector accelerated slowly. "Oh, James, is that all she's got?" Jivvy complained.

"I've got the accelerator down! Citizen vehicles are designed to be slower than chasers, Jivvy. I can't outrun them!"

Adam looked ahead and saw that the highway entered into a tunnel through the side of a mountain in the distance. "James, there's a tunnel ahead. Try and stay in front of the chasers, and let's get into the tunnel before they do."

One of the chasers pulled up alongside the left side of the Vector. "This is the Federal Police. Pull your vehicle over, now!" a voice blared from the chaser's speaker.

"Droven, I didn't copy!" James yelled.

"Pull your vehicle to the shoulder," the voice blared once again.

"Droven, we're being pursued by two chasers, and I can't hear you!"

The other chaser pulled up along the right side of the Vector. After a moment, it began accelerating and making a move to get in front of the Vector. James turned the wheel slightly to the right, bumping the side of the chaser. The chaser swerved and slowed down enough to stay behind. The lights from inside the tunnel grew closer as the Vector and its pursuers neared the entrance.

"Droven says not to enter the tunnel!" James had finally understood Droven's warning, but it was too late. Both chasers backed off and took positions behind the Vector as it entered the tunnel. Adam looked ahead and saw flashing lights from additional chasers blocking the tunnel's exit.

"They've got us blocked in, James," Adam calmly admitted. "Slow down so I can get out."

"What!" Jivvy exclaimed. "Get out?"

"Yeah, let me divert their attention and see if I can find a way to get you guys outta here. James, keep going about this speed until we get close to the road block," Adam instructed as he prepared to leap out the door.

"Adam!" Jivvy yelled. "Don't be stupid. They'll kill you!"

"I'll be okay." Adam gave her a confident smile. "Watch this. They won't be able to catch me."

Adam opened the door and leapt out. His feet hit the ground running as he kept pace with the Vector. Four chasers loomed ahead, completely blocking both lanes. He scanned the road block, attempting to count all of the agents. There were ten that he could see. The Vector began to slow as they neared the end of the tunnel. He kept pace with it for a few more moments, then burst to full speed toward the four chasers. The blast of automatic weapon fire rang in his ears as bullets impacted against the concrete wall behind him.

He whipped around the back of the chaser on the left with bullets continuing to fly all around him. Glass shattered as the agents firing at him from the right side of the road block hit the chasers on the left side. Adam heard several agents cry out as they were sprayed with friendly fire. He maneuvered around the rear of the road block, knocking two agents to the ground in clothesline fashion as he zipped past them. One agent stepped out in front of Adam and trained his weapon on him. Adam slid, baseball-style, into the legs of the agent as bullets flew just over his head. The agent went down face first onto the road. Adam got to his feet just in time to receive a crushing blow to the chest that put him immediately on his back. He rolled onto his side, trying to catch the breath that been knocked out of him. A black leather boot stepped on his chest and pushed him onto his back.

Adam looked up to see the owner of the boot. "Sinclair?" he wheezed.

The man standing above him held a black steel baton in one hand and a hand gun in the other. "Well, look who it is."

"Are you from Europe, Marshal?" Adam squeaked, still trying to catch his breath. "In our culture, you can take an occasional shower. You still smell like an onion."

Marshal Marbury grunted. "Boy, I've missed you. We're going to have us a good time getting reacquainted."

Adam winced, still catching his breath. "I don't know how to put this gently, Marshal, so I'm just gonna say it. I'm not into you. At all. You're gonna make some dude super unhappy someday, but I'm just not—" Adam was interrupted by the toe of the Marshal's boot slamming into his left cheek. Adam tasted blood and turned his head to spit it out. "Oh, man, I was afraid you'd take it that way."

Marshal Marbury grinned down at Adam. "I don't know how you got so fast, boy. You're like a little roadrunner runnin' around. I think I'm going to have to slow you down some."

The Marshal took aim at Adam's right thigh. Adam cringed, anticipating the impact of a bullet ripping through his flesh. Suddenly, a bright light flashed, and Marshal Marbury's body was lifted off of his feet, thrown into a nearby chaser and crumpled to the ground. Adam sat up in time to see more flashes light up the tunnel. He got to his feet, but kept close to the nearest chaser. The flashes began at the tunnel's exit, but there were some coming from behind the Vector as well. After a few seconds, the flashes stopped. Jivvy appeared from behind the Vector holding a long, silver weapon. The agents from the pursuing chasers were all lying still on the street around their vehicles. Adam turned to see Droven emerge from the shadows just outside the tunnel's exit. He was holding the same weapon in his hands.

Adam gave Droven an ear-to-ear smile and pointed at his weapon. "It that one of the new ones?" Droven nodded. "Truth and honor, brother."

"Truth and honor," Droven repeated.

"Hey!" Droven called out to Jivvy as she approached the two of them. "Did you do all that damage over there?"

"Yes, sir," she answered, confidently.

Droven whistled and shook his head. "Well, let's see if we can get you outta here." He ran back out of the tunnel and returned with another device in hand. He pointed it at the front fender of one of the chasers in the center of the road block and activated it. The chaser's wheels screeched as the rear of the vehicle pivoted, opening up a path wide enough for the Vector to pass through. James maneuvered through the gap and stopped to pick up his passengers.

"Hey!" Adam called out to Droven before getting in the Vector. "Thanks for showing up. I was about to get a bullet in the leg."

"Of course, brother." Droven smiled then turned and ran back to the solo-rider he had ditched outside the tunnel.

"That was crazy." James was shaking his head. His breathing was heavy as he gripped the steering wheel tightly with both hands.

"Aw, James, you have Jivvy riding with you." Adam reached up and patted Jivvy's shoulder. "You obviously have nothing to worry about."

James pulled up behind Droven and accelerated away from the tunnel as fast as the Vector would go.

Adam turned to face Melena. The blood was drained from her face, and her eyes were wide. "What just happened?"

"It's called a Lightning Rod." Jivvy held up her long, silver weapon for Melena to see. "Pretty self-explanatory—it delivers a charge about a third as powerful as a bolt of lightning. Nice part is it finds the target for you so you really can't miss. Those agents will wake up in about an hour, but they won't wake up happy."

"How did Droven move that chaser?" Melena asked.

"Magnetically," Adam answered. "The device he used locks onto a metallic object and takes control of it."

"You look terrible." Melena reached up and turned Adam's head to get a better look at the gash that had opened up above his cheekbone.

"That was a gift from my old buddy, Marshal Marbury."

Melena's eyes widened. "Seriously? He's here?" She turned to look out the back window. "This isn't over if he came personally. I can guarantee you there are a lot more agents out there and probably air support as well."

Adam leaned forward. "James, I don't think this is gonna work anymore. Tell Droven we're gonna have to find alternate transportation. Where do we have friends?"

"Rock Springs is the closest base."

"We can't use these vehicles anymore if they're gonna come at us from the sky. Let's meet up with Droven in Green River and figure out how to get to Rock Springs."

Chapter 14

In Green River, James parked the Vector next to Droven's solo-rider on the third level of a four-level parking garage with poor lighting.

"How far is Rock Springs from here, Adam?" Melena inquired.

"It's about twenty-five or thirty kilometers, I think," James answered.

"Are we walking thirty kilometers tonight?" Melena's nerves were frazzled, and she didn't think she had the energy for such a trek.

"No, I think we'll …" Adam paused, staring at the ground with his brow furrowed. "What is that?"

"What's what?" Droven leaned over. "What are you looking at?"

"No, I don't see anything, I hear something—a buzzing sound."

Droven paused to listen for a moment and then threw the black bag from his solo-rider, which apparently contained various weapons and devices, over his shoulder. "I don't hear anything, man. Let's get going."

"Just trust him," Melena advised. "If he says he hears something, he hears something."

Adam continued staring at the ground. "It's getting closer. Let's get moving. We need to stay outta sight."

The group headed for the stairwell. Melena's ears began to detect the buzzing sound as well. A gust of wind kicked up dust and garbage inside the parking garage. The buzzing grew louder as they reached the door to the stairwell. Melena turned around to see if she could find the sound's origin. Just then, a spotlight appeared on Droven's solo-rider just before it became a huge ball of fire. Melena recoiled at the deafening explosion, bright light and heat. She opened her eyes just in time to see the Vector meet the same fate. Fiery debris scattered throughout the parking level.

"Go, go, go!" Droven shouted.

Melena turned and ran down the stairs right on Jivvy's heels, with the three guys following close behind. Another explosion rocked the structure. At the bottom of the first flight of stairs, Melena glanced out the window. James stopped behind her and looked over her shoulder. "What *is* that?"

"It's a Hummingbird! Move!" Melena instantly recognized the craft hovering just outside the parking structure and resumed racing down the stairs.

"What's a Hummingbird?" Adam called out to her from behind.

"It's a new multi-directional aircraft. It hovers, it moves forward and back and—" Another blast interrupted Melena's explanation and sent several concrete chunks hurling down the stairwell, impacting on the stairs right in Jivvy's path.

"Go, Jivvy!" Adam shouted once the stairs became clear of debris.

Jivvy reached the bottom and burst through the door onto ground level. Explosions in levels above continued to shake the structure.

"Don't go out into the open!" Droven directed, as they filed through the door. "Stay inside until we get to the back!"

Jivvy led the group around two corners and then out the back door into an empty field. Melena heard shouting and turned to see Federal Police agents surrounding the parking garage.

"Keep running," Droven whispered. "Don't stop."

Melena's heart was racing, not just from running, but from watching the vehicle she had been sitting in just moments earlier being obliterated. What if she had still been inside? It certainly looked more like an assassination attempt than a rescue. Didn't her father care that her life was in danger? She wondered if he knew that his agents were recklessly firing upon her as well as their actual targets.

Jivvy began to slow her pace as the light from the parking garage faded in the distance. She was obviously having the same problem Melena was—navigating through the field and the industrial waste that was scattered about in the darkness of a moonless night.

Adam moved to the head of the group. "Let's pick up the pace. Stay close behind me."

He led them through the large field and then through several parking lots adjacent to decaying old buildings. Looking over her shoulder, Melena could see spotlights searching the area surrounding the parking structure. There appeared to be three separate sources of lights now. There were likely three Hummingbirds in the area, she thought. Knowing the capabilities of these unique aircraft, she feared that their chances of escaping them were slim.

Adam stopped, abruptly, at an open bay door of an old auto body shop. "Get in! Go!" He filed everyone inside and then slipped in himself. Melena could hear the eerie buzzing of one of the Hummingbirds. Just as Adam cleared the doorway, a blinding light flooded through it as well as the two broken glass windows of the building.

"Stay near the wall and in the shadows!" Droven directed over the sound of the Hummingbird's engines.

After five or six seconds, the bright lights moved on, and Adam led the group back out into the night. After running for a few hundred meters, he turned and faced his companions. "There's a slow moving freight train about three hundred yards in front of us. It's heading east toward Rock Springs. Let's see if we can jump it."

By the time they reached the train, it was beginning to pick up speed. It was so dark that Melena could barely see the cars moving in front of her, but the rumbling of the wheels on the tracks let her know how close they were.

"There's a white container coming up," Adam shouted over the deafening sound of the train moving over the tracks. "Let's all try and meet up there. Melena, come on. I'll help you find a good place to get on."

He ran alongside her holding her by the hand. "There's a railing on this one. Grab on!" He picked her up under the arms midstride and hoisted her toward the train. Melena reached out and caught hold of the metal railing toward the rear of one of the freight cars. He grabbed onto her legs and pushed them up toward the railing until she was able to climb over it and onto the small platform behind the car. "Stay there, Melena!" he shouted. "I'll come back for you!"

Melena stood on the platform gripping the railing with both hands for what seemed like an eternity. She wondered if the others had made it onto the train all right. It felt like it was moving substantially faster than before. She knew she was ahead of the white container and wondered if she ought to try and climb over or around the cars behind her in order to meet the group there.

After waiting another thirty seconds, she decided to move. She carefully stepped across the hooks that linked the cars together and grabbed hold of the railing of the next car back. The dark-colored container had a ladder leading up to the top of it. She climbed the ladder and crawled along the top of the container, then climbed down a ladder on the opposite end. The next car was the same, and she was able to make it up and over it as well. The night seemed exceptionally dark with no light to help her see where she was going, aside from the searchlights of the Hummingbirds hovering around Green River with an increasing perimeter.

As she crossed over the hooks connecting the cars, she didn't find the same type of railing that the previous two cars had had. Losing her balance, she lunged forward and caught hold of a bar on the front of what appeared to be some kind of tanker car. It felt cylindrical and didn't have a ladder on the end as the others had. The bar she had found left three or four centimeters in between it and the tanker so she was able to keep a good grip with both hands. It extended around the side of the cylinder. There was a square metal strip running close to the bottom of the tanker that she figured she could step on with her toes to climb across while keeping hold of the bar with her hands.

Melena moved slowly across the side of the tanker, sliding the toes of her boots forward a few centimeters at a time and then catching up with her hands. She took a small step with her right foot, and her toes slipped off of the edge. Her weight shifted forward, and her right hand lost its grip on the bar. The toes of her left boot slid off of the edge as well. She screamed as she dangled from the tanker by her left hand. She held on for a moment, but her fingers slipped. Closing her eyes in terror, she anticipated the impact with either the ground or the train wheels. The impact she felt came quicker than she had expected, but it wasn't the ground. The front of her body slammed into someone else's as two strong arms reached around her and pulled her in. After a second, however, she felt herself and her rescuer begin falling forward. Both bodies toppled to the ground with Melena's initial fall being broken by the other body. She rolled into a patch of tall grass and weeds and skidded to a stop.

"Melena! Are you okay?" she heard a familiar voice call out. Adam knelt down beside her and gathered her up into his arms. "Are you hurt?"

Melena paused to listen to her body for any screaming pain. None came. "No, I think I'm okay."

"I'm so sorry. I had you, but I tripped on one of the railroad ties. I'm so sorry." Adam gently ran his fingers over her arms and knees searching for scrapes.

For Melena, time seemed to move in slow motion as she gazed through the dim light at the face of this incredible man, who was frantically assessing her for injuries. He had told her he would come back for her, and he had—and not a second too soon.

"I'm okay," she assured him, without taking her eyes off of his face.

Once satisfied that she was uninjured, his eyes met hers. Their faces were just centimeters apart. Even at this close proximity, she could barely make out his features, but the sparkle in his eyes shone through the darkness. She leaned in toward him and closed her eyes. Just as she anticipated her lips touching his, Adam quickly lifted her up onto her feet and jumped to his own.

"We gotta move! A Hummingbird's coming!"

Jarred back into reality, Melena took hold of Adam's hand and began chasing the train again. After running alongside it for a few seconds, it was apparent that Melena was not fast enough to catch up with the advancing cars.

In mid-stride, Adam lifted Melena into his arms. "Hang on tight."

She wrapped her arms around his neck, placing her face between his shoulder and neck. As soon as she was secure, Adam lurched forward and began sprinting alongside the train. Before long, he was outrunning it. It was exhilarating for Melena to be able to move at Adam's blazing pace along with him. She held on tightly around his neck. She couldn't really see where they were headed, but had complete trust in him. The Hummingbird he had heard made regular passes behind them, shining its spotlight on several train cars at a time. After racing past what seemed like fifteen or twenty train cars, Adam gradually moved closer to the train. Thanks to the advancing Hummingbird's spotlight, Melena could see the white container above her.

"Melena, take my hand!" James was leaning over the edge of the flatbed platform the container rested on with one hand outstretched to her and the other holding onto the container. Melena reached out and grabbed James' hand. He pulled her up onto the platform and then reached out to help Adam.

Adam waved him off. "Get inside!" he yelled over the clamor of the train and the buzzing of the Hummingbird.

Melena turned and saw Droven holding the container door open and motioning for her to get in. Looking behind her, she saw the Hummingbird's spotlight closing in. She turned back to where Adam had been, but he had vanished.

"Come on!" James grabbed her hand and pulled her into the container and shut the door.

Light poured through the crack in the door as the spotlight passed over it. Once it passed, Melena opened the door and stepped out, searching up and down along the side of the train for Adam. He was nowhere in sight. "Adam!" she called out into the darkness. There was no answer. A second later, she heard a grunt and then a thud as Adam landed hard on his stomach on the platform.

He looked up and smiled at her. "Hi."

"Hi." She returned the smile and helped him up.

Droven poked his head out of the container. "Come on."

Melena climbed back into the container with Adam following right behind. He shut the door, and they both turned around. Melena hadn't noticed before, but they were not alone in the container. There must have been twenty or more people stowed away on top of crates and boxes. An elderly man was holding a flashlight, which provided adequate light to see throughout the small container. Jivvy was feeding a nutrition bar to a little girl who couldn't have been older than two. The little girl was devouring it. Her clothes and face were filthy, and her black hair was matted against her head. Seven other children were scattered throughout the container. Several of them sat staring at Melena. Droven retrieved more nutrition bars from his bag and distributed them to the other children and a few of the women until he ran out. Melena wondered where these people had come from. What were they doing on a freight train?

"Where are you folks headed?" Adam asked. No one answered. "We can help you. Are you all traveling together?"

After five seconds of silence, the mother of the little girl Jivvy was feeding spoke up. "There are no jobs in the west and no food. We don't know where we're going. We just had to leave. They're making three or four families share one housing unit."

A tall, young man with sunken eyes stood up from the crate he was sitting on. "The President promised us that his new program would increase taxes, but would help to create new jobs. So far, all we've seen is more taxes. He promised he would help us, but his promises are empty. The way things are now, we can't even help ourselves."

"Have any of you prayed for God to help you?" Adam inquired. Several people shook their heads. "Do you believe He can help you?"

"Do *you* believe He can?" asked the man holding the flashlight.

"I know He can, but He wants us to ask. Can I teach you how to pray to Him?"

A number of heads bobbed up and down.

"Our Father in Heaven," Adam began, "we thank you for our lives. We thank you for this land, which was once great. There are those among us who are hungry and without a home.

They are without hope. Father, bless them with hope. Protect them and lead them to a better life. Help them to know of your love for them and the joy that awaits the faithful."

Melena's eyes burned. She felt a quiet peace. As Adam prayed, it sounded to her as though he was speaking with someone he knew. A tear escaped her eye and ran down her cheek as she gazed into the gaunt faces of the children and their parents.

Adam went on. "Bless the people of this land that they may once again desire freedom and that their hearts may turn to you. Bless those of us who are in a position to help, that we may be instruments in your hands. These blessings we humbly ask in the name of your Beloved Son, Jesus Christ. Amen."

"Amen," echoed Droven, Jivvy and James.

"Amen," Melena whispered.

"My brothers and sisters …" Droven stepped forward. "God is about to perform a great work among us. He's going to help us restore this nation to its former greatness, but there is much to be done. Do you want to be free from the tyranny of this government?"

Most of the heads of the adults nodded.

"Do you want the opportunity to work and to be rewarded according to your efforts?"

"Yes," several answered quietly.

"God hasn't forgotten His people, His people have forgotten Him. Will you join us in inviting God back into this nation and the hearts of its people?

"Yes." The response was slightly more enthusiastic this time.

"Will you invite God into *your* hearts?"

"I will," one voice spoke up. "Yes," another called out. More affirmative responses followed.

Droven's eyes sparkled as tears welled up. "He stands at the door and knocks. All you have to do is open up and let Him in."

Adam nodded his agreement. "Folks, there's a place where you can find food and opportunity, and where you can pray to God without fear of the government. We're traveling there, and we would take you, but we're being pursued by the government and don't want to put you in harm's way. If you desire to join us in this place, continue on and make your way to Kansas City." He stepped to Droven and held up Droven's right arm. "Look for someone with a bracelet that looks like this." Droven had on a thick, silver bracelet with the letters IGWT etched into it. "Ask them this question: '*Does liberty live?*' If they respond by saying: '*It lives in our hearts*', you can trust them to lead you to the place we've spoken of." He looked around the container at each of the stowaways. "What question do you ask?"

"Does liberty live?" the mother of the young girl responded, echoed by several others.

"That's right. And it does live in our hearts."

Melena was confused by her feelings. Somehow, she knew what Adam and Droven had told the people was right, and that it would help them. A few days earlier, she had been repulsed by Adam's faith—both in his God and in restoring America. Now, she wasn't sure. It was certainly an inspiring idea. She felt that something ought to be done to ease the suffering of the people. She had been so insulated in her life of education and politics that she was somehow unaware of the depth of the widespread poverty that suddenly seemed very real and very close. The state-controlled news media had certainly not been reporting on stories like the ones these people were telling.

The train began to gradually slow. James opened up the door and looked outside. “I can see the lights of Rock Springs. We’d better bail.”

Droven nodded. “My brothers and sisters, we need to go before we’re discovered. I hope to see you all very soon. May God bless you and protect you.”

Chapter 15

The lights from Rock Springs provided enough illumination so that Melena could see the outline of nearby buildings. The train had slowed enough as it entered the city to make it appear that jumping off wouldn't be quite so dangerous.

"Let's go." Adam leaped off of the platform and into the tall grass that bordered the tracks. His feet hit the ground, and he rolled onto his back and stood back on his feet. He ran back to the platform where the others remained. He reached out for Jivvy. She sat on the edge of the platform and then scooted off into his arms. He held on to her until he could slow enough to safely set her down. Easily catching back up to the train, he came for Melena. She followed Jivvy's lead by sitting on the edge.

"I promise I won't trip this time," Adam called out to her.

She smiled and pushed herself off of the platform and into his arms. He set her feet safely on the ground and then caught up to the train again. James and Droven didn't wait for Adam to help. They both jumped off on their own and rolled like Adam had done.

Droven stood up and brushed himself off. "We're good, man. You can carry James and me around some other time."

James led the group through the streets of Rock Springs. The searchlights of the Hummingbirds were still a fair distance behind, but they appeared to be widening their search.

Eventually, the group arrived at a small diner. James led them to the rear of the building where there was a concrete stairway leading to the basement door. James knocked. There was silence for thirty seconds.

"Do you want to knock again?" Melena suggested, lifting her fist.

James put his hand up. "It's okay. Just hang on. Someone will come," he assured her.

After a few more seconds, Melena heard footsteps coming toward the door.

"What do you stand for?" a female voice on the other side of the door asked.

"Truth and honor," James responded.

Melena could hear a security mechanism working inside the door. After a moment, a woman, appearing to be in her mid-to-late forties with black hair and dark skin, pulled the door open. "Come on in." She waved them in with her hand. "I understand you've had quite a night." Once they were all inside, she placed her fingertips on a glowing orange pad on the wall and reactivated the security system.

James stepped forward and embraced the woman. "Mary! How are you?"

"Oh, I'm just fine, James. I haven't seen anywhere near the action you have lately."

James turned to the others. "Everybody, this is Mary Gathers. Mary, this is Droven, Jivvy, Adam and Melena."

"How are you, ma'am?" Adam offered his hand.

"Oh, no, you get over here." She took Adam's hand and pulled him in for a hug.

"Good to meet you." Droven was embraced as well.

"Hi." Jivvy smiled as Mary pulled her in for a squeeze.

Mary moved in front of Melena and held her by the shoulders. "So, this is Melena, the kidnapping victim."

Melena smiled awkwardly and shrugged. "Nice to meet you, Mary."

Mary belly laughed and then hugged her as well. “It’s nice to meet you, too.”

Melena looked around the room. It appeared to be a music room. It was beautifully decorated with portraits of famous composers on the walls. A glossy, navy blue grand piano was the center piece with a cello and a wooden chair in one corner and a tympani in another.

Droven removed the bag from off of his back. “We really appreciate your help.”

Mary walked over to the cello and picked up the bow. “Well, of course. We’ve been pretty busy monitoring things tonight. You all have stirred up quite a fuss out there.” She took the cello and sat in the chair. Then lifting the bow, she began playing a beautiful melody. Melena recognized it, vaguely, but couldn’t quite put her finger on what the tune was called.

“What are you playing, Mary,” Melena asked. “It’s beautiful.”

“You almost got it, Melena. It’s *America, the Beautiful*.”

Melena nodded. She had heard the song once before in a university history class.

As Mary played, a panel on the wall slid up into the ceiling, revealing a hallway behind it. “Go on in,” Mary instructed. “I want to finish the chorus.”

Behind her, Melena could hear Droven singing softly. “America, America, God shed His grace on thee …”

Melena filed through the opening behind Jivvy and James. After a few meters, the hallway turned to the right, and a stairway appeared. Melena could hear voices coming from downstairs. As she descended the stairs, the room below began to open up. A large office with more unfamiliar tech, including a similar, though much larger, map like the one in Rexburg, sprawled out in front of her. Thirty or so people were milling about, performing various tasks and talking with one another.

A short, portly man with thinning gray hair and a gray mustache broke away from his workstation and came to greet the group. "Well, it appears you five have had quite a night. I'm Christian Stoker. I'm the Director of this facility."

"Director Stoker," Droven held out his hand, "Droven Harper. Thanks for taking us in." He turned to introduce the group. "This is the stunning Jivvy Luna. I think you already know my twin brother, James Thomas. Then there's the lovely Melena Jaxon and *The Roadrunner*, Adam Winter."

Director Stoker's round body bounced with laughter at Droven's introductions. "We're honored to be in the presence of such esteemed guests. You'll have to excuse me and my colleagues. With all the activity nearby, we're quite engaged at the moment. Please find your way into the kitchen and lounge. It's just through that door in the corner. You can brief us on your situation later."

"Thank you so much." Jivvy smiled and shook the man's hand.

"Thank you," Adam, Melena and James echoed.

The group headed for the door to the kitchen. Before going inside, Adam took Melena by the arm. "Can I talk to you for a second?"

"Sure." Melena stopped and allowed James and Droven to go ahead of her. She figured Adam wanted to emphasize the security risk he was taking bringing her into this base.

"Melena, I want you to know that I've felt compelled to bring you along with us. I believe that it's God's will that you learn about our mission and the good that it will do for this nation. We're closer to making a difference than you might think."

Melena wasn't sure she could get completely on board with Adam's agenda, but she definitely found herself questioning many of her long-held philosophies. She reached out and took his hands in hers and looked up into his kind, brown eyes. "Thank you for trusting me."

Adam smiled and looked back toward the kitchen door. "Let's go see if they have any bunny rabbit in there. I understand it's your favorite."

"Gross!" Melena hip-checked him. "That was a one-time thing. There'd better be a big salad in there for me."

"I'm sure there is. You can wash it down with a little creek water." He tried not to smile, but the corner of his mouth turned up just a little.

"Oh, knock it off. You're going to make me sick!" She held onto his arm and headed through the door. "So, how do these people know what's been going on with us? Are they tracking us?"

"Droven gave them a heads up that we were coming," Adam replied, "but no, they haven't been tracking us. Let's just say they take notice when three government aircraft come sniffing around their backyard."

"So, this place is a base for intelligence operations?"

Adam nodded. "Among other things. Our organization is larger than you think. It's not just Independence."

Melena pointed at Droven's wrist. "You guys told the people on the train to look for someone with a bracelet like Droven's. What does IGWT stand for?"

"Have you ever seen any old U.S. currency before?" Droven asked.

"Yeah, I'm sure I have, but I don't remember seeing that acronym," Melena answered.

Droven held his arm up so she could see the bracelet. "In God We Trust."

Jivvy took several bottles of water out of the refrigerator and held one out to Melena. "Do you want some water, Melena?"

"Yes, thanks." Melena took the bottle from her, took a long swig and then continued her inquiries. "So, how is your organization related to The Response?"

"Not at all," Droven answered. "They're motivated by a lust for power, just like those who have it. They're basically anarchists."

"Then why did Adam meet with them? Why did they put that stamp in his head?"

"The Response obtained the stamp on their own, though I'm not sure exactly how," Adam explained. "They weren't sure they had the resources to adequately exploit the data on it and figured we'd be interested, so they offered it to us. I went to Rugby expecting to get the stamp from them, but I didn't expect it to be implanted in me. I'm not sure why they did that. I certainly didn't volunteer."

"Lucky for Adam, he's a remarkable healer." Jivvy reached down and pulled on Adam's torn pant leg. "By the way, what happened to your leg?"

Melena hadn't noticed the ripped fabric or bloodstains on Adam's pants.

"Oh, I did a little baseball slide into one of the Fed's legs back in the tunnel in Green River." Adam demonstrated the slide without going all the way down to the floor. "Concrete highway isn't the best surface for such a slide, however. I learned that the hard way."

"Are you okay?" Melena was alarmed at the amount of blood that had soaked into the dark fabric.

"Yeah, I'm good," Adam replied. "It's all closed up now."

"You can't hurt Adam." Jivvy stepped forward and punched him in the stomach. "I've been beating on him for years, and he just keeps coming back for more."

"You *have* been beating on me for years!" Adam laughed. "You need to invest in a punching bag."

She took a couple more jabs at his midsection. "What are you talking about? I already have a punching bag right here."

Melena thought Jivvy's playfulness with Adam was sweet, but she felt a hint of jealousy watching them interact. She wondered what their history was. They had obviously known each other a long time, but was there more than a friendship between them? She remembered their kiss at the charging station. It had been surprisingly difficult for her to watch. Thinking about it caused a pit to form in her stomach.

James brought some bread and condiments out of the refrigerator and set them out on the countertop. "Anyone want a ham and Swiss?" he offered. "Melena, what'll it be?"

"She'll take a half-pound ham sandwich, hold the bread." Adam answered for her.

"No, thank you, James." She elbowed Adam in the ribs. "I'll find something myself."

"Okay. Jivvy, how about you?" James asked.

"Thanks, James." Jivvy put her arm around his shoulders. "I'd love a ham and Swiss with lots of mayo, please."

"You got it." James went to work making sandwiches.

Jivvy turned her attention back to Adam. She reached up with her thumb and rubbed it on his cheek. "Your little skeleton tattoo is looking a little ragged. I'm not sure this is going to fool anyone anymore."

Adam ducked out of her reach. "Leave it alone, Jiv. I'm leaving it there. In fact, I might get it put on permanently." He tightened his jaw and squinted his eyes. "Tell me I don't look like one tough, crazy fool with this thing on my face."

"Melena, your tat looks hot," Droven commented. "And not just because I did it and not just because it's fire. You may want to consider making yours permanent too."

"Thank you, Droven. Is it smudged?" She turned her head from side to side so he could examine it.

Droven took her by the shoulders to get a closer look. "Not at all. It looks great. Adam sweat all over his, and Jivvy's a sloppy kisser, so that didn't help either."

Jivvy's jaw dropped, and her eyebrows shot up. "What?" She went after Droven, pounding him with both fists. "Am not! How would you even know that? Big jerk!"

"I'm sorry!" Droven tried to cover up with his arms to deflect some of the blows. "I'm just playin'. I'm just playin'."

Jivvy made a pouty face. "I was going to kiss you too, Droven, but not now. You'll never know whether I'm sloppy or not."

Droven grabbed her around the waist and pretended to try and kiss her. "Aw, don't do that to me. Come here."

Just then, the kitchen door flew open, and Director Stoker poked his head inside. "You all may want to come out here and see this."

Melena made it out of the kitchen just in time to look up at the large monitor on the wall and see her own face on it. A reporter's voice narrated. "Melena Jaxon, daughter of Senator Cai Jaxon, was abducted Tuesday by this man …" An image of Adam's face at the lab appeared on the screen. "Adam Winter, a convicted rapist and murderer."

"What!" Droven yelled at the monitor.

The reporter went on. "Earlier tonight, Adam Winter, along with several unknown accomplices, led Federal Police Agents on a high speed chase, ending in this tunnel near Green River." Video images of the tunnel showed police chasers with lights flashing and police agents lying on the road beside them in pools of blood. "At least a dozen Federal Agents were gunned down, mercilessly, with automatic weapons."

"Come on!" Jivvy shouted. "They shot each other! And there were only two or three who were even hit!"

"The kidnapper remains at large," the reporter continued. "If Ms. Jaxon is still alive, she is considered to be in grave danger. We've learned that an enormous ransom has been demanded of Senator Jaxon in exchange for his daughter's life."

Marshall Marbury appeared on the screen with a microphone in front of his face. "Our only hope for Ms. Jaxon's safe return is that some honest citizen will come forward with information that will lead us to her and her abductor." He appeared very concerned. "We just want our dominion's Scion returned home, unharmed."

The reporter concluded. "If anyone has any information as to the whereabouts of Ms. Jaxon or her ruthless captor, they are invited to contact authorities immediately. The government is offering a thirty percent increase in monthly appropriation for any citizen who provides information leading to the safe return of Melena Jaxon and the arrest of Adam Winter and his accomplices."

The room fell silent as the broadcast concluded. Melena felt sick. She couldn't believe the news media and the government would stage a crime scene and fabricate a criminal history for Adam. Now every citizen in the dominion would be looking for them. How on earth could they possibly continue travelling? She knew what had to happen now. "I have to go back," she announced. "It's not safe for any of you anymore."

"I hate to point this out, Melena," James spoke up, "but, those Hummingbirds would have killed you too if they would have arrived fifteen seconds earlier. I'm not really sure how safe it is out there for you either."

Droven nodded. "That's a good point. It appears that taking Adam out is the top priority, and if you survive, they'll just force you to lead them to him."

Melena was so confused. She couldn't believe she had gotten herself into this predicament. She knew what they were saying was true, but thought that if she could distance herself from the group, perhaps they could escape without her. She especially didn't want to put Adam into any more danger than he was already in. And where was her father in all of this, she wondered? How could he let the police put her in harm's way? Did he really want to pass the leadership of the Dominion on to Hava instead of her? She couldn't believe that was possible. She was his daughter!

"I don't know how staying together can be a possible option now." Melena shook her head. "By tomorrow morning, everyone in the Dominion will have seen that broadcast and will be searching for us. They just created an army of bounty hunters. What are the chances that we won't be seen between here and Independence?"

"Actually, pretty good." Adam looked at her and smiled. "I told you I'd take you to Independence, Melena, and that's where we're going."

"Yeah, but—" Melena began to protest.

"Don't worry. We're not driving from here. We're flying." Adam looked confident, but what he was saying was ridiculous.

"Flying?" Melena repeated. "We can't fly from here. We'll be identified even easier. Do you honestly think we can set foot in an airport after what we just saw?"

"No. I agree with that." He pointed at the floor with both index fingers. "What I'm saying is that we'll be flying … from *here*."

Chapter 16

Adam found himself back in the tunnel in Green River. He burst out from behind the Vector, but his legs were sluggish. He willed them to run, but they were so heavy. He flinched as the sound of gunshots bounced off of the tunnel walls. He felt a painful pinch in his right arm and then one in his shoulder and then another and another. He turned away and felt pinches all over his back. He was being shot! He fell to the ground. Looking up, he searched for his friends. Marshall Marbury was holding Droven's limp body up while police agents beat him, viciously. Adam turned the other way toward the Vector. It was being blasted to pieces by gunfire. The driver side door opened, and James rolled out, his eyes and mouth open wide and little red circles dotting his body. Jivvy's door opened, and she ran to Adam. She reached out her hand, but just before her fingers reached him, she was struck from behind. She fell forward in slow motion, and there behind her stood Melena—a smoking gun in her outstretched hand. She walked slowly toward Adam, keeping the gun trained on him. She opened her mouth to speak, but no words came out. Instead, numbers began spilling out of her mouth until, eventually, she and the tunnel faded away, and lines of code sped across his vision.

After a moment, the symbols of the code slowed and came to a stop. Once they were still, a pattern in the code revealed itself. Adam began arranging pieces of the code when a familiar buzzing noise began and grew continually louder. Suddenly, a Hummingbird appeared over his head, its four horizontal propellers chopping the air. A bright searchlight circled the ground around him and then rested directly on him.

The light was intense as he looked up into it. He wanted to look away, but couldn't force himself to.

"Hey!" a voice called out. "Adam!"

Adam's eyes flew open, but the light in the room forced them shut again. He turned his head away and opened his eyes again. The bright light began to dissipate. He lifted his head and looked around.

"You okay, man?" It was Droven's voice.

"Yeah," Adam breathed. "Yeah, I'm okay." He rubbed his eyes. "Sometimes my eyes don't adjust right away."

"Is that why you were moaning and thrashing around?" Droven asked.

"Uh, no, I was just having kind of a crazy dream," Adam explained. He sat up and looked across the lounge room. Jivvy and Melena were still asleep on the sofa on the opposite side. "Where's James?" he whispered to Droven.

"I think he's in the office talking to the director."

"Are the four Chameleons still available?"

"Far as I know. James volunteered to stay here." Droven reached his arm around his neck to scratch a hard-to-reach spot in the center of his back. "If I'm being honest, I'm not really sure about your plan, man. You really think we can teach Melena to fly a Chameleon?"

Adam looked up at the ceiling and sighed. "I don't know. It took me weeks to get the hang of it. Jivvy picked it up really fast, though. Maybe James can fly her remotely or at least get her launched. I don't know."

"Guess we're about to find out, huh?" Droven smiled. "Have you heard from Gildrich?"

Adam nodded. "Talked to him last night before I went to sleep. He agrees that Melena should come to Independence."

"I spoke with him as well. He said that projections of you are scheduled to appear in Jackson, Denver and Cheyenne this morning."

"That ought to keep the bounty hunters busy," Adam chuckled.

"The projections won't have your skeleton-face tat, though. They'll just be little wussy Adams runnin' around." Droven's shoulders bounced as he tried to laugh silently.

Air burst out from between Adam's lips as he gave up trying to hold it in.

Jivvy's head lifted up from off of the sofa. "What's going on over there?" Her eyes were only half open. A lock of her long, blond hair was stuck to her cheek and bottom lip and moved up and down when she spoke.

Adam held up his hand. "Sorry, Jivvy. Droven told me he went on two dates with the same girl back home, and I couldn't hold it in."

"Come on, man." Droven slapped Adam's shoulder with the back of his hand. "Don't make me bring Beth Hannover into this."

"Who?" Jivvy wondered, groggily.

"Beth Hannover?" Droven feigned a confused look, as if Jivvy should have known exactly who he was talking about. "Adam's most recent girlfriend."

"Stop," Adam warned.

Droven put his hand in front of Adam's face. "We figured that Beth had asked Adam out a total of thirteen times. He finally came to his senses a while back and actually said yes."

"Really?" Jivvy smiled and rubbed her eyes. "Wait, is this the mechanic who works over on tenth?"

"One in the same," Droven answered.

"Wow. She's really cute, Adam." Jivvy's smile grew even wider.

Droven nodded, vigorously. "Oh, she steams when it rains."

Jivvy laughed. “So what did the two of you do on your date?”

“Well,” Adam began, “I thought we were gonna eat at a fancy restaurant and discuss sixteenth century European literature, but instead we played one-on-one basketball in her parent’s backyard.”

“How did that go?” Jivvy managed to ask between intakes of breath as she fully cracked up.

“I’ll tell you what—I gave her a run for her money.” Adam started to laugh also. “She did play me very physically under the basket.”

“She dunked on him!” Droven blurted out.

Adam turned to Droven with a stern look on his face. “Droven! We both agreed that we would leave that part out of the story!”

Jivvy was doubled over with laughter. Finally, she caught her breath. “How much taller is she than you, Adam?”

“According to the University team roster, she is six-foot-eight. That would make her a good six inches taller than me, but she’s got at least a seven-foot wingspan.”

All of the laughing and commotion had stirred Melena. Her eyes fluttered open, and she looked around, trying to discern what was going on.

“Sorry Melena,” Adam whispered loudly. “Droven’s just making up stories about me.”

“So, are you going out again when you get back to Independence?” Jivvy asked.

Adam’s face became serious. “Well, Jivvissa, she is a beautiful young lady and a very competitive athlete—and thanks for asking—but a woman’s ability to bump me out of the key when playing ball happens to be a deal breaker for me.”

Jivvy reached over and put her hand on Melena's shoulder. "Take note, Melena. Adam doesn't like girls who can beat him at sports."

"What?" Melena was still rubbing the sleep out of her eyes.

"I never said that!" Adam tried to defend his position. "As an above-average-sized, athletic male, I'm just not comfortable being dominated by a bigger, more powerful woman." He threw his hands up. "Sorry. That's just how it is."

James came through the door as the laughter was dissipating. "Sounds like I missed something funny."

"Nothing is funny, James. Believe me," Adam assured him. "Anything new from Director Stoker?"

"Well, the Hummingbirds have bugged out. There's a large Federal Police presence here in Rock Springs, though," James informed them.

Droven shook his head. "That probably means we're only gonna get one shot to launch."

"Adam, can I talk to you in private?" Jivvy asked.

"I don't see why not." Adam stood up and followed Jivvy down the hall into an empty office.

She shut the door behind them. "Sorry. I just wanted to talk to you really quick before we launch." Her hands fidgeted, nervously.

"Okay. What are you thinking about?" Adam had a good idea of what she might be concerned about, but let her explain herself.

"Adam, I know you think that Melena is …" She trailed off and looked up at the ceiling. After a moment, she started again. "I know you feel a connection with Melena, and you want her to see things the way you do, and bringing her to Independence will help her see what this country is supposed to be like. And maybe that will happen." She was looking everywhere except at Adam's face. "And I think you hope she'll find God and everything." Her words began coming faster. "I just don't want to see you get hurt if things don't work out the way you hope or think they will." She finally met his eyes. "Do you know what I'm trying to say?"

Adam could see by the look in her eyes that she was sincere. She was usually so tough, even slightly aloof. Showing her serious side made her seem much more vulnerable.

He held her gaze and smiled. "I do know what you're saying, and, believe me, I know it's a lot to expect from someone with Melena's background. I do appreciate your concern for me, and I understand why you're concerned." He paused to gather his thoughts. "I don't really know why I feel so strongly that this needs to happen, and maybe it's a mistake, but I just feel like it's what we should do. Do you think you can try and trust me on this?"

"Trust *you*?" She lifted her eyebrows and then looked to one side and then the other as if making a difficult decision. "Of course I trust you, Adam. Just be careful."

"Please, Jiv. I'm always careful." His smiled widened. "Come here." He pulled her in and hugged her. "Should we go see if you can get her to fly a Chameleon?"

"We should," Jivvy answered, flashing him a charming grin.

Just then, the door swung open, and Melena walked in. "Adam, are we going to be able to take any—" She froze when she noticed the two embracing. "Oh." She retreated back out the door. "Sorry. I was just wondering if we should pack some food and water to take with us." She turned on her heel and went back the way she came. "We can just talk when you're … done," she called over her shoulder.

"Melena," Adam called after her. "We *are* done—done talking. We were just about to come back and talk to you about the aircraft."

She turned back to face the two of them. "Okay. I mean, whenever you're ready we can figure out what's going on."

"Let's figure it out right now." Adam let Jivvy step out of the office in front of him and they both followed Melena back to the kitchen and lounge area.

Droven got up from off of the sofa as the trio returned. "Are we ready to get this thing going?"

"Yep," Jivvy answered, "we're ready."

"So, I'm not really sure I understand," Melena admitted. "The aircraft that are being stored here require only a single operator in each craft?"

The awkwardness that hung in the room subsided only somewhat as Melena focused on the task before them.

"Yeah," Jivvy responded. "The engine is what's known as a cold engine. It's not really *cold*, it just doesn't produce enough heat to create a signature on police infrared surveillance scanners. The structural material they're made of is kind of soft and is really low-friction so it doesn't produce heat either. It works great for a one-man, or one-woman craft, but can't be any larger without creating a heat signature that the government can pick up on. They're pretty easy to pilot, too. The controls are intuitive and you can kind of just … *feel* how to handle them."

"So, they're camouflaged?" Melena asked. "You guys were calling them *Chameleons*, right? How do they get past visual scanners or radars?"

"The material the craft is made of works as kind of a projection screen," Adam explained. "Cameras on either side record what is seen on the opposite side and project it onto the screens. The cameras are so precise that it creates a seamless visual from below and from above. As for the radar, there's a device mounted on the nose that basically absorbs radio waves so nothing is deflected back to the source."

"Okay …" Melena appeared unsure.

Adam shrugged. "I don't completely understand it all, but so far, they've effectively evaded detection. The only downside is that we don't have a simulator or opportunity for test flights to get you comfortable flying one. I think you'll do great, though."

"Oh, I knew Melena was meant to fly the moment I saw her," Droven flattered. "Today's the day she finally gets her wings."

Melena laughed. "That's right. Thanks, Droven."

"Should we go check them out?" Adam asked.

"Yeah, let's see what we're dealing with here," Melena answered without looking directly at him.

Director Stoker and James led the group into an underground garage. There were several armored all-terrain vehicles as well as two fancy solo-riders that Adam didn't recognize, but he thought they looked fast. It was too bad they were in a hurry. Otherwise, he would have arranged a test drive.

Eight black suits hung on hooks on the wall, with eight helmets resting on a shelf above them. Droven went to the suits and began checking the sizes on the back of the collars. "These suits will keep your body heat locked in," he explained to Melena. "They need to fit pretty snug. Let's see, this one is size *super-sexy*. It must've been made for me." He found two smaller suits and handed them to Jivvy and Melena. "Now, let's see if I can find a husky, roadrunner-sized suit for Adam."

"A *husky* one?" Adam clarified.

"Yeah, one with a little extra room around the middle, you know, for a spare tire." Droven couldn't help smiling to himself as he searched for Adam's size.

"A spare tire?" Adam laughed. "You know what? I actually don't think this is gonna work out because I think the chances are pretty slim that we're gonna find a helmet big enough for your head."

Droven looked up with a hurt look on his face. "Oh, Adam, you know how sensitive I am about my noggin." He reached up with his free hand and patted his bald head as if to sooth it. "You shouldn't have gone that far, man. You can't bring my slightly-over-sized dome into the conversation just to get even. That's just wrong."

"I apologize. I'm a little sensitive as well." He patted his stomach. "You know, about my *problem area*."

"Okay, boys and girls," Director Stoker broke in. "I don't think I need to explain that this is an extremely dangerous situation. Also, these aircraft are very expensive, and their design is even more valuable than the aircraft itself. They can't fall into the wrong hands, okay?" He looked the four of them over. "God bless you and protect you. Have a safe trip."

"I'll be monitoring you from here," James informed them. He turned to Melena. "There's a communication system built in to the helmet. You'll be able to hear each other and me, okay?"

Melena nodded.

"If you have any questions or problems, I'll help you through," James offered.

"Are you sure you don't want to go, James?" Melena asked. "I could really just stay here and lay low for a little while."

"No, thanks," James answered. "They can use my help here for a while, and I want to make sure you all make it safely to Independence. Maybe I'll catch up with you later."

Melena went to James and hugged him. "Thanks for everything, James. It was so nice to have met you. I hope I'll see you again soon."

"I think you will." James smiled. "It was nice getting to know you, too."

"Bye, James." Jivvy also had a hug for him.

Droven shook James' hand and pulled him in for a pat on the back. "Always a pleasure, man. You take care of yourself."

James nodded. "You too, Droven."

Adam walked up to James and embraced his friend. "I'm sorry about your car." They both laughed, and then Adam's face became serious. "You really put your neck out for me this time, James. Thank you."

"Truth and honor," James replied, placing his right hand over his heart.

"Truth and honor," Adam repeated.

Chapter 17

"Come over here, Melena." Jivvy motioned for Melena to follow her. "Let me show you the controls." Adam had mentioned earlier that Jivvy would be their flight captain. Melena decided it would be best if she put her feelings about Jivvy and Adam aside for the time being so she would be able to focus on flying.

The four Chameleons were lined up in single file, the lead aircraft facing a ramp that led into a narrow tunnel. They were about three meters long with stubby wings and a tall fin in the rear. They looked more like missiles to Melena than manned aircraft. Jivvy walked to the lead Chameleon and pulled a handle on the side of it. The entire craft split in half like a clam shell, with the top half lifting open. Jivvy climbed inside and put her knees into two padded spaces and then dropped onto her stomach with her arms stretched out into each of the two short wings. The position wasn't too different from piloting a solo-rider, except for the outstretched arms. The nose of the Chameleon, now occupied by Jivvy's head, was transparent, allowing the pilot to have a three-hundred-and-sixty-degree range of vision. The craft was so small that Jivvy's body almost filled the entire interior.

"There's a stick in either wing." Jivvy lifted her hand to show Melena one of the control sticks. "You take one in each hand, and use the two together and they'll balance you out. The thrust control is this pedal under your right foot and air brakes are under your left. There will be a red line across the center of the nose window. It's your horizon. James has programmed your aircraft with more detailed controls and instructions. It will basically tell you what to do."

Melena nodded. It sounded fairly simple, but she was still a little apprehensive. It didn't look like the aircraft could provide much protection if there were a crash. It seemed so small and fragile.

Jivvy sat back up and continued her instructions. "James will launch and land your craft via remote control so you won't have to worry about that. Your call sign will be *Ghost Two*, okay? Once we're airborne, we all need to keep a thirty-foot—I mean a ten-meter—buffer in between one another. We'll fly in a V formation. I'll take the lead, and you will flank me on the right. Droven and Adam will flank me on the left. Make sense?"

Melena was relieved that she wasn't going to have to try and land the thing. "Yeah, I think so. Will James be able to take control of the aircraft if I'm having problems?"

"Yes, when you're not flying at high speeds. As the pilot, you have the ability to grant or refuse remote access. When you allow him, James can help you remotely," Jivvy explained. "Don't be nervous. I know it doesn't look like much, but the hull of this craft is extremely durable. It's airtight and buoyant in the event of a water landing and will hold its form in case of a hard ground landing."

"Well, I'm not interested in verifying those claims." Melena smiled. "Should I get in mine?"

"Yeah, of course. Most of your instruction is going to take place in the sky so you might as well get in." Jivvy pointed to the Chameleon directly behind hers. "This one's yours. Put your helmet on before you get in. The helmet is really part of the aircraft. It'll provide visual and audio instruction as well."

"Jivvy's a great instructor, Melena." Droven adjusted the chin strap on his helmet. "She'll take good care of you up there."

Melena nodded. "I believe you. She certainly sounds like she knows what she's doing."

"She's a showoff, though. Don't try and mimic her maneuvers," Adam warned.

Jivvy smiled at Melena. "Actually, I prefer *hot dog*."

Melena pulled her helmet on over her head and then pulled up on the handle, as she had seen Jivvy do, and the little craft opened up. She climbed over the edge and placed her knees down into position and adjusted the pedals to the length of her legs so her feet were directly over them. The padding below her seemed to mold to the shape of her body as she settled herself into flight position. The helmet came to life as soon as it entered the cockpit.

"Welcome Melena," the helmet greeted her in a pleasant female voice. Its visor lit up, displaying the outside temperature, a compass, a throttle indicator and an airspeed indicator.

"Uh, hi." Melena wasn't sure if the helmet expected a response or not, but figured she'd be friendly either way.

"Are you ready to seal the aircraft?" The voice asked.

She took a deep breath and let it out slowly through her mouth. "Yes, seal the aircraft," she finally responded. The top half closed down on top of her and sealed itself together.

"Melena, do you copy?" James' voice came in over the helmet's audio system.

"I copy, James," Melena answered. "So, you're going to launch this thing for me, huh?"

"That's correct," James confirmed. "My call sign will be *Coyote* in our transmissions, okay? Don't be nervous. I'll take good care of you."

Melena smiled to herself. Her new friends were some of the most genuine, selfless people she had ever met. It was becoming difficult for her to imagine being at odds with them on any issue. "I know you will, James—I mean, Coyote. I'm not nervous." She was lying. She was nervous. Not just about piloting an aircraft, but about going to Independence. What would the people there think of having a future S.O.U. Senator in their midst. Her father considered the people of Independence enemies of the Federal Government. Didn't it stand to reason that they would consider him an enemy as well? What if they held her as a political prisoner or turned the tables and decided to interrogate *her* for classified information? She tried to imagine Adam or Droven or even Jivvy betraying her once they had her inside the walls. She couldn't. Maybe Independence really was all that Adam had professed it to be. Perhaps there was something to be learned from a different system of government and a different way of life. So far, she greatly admired the character of the people it had produced.

"This is Ghost One ..." Jivvy's voice came in over the audio system. "All wings report in."

Melena guessed that since she was Ghost Two it was probably her turn. "Ghost Two is standing by."

"Ghost Three standing by," Droven reported. "Ready to head home."

Adam came through next. "Ghost Four should have used the restroom before sealing the lid, but is standing by."

Jivvy laughed. "Do you want to get out, Adam? We can wait."

"Just go," Droven suggested. "You can empty your suit when we get home."

"Thank you, one and all," Adam laughed. "I can certainly hold it for thirty minutes."

"Thirty minutes?" Melena asked. "How fast do these things go?"

"Right around twenty-five hundred kilometers per hour," Jivvy answered. "But we won't go that fast the whole way. We'll slow down well before we reach Independence. These babies can move, though."

"Is this how you and Droven got to Rexburg so quickly?" Melena asked.

"That's classified," Jivvy chuckled, "but a very good guess."

"Prepare for launch," James' voice cut in.

The tunnel in front of Jivvy's Chameleon lit up. A slight vibration permeated the air. Melena assumed it was from Jivvy's engine.

"Ghost One is clear for launch." James sounded so official. Melena wondered how many times her friends had done this before.

"Copy that," Jivvy answered. "Launching in five, four, three, two, one."

The vibration intensified for a fraction of a second before Jivvy's Chameleon disappeared into the tunnel.

"You're up, Ghost Two. Just relax. You're going to be moving pretty quickly, so be prepared for that, but I'll get you airborne, okay?" James sounded confident and gave Melena some comfort.

"Copy. Ready when you are," Melena answered.

Adam's voice came over the audio. "Melena, it's okay to be afraid. Your suit really will hold it in if you pee, so don't sweat that, okay?"

The tenseness in her body lessened. "You're a moron, Adam." She smiled to herself. For the past few minutes, she had almost forgotten about seeing Adam and Jivvy together earlier. Her smile faded. It was obvious that something was going on between them. So why was he stringing her along? Was he determined to get her to Independence for strictly political reasons, she wondered. Was he just looking for a new convert to his faith?

James' began her countdown. "Ghost Two launching in five, four, three, two …"

Melena gripped the control sticks and gritted her teeth.

"One."

For the next three or four seconds, everything was a blur. The pressure the g-force exerted on Melena's body almost overcame the euphoria of being in flight, but as her eyes focused on the ground below, she became exhilarated.

"Ghost Two, this is Coyote. You okay up there?"

Melena was so enthralled in watching the buildings and roads shrink below that his words almost didn't register. Finally, she realized that James was speaking to her. "Yes, Coyote, I'm okay. This is amazing."

A fuzzy area in the blue sky appeared in front of her. After studying it closely for a moment, she determined it must be Jivvy's Chameleon. The image on the monitor in the nose of the craft confirmed that *G-1* was at her twelve o'clock. The fuzzy spot seemed to swirl for a second. It slowed and then banked in on Melena's left and assumed a forward position. Once it was closer to her, she could vaguely make out the shape of the aircraft.

Jivvy's voice was in her ear. "You ready to drive, Ghost Two?"

"Yeah, let's do it." Melena had flown frequently as a passenger on air conveyers, but that was about as exciting as riding on a commuter train. This feeling of freedom was something she had never felt before. And she adored it.

James' voice came through again. "Once I release you, you will be in control until you accept remote access through verbal confirmation, all right?"

"All right," Melena affirmed. "Sounds good."

"Okay, get a good grip on your control sticks," Jivvy instructed. "Pushing forward will push the nose downward. Pulling back will lift the nose higher. Left and right are self-explanatory. Just take it easy. A hard left or right might send you into a roll. That might be fun later, but let's just try straight and level for now, okay? Keep an eye on your horizon at all times."

"Got it," Melena responded.

"Okay, request manual control from Coyote," Jivvy directed.

Melena took a deep breath. "Coyote, this is Ghost Two requesting manual control."

"Copy that, Ghost Two. Coyote is disengaging remote pilot."

Suddenly, Melena felt the aircraft rock back and forth. Her heartbeat increased as she realized she was in control. She tried to steady her hands. She felt her speed decreasing and Jivvy pulling away from her. She applied a small amount of pressure to the pedal under her right foot and felt herself picking up speed. She eased back into position beside Jivvy.

"Looking great, Ghost Two!" Droven's voice came through just as his Chameleon assumed its position to Jivvy's left on Melena's monitor. At a slightly greater distance, it was much harder to make out visually than Jivvy's was.

"Thank you, Ghost Three. I'm okay at flying straight so far," Melena reported.

"See, I told you. I said this girl was born to fly."

Melena thought maybe Droven was right. The speed and danger were intoxicating to her. "Woohoo! I never even knew what I was missing."

Droven laughed. "This is pretty great, right?"

"I think it's about the closest thing there is to being a bird. Well, if the bird could go Mach two." Melena laughed to herself.

"This is nothing, Ghost Two," Jivvy broke in. "Wait until Ghost Four arrives. We'll bank around to the east, and then we'll open these babies up."

"Copy that, Ghost One."

"What do you mean wait for Ghost Four?" Adam chimed in. "Let's do it."

Melena looked beyond Droven's position, but couldn't see Adam. "Ghost Four, you're on my monitor, but I don't see you."

"Exactly," Adam answered. "I'm here. Look at my position."

Melena turned and looked at the spot in the formation where Adam was supposed to be. At first, she saw nothing. Then the air around the position appeared to swirl like it did when Jivvy was in front of her earlier. "What did you do, Ghost Four? It just looks like some kind of disturbance in the air."

"Just a little roll. Maybe you can try one when we get closer to our destination."

That sounded exciting to her. "Yeah, I want to try that."

"All right, Ghost Team, stay in formation. On my mark, bank right to point zero-seven-six. Ghost Two, watch the readout below your compass. Nice and easy," Jivvy coached. "Mark."

Melena eased her right hand control stick to the right, and the aircraft responded by gently lifting the left wing and banking right.

"Give it a little bit more, Ghost Two, you're getting a little too close." Jivvy was a patient instructor. Melena could see from the monitor that she was well inside the ten-meter buffer and was dangerously close to Jivvy.

"Sorry." She used her position on the monitor and the readout beneath the compass to correct her position and complete the turn. Her confidence grew with each passing minute as she seemed to be catching on remarkably well.

"All right, we're on course. Time to cook. " Jivvy sounded excited. Melena could tell that Jivvy enjoyed flying as much as she did. "Break formation. All wings parallel. Ghost

Two, don't get behind anyone. We all need to stay together. Got it?"

"Got it."

"Accelerate to twelve hundred knots and hold."

Keeping her eyes on the monitor, Melena pushed the throttle pedal down and tried to stay alongside Jivvy. The acceleration felt amazing. Suddenly, Melena felt the Chameleon's nose dip. Her heart dropped, but she maintained control. She looked at the ground below and noticed how much faster they were passing cities and fields.

"Are we going to hear a sonic boom when we break the sound barrier?" Melena asked no one in particular.

"No," Adam answered. "That was it. Did you feel that little jolt?"

"Yeah."

"We don't hear the boom because it's behind us, and the sound waves won't catch us."

"I see."

"Hold formation and airspeed for approximately twenty-three minutes," Jivvy instructed.

Once the team had reached their desired airspeed, the flight became less interesting for Melena. She thought about Independence and whether or not Adam would be different once they were on his home turf. She wondered if everyone there was going to talk about God all the time. Adam and Droven obviously had conviction, and Melena couldn't deny that she had felt something stir inside of her when they spoke to the people on the train about God and freedom. But what did that mean? Was it her admiration for them, or was it something else?

Melena checked her horizon and her position on the monitor. Everything seemed steady so she allowed her thoughts to wander once again. She wondered about her father. It hadn't really crossed her mind before, but was there a possibility that he actually thought she had been abducted? If only she could contact him and let him know she was okay. Knowing her father, if it wasn't worry he was feeling, it would have to be rage. If he believed his daughter was intentionally giving aid to a fugitive and an enemy organization, he must be furious with her. Perhaps he knew she had been attacked by the Federal Police and felt it was justified because she was a traitor to her government. Maybe he wanted her dead. Not knowing what her father did or didn't know was driving her insane. She thought that maybe once they were safe inside the walls of Independence, she could contact him and see where she stood with him.

Thoughts about her father, Independence and Adam continued throughout the duration of the flight. There was some chatter between the team, but overall, communications were minimal.

Melena was forced out of her thoughts by Jivvy's voice in her ear. "Begin deceleration and resume original formation. We'll start our descent in a few minutes."

Melena had to admit to herself that she admired Jivvy. She had been a very conscientious flight coach and was obviously an accomplished pilot. Add that to her dazzling good looks and how could she blame Adam for being attracted to her?

Jivvy's voice sounded in her ear. "Ghost Two, are you ready to try a roll?"

The excitement for flight that Melena had felt earlier returned. "Oh, yeah."

Jivvy walked Melena through the process and which sticks and pedals to use. "Okay, let's try a single roll to your right."

Melena executed the roll successfully, but became slightly disoriented once she came out of it.

"Find your horizon, Ghost Two!" Jivvy shouted.

Melena quickly recovered and steadied the aircraft. Performing the roll was a little scary, but exhilarating as well.

"I want to do one more," she told Jivvy.

"All right, but take it slow."

Melena's second roll was even better than the first. She recovered easily. She couldn't help but shout out a "Wooo!" to her companions.

She could hear Adam chuckling. "Well done, Ghost Two. You're a screaming banshee."

Jivvy's voice broke in to spoil her fun. "We're about to begin our descent. Ghost Two, Coyote will be requesting remote access shortly. He'll bring you down."

Melena didn't know if she would ever have the opportunity to fly a Chameleon again. She was disappointed that her flight was coming to an end. "Let me try one more roll before Coyote takes control."

"One more, Ghost Two. Make it quick."

Melena's confidence was high, and the thought of this possibly being the last time she would fly made her a little more daring. "I'm going to try a double roll this time."

"Negative, Ghost Two!" Melena heard Jivvy order as she began the stunt. She executed the double roll perfectly and brought the aircraft back into position. She watched the horizon level out on her monitor, but something didn't feel right. Her head felt light. She looked down at the ground below her. Everything she could see took on a gray tone until it all sort of blended together and turned to black.

Chapter 18

"Ghost Two!" Adam shouted as he watched the *G-2* icon on his monitor begin to lose altitude. "Ghost Two, do you copy?"

Melena's Chameleon was going down. Adam pointed the nose of his aircraft toward the ground and dove straight down toward her.

"Coyote, assume control of Ghost Two!" Jivvy yelled in his ear.

"Ghost Two is unresponsive, and the system won't allow me to assume control without her giving it to me!" James shouted back.

"Melena!" Jivvy shouted.

Adam's dive was deeper than Melena's so he was gaining on her. He wasn't sure exactly what he could do, but he wasn't going to just let her fall out of the sky. He eased toward her aircraft as he caught up with her in a free fall. He thought that if he could get his Chameleon beneath hers, perhaps he could break her fall or land with her on his back. He waited until her spin brought her around to face the same direction as he was.

"Scoot over, Ghost Four. I got her." Jivvy's Chameleon appeared out of nowhere and slipped under Melena's. The two aircraft collided, the falling Chameleon bouncing off of the rescue one, causing pieces of both aircraft to break loose and fly away. Jivvy's camouflage system deactivated. Her aircraft suddenly appeared a stark gunmetal gray in the azure sky. She came up more gently the second time until the aircraft above her rested on the back of her own. "Gotcha," Jivvy whispered. "Ghost Four, pull up. I'm taking her down."

Adam didn't want to leave either of the two women in such a dangerous situation. "Negative, I'm going down with you."

"Pull up!" Jivvy shouted back at him. "You can't help us now. We don't need three Chameleons downed outside the walls. I can handle this. We're not far from home. Track our landing and send out a recovery team."

"Jiv, you're damaged. You're visible!"

"Oh, really?" She snapped. "I guess that's why there's a bunch of blinking lights and beeping in here. I'll have to destroy both aircraft once we're on the ground."

"I'm coming with you."

"No! I said pull up. Land inside the walls, and I'll contact you from the ground. Go! I've got her."

"Come on, Ghost Four," Droven's voice piped in. "We'll go get them once we've landed.

Adam was torn. He knew what Jivvy was telling him to do was the right thing, but he wanted to protect them somehow. The ground was coming up quickly. He had to make a decision. He said a silent prayer and asked God to protect Jivvy and Melena until he could reach them. He quickly pulled his Chameleon out of the dive and back to a safe altitude.

He watched, helplessly, as Jivvy struggled to keep Melena's Chameleon on top of her own. The only comfort he could take was in the fact that Jivvy was a better pilot than he was, and their chances of landing safely were better than they would have been if he were in Jivvy's place. Jivvy headed toward an empty field with a long, straight dirt road running along the edge of it. As soon as Jivvy's landing gear made contact with the road, Melena's Chameleon launched off of the top of it. It skidded down the road on its belly, spinning out of control and creating a huge dust cloud behind it.

"Ghost One, you okay?" Adam asked once Jivvy had rolled to a stop.

"Yeah. I'm good."

Adam circled around the landing site. He watched Jivvy jump out of her Chameleon and run to Melena's and pull it open. "How is she?" he asked.

Jivvy was breathing hard. "She's alive. Looks a little banged up from the crash, but she's breathing. Now, get outta here and land those stupid things. I'll head to the southwest corner of the wall. If I don't see you before I get there, I'll try and get inside on my own."

"All right, Ghost One, hang on. Ghost Four, let's go!" Droven shouted.

Adam was relieved that Melena was alive, but remained anxious about her condition. He wondered if it might have been a mistake to try and bring her to Independence after all. She probably would have been fine if he would have just helped her get back to Rugby instead. Now, she and Jivvy were out in the open without protection. Jivvy's camouflage had failed, and there was a good chance that she was spotted. All he could do now was assemble a rescue team and try and get to them as soon as possible. He offered another silent prayer, thanking God that both women were still alive.

Chapter 19

Melena raised her hand to answer the professor's question about … what? She realized she didn't know what he had asked.

"Yes, Ms. Jaxon."

She froze. She could feel the eyes of her classmates on her.

"Ms. Jaxon?"

Melena's tongue was stuck to the roof of her mouth. She tried, desperately to remember what the lecture was about, but nothing came.

"Melena?"

This voice didn't sound like the professor's voice. It was female.

"Melena!"

There it was again. And what was the awful smell in the room?

"Melena!"

Her eyes flew open, and she sat up.

"Hey. It's okay."

Melena's eyes found Jivvy leaning over her.

"You're okay."

Melena surveyed her surroundings and became even more confused. She also became aware of a dull pain in her right hip and a sharp pain in her left shoulder. "Oh, crap. What happened? And what was that smell?"

Jivvy held up a small cylinder. "Smelling salts from the first aid kit."

"Where are we?"

"Well, we're in the middle of a field because this was as close as I could get to Independence with your sorry butt balanced on my back."

"What?" Suddenly, Melena remembered that she had been flying. She looked around to find the Chameleons. Behind her, two smoldering heaps sent black smoke into the sky. "How did we get on the ground? I don't remember landing."

"No kidding." Jivvy shook her head. "You didn't land. You fell."

Melena looked back at the black, burning wreckage. "You mean, we crashed?"

Jivvy's mouth curved into a smile. "No, *you* crashed. I had a fantastic landing."

A terrible thought entered Melena's mind. "Where's Adam?" She searched the wreckage, hoping not to find a third heap.

"He's fine. He and Droven have probably landed inside the walls by now. He tried to help you, but he wasn't as quick as I was."

Melena was relieved that Adam was safe. At the same time, she couldn't believe that she was alive, considering how high she had been flying. "I fell from six thousand meters and survived?" She was more impressed with her little Chameleon than ever.

"You fell most of the way, but you were on my Chameleon's back by the time we reached the ground, and then you had a much smaller crash than you would have had otherwise."

Melena was still confused, but gathered that Jivvy had somehow rescued her. "What are you saying? You caught my Chameleon on top of yours and brought it to the ground?"

"Yeah." Jivvy pressed her lips together. "Pretty much."

She couldn't believe it. Certainly, Jivvy had risked her own life to save Melena's. "Oh, my … thank you."

An irritated look crossed Jivvy's face. "I told you not to try that double roll, you idiot. You always obey your flight captain when you're in the air."

Melena remembered performing the stunt and then … "I blacked out, didn't I?"

"If you would have waited twenty more seconds before blacking out, James would have taken control of your aircraft and landed you."

Melena looked back at the burning aircraft. "If you didn't crash, why is your Chameleon burning?"

"Well, it got messed up from trying to catch you on my back, and yours wasn't pretty either. I wasn't about to let the government get their hands on either of them." She held up a lightning rod. "I had to destroy them. Speaking of the government, I'm sure Feds are nearby. We need to get outta here."

Melena realized her recklessness had cost them two Chameleons and almost two lives. "I'm so sorry, Jivvy. I'll pay for them. I really thought I could handle it."

"We can talk about that later. Can you stand up?"

Melena held out her hands to Jivvy to help her up. As soon as Jivvy began pulling, pain shot through her left shoulder. "Ahhh!" She let go of Jivvy's hands and reached her right hand up to her left shoulder. She could feel that something was definitely wrong.

"Let me see." Jivvy unzipped Melena's flight suit and pulled it down off of her shoulder. Her fingers examined the area. "I think your shoulder's dislocated."

Melena tried to lift her arm, but the pain was excruciating. "Yeah, I think that's a good guess."

"Come here." Jivvy took hold of Melena's wrist with one hand and gripped her arm just above the elbow with the other. "What's your favorite color, Melena?"

"My favorite color?" Melena thought that was an odd question, but figured she would play along. "I guess I would have to say—aaahhh!"

Jivvy jerked Melena's arm up and back, causing intense pain. Melena heard a soft *pop*, and instantly the worst of the pain subsided.

Melena glowered at Jivvy. "Yellow!"

Jivvy covered her mouth with her hand and tried not to laugh.

Melena's hand went up to her shoulder and massaged it, gently. She felt sore, but the pain was bearable now. "Thanks … I guess. You could have warned me you were going to do that."

"Naw, I think it's better when it comes as a surprise. You're more relaxed."

"Whatever you say." Melena stood up, and the pain in her hip replaced what had been in her shoulder. She stepped gingerly on her right foot. She felt pain, but it felt more like a bruise than anything serious.

"Can you walk?" Jivvy asked.

Melena limped a few more steps. "Yeah, I can walk."

"We're only two miles or so from the walls. Can you make it that far?"

"Doesn't look like I have a lot of options. I'm fine, really."

"We need to put some distance between us and the Chameleons. There's no way my descent and that smoke got past their surveillance."

Jivvy picked up the lightning rod and slipped the small first aid kit into a pocket in her flight suit and began walking. Melena tried to keep up.

They walked about a kilometer through several fields without speaking until Jivvy broke the silence. "So, Melena, why did you decide to come to Independence? I mean, besides Adam's persistence."

Melena wasn't sure she had a good answer for her. It's what she kept asking herself. She guessed that it had something to do with her curiosity about the city and its inhabitants. It also had to do with her not wanting to be in the custody of the government with the possibility of them using her to track Adam down. And it maybe had more to do with her wanting to be with Adam, but that wasn't something she was anxious to share with Jivvy. "Well, I guess I thought it would be the safest option for Adam and you and Droven. I'm sure they would have tried to use me to help capture all of you if I'd turned myself in. Part of me is curious to see what Independence is like, I suppose. Adam's told me some things about it that I'd like to see for myself."

Jivvy kept her eyes straight ahead. "It doesn't have anything to do with your romantic feelings for Adam?"

For some reason, Melena felt instantly defensive. Their relationship—whatever it was—was none of Jivvy's business. "What do you mean? No. I *am* trying to help him. I feel responsible for him being in the mess he's in."

Jivvy glanced at her. "He's very serious about his faith, you know. He would never really want to be with someone who thought it was silly, let alone *criminal*."

Melena could feel her face getting hot. She had to fight the urge to catch up to Jivvy and slap her. "Oh, okay, well, it sounds like the two of you are just perfect for each other then. So sorry to have gotten in the way."

Jivvy stopped and turned to face Melena, her eyes narrowing. "What was that supposed to mean? I didn't say anything about me and Adam."

"Oh, I know. You didn't have to say a word—your little make out back in Blackfoot, your banter back and forth, taking him into a private room at the Rock Springs base to do … whatever you were doing. I can see that I've made some waves in your plans for the two of you, so I can see why you're jealous."

"Jealous?" Jivvy repeated, looking appalled. "Adam is one of my oldest friends, and that's what we are—friends. I just have a small problem with the woman who held him against his will, interrogated him with dangerous drugs and put his life in jeopardy, and who is responsible for having the entire continent hunting for him acting like she and he are a couple or something."

Melena was furious. She stepped up close to get right in Jivvy's face. "How dare you talk to me like that? Adam is only alive because I helped him escape from that lab."

Jivvy gave her a curt smile. "Keep telling yourself that." She turned on her heel and resumed walking.

There was no way Melena was going to let her get away with making those accusations against her. She limped up behind Jivvy and shoved her hard in the back with her good arm, knocking her to the ground. "I *will* keep telling myself that!"

Jivvy turned over onto her back, lifted her hips and kicked her feet into the air, propelling herself onto her feet. Before Melena knew what was happening, Jivvy landed a right hook to her left cheekbone, flattening her to the ground. Melena rolled onto her back as Jivvy bent over her and reached for her hair. Melena threw her right elbow toward Jivvy's face, connecting with it just over her right eye. Jivvy went to her knees, holding her face in her hands. Melena scrambled to her feet, preparing to deliver another blow.

"Put your hands in the air!" a voice behind them commanded.

Melena wheeled around to find three police agents with their guns trained on her from several meters away. Her eyes widened with surprise. She lifted her right arm and propped her weakened left arm against her pelvis with both hands outstretched.

"You too!" One of the agents pointed his barrel down at Jivvy.

Jivvy stood up slowly, raising both hands into the air. Blood trickled into her eye from a small cut that had opened up just above her eyebrow. Melena felt momentary satisfaction that she had done some damage. Her own cheek was throbbing, and she could feel it swelling up.

One of the agents, a large man with a blond Fu Manchu mustache and a shaved head, spoke into his transmitter. "This is M-Seven-Four-One. We've apprehended two females approximately one kilometer from the fire site. Recommending a sweep of the surrounding area for additional suspects." He paused to listen to the response in his ear piece. "Yes, ma'am, we'll bring them in."

Out of the corner of her eye, Melena noticed Jivvy looking over at her lightning rod, which had landed a few meters away. One of the agents followed her eyes to the long, silver weapon. Keeping his gun trained on Jivvy's head, he slowly walked around her and picked it up off of the ground.

"Get on your knees," the agent who had reported on their capture barked. "Put your hands behind your back."

Both women complied. Hand cuffs were fastened, and the police agents jerked them to their feet.

"Do you know who I am?" Melena asked the big agent who seemed to be in charge. "You may want to reconsider your manhandling of me."

He took a few steps in Melena's direction and stuck out his chin. "Why don't you tell me who you are?"

"Who are you looking for?" Melena asked, her tone dripping with defiance.

"Maybe the more important question is who your little girlfriend here is."

Jivvy gave him a sarcastic smile and then turned on her best southern drawl. "Oh, how rude of me. My motha would be so ashamed a me for not introducin' myself to ya'll earlier. I'm Martha Washington. How do ya'll do?" She gave a slight curtsy.

The agent gave her a menacing grin in return. Then he stepped over to her and took her chin in his hand, squeezing her cheeks together. "Well, I'm doing fine, Ms. Washington. There's nothing I love more than a little southern comfort. I think you and I need to get a little better acquainted before we part company."

Jivvy pulled her face loose of his grip. "Well, let's not go assumin' that desire is reciprocated."

He grabbed her by the arm and pulled her close to him. "Oh, I'm sure it will be." Keeping his grip on her arm, he spun her around and pushed her forward. "Let's go."

One of the other agents took Melena roughly by the left arm and pushed her on as well.

"Ouch!" Melena's shoulder was still tender. "Get your hand off of me. I can walk all by myself." The agent refused to ease up and continued pushing. "What's your name, agent? I want to let my father know who was responsible for my *rescue*." He didn't respond.

Melena and Jivvy were led up a dirt road where a police transport vehicle was parked near what remained of a decaying barn. The big agent opened the rear door of the vehicle, then took Jivvy and tossed her inside.

He turned and looked at Melena. "Take her over there." He gestured with his head to an area a few meters away. "This one needs further questioning." He turned back toward the open door.

The two agents began dragging Melena away. "No!" she screamed. "Stop! Don't!" She struggled to break free of the agent's grips on her arms, but they only held her tighter. "Let go of me!" Hot tears erupted from Melena's eyes as she desperately hoped that what she feared was about to happen wouldn't happen.

The big agent stepped up onto the running board of the vehicle. In her periphery, Melena saw a flash of color moving rapidly toward the vehicle. Suddenly, the agent's mustached face slammed into its metal frame, just above the door opening. His head whipped backwards, spurting blood in every direction. His heavy body landed flat on its back in the dirt and gravel with a thud. Adam stood over him for a split second and then disappeared behind the vehicle. The two agents with Melena started to raise their weapons, then, unexpectedly, their grip on her arms loosened, and they both crumpled to the ground. Melena looked down at the two bodies at her feet, wondering what had happened to them and after a moment spotted the tiny darts protruding from their necks. She turned to see Droven and a girl with long, dark hair and skin perched on the roof of the old barn holding sniper rifles.

Adam returned to the open door of the vehicle and lifted Jivvy out. "You okay?" he asked, gently.

She tried to push past him, her face blazing with fury. "Where is that big, stupid—"

"Hey," Adam pulled her back and held her by the shoulders. "It's okay. You're okay."

Jivvy looked down at the man on the ground. He was out cold. A large gash over the bridge of his nose had distributed crimson all over his face and the front of his gray police fatigues. She kicked the toe of her boot into the ground near his head, sending a cloud of dust and rocks over it, the reddish-brown dirt sticking to his blood-soaked face.

"All right." Adam's voice was soft, but firm as he led Jivvy away from the unconscious police agent. "Let's go."

Jivvy took a few steps before shrugging out of Adam's grip and spinning back toward the downed man. She kicked him twice in the ribs with the toe of her boot before Adam could take her by the shoulders and pull her away again.

Droven and the girl with him had climbed down from the barn's roof and were running toward Melena.

"Melena!" Droven called out. "You okay?"

Melena turned her head and wiped her face on the sleeve of her good shoulder. "Yeah, I'm okay."

Droven embraced her. "Thank goodness. I'm so glad you two are all right." He turned to the girl standing next to him. "Heaven, take the engine out."

The girl nodded and ran back to the police vehicle. She pulled a device from a holster at her waist and pointed it at the front of the vehicle. The rectangular metal sheet covering the engine snapped loose and was thrown clear. There was an awful screeching sound of metal scraping against metal as the entire engine broke loose and was lifted out of the vehicle and placed on the ground next to it. Melena's jaw dropped. This girl could really take orders, she thought. She had literally taken the engine out of the vehicle.

Adam brought Jivvy over to where Melena was standing. "We're ready," he announced to no one in particular.

Off to her right, a large vehicle emerged from behind a grass-covered hill and sped toward them. It looked like a tank to Melena, except that there was no cannon on top and it was fast. Its wheels, if it had any, were concealed behind a sheet of armor. It pulled up alongside the five of them, and a door slid open.

"Jump in," Droven directed as he reached down and picked up the lightning rod that lay next to the downed police agents and then pulled the darts out of their necks.

The girl Droven had called *Heaven* ran to the vehicle and hopped inside. Adam helped Jivvy and Melena, who were still in hand cuffs, up into the tall transport and then got in. Droven paused to scan the area before jumping in and sliding the door shut. The passenger area of the vehicle was separate from the cab so Melena couldn't see the driver. It was also void of windows, but had a row of white lights along the ceiling. It had two black leather benches facing one another. There was a man who, by the look of his graying, receded hair and dark, aged skin, appeared to be in his mid-to-late fifties sitting at the far end of one of the benches. Heaven sat down next to him, and Droven plopped down next to her. Jivvy, Melena and Adam sat down on the bench opposite the others. The vehicle lunged forward, and Melena could feel it picking up speed.

"Hi, Melena." The man gave her a warm smile. "I'm Peter Gildrich."

"Hi." Melena could only muster a half-hearted grin. "Nice to meet you."

Peter Gildrich put his arm around the young woman sitting next to him. "This is my daughter, Heaven."

"Hi, Heaven. Thanks for your help out there."

Heaven nodded and then reached into the holster at her hip and pulled out the device she had used to remove the police vehicle's engine. She twirled the index finger of her other hand in a circle. "Turn around. Let's see if we can't get you outta those cuffs."

Melena turned and knelt on the bench, bending so that her hands were up in the air behind her. She heard a click, and the cuffs loosened around her wrists. She pulled her hands away from one another, and the cuffs fell to the metal floor with a clank. Whatever Heaven's device was, it certainly had a way with metal objects. Jivvy turned around to have hers removed as well. Her expression was even, but her eyes glistened, and tears stained her cheeks. Once her cuffs were removed, she sat back down and stared at the floor.

Adam squatted down in front of her and put his fingers under her chin, lifting her face up even with his. "Let's get you cleaned up a little here."

Jivvy reached into her pocket and pulled out the first aid kit from the Chameleon and held it out to him. Adam took it from her and unzipped it. He removed some gauze and rubbing alcohol, dowsed the gauze with the alcohol and began wiping the blood away from Jivvy's eyebrow.

"Looks like those police agents roughed the two of you up a little, huh?" Peter asked, unaware of what had actually happened.

Jivvy glanced at Melena as Adam dabbed at the cut over her eye. "Yeah, they did."

Adam looked over at Melena and held up his bloody gauze. "You're next, Melena. Are you okay?"

"Yeah, I'm fine."

"She dislocated her shoulder in the crash," Jivvy informed them.

"Jivvy set it for me, though, so it's okay now."

Peter shook his head. "It's only by the hand of God that you two girls are alive right now. I can't believe you were able to bring both aircraft down, Jivvy. That was truly amazing."

Jivvy pursed her lips together, but didn't say anything.

Outside the vehicle, Melena heard gunfire and the sound of bullets hitting and ricocheting off of the vehicle's armor. Everyone's heads came up as they became aware that they were under attack. An explosion outside shook the vehicle, but it didn't lose any speed. The gunfire continued, accompanied by two more explosions. After a few more seconds, the noise outside ceased. The vehicle slowed down and came to a stop. It idled for a few seconds and then crawled forward, picking up speed again. After driving for another twenty seconds or so, it came to a stop.

Peter stood up and slid the door open. “Welcome to Independence.”

Chapter 20

Melena squinted as she stepped out onto the pavement and looked up at the sky. It looked just as blue as it did when she was flying earlier in the day. She wasn't sure what she expected it to look like from the inside, she just assumed something would be different. The station their enormous armored truck had pulled into was surrounded by large trees, which obstructed her view of the city.

Adam came up behind her and put his arm around her waist. "Melena, we need to have a doctor take a look at your shoulder."

She nodded, absentmindedly, still taking in her surroundings. The manicured lawn and flower gardens at the station were vibrant and fresh. A light breeze tempered the summer heat and thick humidity. A quiet street lay just beyond the station. A row of modest, but beautiful homes lined each side of the black paved road. Each home looked unique and colorful with large front lawns and bright flowers. Many of the trees in the yards looked quite young, indicating that the homes had likely been constructed recently. Some of the driveways were occupied with vehicles, but Melena didn't recognize any of the models. Most of them were considerably larger than the ones the government produced for the citizens of the S.O.U.

Peter had gone into the station's garage and was now backing out what appeared to be a miniature bus. A door on the side slid open automatically. Peter's window lowered, and he leaned out of it. "You ladies and Adam climb in. I'm taking you to the clinic. Jivvy, your mother will meet us there. Droven, you need to be debriefed inside."

Droven waved to his friends. "I'll catch up with you guys later." He turned and headed toward the station.

The three of them climbed into the little bus, the sliding door closing behind them. Little was said during the five minute ride to the clinic. Peter was busy discussing Melena's and Jivvy's condition with someone who must have been on the other end of the earpiece she assumed he had, but couldn't see. With Adam wedged in between the two women, each stared out of her respective window, though Melena wasn't necessarily trying to avoid conversation, she was just curious about the buildings and parks they were driving past.

There seemed to be a common theme among the homes and businesses and parks she had seen so far—they were clean. None of the litter and graffiti she was accustomed to seeing in residential areas was present here. People moved about freely, and none of them seemed afraid of one another. Something even more unusual than that was the number of children she had seen. They seemed to be everywhere. There was no shortage of parks and they were filled with children. Some were running and chasing one another, some were kicking balls or playing on swings. She even saw a large group of young boys wearing helmets and shoulder pads lined up opposite one another.

The vehicle slowed and pulled into the parking garage of a tall, glass building. An attendant approached the vehicle holding a thin, square pad. Peter lowered his window, and the attendant held out the pad. A blue orb appeared from out of the pad and made a pass around Peter's head, slowing in front of his eyes and then returned into the pad and disappeared. The attendant waved the vehicle forward onto a silver-colored rectangle that was just slightly larger than the vehicle. When they stopped on top of the rectangle, it slowly lowered the vehicle into the ground. It was dark outside the windows for a few seconds, and then another parking level appeared. When the elevator stopped, Peter pulled the vehicle a short distance into a parking stall. Two nurses pushing wheelchairs rushed out of a sliding glass door, stopping just outside the mini bus.

Peter turned and looked over his shoulder at the three of them. "I'll see you inside."

The door slid open, and one of the nurses reached for Melena. "I'm fine. I don't need a chair," she protested, but the nurse just smiled and pulled her into it anyway.

The other nurse had also insisted that Jivvy sit down, despite her assurances that her only injury was a minor cut over her eye.

As they approached the glass door, a woman stepped out and hurried toward them. Her long, dark hair waved back and forth behind her as she ran. Her eyes were fixed on Jivvy.

"Jivvissa!" The woman called out.

Jivvy got up out of her wheelchair and shrugged. "Hi, Mom."

Jivvy's mother threw her arms around her daughter's neck and closed her eyes tightly as she held her. "Are you okay?"

"Yeah," Jivvy whispered.

The woman looked up and noticed Adam standing there.

"Hi." Adam grinned and held up his hand in a wave.

"Get over here," Jivvy's mother insisted, waving him toward her. She embraced him as well. "Oh, Adam boy, you had us so worried."

"Worried? About me?" Adam frowned and shook his head as though the thought of it was absurd.

Jivvy's mother rolled her eyes as she exhaled an exaggerated sigh. Her eyes were a deep blue with long, dark lashes. The skin on her face was smooth, aside from a few subtle wrinkles at the edges of her mouth and around her eyes.

Despite the obvious difference in age, she was just as stunning as Jivvy.

Melena got up out of her wheelchair. Adam moved over to her and put his hand on the small of her back. "This is Jivvy's mom, Emaya Luna." The woman smiled at her and nodded. Melena smiled back.

Adam's hand gently patted Melena's back. "And this is our new friend, Melena Jaxon."

Emaya Luna's smile vanished, and she nearly choked on an audible gasp. Her eyes widened, and she froze. For an awkward few moments, she just stared at Melena.

She was startled when Jivvy finally broke the silence. "It's okay, Mom. She helped Adam escape. She's been with us for a few days."

Jivvy's mother's eyelids fluttered as she seemed to wake up from whatever trance the mention of Melena's name had cast upon her. "I'm sorry." She managed a nervous smile. "Hello, Melena."

"It's nice to meet you," Melena responded.

"It's very nice to meet you as well." Emaya stepped slowly toward Melena and held out her arms. "May I?"

Melena stepped toward her. "Of course."

Jivvy's mother embraced Melena gently and then pulled back and locked eyes with her again. "Thank you for whatever help you gave to Adam." Her dark blue eyes glistened with emotion.

Melena blushed, slightly. "It was the right thing to do."

"Melena dislocated her shoulder in the crash," Adam informed her. "We ought to get her inside to have it checked out."

"Actually, Jivvy set it for me," Melena told Emaya. "She's quite the field doctor."

"Is that right?" Emaya's attention returned to her daughter. "It looks like you could use a few stiches on that cut too, Jivvy."

"It's not a big deal." Jivvy glanced at Melena quickly and then back at her mother. "Let's just go get it over with."

Jivvy and Melena both ignored the nurses with the wheelchairs and walked into the clinic on their own. Melena couldn't help noticing Emaya staring at her as they made their way to the lobby. This was one of the things she feared before coming to Independence—people being afraid or uncomfortable with her presence as the daughter of the Senator that opposed their very existence. She tried to ignore it.

The interior of the clinic was immaculate and beautifully decorated, though the floor they had descended to didn't seem to be available to the public. Melena didn't see any other patients waiting to be seen. Only celebrities and government officials in S.O.U. territory were spared the unbearable waiting for medical treatment that the general public had to endure. Perhaps this was something similar.

A young female doctor in a white lab coat approached Melena. "Ms. Jaxon?"

"Yes."

"Do you want to come with me? I'm going to examine your injuries." She smiled and turned toward a hallway with several examination rooms.

Melena followed the doctor a few steps and then looked over her shoulder at Adam. "Are you coming with me?"

"I think I better let the doctor look you over without me there, but I'll come check on you in a few minutes," he replied.

Melena smiled to herself. Adam was so proper and old fashioned. If he were someone else, it may have been a turnoff, but to Melena it was an endearing quality in him. In reality, she enjoyed the respect and thought that perhaps his brand of gentility should never have gone out of style.

Chapter 21

Once Jivvy and Melena were being attended to, the medical staff's attention turned to Adam.

Peter had joined him in the lobby. "All right, my brother, we're going to see if we can't figure out what is going on with you."

A pair of doctors came out of their offices to greet Adam and Peter. The first introduced himself as Dr. Kimura. He looked to be in his early forties. He was thin and average height with short, black hair. He told Adam he had immigrated to Independence just seven years ago from Japan. The other was Dr. Azevedo, who appeared to be a few years younger than his associate. He was tall and barrel-chested with an easy smile. He explained that he was a second-generation citizen of Independence. His parents had come from Brazil during the time the wall around the city was being constructed.

The two doctors led Adam and Peter deeper into the clinic and through a security checkpoint. On the other side of the checkpoint, they entered a large laboratory-type facility. It was filled with lights and instruments, almost resembling an operating room, but with a chair in the center rather than a table.

Two gray-haired men in a dark suits sat at desks in the rear of the room. Both men stood when Adam and Peter and the two doctors entered, then walked across the room to meet them. "Good to see you, Peter." The younger of the two men shook Peter's hand and then turned to Adam. "Adam Winter?" He held out his hand.

"Yes, sir." Adam took his hand and tried to match the firmness of his grip.

"I understand you've had quite an eventful few days." The man gave him a tight-lipped smile, keeping his iron grip on Adam's hand.

"Well, the Lord's been mindful of me," Adam replied. "And here I am in one piece."

"And we are certainly grateful for that." The man's smile widened. "My name is Andrew Kent." He gestured to the man beside him. "This is Louis Green, Chairman of the Independence Security Council."

The older man shook Adam's hand. "Mr. Kent and I are here to observe the examination that these good doctors are here to perform. I hope you don't mind."

"Not at all," Adam answered. "I think we're all interested in finding out what's happened inside this old noggin." He tapped his forehead with his index finger.

"Yes, we are." Louis Green smiled and released Adam's hand. Both men returned to their desks at the back of the room.

Adam had heard of Mr. Green. He was somewhat of a celebrity in Independence, having taken part in the design of the city's defenses. Adam recognized the name Andrew Kent as well, but wasn't exactly sure who he was. Someone in the Independence leadership circle, he assumed. He was impressed with the strength of Mr. Kent's handshake. His firm grip wasn't intended to intimidate Adam, it was more a sign of respect.

Dr. Kimura pointed to the chair in the center of the room. "Adam, please have a seat."

Adam complied and took the chair in the center of the room. He felt awkward being the object of everyone's attention.

Dr. Kimura sat on a tall stool behind a sort of lectern and held a small remote control in his hand. He pushed a button, and a large, white ring descended from above the chair in the center of the room, stopping just above Adam's head. The lights in the room dimmed.

"You can watch this too, Adam." Dr. Kimura pushed another button on the remote, and a large three-dimensional image of Adam's brain appeared about ten feet in front of him. A smaller image of the floating brain appeared above Dr. Kimura's lectern. Dr. Kimura reached up and began manipulating the image with his fingers. He removed brain tissue from the small image, which corresponded with the larger image, until he had revealed the data stamp. The tissue surrounding the small, flexible electronic component had grown in around it.

"Your brain tissue has accepted the stamp. It is actively communicating with your brain," Dr. Kimura explained.

"So, this stamp was intended to be surgically implanted in the brain?" Adam asked.

"Yes," Dr. Kimura replied. "It's designed to communicate with a human brain rather than with an artificial one."

"Why do you think the Response's surgeon implanted it inside *me*? My understanding was that I was to simply retrieve it and bring it back here."

"The stamp was intended for you, Adam," Andrew Kent explained. "But we wanted the procedure done here, rather than in a crude apartment. For that, I apologize. The Response agent overseeing the transfer became aware that their team had been compromised—that they were being observed by the government. He made the call to have the stamp implanted prematurely to increase its chances of reaching Independence. He thought that implanting the stamp in your brain would conceal it, and that they could then distance themselves from you before being apprehended so the government wouldn't know about your involvement. He misjudged the situation. Fortunately for you, the government didn't know at the time exactly what your meeting with The Response was about. Everyone else who was involved was killed."

Adam felt anger boiling up inside of him. "Respectfully, sir, don't you think I should have been consulted about having this thing implanted in me before going to Rugby in the first place?"

"Like I mentioned, we did not intend for an implantation to occur without your consent," Mr. Kent explained. "The Response took a great liberty in sedating you and performing the surgery themselves. I'm sorry."

Adam's blood pressure lowered, somewhat.

"Have you noticed data being presented to your subconscious, Adam?" Dr. Kimura asked.

Adam recalled the dreams he had been having. "I think so. I've had some strange dreams the past few nights with strings of numbers and other characters involved."

Dr. Kimura nodded. "The stamp communicates with your subconscious. It has essentially integrated itself into your thoughts. Don't worry though, Adam, it can't manipulate you, it just provides you with information."

"What kind of information?" Adam asked. "What's the purpose of having the thing in my head?"

"All of that will be explained to you in the near future, Adam," Mr. Kent answered. "We're here today to observe your physiological condition."

Dr. Azevedo took Dr. Kimura's spot on the tall stool and removed some additional tissue from the image. "We were told that you have developed some hyper-sensitivity in your basic senses, Adam. Is that accurate?"

"Yeah," Adam confirmed. "Mainly my vision, smelling and hearing have been enhanced. After the surgery, I could hardly bear light or loud noises, but gradually I've been able to learn to control it, or at least deal with it."

Dr. Azevedo reconstructed Adam's brain image. A section of tissue in the image turned red. "This is your sensory cortex." Dr. Azevedo pointed to the red area, which was located just above the stamp. Another section a short distance from it filled in with red as well. "It appears that the Response's surgeon, in his haste, inadvertently created a canal from your sensory cortex into a dormant section of your brain. It looks like the tissue here has duplicated the function of the sensory tissue." He looked up from the image. "Amazing!"

"So, if I understand this correctly, more of my brain is performing sensory functions than before?" Adam asked.

"Yes, that looks to be the case," Dr. Azevedo confirmed.

The doctor continued probing the image in front of him. He pushed a button, and the ring above Adam retracted a few feet back toward the ceiling. "Would you mind standing up, please, Adam?"

Adam got up from his chair, and the image in front of him enlarged until it included his entire body.

"From what I understand from my briefing, you also have increased motor skills and speed. Is that accurate?"

"Yes, that's accurate. I would guess my foot speed has doubled or tripled."

Dr. Azevedo studied the image for a few moments. "Adam, would you mind running in place—maybe three-quarter speed?"

Adam complied. After thirty seconds of running in place, Dr. Azevedo held up a hand, signaling for him to stop. "Can you just start and then stop a few times?"

After the second start and stop, the nervous system in the image of Adam's body flooded with a blue color, detailing hundreds of tiny branches reaching to every part of his body.

"Dr. Kimura, would you come and take a look at this?" Dr. Azevedo waved his associate over to him. "Again, please,

Adam." The two doctors studied the image for a while longer, speaking softly to one another and pointing out different areas of the image as Adam continued his start and stop running exercise.

Finally, Dr. Kimura directed his attention back to Adam. "Adam, it appears that your increased agility is a function of the stamp. I'll try to explain this in simple terms. When your brain decides it wants your body to move, the motor cortex communicates with other parts of the body to regulate movement. The basal ganglia are a neural structure located deep within the cortex. The basal ganglia receive instructions from the cerebral cortex and basically forward them to the motor areas via the thalamus." He paused to see if Adam was following. Adam's expression must have convinced Dr. Kimura that he was with him so far. He continued, "The stamp is emitting a signal that basically speeds this process up. Your brain is communicating with your body at an extremely high rate. That accounts for quickness and agility in your limbs, but there seems to be another factor at play in your raw speed. Your medical file makes mention of a virus your father modified and developed as a health supplement for you. Is that correct?"

Adam nodded his head.

"It appears that your muscles do not fatigue the way someone else's would due to the effects of this supplement. Their rapid recovery, in tandem with your increased neurological communication, may be responsible for your incredible speed. This is, of course, a working theory. Dr. Azevedo and I will continue to study the recorded imagery from today."

The ring over Adam's head retracted all the way to the ceiling and the lights in the room returned to normal.

Chapter 22

Adam and Peter met Emaya outside a waiting room where Jivvy and Melena were waiting for them.

"Looks like the girls are all fixed up," Emaya informed them. "Adam, will you excuse Peter and me for a moment?"

"Sure." As Adam entered the waiting room, Melena's and Jivvy's heads came up, and each presented a smile that would have impressed any beauty pageant judge.

"What was that all about?" Jivvy asked. "I thought we were here to get stiches for me and a sling for her." Jivvy pointed to Melena with her thumb. "We've been sitting here forever waiting for you, you prima donna."

Adam laughed. "Prima donna? Be honest, did you or did you not have a plastic surgeon apply your three stiches rather than a regular doctor?"

Jivvy smiled, innocently. "I wasn't given the option. I just sat there while the plastic surgeon did her thing."

Adam took a seat next to Melena and turned to face her. "How are you feeling?"

She laid her head on his shoulder. "I'm fine. They said that Jivvy did an outstanding job resetting my shoulder and that the pain should subside soon. I did get this cute sling out of it, though." She held out her bent arm for him to admire. Her sling was pink with tiny cartoon penguins sliding on their bellies.

"Did you pick that out yourself?" Adam asked.

"Well, they gave me a dark blue one first." A childish grin appeared on her face. "I asked them if there were any other options and ended up with this one."

"It's adorable." Adam smiled back at her. He imagined Jivvy's eyes rolling, but he didn't look at her.

As Adam sat back in his chair and let out a long sigh, he overheard Emaya and Peter's conversation out in the hall.

"I still can't believe you didn't tell me who she was!" Emaya was whispering, intensely.

"I'm sorry," Peter defended. "I didn't know quite how to tell you, and I thought you would have seen it on the government's news broadcasts anyway."

"I've been buried in campaign analysis, Peter. You know that. I've barely been up for air."

"I'm sorry. I should have given you a heads up, but she's here now, Emaya. What are you going to do?"

"I'm not sure. I really wasn't prepared for this."

"Adam?" Melena's voice finally registered in this brain.

He turned to face her. "Sorry. What?"

"I asked if they were able to provide any answers on your condition."

"Uh … yeah, yeah, the doctors were brilliant. I think they have things pretty well figured out." Adam's attention was divided as he tried to pick up the conversation going on in the hall again, but it had apparently ended because just then, Emaya pushed the waiting room door open, and she and Peter entered the room.

"All right, let's get you folks out of here." Peter clapped his hands together. "Melena, we have a hotel room reserved for you just down the block, which I think—"

"Actually," Adam interrupted, "I thought she could stay with my aunt and uncle tonight."

Chapter 23

Melena bit down on her lower lip let her gaze wander anywhere except at the tall walnut door in front of her.

"You don't need to be nervous." Adam's voice was soothing. "They'll be happy to meet you and glad to have you stay. Trust me."

Melena said nothing, but looked up into his soft brown eyes for a moment to draw a little comfort. So far, everyone in Independence had been warm to her, but this was Adam's family, and she was the woman who had taken him bound and sedated to a hidden laboratory inside of a mountain to manipulate his brain in order to glean information from him. It was a little different than bringing home a prom date.

The heavy door's lock release beeped, and it popped open a few centimeters. Melena finally brought her eyes forward, but saw no one at the door. Just then, a little blond head appeared from around it. Two big, blue eyes widened, and a broad grin split chubby little cheeks. "Adam!"

"Hi, bud!" Adam squatted down just in time to nearly be bowled over by his little cousin. "What've you been up to?" He scooped the little guy up and brought him to Melena's eye level. "This is my friend, Melena. Can you say hi?"

The big blue eyes studied her for a moment. "Hi."

"Hi. What's your name?" Melena had spent very little time around children and wasn't quite sure what to say to him.

"Aaron." The little guy stared at her for another second, and then his mouth began working at a feverish rate. "We were playing builders, and I was Mr. Gus, and he's in charge of all the building, and mommy was a helper, and we made a big fort with a ginormous blanket on top, but then it was too dark inside so we took off the roof, and we ate popsicles inside, and then mommy said we could build another fort tomorrow, but I had to get my jammies on and brush my teeth, and then Dad read me my *Charles Monkey* book, and he was talking like Charles, and then I heard 'beep boop,' and I beat everybody to the door and—"

"Okay, bud." Adam grabbed his face and smushed his cheeks together. "You gotta take a breath. You're gonna make Melena dizzy."

Melena laughed. It was love at first sight with this little man. She was so enthralled with Aaron's adventures that she hadn't noticed the doorway fill up with more children.

"Adam!" A toothless smile appeared on a pajama-clad little girl's face as she ran to greet her cousin. Her wet, auburn hair whipped Adam's face as he bent down to pick her up with his free arm.

Adam groaned as he stood up. "Oh, Lizzy! You're too big to be in this tree." The little girl giggled and hugged his neck.

"John said you were in jail, Adam," a freckle-faced girl with wide, brown eyes and wet red hair commented from the doorway.

"No I didn't!" the thin, awkward boy standing next to her countered, slapping her shoulder with the back of his hand.

"Okay, guys. Let's let them inside. It's hot and muggy out there." A woman with short, blond hair appeared and gathered the two older children back into the house, making room for Adam and Melena to enter.

Adam set the two younger children down and bear hugged his aunt. She closed her eyes and buried her face in his neck, holding him tightly. "Oh, Adam boy, I'm so glad you're home."

He smiled at her and then turned to Melena. "Aunt Esther, this is Melena Jaxon."

Esther's blue-gray eyes found Melena's and held them for a moment. "Hello, Melena."

"Hello." Melena smiled nervously and went up onto her toes and back down. "It's nice to meet you." She held out her hand.

Esther ignored it and hugged her instead. "It's very nice to meet you also. We're so glad you're both safe."

A tall man with thick dark hair and a double chin appeared from around a corner. "What's going on out here?" he boomed. "Oh, it's Adam. I thought I smelled something."

"Oh, Paul, we don't wanna hear about what you've been smelling," Adam called back to him.

The man looked at Melena and then back at Adam. "Wait a second. This girl must be lost. She's way too pretty to be seen with Adam."

Adam turned his head to look at Melena. "I don't disagree with that. She is, unfortunately, homeless. I picked her up out on the street and offered her a place to stay."

"Okay." Paul nodded his head. "We'll trade you for her."

"Dad!" The redhead shot her father a warning look.

"Oh, sorry. We'll trade Adam and Joy for the homeless girl."

The redheaded girl, Joy, gasped and crinkled her freckled nose at him, deeply offended.

Melena smiled, feeling much more at ease. "The homeless girl's name is Melena." She offered him her hand. He took it and then pulled her in for a one-armed hug.

"Welcome, Melena." He looked down at her and smiled, warmly.

"Get over here, tough guy," he growled, reaching for Adam. The two men created a chorus of deep thuds as they slapped each other on the back in a manly embrace. The tall man took a step backwards. "So, I hear you two had a pretty boring day."

Adam and Melena both laughed and nodded their heads.

The older boy, John, looked at Melena. "My friend said that they said on the news that Adam kidnapped you."

Melena chuckled, awkwardly. "I know. They've been saying a lot of crazy stuff on the news lately."

"John …" Esther glared at her son. "That's enough."

"What did you tell your friend?" Adam asked.

John shrugged and looked up at Adam through several locks of his shaggy dark hair. "I told him that you wouldn't do that."

"He didn't!" Joy insisted. "Right, Adam?"

Adam nodded and tried to keep a straight face, but let a short laugh escape. "Actually, Joy, they kinda got the story backwards."

Melena felt her face flush as she looked down at the floor.

"But, it all worked out," he continued. "Now, we're friends."

Melena looked up and met his eyes. "Right." She smiled.

The younger girl walked up to Melena and gently reached out her index finger to touch one of the penguins on Melena's sling. "Did you break your arm?"

"No, I just hurt my shoulder a little, but it'll be fine in a few days."

"All right, you kids, it's time for bed. We let you stay up so you could say hi and now you've said hi. Give Adam a hug, and go hop into bed," Esther commanded.

"Hold on, Sweetheart." Paul got down on his knees. "We need to have family prayer first." He looked up at his guests. "Would you two join us?"

Adam looked at Melena and raised his eyebrows.

"Yeah." She knelt down and took Adam's hand and pulled him down beside her.

Aaron darted across the room and knelt down next to Melena, taking her other hand. The family formed a circle and all joined hands.

"Elizabeth?" Paul leaned over and looked at his youngest daughter. "Would you say the prayer for us?"

Elizabeth nodded and then closed her eyes, tightly. "Heavenly Father," she began, "thank you for the day we had. Thank you that Adam and Ma … and Mel …"

"Melena," Esther whispered.

"Thank you that Adam and Melena could get home safely. Thank you for Jesus. Bless us to sleep good tonight. Bless that Daddy will let us have a puppy. Help us do what's right. Bless Adam to get married soon. In Jesus' name, amen."

"Amen," everyone echoed, followed by snickers from the older children at Elizabeth's latter request.

Esther clapped her hands together. "All right, into bed all of you kids!"

After some brief whining and mild resistance, each of the children hugged their parents and then went to Adam and Melena. Aaron jumped to Adam, who snatched him out of the air and gave him a big squeeze. He reached out for Melena and Adam leaned him over to her. He hugged her neck and then planted a soft kiss on her cheek.

Melena grinned. "Aw, thank you. Good night, Aaron."

Joy hugged all of the adults and then took Aaron's hand and led him down the hall to his room. Elizabeth hugged Melena timidly and Adam enthusiastically and then gave Melena a broad smile from over her shoulder before retreating to her room. Melena could only assume her smile had something to do with the desire she had expressed for her older cousin to settle down. Apparently, she had gained Elizabeth's approval to help him out with that.

John wandered toward the two of them with his head down. "Good night," he muttered.

Adam grabbed him by the arm as he passed and wrestled him to the floor. John winced and smiled simultaneously through the headlock Adam had him in.

"It's good night for you right now, Johnny boy!" Adam held him in a loose sleeper hold for a few seconds and then released him, rustling the bushy mop on his head. He ducked away from Adam and got to his feet.

"It was a pleasure meeting you, John." Melena tried to meet his eyes.

He glanced up at her briefly. "It was a pleasure meeting you, too."

"Your brother and sisters had a hug for me. What about you?"

He blushed, instantly. "Okay." He leaned into her as she patted him on the back and then hurried down the hall to his room.

Melena smiled at Esther. "You have sweet children."

"They are sweet," Esther agreed. "They're really what life's all about." She looked up at her husband. He winked back at her.

"Sit down, you two," Paul insisted. "You've got to be exhausted."

Esther and Paul stepped to an over-stuffed love seat and sat next to each other, Esther taking one of Paul's hands in both of hers. They made a cute couple, Melena thought. He was big and loud, but gentle and affectionate towards his wife. She was short and slight of build, but could obviously take charge of a situation. Melena and Adam backed up to the larger sofa behind them and sat down. Melena decided to leave a little space between them, even though she wanted to be closer to him. Although they were very warm toward her, she wasn't exactly sure how Adam's aunt and uncle felt about her.

Paul smiled at the two of them. "So, this is an interesting situation, isn't it?"

Adam nodded and then glanced over at Melena. "A little bit."

"So, what's your plan, Melena?" Esther asked, getting right down to business. "Do you plan on staying in Independence for a while?"

"I'm not really sure what I'm doing," Melena answered. "I need to get in contact with my father soon. I'm not sure whether he's worried about me or ready to hang me for treason." She pressed her lips together and shook her head, her emotions beginning to surface. "I'm not sure what he actually believes." Her voice broke. "All I know is that it's been as dangerous for me as it has been for Adam and the others since … well, the past few days."

"Well, you're safe now," Esther assured her. "You're welcome to stay here as long as you want. Peter told us that you helped Adam escape from a life-threatening situation so we thank you for that."

Melena wiped a tear with the back of her finger. "To be honest," she sniffled, "I saved his life once, but he's saved mine half a dozen times since."

Adam put his hand on her shoulder. "Your saving my life is what created the life-threatening situations that followed. I know there's a reason for all of this, though. You're supposed to be here. We'll figure out what happens next, but I think the best thing to do now is to get some rest."

"There's a guest bedroom and bathroom at the end of this hall, Melena. You're welcome to it," Paul offered. "It's actually Adam's old room."

"Thank you. I don't want to be a burden on you. They had a hotel room booked for me, but Adam insisted I stay here instead."

"A self-serving gesture, really." Paul looked over at Adam and shook his head. "He just wants to come back in the morning for breakfast. He knows that I always make my famous aebleskivers for breakfast when we have guests."

Adam put his hands up. "No contest."

"Aebleskivers? That's a Danish pastry, isn't it?" Melena asked. "Are your ancestors Danish?"

"Impressive. Yes." Paul smiled. "Have you had them before?"

"A long time ago in Copenhagen, but … I'm sure yours are better than the ones I had."

Paul laughed. "I guess we'll find out in the morning."

The four of them stood. Esther and Paul said goodnight and left the room together. Adam headed for the door.

"I'll walk you out," Melena offered and followed him out onto the front porch. "Can't I just stay wherever you're staying?" she whispered.

Adam smiled and shook his head.

"Well, can't you just stay here with me?" she asked.

Adam shook his head again. "I won't be far. Droven and I have a place a few blocks away. I'll be back before you wake up."

Now Melena was shaking her head. "I don't get it."

Adam chuckled. "I know."

She stepped toward him and looked up into his eyes. "Everything's going to be okay, right?"

"Come here." He held out his arms. She leaned into him, pressing her cheek against his chest. She wrapped her good arm around his waist. His embrace felt like a warm blanket. It was the safest she had felt since leaving Rugby. She closed her eyes and inhaled through her nose, savoring his scent. She lifted her head to find his eyes again. Her face was close enough to his to feel his breath. Her heart pounded as she stared intensely into his dark eyes. She wondered what he was waiting for. Finally, he began to move in, but his lips missed hers and ended up next to her ear. “Get some sleep,” he whispered. “I’ll see you in the morning.”

Chapter 24

Adam joined in the audience's thunderous applause. Droven got to his feet, and Adam joined him. Jivvy and Melena decided to give the cast a standing ovation as well. Adam stole a glance at Melena's face as the house lights began coming up. Her eyes sparkled, and she appeared to be trying to keep her emotions in check. Adam struggled with the same endeavor, but was less successful. He pressed his sleeve to his face to soak up the tears that streaked down his cheeks.

On stage, Joseph's beard was beginning to peel off in front of his ear, but he and Mary both smiled and waved to the crowd as they were rewarded for their performances. Peter and the other apostles patted each other on the back and smiled at each other and the audience.

Outside the theatre, Adam walked slowly alongside Melena. The night air felt heavy and thick, and he could feel sweat beading up on his forehead. Melena had been relatively quiet since the production had ended and they had said good night to their friends. Now she looked reflective as the moon cast its blue light on her face. She wandered to a bench carved out of a large boulder and sat down.

"So you really believe that all those things actually happened?" she asked, finally breaking the silence. "I mean like angels appearing, him healing people, his body reviving after being dead for three days?"

"I know they did," Adam replied, trying to meet her eyes.

"What do you mean you *know*?"

He paused and tried to collect his thoughts. "Well, I believe that we are both physical and spiritual beings. Some things we experience appeal to our physical senses and some things are communicated to our spirits." He sat down next to her and looked up at the stars. "The things that have had the most lasting effect on me have been things that I have learned in a deeper way than just through my eyes or ears. It's more difficult to discern spiritual knowledge than temporal knowledge, but it's also more powerful. I know that the events depicted in the show we watched are true because I feel it."

Melena narrowed her eyes. "Isn't that just an emotional response?" At first, it sounded critical, but he knew her question was sincere. What she was really wondering about, Adam knew, was her own response to what she had seen and felt.

"Many people, myself included, become emotional as a result of being touched spiritually. It's a reaction to that communication. Sometimes, that's how you can recognize that it's happening." She was looking at him intently. "How did you feel tonight?"

She looked down at her hands for a few seconds before responding. "Do you remember when we found those stowaways on the train and you and Droven spoke to them about God?"

"Yeah."

"Tonight, I felt the same way I did that night. Warm. Peaceful."

Adam let his breath out slowly, trying to choose his words carefully. "Truth is accompanied by a spiritual confirmation. Maybe your spirit learned something that's true."

She turned her face toward his and just stared for a moment, then smiled and looked back down at her hands. "I don't know about all of this." She nudged him with her shoulder. "Are you sure you're not just crazy?"

Adam laughed softly. "No. I've never been sure I wasn't crazy."

Melena laughed at that and laid her head on his shoulder. He turned his face toward her, taking in the smell of her silky dark hair and feeling its smoothness on his cheek. He smiled to himself. Melena always smelled good, and as someone with ridiculous olfactory sensitivity, he was grateful for that. She reached over and took his hand, interlocking their fingers. The chirping of crickets rang in Adam's ears as they sat in silence.

Melena leaned back so she could see his face. She locked her big, radiant blue eyes onto his, and her full lips curled into an adorable grin. "So, are you ever going to kiss me, Mr. Winter?" she murmured.

He held her gaze for a few seconds before smiling back at her. "Probably."

"*Probably?*" she repeated in almost a whisper.

"Come on." Adam stood up and pulled on her hand. "You've got a big day ahead of you tomorrow. You'd better get a good night's rest before talking to your dad. Who knows what kind of wrath you'll have to endure."

Reluctantly, Melena got to her feet, looked up at Adam and sighed. "Whatever you say."

Chapter 25

Adam watched as the middle-aged security technician picked at the salad in front of her on the desk with her fork. She had separated the croutons, cucumbers and radishes into piles. Her fork would then spear several pieces of lettuce and then one item from each of the piles before being lifted into her mouth. Adam didn't mean to be intrusive, he was really just testing his vision. The woman was in the office building next door—a distance of about two hundred feet, he guessed.

Adam and Peter had been waiting outside a confidential communications office for the past thirty minutes and had run out of things to talk about. Inside the office, Melena was having a private conversation with her father, Senator Cai Jaxon. The room was soundproof, even for Adam, so he had no idea what could be taking her so long. Peter began dictating a communication to the director of a base of operations in Jacksonville through his sphere—a small, intelligent orb. The sphere was his preferred method of communication because it physically traveled through the air to its intended recipient rather than through radio waves or a cellular network and was worthless to anyone who intercepted it. It would only communicate to its intended recipient once it identified him or her. Adam had to roll his eyes every time Peter called it his *homing pigeon* because that meant a lengthy explanation of where the nickname originated, and he had heard it a million times.

Adam focused back on the security technician in the adjacent building. She had finished her salad and was now arranging small candies on her desk according to their color.

Adam heard the door to the communications office beep and pop open. Melena emerged from the room slowly, her head down. Her face was white, and her eyes were red from crying. She walked straight to Peter.

"Can you arrange transportation for me to Kansas City right away?" she asked him in a weak voice without looking at Adam.

Peter's sphere retreated into the small box he stored it in, and he looked up at her. "Is everything okay?"

"It will be. I just need to get to Kansas City as soon as I possibly can."

Adam stood. "What happened? What did he say?"

She continued to avoid eye contact with Adam. "I can't say, but it's important that I leave."

He stepped in front of her and took her by the shoulders, his voice gentle. "Hey, what's going on? Did he threaten you?"

"No. I'm sorry. I wish I could explain more, but it will only make things worse. Please just trust me. I have to go. Now." The concern on her face was apparent. Whatever she had been threatened with, Adam thought, it was having its desired effect.

"All right," Adam nodded his head, slowly. "I'll take you to Kansas City."

"No!" Her intensity startled him. "I'm sorry." She took a deep breath and exhaled through her mouth. "No, Adam, you need to stay here. Please don't leave Independence. Stay with your family." She turned back to Peter. "Peter, can you help me?"

Peter got up. "Yeah, yeah, I'll help you. You don't have to stay here if you don't want to."

"Melena, what are you going back to?" Adam asked with obvious concern, "Are you gonna face charges? Are you sure it's safe?"

She finally made eye contact with him, but only for a moment. “Yes. I’ll be fine, but I can’t linger here anymore.” She turned to Peter. “I’m ready now, if you can take me.”

“Melena …” Adam began.

“Adam, please!” She shot back at him. Her eyes were wide, pleading. She stared up at him for a second and then looked away. “Peter?”

“Okay, let’s go.” Peter turned and headed for the hallway with Melena following close behind. She didn’t even look back to say goodbye.

Chapter 26

Adam opted to walk back to his apartment through the city. The sky had grown dark and thunder from an approaching storm rumbled in the distance. The weather seemed to mirror the frustration he was feeling. He hated how helpless he felt. It drove him crazy not to know what Senator Jaxon had threatened his daughter with. The more Adam thought about it, though, the more it made sense. Melena had grown up in the most comfortable of circumstances. She had wealth, privilege and was a Scion—heir to the Senatorial seat of the Great Plains Dominion. Could Adam really expect her to walk away from that life? But if that was the reason she had left—to avoid being cut off by her father—then why had he felt so strongly about getting her to Independence in the first place? She had only experienced a glimpse of what the city had to offer.

As much as he hated to admit it, what was really gnawing at him was that he had developed feelings for Melena. They had only known each other a short time, but he felt deeply connected to her, and he had never expressed it or really reciprocated her affection. Now, she was gone. The opportunity had passed. Once Melena was back in Rugby, safe in the Senator's mansion, there was little chance they would ever meet again. The news media would likely report that Melena had escaped or that a ransom had been paid to secure her release. She would be endeared to the public, and Adam would be hated by them.

A large raindrop splattered on the tip of Adam's nose, startling him. More rain began falling from the sky and soon it was pouring down in buckets.

By the time Adam reached his apartment, he was soaked through. He opened the door and found Droven and the man he had met at the clinic, Andrew Kent, seated in the living room.

Mr. Kent stood as Adam entered the room. “Adam, looks like you forgot your umbrella.” He held out his hand and delivered another firm shake.

“Yeah, I guess I forgot to check the forecast.” Adam smiled, weakly.

“Can I speak with you for a few minutes?” Mr. Kent asked.

“Sure,” Adam answered. “Just let me grab a towel.” He walked down the hall to the linen closet, pulled out a towel and patted himself down with it.

Droven stood up. “I’ll give you two some privacy.”

“Actually, Droven, why don’t you stay?” Mr. Kent asked. “This concerns you as well.”

“All right.” Droven sat back down as Adam returned and sank down next to him on the sofa.

Mr. Kent reached into the pocket of his slacks, pulled out a small black device, held it up for a moment and then returned it to his pocket. “I can’t imagine that there would be any eavesdropping devices in your apartment, but just for good measure, if there are, they are now destroyed.” He smiled and continued. “The stamp that was implanted into you, Adam, was originally intended for a high-ranking government intelligence agent. For efficiency purposes, the government has produced these stamps for an elite group of operatives to give them instantaneous access to classified data.” He paused and looked at Droven, then at Adam. “They provide complete access to the Central.”

Adam narrowed his eyes. “The stamp provides access to the Central? How?”

"I suppose that's something you're going to have to discover for us. Our intelligence has confirmed what the purpose of the stamp is, but unfortunately we don't have an owner's manual."

"How was The Response able to obtain the stamp?" Droven asked.

"They had a man on the inside—a double agent," Mr. Kent explained. "Unfortunately, the double agent has since been discovered and executed. The government only discovered the stamp was missing after Adam had already escaped from their lab. If they had known he had it before then, they would have terminated him immediately and taken it from him."

Adam considered that a moment. "Wouldn't they have included some safety measures in the stamp? Self-destruct? A tracking device?"

"Yes," Mr. Kent affirmed. "It had both originally, but The Response's man disabled them before it was delivered to you."

"So, what's our next move?" Droven asked.

"Well, we need the two of you to figure out how to access the Central using Adam's mind and the stamp. As you are aware, we are approaching Senatorial elections and have three candidates preparing to enter their respective races; the TexMex Dominion, the Mountain Dominion and the Great Plains Dominion. The information you could potentially provide could be invaluable to our efforts. We will need evidence of the fraudulent tactics used by the incumbents and the Federal Government so we can provide them to the public."

Droven glanced at Adam, then back at Mr. Kent. "We'll figure it out, sir."

Adam nodded. "We'll get to work on it."

Mr. Kent smiled and got to his feet. "You men have a larger role in restoring this great nation than you realize. God bless you for your service." He shook their hands and began walking to the door. He paused and turned back to them. "The information I shared with you is sensitive. Even my superiors are unaware of the full significance of the stamp you have. Let's keep it confidential."

"Yes, sir," Adam and Droven responded in unison.

Chapter 27

Melena studied the various patterns in the textured ceiling as she had done hundreds of times before as a young girl. Her bedroom in the Senator's mansion had been preserved just the way she left it. Shelves filled with futbol trophies—or *soccer* trophies, as Adam would call them. Sashes won in pageants lined the wall to her right. The enormous oil portrait of her as a ten-year-old girl—the one she hated—still hung on the wall to her left. The artist had made her look like a queen looking out over her kingdom. Her chin was high, and her nostrils flared. She didn't remember ever posing for the thing, so the artist must have taken some liberties.

The tall, over-sized bed she was lying on still had the beautifully embroidered quilt she had been given by the Scion of the British Isles Dominion spread across it. She remembered the boy. He was pudgy and smelled like boiled cabbage. They had been forced to dance together at a party in the capitol when she was eight. She was sure he had had nothing to do with the quilt's design or production, but it was a gift from *him*, nonetheless.

Melena had been back in Rugby for two days and had not yet seen her father. She had been ordered to stay in the Senator's mansion for security purposes, rather than returning to her own house. The Federal Police officials who had picked her up in Kansas City and brought her home told her it was for her safety, but now she felt like a prisoner in her former home. She had not been allowed to leave or to contact any personal acquaintances. The use of electronic devices was also forbidden.

There was a quick knock on her door before it cracked open and Agent Martinez, the head of security for the mansion, poked her tattooed face inside. "Ms. Jaxon, your father has asked that you see him in his office." Agent Martinez had large eyes tattooed around her actual eyes, giving the appearance of one set of huge, surprised eyes. Her bottom lip was tattooed dark red, and the ink extended nearly all the way to her chin, making her appear to have a giant bottom lip. She looked like an animated character of some kind. Melena often caught herself staring at the woman.

"Thank you," Melena answered.

Agent Martinez nodded once and disappeared, leaving the door open behind her.

Melena took a deep breath before exiting her old room and joining the two police agents who were waiting to escort her downstairs to her father's office. Why the escorts were necessary for her in the home she had grown up in was beyond her. She was certain she still remembered the way.

Upon arriving at the door to her father's office, one of the agents spoke into his transmitter. "Ma'am, she's here."

The tall door creaked as one of the agents pushed it open and then stepped aside. The office was fairly dark, except for a small desk lamp and a few shafts of evening light spilling in from between the blinds on the three-meter-tall window. Melena's father sat behind his huge and ornately carved solid cherry wood desk. Beside him, to his left, stood a dark, feminine figure.

"Hello, Ms. Jaxon," Hava cooed. She motioned to the agents at the door. "That'll be all."

Melena heard the door close behind her. Her father's elbows rested on his desk, his index fingers pressed together in front of his lips. His eyes were zeroed in on his daughter's.

After several moments of awkward silence, Melena's father spoke. "I'm pleased you've returned safely, Melena."

"Yeah, thanks," she murmured back. "After no shortage of close calls."

Senator Jaxon rose to his feet and walked past Hava and around to the front of his desk and sat on the edge of it. "You've done well, Scion," he began, his voice sounding light, but insincere. "Lucky for us, our prisoner wasn't killed before revealing the secrets we've been working for years to obtain. Congratulations on your foresight and clever infiltration of such a traitorous group."

Melena held his eyes, but didn't respond.

"As I mentioned during our last communication, we now have the information we previously lacked to enable us to penetrate the walls of the enemy's stronghold." He stood up and slowly paced in front of the desk. "We still have a few questions for you, however."

"I already told you that I don't know how to get into the city," Melena admitted, losing her patience. "I don't really have any useful information."

Hava stepped forward and smiled through her mess of tattoos. "Ms. Jaxon, you have a very unique opportunity to serve your government and yourself here. Everyone knows of your unfortunate plight—being held at the peril of your life by a violent criminal and then making a brave escape. It's inspiring. What's even more inspiring is your willingness to bravely step forward and help hunt down the traitors who taunted and tortured you, as well as the organization they belong to. You're a hero."

Melena narrowed her eyes. "I'm a little confused. Are you suggesting I turn *you* in to the authorities—the person who attempted to kill me multiple times?"

Hava let out a curt laugh. "Let's not play games, Melena. Your father is offering you a pardon for treason, which I think is more than generous. He's not even asking a lot in return. He's just asking for your cooperation."

"Play games?" Melena countered. "He threatened to kill an innocent family with four little children if I didn't return home immediately!"

"Innocent?" Hava raised her eyebrows. "Enemies of this government who willfully rebel against its laws? They're fortunate it didn't happen anyway, but the Senator is a man of his word."

Melena's voice rose in frustration with the conversation. "How about we just leave things as they are and move on with our lives?"

"Leave things as they are?" her father roared, causing Melena to flinch. "You don't have any idea as to the damage you've done here. Damage to yourself in my eyes! The only positive aspect of this whole debacle was inadvertent—tracking this Adam Winter into Independence." His eyes grew dark, hooded by scowling eyebrows as he spat the words out. "I'm trying to protect the Scion of this dominion, but make no mistake, your actions are unforgivable. You're fortunate I haven't ordered your incarceration, or worse."

"*My* actions are unforgiveable?" Melena shouted back. "So the way we govern here is to just kill people if they stand in the way of our interests? Hava gets to decide if someone lives or dies? No trial? Do I understand that correctly?" She let her words sink in before continuing. "When I took him from the lab, I was doing what I felt was right. I'm beginning to see that maybe I'm alone in actually caring about right and wrong around here."

Senator Jaxon's face softened, and Melena thought for a second that perhaps she had gotten through to him. Perhaps there was a small pang of guilt in those hard eyes of his. He looked away and let out a long sigh. "Melena, I'm sorely disappointed. I had hoped you were better prepared to lead. Because you are my daughter, I have been giving you the benefit of the doubt, but you have proved yourself naïve and short-sighted. A true leader does not lead with his or her heart. Reason, logic and a willingness to serve the greater good are required." He turned back to her, his eyes cold. "I had hoped it would not be so all of your life, but it turns out you are hopelessly stubborn, defiant and foolish … just like your mother."

A lump formed instantly in Melena's throat. She felt her eyes getting warm. Her father had not mentioned her mother since Melena was a small child, and his words stung her now. She felt tears welling up in her eyes. She stared for a few seconds at the man who had always been too important to pay any attention to his only daughter. She realized more than ever before that he didn't know her at all, and she didn't know him. Now, she didn't care to know him. All she wanted to do was to get away from him.

Without another word, Melena turned to the door and pulled it open. The two agents waiting in the hallway stepped in front of her.

"Get out of my way you pathetic slaves," Melena growled through clenched teeth.

The agents looked past her into the office momentarily and then stepped aside just as she stormed through the space in between them.

Chapter 28

Adam sighed and leaned back in his chair. Images from his three-dimensional monitor continued rolling across his desk. So far, he and Droven had been unsuccessful in their attempts to access the Central. Adam was beginning to wonder if the stamp in his head could actually do what Mr. Kent had told him it could do. He lifted his hand with his fingers extended and then closed them into a fist, signaling his display to dematerialize. The images dissolved, leaving only the bold, red digits of the clock in their place. Eight fifty-six, the display read.

There was a soft knock on the glass of his office door as it opened.

"Are you still here?" Jivvy took a step into the doorway and leaned her shoulder on the frame. Her wavy blond hair was pulled up into a twisted bun on the top of her head with a pen pushed through it to hold it in place. Several locks of it had escaped and fallen in front of her ears down to her chin, framing her delicate face. She wore a white button-up top, tucked in just below the ribs to a black calf-length skirt. Her tall, emerald green heels made her appear several inches taller than she actually was.

"Yeah, I'm still here," Adam yawned. "What are *you* still doing here?"

"Just trying to catch up on some stuff." She glanced at the empty desk across from Adam's. "Is Droven here too?"

"No. I made him go home an hour ago. I didn't plan on staying either, but …" he trailed off.

She leaned her head against the door frame. "Is your assignment not going well?"

"Oh, just a little slower than I'd hoped, but I'm sure we'll get things figured out eventually."

She took a few steps into the office and stopped in front of him, wringing her hands. "So, I never really said thank you for what you did for me." She paused. "You know, with that slimy Fed after the crash."

"Honestly, Jiv, I'm just sorry you were in that situation at all." His voice softened. "I should have gotten there sooner."

"You were right on time." A tiny smile appeared on her glossy lips. "My dashing hero—who was literally *dashing* to the rescue and then *dashed* that jerk's face into the truck."

"Actually, I think that jerk was lucky I got to him first." Adam smiled. "I don't envy anyone who finds himself in your crosshairs."

She let out a short laugh and then wrinkled her nose, making a tough face. "You got that right." Her face softened, and she looked away. "Anyway, thank you for being there."

"I'm just glad you're okay."

Jivvy went to Droven's desk and wheeled the empty chair around in front of Adam's and then plopped down into it and crossed her legs. "So, are you missing your little girlfriend?" she prodded.

Adam put his hands behind his head, interlocking his fingers and leaned back to the chair's full capacity. "My *little girlfriend*?" he repeated with raised eyebrows.

"I'm sorry." She pressed her fingers to her lips. "I meant to say … Have you heard from her since she left?"

Adam took a deep breath and exhaled slowly through his mouth. "No, Jivvy, I haven't heard from her. She wouldn't even have a way to contact me if she wanted to. I'm sure she had her reasons for leaving. You have to admit, it took a lot of courage for her to even come here in the first place." He rocked forward and rested his elbows on his knees. "I don't know. Maybe we've seen the last of Melena Jaxon."

"Well, I'm glad you've come to terms with it." She leaned forward until their faces were only separated by a few inches. Her playful green eyes stared into his. "I'll let you get back to your assignment now," she whispered. "Maybe what you've been searching for has been right in front of you all along."

Adam's heartbeat quickened; firstly, because he thought Jivvy could be giving him a useful clue about his assignment; secondly, she could be referencing herself as what he had been searching for; and thirdly, there was the close proximity of her lips, which he stole a quick glance at.

"Do you know something about my assignment that might help me?" he muttered, meeting her eyes again.

Jivvy smiled at him and then stood up. "No. Sorry. That was just something people say in movies and stuff. I really have no idea. Good luck, though." She walked to the doorway and then turned and gave him a flirtatious wave with her fingers before exiting the office.

Adam watched her leave and then turned back and stared at the empty desktop. After a few seconds, he decided to take one last look at the Federal Government's locked domain before heading home. He reached out his hand with his fingers and thumb all touching together and then spread them apart, reactivating the three-dimensional display. He brought up the government's domain, and the great seal of the S.O.U. appeared in spherical form, revolving like a globe. Adam rested both of his hands on the image he had been trying to penetrate for the past few hours as if to strangle it in frustration. He wondered what he could be missing that would allow him to access the domain. After ten seconds without any revelations on where to go, Adam began to notice how exhausted he felt after such a long day. He let his eyelids slide down over his eyes. A moment later, they flew back open. "Whoa!"

Chapter 29

“Let’s move on to the Great Plains Dominion.” Andrew Kent flipped to a clean page in his old-fashioned paper notepad.

“Adam, can we start with agriculture and food storage?” Peter Gildrich asked. “We’re mostly interested in production levels and exports.”

Adam shut his eyes tightly and took a deep breath to try and clear his thoughts. Once he felt like he was ready, he placed his hands on the virtual sphere once again and focused his mind on food production. A variety of letters and numbers swirled around on his mind’s stage and then arranged themselves into words and images.

“I’ll begin with the wheat crop from last season.” Adam’s eyes remained closed as he let his mind ask questions to which the Federal Government’s *Central* responded. “Between hard red winter, hard red spring, soft red winter and Durum, the G.P.D. produced three hundred and seventeen percent of the continental quota. Corn produced was one hundred and ninety-three percent. Barley production was three hundred and forty-one percent of the continental quota. Soybeans were two hundred and seventy-six percent. Dairy production in the G.P.D. was four hundred and twenty-nine percent of quota. Do you want the specific amounts of surplus?”

Adam could hear Mr. Kent’s lungs heave a heavy sigh. “Not right now, Adam. Thank you.” The pen in Mr. Kent’s hand scratched some notes onto the paper. “Unbelievable.” Adam heard Mr. Kent whisper to himself.

"Adam?" Peter called out. "Can you tell us where the surpluses are being stored and if there are exporting orders attached to them?"

"Yeah." Adam began digging deeper into the data that appeared in his mind as his thoughts requested it. "The majority of the wheat surplus is being stored in Rugby and Bismark. Twenty percent is slated to ship to Europe and eighty percent to China."

"Did you say eighty percent is going to China?" Mr. Kent asked, astonished.

"Yes, sir. China," Adam answered. "The corn surplus is in Des Moines and Springfield and eighty percent of it is allocated to ship to China. Barley is in Rugby and eighty percent of it is allocated to China. Soybean storage is in Omaha with eighty percent allocated to China. The dairy production is currently higher than last year and ninety percent of the surplus is scheduled to ship to Russia."

"Wow." Peter sounded disgusted. "The people were told that the majority of the crop was destroyed by floods when clearly there's plenty. They're selling an enormous surplus to China and Russia while the people who harvested it and the rest of the public go without."

Mr. Kent finished scrawling on his notepad. "We need photographic and printed evidence of the surpluses to show to the public, Peter. Can your team provide that for us?"

"Yes, sir," Peter answered. "Adam, can you get accurate locations for the surplus storage facilities and find out how to gain access?"

"Yeah. Give me a second."

Adam sifted through data until he located each of the facilities and their security specs. Additional data on imports caught his attention as well.

"It looks like Omaha is receiving a hundred and eighty-eight metric tons of cocaine and seventy-five metric tons of trigger from South America," Adam reported. "Rugby has a similar order."

"It's been obvious that the government has been distributing drugs to the public, but it's been difficult to find evidence." Peter let out a sigh. "It just seems all the more pathetic that the government would stoop to such lows in order to control the people."

Adam continued searching through the import records until he came across something unusual. "That's interesting. Rugby received scientific equipment and personnel from the Glacier Mountain lab yesterday. That's the lab where they interrogated me."

"Where in Rugby was it delivered?" Mr. Kent inquired.

There was a pause while Adam searched. "The Senator's mansion."

Chapter 30

Melena was lost in her thoughts as she stared into the mirror of her bedroom vanity. She smiled to herself as she recalled the time she had spent with Adam—the warmth she felt as he snuggled up to her that night in the woods under a blanket of pine needles and leaves. She pictured him sitting there with his cocky grin on the solo-rider he had stolen from Hava at the train station in West Glacier, somehow knowing that Melena wouldn't be able to resist climbing on the back and racing away with him. Her heart quickened as she remembered how close she had been to kissing him after falling off of a moving train and landing right in his arms before tumbling to the ground together.

Her memories of him were the only pleasant thing in her life at the moment. Still confined to the mansion and under the close supervision of Federal Police agents, she was literally her father's prisoner.

After a quick rap on Melena's bedroom door, Agent Martinez poked her bizarrely tattooed face around it. "Ms. Jaxon, you are to report to the basement level immediately."

"What for?" Melena wondered aloud.

"You will be briefed upon your arrival, Ms. Jaxon."

Melena exhaled loudly to communicate her annoyance, and then stood and followed Agent Martinez into the hall to the elevator. The door slid open, and the two women stepped inside.

"This assignment must be thrilling for you." Melena's tone lacked nothing in the way of sarcasm. "Years of training, high marks at the academy, and then you're assigned to babysit the Senator's adult daughter and, finally, all of your dreams come true."

Agent Martinez kept her eyes forward, staring at the elevator door without reacting.

"Anyway, enjoy it while it lasts. Someday, you'll gather your grandchildren around you and tell them ..." Melena's thoughts stalled as the elevator reached the basement level and the door slid open.

The two agents waiting outside the elevator reached in and pulled Melena out, bending her arms behind her back.

"Ouch! What are you doing?" She tried to shake them off, but her struggling only sent a wave of pain coursing through her injured shoulder.

The two agents led her through a heavy metal door into the large underground garage where her father's fleet of personal vehicles resided. A large space in the center of the garage had been cleared, and the two people standing near it turned as they heard the door open.

"Over here, Melena," Hava's low voice echoed off of the concrete walls.

Shock registered on Melena's face as she recognized the man standing next to Hava. "Dr. McArthur?" Melena's former professor said nothing and failed to meet her eyes. "What are you doing here?" Melena asked. He didn't respond. Suddenly, the blood drained from her face as Melena looked beyond the two of them and noticed the equipment set up behind them.

Hava let out a sharp cackle. "Is anyone else having déjà vu?"

Chapter 31

Adam gave the thumbs up signal to Heaven Gildrich. Heaven nodded and pulled the black goggles that hung around her neck up over her eyes. From the rooftop of an apartment building adjacent to the Great Plains Dominion Senator's mansion, she aimed her device. A small, green bead of light appeared on the surface of a surveillance camera mounted on top of the wall that surrounded the mansion. The goggles she wore identified additional cameras positioned throughout the rear of the estate. When the green light from her device hit each camera, it froze the image the camera had been broadcasting, effectively disabling it without alerting the person monitoring it.

Droven walked confidently across the street toward the mansion to a booth where two guards monitored a fifteen foot void in the wall. Without a word, Droven removed his right hand from his pants pocket and flung a tiny capsule through the open window of the booth. As soon as the capsule made contact with the floor inside, thick white smoke erupted from it, choking the guards and causing them to collapse almost instantly. A light breeze carried the smoke toward the void in the wall, revealing ten red lasers that crisscrossed the length of the rear entrance to the mansion. Droven pulled a small mask over his nose and mouth and reached inside the doorway of the booth. He pressed a button on the panel just inside. The lasers disappeared, and Droven walked safely through the opening. He held up his hand and signaled for Adam to join him.

In an instant, Adam was across the street and at Droven's side.

Heaven's voice broadcast through Adam's earpiece. "You've got two more guards back there, one on each corner of the building. I'm neutralizing the one to the north now."

Adam heard a soft grunt, and a body hit the ground as Heaven's tranquilizer found its mark.

"Nice shot," Adam whispered.

"The guard to the south is about to go down too," Heaven predicted.

The second guard only let out a heavy breath before toppling to the ground.

"You boys are clear as far as I can tell."

"Nice work," Droven whispered back. "Keep us covered."

"Roger that."

Adam and Droven made their way silently up the drive to the rear of the mansion and began moving through the gardens to the rear of the estate when Adam stopped, abruptly. He turned and took several steps back the way they had come and then walked slowly toward a ramp at the end of the drive that led to the basement level of the structure.

From the top of the ramp, Adam heard voices coming from below. They were muffled at first, but as he crept down the ramp, they became clearer.

"After your communication with Senator Jaxon, what did you do?" an eerily familiar voice asked.

"I told Adam and Peter I needed to leave immediately."

Adam recognized Melena's voice. He motioned for Droven to join him and crept down the ramp.

"Were you able to leave Independence right away?" Hava's deep, rich voice was unmistakable. In an instant, Adam knew what was taking place on the other side of the garage door at the bottom of the ramp.

"Get rid of this door," Adam whispered to Droven. "We need to get in there. Now."

Droven pulled his t-shirt up, revealing a belt around his waist that held various instruments. He selected a device, yanked it from the belt and pointed it at the garage door.

"Yes. Peter agreed to take me to Kansas City," Adam heard Melena answer.

"Tell me about how you got from Independence to Kansas City," Hava continued probing.

"Now!" Adam whispered.

Droven activated the device and the metal door screeched in protest as it began to crumple into its center. As soon as a space large enough for Adam to fit through opened up, he darted into the garage and ducked behind a shimmering silver sports car. He looked back toward the door. It lay in a crumpled heap on the ground, and Droven was nowhere in sight. Three Federal Police agents rushed to the doorway, weapons raised. When they saw no one inside the garage, they fanned out and headed up the ramp. Adam saw three quick flashes of blue light come from beneath the crumpled garage door and heard three bodies hit the concrete.

Adam scanned the garage. He didn't see any additional police agents, only Hava and a tall man with a white goatee who was standing around monitoring equipment and, Adam assumed, the chemical tank, though he couldn't see it from his angle. Adam recognized the man with Hava as Dr. McArthur from the Glacier Mountain lab.

"Hava?" Adam's voice echoed off of the concrete walls. "Is that a new tattoo under your left nostril or do you just need a tissue?"

Hava's head swiveled back and forth as she tried to locate the voice's origin.

"Hey," Adam called out. "How do you make a tissue dance?"

Hava couldn't see Adam, and it took a moment for her to recognize his voice before her cackle bounced off the walls in response. "I never really thought you were all that clever before, but I hadn't considered that you would be stupid enough to come here."

"Haven't you heard this one? It's an oldie, but a goodie. My cousin told it to me—she's six years old."

"I didn't expect you to turn yourself in." Hava's eyes searched back and forth across the garage. "But I guess it saves us a trip."

Adam emerged from behind the car and began walking toward Hava and Dr. McArthur. "Put a little *boogie* in it."

Hava took a step toward Adam and then stopped, searching the garage behind him with her eyes. Adam smiled as Hava quickly wiped at her nose with the back of her hand.

"Dr. McArthur, you're looking good—like a cowardly puppet—just how I remember you." Adam called out in a mock-friendly voice.

Dr. McArthur just stared in shock at the sight of Adam.

"What are the two of you up to?" Adam asked, closing in on them. "Another *scientific experiment*? I heard the last one went really well."

Hava narrowed her eyes and cocked her head to one side. "Is that what you heard?" She reached behind her back and produced a hand gun that she raised to Adam's face.

Adam froze about fifteen feet from the barrel of Hava's gun.

An arrogant grin played on Hava's dark, inked lips. "The public would have enjoyed your trial, Adam."

"Really?" Adam replied, calmly. "I think the public would find this whole thing a bit … *shocking*."

An instant later, Adam felt the hair on his head and neck stand on end as a bolt of electricity flew past him, hitting Hava square in the abdomen. She flung the gun backward as her body slammed against several crates of equipment, convulsed once and then lay limp on the concrete floor.

Adam looked back toward the crumpled garage door and then turned back and smiled at Dr. McArthur. "I swear, Doc, that was completely unrehearsed." He laughed and turned back to the metal heap. "We're like twins, man. *Shocking*? I love that you caught that. Ha! That's gonna make a great story."

Dr. McArthur lifted his hands above his head as his eyes moved from Hava to the hunk of crumpled metal across the garage.

"I would seriously consider holding very still," Adam advised Dr. McArthur as he moved past him toward the chemical tank.

Melena's eyes were closed, and her dark hair floated on the surface of the liquid around her face, as Adam looked down on her. He began working quickly to remove the cables and wires from the tank before lifting her out of the amber-colored liquid.

"Did you bring a towel or something?" Adam asked Dr. McArthur, holding Melena's dripping, unconscious body in his arms.

"Over there." Dr. McArthur pointed to chair with a folded white cotton robe sitting on it.

Adam spread the robe out on the chair with one hand and then sat Melena in it, placing her arms in the sleeves before wrapping it around her. His ears perked up as he heard boots moving across the floor in the adjacent room.

"Get in the tank, Doc," Adam ordered.

"What?" Dr. McArthur exclaimed, his eyes wild with fear.

"Lie down in that tank or you're gonna be lying next to Hava in the same condition!"

Dr. McArthur hurried to the tank and sat down in it as Adam picked Melena up again.

The sound of boots on the floor grew louder in Adam's ears. "Jivvy, we're ready for extraction," he called out.

Suddenly, Droven burst out from underneath his crumpled metal shell and headed up the ramp. In two seconds, Adam was by his side, carrying Melena over his shoulder.

"Why did you make the old guy get in the tank?" Droven asked as they sprinted down the drive.

"No reason. I was just trying to freak him out."

Droven guffawed, shaking his head. Suddenly, gun shots echoed off of the estate walls as the three of them reached the end of the drive. A white Vector screeched to a stop in the street in front of them.

"Let's go!" Heaven shouted out the passenger window.

Adam opened the rear door and tossed Melena onto the seat and then jumped in next to her. Droven ran to the opposite side of the vehicle and climbed inside. Adam's window shattered as a bullet whizzed past his face and exited through the window on Droven's side. Droven flinched and then covered his head with his arms. "Go, go, go!"

The Vector's tires screeched and spun until they found traction and launched the vehicle forward. Droven's head was like a pinball, slamming into the driver's seat head rest and then into the head rest above his own seat.

He rubbed his forehead with the palm of his hand. "Jivvy, where did you get a Vector with this kind of power?"

Jivvy laughed. "I kinda … made it. I brought my own power source."

The Vector skidded around a corner and headed down the ramp toward the four-lane highway. Jivvy slowed the vehicle down and carefully merged into a river of white, silver and black Vectors.

Chapter 32

Adam leaned over and brushed aside a strand of chestnut hair that had fallen across Melena's eyelids. He took her hand and held it in both of his. Although she had been sleeping for nearly twelve hours since being recovered from the basement of the Senator's mansion, he had enjoyed just being in the same room with her. She stirred a moment, then her eyes flew open, and she sat up suddenly. Her eyes were wild as they scanned back and forth before settling on Adam.

"Hey," Adam soothed, "you're okay."

Melena stared, open-mouthed, for a full three seconds before reaching up to touch his face.

"Adam?"

"Yeah, it's me."

She scanned the room, but nothing she saw was familiar. "What's happening?"

He smiled warmly at her. "Nothing. I've just been sitting around waiting to see those eyes."

Her expression was one of utter confusion. "Is this real? How did you get here? How did I get here? Where *is* here?"

Adam rubbed his chin with his fingers. "Well, let me see. First of all, you got in the old hot tub from the lab without me—which I was a little upset about—then Hava got all bothered because she didn't want you to leave, but I got you out and then Dr. McArthur got in, but there really wasn't any purpose in that …"

"What?" Melena exclaimed in pure bewilderment. Then, her eyes widened with recognition, and she gasped. "Adam, what did they do to me? What did I tell them?"

"It's okay." Adam caressed her hand to calm her down. "I don't think you told them much at all. I think we got to you just shortly after they started interrogating you."

"Adam, they're tracking you! The stamp has a tracking device. They tracked you into Independence. My father says he knows how to get into the city."

Adam didn't react. He just smiled. "Does he? Then why were you being interrogated? Why did he go through the trouble of shipping the equipment and Dr. McArthur to Rugby from the lab?"

Her eyebrows furrowed. "How? How did you know? Did you take me from the garage? How did you get into the mansion?"

Adam grinned broadly, ignoring her questions. "It's good to see you."

Slowly, Melena's face softened, and she smiled back. "It's good to see *you*."

"You never said goodbye."

"I didn't want to say goodbye."

"Well …" Adam shrugged. "Here we are."

"Here we are—where?"

"Still in Rugby. I figured they'd be expecting us to run back to Independence. Plus, we have a job to do here."

"We? We, who?"

"Droven, Heaven, Jivvy and me. And you if you want."

"They came with you? They came to help me?"

"Actually, we were ordered not to go anywhere near you or the Senator's mansion. We came to Rugby for a recon mission, but we decided to come after you anyway. Everyone agreed."

"Even Jivvy?"

"Of course."

Melena looked around the small bedroom. "Where are they?"

Adam glanced at the door. "This is our Rugby operation. They're right out there."

Melena swung her legs over the edge of the bed and stood up, adjusting the cotton robe she wore. "I can't believe they would do that for me. I need to thank them."

She headed for the door, but Adam caught her hand, stopping her.

"Hang on." He got up from the chair he had been sitting in and turned her around to face him. Placing his hands on her waist, he pulled her in close and found her sparkling sapphire eyes. Heart racing, he closed his eyes and gently pressed his lips to hers. Her lips were soft and warm, and the touch of them sent warmth throughout his entire body. He savored the moment before slowly pulling away and finding her eyes again. "Okay." He nodded toward the door. "You can go."

Melena stared at him for a moment and then wrapped her arms around his neck and smiled. "About time." She pulled his head down and kissed him again—this time with greater intensity.

The rapid beat of her heart sounded in Adam's ears in unison with his own. He could smell the unique scent of her skin through the chemical residue from the tank.

Finally pulling away, Melena took his hands in hers and looked up at him with a tender smile. "I can't believe you came for me." Her smile disappeared, and her eyebrows pulled together. "It was awful, Adam. I was a prisoner in my own father's house. I haven't been able to leave or speak to anyone. My father is …" She closed her eyes and shook her head. "Anyway, it doesn't matter. I'm just glad to be away from him."

Adam pulled her to him. "I'm sorry, Melena. I'm sorry for this whole thing. I mean, I'm not sorry we met or that I'm still alive, but I'm sorry for what's happened to your life."

Melena went up on her toes and kissed him again. “Please don’t be sorry. I’m not sorry. I don’t like where my life was going before all of this.” She paused, looking deep into his eyes. “But I like where it’s going now.”

Adam continued holding her. “Oh, yeah? And where’s it going now?”

“It’s going wherever you’re going.”

“Does that mean you’re ready to join my team?”

“Your team?”

“Yeah, my team. We’re called The Knights of Liberty.”

Melena was obviously suppressing a smile. “Wow. That’s what you’re called?”

Adam nodded, straight faced then shook his head slowly. “No. We don’t really have a team name. It’s just … my team. We do have a recon mission, though. Do you feel well enough to come along?”

She grinned and planted one more kiss on his lips. “Try and stop me.”

Chapter 33

Droven removed his dark glasses and repeated himself to the guard at the entrance of the grain storage facility. "I said, I'm here to tour the facility. My assistant arranged it with the director."

The guard, a heavy-set man with a bushy, blond mustache that looked like it consisted of more nose hair than lip hair, looked confused.

"Your assistant spoke with him? And who are you?"

Droven let out a short laugh and raised his eyebrows. "Are you serious?"

Heaven stood at Droven's side in ridiculously tall platform shoes and a pink jumpsuit with strands of glowing green light running up the legs and down the sleeves. Her hair made a tall spiral on the top of her head. She looked up from the small page her eyes had been glued to since their arrival and lowered her dark glasses to look at the guard incredulously.

The guard eyed Droven. "What's your name, sir?"

Droven sighed and looked annoyed. "I'm Birchi Neville, the Scion of the Dixie Dominion. We're going to build a bigger, better storage facility in the south for cotton and rice. I understand this facility is a disaster. I'm basically here to learn what not to do when designing ours."

The guard scanned the page on his clipboard for a moment and then looked up. "I don't have any sort of confirmation for your visit today. You say your assistant set up a tour with the director of the facility?"

Droven glared at the guard in disgust. “Not the director of the facility, you idiot!” he yelled. “—the Director of Agriculture!”

Heaven looked up again from her page, her jaw laboriously working the wad of gum in her mouth. “Birchi, are you almost done?”

“Am I almost done?” Droven turned and shouted at her. “Do you *think* I’m almost done? Baby, we just got here!” Heaven lowered her glasses and challenged him with her eyes. Droven immediately backed down. “I’m sorry, Baby, I didn’t mean that. I’m just tired of standing here while this man tries to figure out what on earth his job is!” He turned back to the guard and resumed the glare.

From his position across the parking lot from the storage facility on a brush covered hill, Adam chuckled and turned to Melena. “They’re so good.”

“What are they saying?” she asked.

Adam chuckled again. “They’re just a couple of characters. You should see Heaven. She’s a great actress. She looks about as high-maintenance as you can get. And Droven is really giving the guard the business.”

“I’m sorry, sir,” the guard answered back to Droven, “nothing was scheduled for today.”

“Oh, okay.” Droven turned to Heaven. “Nothing was scheduled for today, Baby. Let’s head back to Tallahassee.”

“Okay,” Heaven replied without looking up from her page.

Droven turned back to the guard. “Are you kidding me!” he shouted. “I don’t care what your little schedule says. You are wasting my valuable time!”

Just then, Jivvy walked up to the entrance from the parking lot dressed in an employee uniform. She did a double take at Droven and Heaven and froze. Her hand shot to her mouth, and she gasped. "Oh my gosh!" she gushed. "I was just listening to your record in my Vector."

Droven smiled and nodded. "Of course you were, Baby."

Jivvy reached into her pocket and unfolded her page. She held it out to the guard. "Will you take an image of us together?" She turned to Droven and Heaven. "Do you mind?"

"Naw." Droven motioned her over with his hand. "Hurry up, though."

Jivvy nestled herself in between Droven and Heaven and smiled her giddiest smile. Droven made a serious face, and Heaven assumed her best red-carpet pose. The guard hesitated, then pointed the page in their direction and took the image. Jivvy ran back to him and took her page from him, retrieving the image so she could view it.

"Thank you!" she called out in excitement. "This is the only way my friends would ever believe that I met you. You're amazing!"

"All right," Droven replied, nonchalantly, turning his attention back to the guard.

The guard smiled, awkwardly. "You're a Scion and you do music as well?"

Droven shook his head. "Didn't you hear me? I'm Bir-chi Ne-ville." He pronounced each syllable of his name as if he were speaking to someone who didn't understand English.

The guard fumbled with his clipboard. "Oh, yeah, Birchi Neville. My son listens to that kind of—I'm not really familiar, but …" he trailed off.

"What's *your* name?" Droven leaned over to look at the guard's name badge. "Preston?"

"Yes, sir, Preston Thorn."

Droven nodded. "Preston Thorn, I have good news. Even though you have wasted my time, I am going to let you be our tour guide today. I hope you know the specifics of this facility."

Preston perked up. "I've been here for thirteen years, sir. I know everything there is to know about this place."

"Well, that's good, Preston, cause I don't want this to take long. Now, let's get going."

The guard leaned his chin toward the transmitter on his lapel. "Farber?"

"Yeah?" a voice answered back through the device's speaker.

"I need you to take the main entrance. I have a VIP tour."

The speaker crackled. "I'll be right there."

Droven took Heaven's arm and led her toward the entrance. Jivvy was still admiring the image the guard had taken and fell in behind them. The guard stepped up to the security pad and placed his palm on it. The door slid open, and Droven, Heaven and Jivvy stepped inside, followed by Preston Thorn. A young, slim guard slipped past the group, replacing Preston Thorn outside. He turned to admire the VIPs as they disappeared into the building.

Chapter 34

Adam held the sphere, or "homing pigeon", out in front of him and concluded his message to Peter Gildrich. "There is a file of images of the storage facilities included in this transmission. Everything revealed to me by the Central is confirmed—images of the physical inventory as well as shipping orders. Our mission is complete. We'll make preparations for our return trip this afternoon."

Adam verbally instructed the sphere to return to Peter and provided the necessary passcodes. The sphere chirped and disappeared.

"Did you get those images sent off?" Jivvy asked, entering the office Adam was using at the Rugby operation.

"Yeah, I just sent them," he answered. "I guess we're done here."

"Too bad your face is so infamous these days. I have to admit, it was strange having you in the background the whole time. You know, you could have been Birchi Neville's manager or bodyguard or something."

Adam got up from his chair, looking offended. "What are you talking about? *I* would have been the rock star."

Jivvy laughed and nodded. "Oh, you think you're a rock star?"

"Are you implying that I'm not?"

A crooked smile played on Jivvy's lips, and she punched him on shoulder. "You really think you're something now that you have your little girlfriend back, don't you?" Her comment came across with some obvious bite to it.

Adam took on a more sober tone. "Seriously, Jiv, the last thing I want to do is to mess with the chemistry of our team. If you have a concern, let's air it out. Do you have a problem with the way this all went down?"

She sighed impatiently. "No, Adam, I don't have a concern or a problem. It was a great extraction and—"

"Guys, check this out!" Droven burst into the office with Heaven on his heels. He gestured with his hand to make his holographic monitor appear above it and then pointed with his other hand to a news story he had come across. "Melena's dad addressed the Senatorial Campaign Conference in Rugby yesterday."

Heaven pointed to the next paragraph down. "Tonight, there's a special speaker scheduled to address the conference on behalf of the challenger. Look who it is."

Jivvy read what was displayed on the monitor and smiled. "Maybe we can stay here just one more night. I think the Senatorial election in this dominion this go-round may be slightly more interesting than the previous nine were." She looked at Adam as he finished reading.

He nodded his head. "I think one more night sounds fantastic."

Just then, Melena found her way into the office. "One more night here in Rugby?" she asked.

"There's a campaign speech at the conference downtown tonight," Droven answered. "You won't want to miss it."

Chapter 35

"Ladies and gentlemen …" The crowd noise dissipated as the words sounded over the public address system. "I want to thank you all for being here tonight."

Melena gasped when she recognized the attractive, distinguished-looking woman standing in front of the podium at the far end of the square. She turned to Jivvy, raised her eyebrows and whispered. "Did you know she was speaking tonight?"

Jivvy nodded and whispered back. "Yeah."

The team watched through the open twelfth-floor window of an office building overlooking Rugby Square where thousands had gathered for the Senatorial campaign event.

The woman at the podium continued. "It is a great blessing that we are still able to assemble together and hear from those who aspire to lead us. Yesterday, we heard from Senator Jaxon. He is campaigning for his fifth term as the S.O.U. Senator over the Great Plains Dominion—the same seat possessed by his father before him. We have become a nation of aristocracy, but at least in theory, we are still allowed a vote and a voice. As citizens, the future of this dominion and this entire land is in your hands. In order to create the best possible future, it is necessary for all of us to understand our past."

"This could get ugly," Droven whispered to no one in particular.

"Nearly three hundred years ago, a handful of men recognized the unique opportunity they had to shape a new nation. As victims of tyranny themselves, they sought to form a system of government that would protect the rights that couldn't be granted by government or any mortal entity. They didn't seek control over those whom they would govern, they only sought to protect the liberties that they believed had been granted by their Creator."

Melena heard a general commotion in the crowd at the mention of Deity.

The woman at the podium paused to let the crowd simmer down before going on. "With the intent to limit the size, power and scope of the Federal Government, they established the Constitution of the United States of America and what would eventually become the greatest nation in the history of the world. Though the fledgling nation suffered wars and strife in order to keep its people free, the people came together and became prosperous and industrious. Men and women found opportunities to succeed by the sweat of their brows. They created farms, businesses and technologies. They competed with one another in order to offer one another the best products and services possible. They worked for what was then known as *The American Dream*—homeownership, property ownership—a little piece of this earth that they could call their own and do with what they pleased. The nation grew and expanded.

"Eventually, the evil of slave ownership was acknowledged, and after the shedding of much blood, slavery was abolished. People from every part of the world came to claim their freedom and their chance to make something of themselves, regardless of their race or the social class they came from in their former countries. They all became Americans."

"Get on with it!" someone shouted from the crowd. "We don't need a history lesson!" Others shouted in agreement.

The woman smiled, patiently. "I wish that were true. The history lesson you need to hear most is not one that they teach you in your government-controlled schools. It is the story of the downfall of the United States of America.

"Once a thriving economy, the citizens of this land began to abandon the principles that had made them great. Those who had less began to envy those who had more and began to demand that the government take from those who had and give to those who wanted. They expanded welfare policies that were intended to help the poorest of the poor and the disabled or disadvantaged, to benefit those who simply didn't want to work for their own support. The federal government grew larger and larger as the people demanded more from it. Out of necessity, those willing to work took home less and less of what they had earned in order to support government programs and employees. Massive debt began to accumulate as the government spent far more on social programs than it brought in through taxation and other revenues.

"Fossil fuels discovered near this very city were vast then and are abundant even to this day. After a short period of extremely successful extraction, these resources were hidden from the public and restricted, as the Federal Government insisted on maintaining its dependency on oil purchased from hostile nations in the Middle East, South America and Russia. Development of these domestic resources would have produced revenue sufficient to pay off the enormous federal deficit and create prosperity for everyone in the country who desired it, but it was intentionally suppressed under the guise of environmental protection.

"In tandem with the economic turmoil that plagued the country, moral decay crept into society. A man or a woman's honor and integrity became less and less valued. Politicians used the growing government machine to intimidate and harass individuals and organizations who opposed them. The Internal Revenue Service became the preferred vehicle for political punishment.

"Individual corruption began occurring at a dizzying rate as well. The traditional family, with a husband, a wife and their children, first suffered ridicule and then ceased to be the central unit in society. Marriage between a man and a woman was redefined to include any number of alternatives and then simply abandoned as an institution. Sexual intimacy lost its sacredness and became casual and perverted. Pornography and prostitution hastened the erosion of the moral character of an entire people.

"International terrorists began preying on the American public, knowing that with each attack, the people would be willing to sacrifice their freedom for security. In order to protect its citizens from being attacked, additional government agencies were formed. They began monitoring the private interactions of citizens and accessing private information that had previously been unlawful to obtain, in order to identify threats. As technology advanced, privacy for citizens diminished. Constant surveillance of the public by the government became commonplace. Almost as damaging as international terrorists, were domestic criminals who committed atrocities against people gathered in public places, such as children in schools, using guns and bombs. Politicians took full advantage of these tragedies in order to restrict the use of guns by citizens and to eventually disarm them completely, robbing them of their constitutional right to bear arms.

"Of all of these missteps, the most egregious and damaging was the expulsion of God from public discourse and the criminalization of religion. At the insistence of the very few, the mention of God in public schools was prohibited. Soon after, plaques or artwork featuring Judeo-Christian figures, words or symbols in public buildings were removed. Next, speaking openly of God and religion in the military became worthy of court martial. Prayer in the legislature ceased. Soon, the mere mention of God or expressions of faith became criminal acts. Once again, politicians took advantage of the fears of the people, blaming all war and conflict throughout history on religion. They propped up science which, ironically, had actually begun amassing evidence supporting the existence of a Grand Creator and the immortality of the human soul. They claimed that only the uneducated and unenlightened believed in such simplistic and archaic things."

The majority of the crowd was silent and listening intently to the woman's message, but near the center of the throng of nearly ten-thousand people, several men and women began heckling her.

"Trident!" one of them shouted. "Get off the stage!

"Shut her up!" another called out. "She's preaching!"

The woman at the podium ignored the hecklers and continued. "In a chaotic political whirlwind, a nation that was once prosperous and free surrendered its sovereignty to an international governing body in order to appease the interests of politicians and corporations. The divinely inspired Constitution was retired as a relic that had outlived its usefulness. The blood of patriots who gave their lives by the hundreds of thousands in order to establish and maintain the great United States of America was forgotten, and the nation died quietly and was quickly buried by the Social Order of Unions."

Melena noticed two lines of Federal Police pushing their way through the crowd toward the stage. A wave of panic came over her, and she grabbed Jivvy's arm, pointing out the advancing agents. "They're going after her!" she whispered. Jivvy just nodded and kept her eyes on the podium.

The speaker continued. "This is a tragic story, but it's *our* story. Fortunately for us, the time has come for us to reverse history. The people of this land have been slaves to politicians and their corporate partners long enough." The woman's voice began to rise. "Change is coming, my brothers and sisters. There is a hunger for freedom, and it is sweeping across this great land. Opportunity is now at your very door. You have allowed yourselves to become dependent on the government for your food, your healthcare, your employment. In exchange for these meager offerings, you have offered up your dignity and your liberty. Do not continue to sell your liberties for government hand-outs. There is another way. New leadership is emerging. Listen for the call of freedom."

The police agents aggressively pushed through the crowd, shoving people out of their path. They were nearing the stage.

The woman continued her speech, oblivious to the danger she had placed herself in. "I have seen corruption, greed and tyranny first-hand, my brothers and sisters. I know the hearts and minds of the rulers of this government. They are not serving you—you are serving them."

Suddenly, the wooden panel behind the podium cracked loudly. Two more pops followed, and Melena saw that three gaping holes had appeared in the panel, directly behind the woman. A scream escaped from Melena's throat, but was swallowed up by the gasps from the crowd. She grabbed onto Adam. To her surprise, the woman at the podium didn't budge. Melena wondered if the sniper had missed his target. From their high perch, Adam began scanning nearby buildings, trying to locate the shooter. The police agents near the stage slowed their advance to avoiding putting themselves in the line of fire.

"I count three gunmen on the roof of the next building over," Adam whispered. "All of them wearing Federal Police fatigues." He shook his head in disgust. "It's the security detail doing the shooting."

The woman at the podium smiled. "I regret that I could not address you in person, but it is obvious that I would have done so at the peril of my life."

Melena gave Adam a quizzical look.

"It's a projection," he explained. "She's probably in Independence right now. This is a live broadcast."

Melena turned back and studied the woman. She certainly looked real to Melena and, apparently, to the rest of the crowd. The police agents finally reached the stage. The first one to the podium attempted to grab the woman, but his hand just swiped through the projection. The other agents surrounded her, weapons raised.

The woman paused a moment, then went on. "My brothers and sisters, my name is Emaya Luna, but some of you may remember me by my previous name … Delyn Jaxon."

Melena's breath caught in her throat.

Emaya went on. "A little over twenty-three years ago, I was driven from this city—from my home—and exiled for possessing the beliefs I just expressed to you. The government and my former husband forced me to leave my precious infant daughter behind and flee for my life. I have been a ghost since that time, but I will be a ghost no longer. Prepare yourselves, my brothers and sisters, for a new dawn. The darkness is subsiding, and light will once again shine upon us. I do not aspire to lead you myself or to pursue political office, but I stand with those who endeavor to restore freedom. Watch and listen for them. Until I have occasion to address you again, may God bless you and may God bless America."

The projection dissolved, and the crowd erupted in a mixture of cheers and boos.

Chapter 36

Melena turned away from the window and leaned her back against the wall. She covered her mouth with her hand and sank to the floor, her eyes welling up with tears. She felt all of the energy she had drain out of her, and her heart sank. Her entire life she had believed that her mother had abandoned her only to find out now that Jivvy's mother—this bold, beautiful, strong woman at the podium—was also *her* mother.

Melena looked up at Jivvy, her vision blurred by tears. "Did you know?" she whispered.

Jivvy shook her head slowly. She looked as shocked and shaken as Melena felt.

Melena turned to Adam. "Did you know, Adam?"

He knelt down next to her and gripped her gently by the shoulders. "No, I didn't know, and I'm sure this isn't how she wanted you to find out. She doesn't even know we're here. We were supposed to return to Independence this afternoon." He rubbed her arms with his hands. "Are you gonna be okay?"

Melena shook her head as tears streamed down her cheeks. Her emotions were a combination of anger and sorrow. Anger that she had been lied to by her father and sorrow that she had lived twenty-three years without a mother—a mother who hadn't intentionally abandoned her as she'd been led to believe—a mother who had wanted her, but was torn from her.

Adam put his arms around her and let her cry onto his neck. She sobbed quietly for a while, then pulled away from Adam and looked up at Jivvy. With Adam's help, she got to her feet and went to her.

Jivvy averted her eyes and tried to look unaffected. Despite her efforts to disguise her emotions, tears were rolling down her cheeks.

Melena wiped at her swollen eyes. “So, I guess it turns out that you’re my little sister, huh?”

Jivvy stared back with an expression that Melena couldn’t read. She shot Adam a quick glance and then turned and walked out of the room, shutting the door behind her.

Chapter 37

Melena trembled as she stared at the sage-colored door in front of her. Despite her nerves, she noted and admired the stylish decorating of the front porch area of the Luna home. Beautifully hand-painted pots, containing blossoms and flowers of every variety lined the concrete slab. A whitewashed wooden porch swing creaked as the breeze gently pushed it back toward the light red brick façade of the house.

Melena heard footsteps approaching the door and suddenly regretted declining Adam's offer to accompany her. The butterflies in her stomach were so unrelenting that it felt like they could burst right through her flesh at any moment.

The door beeped once and popped open. Emaya Luna pulled the door in toward her and stood silently in the doorway.

Melena's lip quivered. "Hi," she croaked, her emotions beginning to surface.

Emaya pressed her lips together, her moist eyes glistening. "Hi, Melena." It was little more than a whisper.

The two women stood frozen for a few seconds before Emaya slowly stepped out onto the porch without breaking eye contact with Melena. Her expression was pained, but hopeful. She reached out to Melena. Melena didn't hesitate. She fell into her mother's arms. Sobs racked her body as she soaked in the loving warmth of the embrace. Emaya stroked Melena's hair and held her close.

"Oh, my baby," Emaya whispered, kissing the top of Melena's head.

Finally, Melena composed herself enough to lift her head off of her mother's shoulder to look at her. "Can we talk?" she asked, her voice breaking.

"Of course, sweetheart. Please, come inside."

"Thank you," Melena breathed.

She followed Emaya to the sitting room just inside the front door and sat down next to her on a firm, white sofa.

Emaya turned and angled herself toward Melena. "Peter told me about you and Jivvy attending my speech the other night in Rugby," Emaya explained. "I had planned on speaking with both of you girls when you were in Independence a few weeks ago. You left before I had the chance. I suppose it would have been a shock either way, but I would have preferred to tell you in person."

Melena nodded. "I understand. It's okay."

Emaya shook her head slowly and smiled, touching her daughter's face with the back of her fingers. "Oh, you're so beautiful, Melena. I've dreamed about this day for so many years. I feared, however, that when this day finally came you would be disappointed to meet me. I can only imagine what your father has told you about me."

Melena frowned. "He's told me very little, actually. You are a topic that has been painstakingly avoided for most of my life."

Emaya looked away. "Well, maybe that's a blessing."

Melena sniffled. "When I was very young and would ask about you, he just told me that you had chosen to leave, and that you would not be coming back."

Emaya's expression was one of excruciation. She bit her lip. A ray of sunlight peeked through an opening in the curtains and illuminated part of her face. Her large, deep blue eyes looked like two prisms in the light as they filled with tears. "Oh, Melena, I promise you that leaving was not my choice, and it absolutely broke my heart." Her tears spilled over and ran down her smooth cheeks. "There hasn't been a day that has gone by between then and now that I haven't thought of you."

"Why didn't you ever come and find me?" Melena asked, a lump forming in her throat.

Emaya responded with an agonized look in her eyes. "Oh, sweetheart, I wanted to. When you were small, I used to travel from Independence to Rugby just to get a glimpse of you at a public event. Once, I was discovered by one of your father's staff members, and I barely escaped with my life. Once I had remarried and had another child, it just became too dangerous a risk to take."

Melena contemplated her response. She didn't want to accept her mother's explanation for staying away, yet she knew it was reasonable and probably the only rational decision to have made. "I'm sorry for what happened to you. I mean, I'm sorry for what he did to you."

Emaya reached up and stroked the dark, satin hair on the back of Melena's head. "I'm sorry too. I'm sorry I wasn't there to see you take your first steps or to see you lose your first tooth. I missed it all. And now, look at you. You're a beautiful, charming, intelligent woman of character, and I'm just now getting the chance to discover you."

Melena's lips curled into a weak smile. "Better late than never, right?"

Emaya smiled back. "Right."

Melena sat back on the sofa and looked around the room and out into the hallway.

"How's Jivvy doing with all of this?" she asked.

Emaya sighed and leaned forward, cupping her hands over her mouth and nose. "Not great," she admitted. "I haven't spoken to her since you both returned to Independence. She has successfully avoided my attempts to contact her."

"I can understand." Melena tried to comfort her. "I don't think it helps the situation that she isn't exactly fond of me."

"Why would you say that?" Emaya probed.

"When we first met, Jivvy was very friendly. She lent me some clothes and was pretty conversational. The closer I've gotten to Adam, though, the more distant she's become."

Emaya nodded, knowingly. "I see. She's quite protective of her friends."

Melena nodded. "Yeah. We actually got into a little … um … altercation that day when I first met you."

Emaya's eyebrows shot up. "You did?"

"Yeah, the cut above her eye was actually from my elbow, not from the crash or the police," Melena confessed.

Emaya's jaw dropped.

"But, don't worry. The big bruise on my cheek was from her fist."

"What on earth were you girls fighting about?" Emaya asked, clearly dismayed.

Melena's eyes fell. "Adam," she admitted.

Emaya nodded, slowly. "Ah."

"Anyway …" Melena moved on. "We've been doing better since then, but she was obviously shaken by your … revelation. She seemed less than thrilled."

Emaya closed her eyes tightly. "I know." She sighed deeply. "I know. But, she'll be all right. She feels betrayed by me, but I only kept it from her for her own safety. I'm not exactly a beloved celebrity out there."

"I'm not sure about that." Melena tried to lighten the mood. "It sounded like the majority of that crowd in Rugby disagrees with that assumption."

Emaya smiled, warmly. "I think it had a lot more to do with the message than the messenger."

Melena shook her head. "I thought it was a very courageous speech, and I'm so glad you weren't there in person. I almost had a heart attack when those shots were fired."

Emaya grunted. “Fortunately, that was anticipated. We are making remarkable progress, but this government is enormously powerful. We’re so blessed to have Independence.”

“Did you come directly here after being driven out of Rugby?” Melena asked.

“Not immediately,” Emaya explained. “I didn’t know much about Independence at the time. I was in hiding near Omaha, and I met a man named Hyrum Winter. He was Adam’s great uncle. He was involved with an underground organization seeking out people of faith. He arranged for me to be taken to Independence.”

“Was that when you changed your name?” Melena inquired.

“Well, I changed it to Emaya Dobbs back in Omaha. Dobbs was my mother’s maiden name. No one in Independence has ever known me by another name besides Emaya.”

“So, you met Jivvy’s father here in Independence?”

“Yes.” Emaya beamed. “He was the Sunday School teacher for single adults at church. I started attending his class just a week after I arrived. He asked me out the first time we met. I wasn’t interested in him, though, so I was relieved to have a good excuse—I thought I was still married. I soon discovered that your father had dissolved our marriage shortly after banishing me, and when that became public knowledge, he asked me out again.”

Melena smiled, enjoying her mother’s story. “So, did you go out with him then?”

“No, I kept making excuses.”

“You weren’t attracted to him?”

Emaya shook her head. “Oh, no, it wasn’t that at all. He was one of the best looking men I had ever met.”

“What was it then? Why did you resist?”

Emaya took a thoughtful moment before proceeding. "Well, he was handsome, charismatic and confident …"

"He sounds awful," Melena teased.

Emaya laughed, hardily. "Doesn't he?"

"So, what turned you off?"

Emaya's face fell. "I think, initially, he reminded me too much of your father. What eventually won me over, however, was his persistence. He wouldn't accept defeat, but he was respectful to me at the same time."

Melena nodded, enwrapped in the tale.

"Attending his class each week and hearing him express his love for God and his devotion to the gospel helped me to see a side of him that was utterly dissimilar to your father. He was tender and loved easily. I fell in love with his heart before I fell in love with his face."

Melena looked into her mother's bright eyes and smiled. "Thank you for sharing that with me. I can't tell you how it feels to finally meet you and know you."

Emaya reached out and touched Melena's cheek. "I've prayed for this day for so long. Thank you, Melena, for coming to see me."

Melena laid her head on her mother's shoulder, and the two of them sat in silence, just enjoying being in each other's presence.

Chapter 38

Adam smiled to himself, identifying the footsteps he heard in the hallway headed toward his apartment as Jivvy's tall brown leather boots. He picked up her scent as she stood outside the door. It was several seconds before Adam heard the bell finally ring.

"Hey, Jiv," Adam greeted, pulling the door open for her to enter. "Do you want to come in?"

Jivvy looked flustered and entered the apartment without saying a word.

"You okay?" Adam asked.

She looked thoughtful for a few seconds before replying. "Do you ever struggle to forgive?"

"Do I struggle to forgive?" Adam repeated. "I guess some times are easier than others. Yeah, I suppose there have been times when I've struggled."

She looked up at him, anger flashing in her eyes. "Have you forgiven the people who killed your family?"

Adam was caught off guard. That wasn't a question he had anticipated being asked. He hesitated before answering. "Yes, I have."

"How?" Jivvy almost shouted. "How can you do that? They tried to kill you too! They were evil people, Adam!"

Before Adam could answer, Jivvy stormed into the living room and threw herself onto the sofa.

Adam turned to her. "Do you really want me to answer that? What are we really talking about?"

Jivvy just stared at the floor. Adam sat down next to her on the sofa and waited patiently for her to say what was on her mind.

Finally, she looked over at him, the anger in her eyes turning to sadness. “Senator Jaxon banished my mom from her home and her baby and then tried to have her killed.” She looked bewildered and disgusted at the same time. “Who does that? Who would do that to his own wife?”

Adam nodded his head, his lips pursed together tightly.

“And then there’s my mom.” The anger returned to her expression. “She keeps this a secret from me until I’m a grown woman?” She grimaced. “Why? Why wouldn’t she have told me about her former life before now? Did she think I couldn’t handle it?”

Adam lifted his eyebrows and leaned toward her. “Have you asked *her* that question?”

Jivvy glared back at him, icily. Adam shrugged and looked innocently back at her.

Jivvy’s face dropped into her hands, and she rubbed her eyes. “I don’t need to ask her.” She stared down at the floor again. “I know why she didn’t tell me. She was trying to protect me—protect me from people on the outside and protect me from myself.”

Adam reached over and put his hand on her back, rubbing it gently.

She looked up at him in frustration. “So, I’m just supposed to forgive everyone now? I’m not supposed to do anything about it?”

“What would you do about it?” Adam chuckled.

“I don’t know. Beat Cai Jaxon to a bloody pulp and not speak to my mom for a while.”

Adam tried, unsuccessfully, not to laugh so as not to further aggravate her, but she noticed his shoulders bouncing.

“Stop it!” She pounded her fist on his knee, a hint of a smile forming on her lips.

“I’m sorry.” He grabbed her hand before she could strike again. “I don’t know what you want me to say.”

Jivvy's eyebrows were lowered, but it was mock anger now. "Just tell me it's okay for me to be mad at them."

"I understand, Jiv. It stinks. It's infuriating to think of your mom being mistreated by anyone. And I would hate being kept in the dark about something that important."

Jivvy sighed and looked around the room. "Where's Droven?"

"I'm not sure. Peter called him in a while ago. I don't know what for."

Her face softened as she stared into Adam's eyes. "Do you have any secrets, Adam? Are you keeping anything from me?"

Adam snorted. "Like what?"

"Like, are you from another planet or something?"

Adam's expression turned serious. "I guess it's time that you knew." He looked up at the ceiling, blowing his breath out. "You see, I don't actually exist, Jivvy. Your brain invented the ideal man as an imaginary friend—handsome, ridiculously intelligent and attentive to your every need."

She giggled and slapped him on the arm.

"I would have told you sooner," he continued, "but I didn't want you to feel stupid. I mean, like you said, you're a grown woman now. It's probably time to let go of me."

Her green eyes danced, and she smiled at him. "No, I don't think I'm ready to let you go."

Adam patted her on the back. "It's gonna be okay, Jiv. Plus, you got a sister out of the deal. That's got to be worth something, right?"

Jivvy leaned in closer to his face, her emerald eyes locked onto his. "I don't want to talk about her right now."

She quickly closed the gap between their faces, her lips meeting his, forcefully. Adam resisted, but she held onto his arm and pulled him toward her. Adam took her hand off of his arm and gently pushed her away, breaking the lip lock.

"I'm sorry, Jivvy," he whispered, a pained look on his face. "I can't."

She stared back at him, expressionless for a moment, before taking a deep breath. "I gotta go," she breathed out, rising quickly off the sofa.

She made a beeline for the door. Adam beat her to it and held her in front of him by the shoulders. "Hey, what's going on?"

She tried to push past him. "Just forget it."

"Can we just talk about it for a second?" Adam pleaded.

"No. I want to go. Let go of me, please."

Adam released her, and she pulled the door open and hurried into the hallway, passing Droven as she went.

"What's going on, Jivvy?" Droven asked, turning around to watch her go.

"Hey, Droven," she called back without turning around.

Droven looked curiously at Adam standing in the doorway. "What was that?"

Adam shook his head. "I honestly don't know."

Chapter 39

"Sit down, gentlemen." Andrew Kent closed the door to his office as Peter Gildrich, Droven and Adam took the three chairs positioned across the desk in the center of the room.

Mr. Kent's office was sparsely decorated with very few personal effects. His desk was empty, with the exception of his old-fashioned pad of paper and an ink pen. A lone print of a watercolor sailboat on a calm sea adorned the wall behind the desk.

Adam settled into the stiff upholstered chair and watched Mr. Kent as he returned to his desk and sat down in his modest leather chair. His wrinkled eyelids hooded his eyes as he scanned the note pad on his desk before looking up.

"Gentlemen," he began abruptly, causing Droven to flinch, "first of all, I would like to congratulate you on your successful errand to obtain incriminating evidence against the S.O.U. We now have documentation proving that the government is paying off China and Russia to prevent them from invading their borders. We've also learned that they are purchasing narcotics from various sources and distributing them to the public through private dealers. We weren't even looking for that, but we happened upon it.

"We have effectively leaked this information into the public information networks, thanks to the access codes provided by you, Adam. The government has been unable to locate the injection sites into their network, hence, they have not been able to shut down the leaking of information."

Adam bobbed his head, acknowledging Mr. Kent's expression of gratitude.

Mr. Kent looked over the three men sitting across from him and frowned. "The reason I asked you men here today pertains to a separate matter, however. We just briefed the Sherriff's office regarding a potential breech in security here in Independence. It appears that last evening one of our gates was opened without a protective projection, and without authorization, and remained open for approximately three minutes before being discovered. Independence was exposed for three minutes."

"Was the gate compromised?" Peter asked.

"No," Mr. Kent answered. "According to our surveillance, nothing passed through while the gate was open."

Peter narrowed his eyes. "Who operated the gate?"

Mr. Kent leaned back in his chair and placed his interlocked fingers behind his head. "We don't know. The authorization code was generated by the system just moments before it was used. No owner was assigned to it. Equally as disturbing, our atmospheric grid has been reset four times in the past thirty-six hours."

Peter leaned forward in his chair. "What? How long was it down?"

"Only seconds each time," Mr. Kent responded. "But I think it is clear that these glitches are related."

"Were the systems accessed from outside the city or inside?" Droven wondered.

"Thus far, we have been unable to determine that."

"What would you like us to do, sir?" Adam asked.

Mr. Kent put his elbows on the desk and leaned over them. "I need you to scan the Central and search for any data relating to the security of Independence; Federal Police initiatives, intelligence briefings or instructions, anything that might clue us in on S.O.U. involvement with the breech."

Mr. Kent tore a sheet of paper from his pad and slid it across the desk to Adam. "Run all of these keywords through the system, and let me know if anything comes up."

Adam retrieved the paper from off the desk. "Yes, sir."

"Droven, I want you and the rest of your team to assist the Sherriff's office in their internal investigation. Spend some extra time in the security center. Keep an eye out for anything unusual. Another team will be watching the external personnel and interviewing officers."

Droven nodded. "Yes, sir."

Mr. Kent rubbed his eyes and leaned even further across the desk. "I don't need to tell you gentlemen how dangerous this situation could potentially become. Between Adam's escape, Melena Jaxon's rescue and Emaya Luna's speech, the government is more than a little motivated to attempt an invasion of the city. The Federal Police are just itching for an opportunity to silence us and put the city down. Obviously, we can't let that happen. Am I correct?"

"Yes, sir," all three men barked in unison.

"Thank you, gentlemen. May God bless us to protect these good people."

Chapter 40

Melena knocked twice on the tall glass door before opening it and poking her head inside. “Hello?”

Adam looked up from the images hovering above his desktop. His face lit up when he recognized her, which made her heart leap.

“Hey! Come on in.”

Melena pushed the door open and wandered into the office. “Peter told me where your office was and said it was okay if I said hello.”

“Of course.” Adam stood to greet her. “Come on over. I’ll grab Droven’s chair for you.”

“Oh, that’s okay.” She walked to him and pushed down on his shoulders until he sat back down in his chair. “I’ll just take this seat.” She parked herself on his lap and put an arm around his neck. His dark chocolate eyes were warm. His lips curled into a smile, and he put his arm around her waist and pulled her in close.

“So, what are we doing?” Melena asked, turning her attention to the images over the desk.

Adam chuckled. “Well, Princess Jaxon, we’re searching for—”

“Oh, I’m sorry,” Melena interrupted, “but we’re not calling me that anymore.”

Adam frowned. “Who’s not calling you that?”

“Um, *you* are not calling me that anymore. I think that leaving my obligations and running away to Independence twice probably results in the forfeiture of any titles for me.”

“Oh.” Adam lowered his brow to make a serious face. “You must have thought I called you *Scion* Jaxon when I actually said *Princess,* so … I don't see any relevance to your objection."

A broad smile grew across Melena's lips. "Well, aren't you sweet?"

Adam nodded slowly. "Yes."

Melena put her hand on his cheek and kissed him gently. She pulled away for a moment to look at him. His lips lingered, so she returned hers to them.

After a moment, Adam opened his eyes and pulled back. "Hey, Droven," he called out without looking away from Melena.

Melena turned her head to see Droven standing in the doorway.

He held up his hand in a quick wave. "Don't mind me." He fought to suppress a smile. "I just forgot my bag."

Melena looked back at Adam. "Did you hear him or smell him?" she whispered.

Adam nodded, almost imperceptibly.

"Both?" she mouthed.

Another slight nod.

Melena covered her smile with her hand.

Droven hurried to his desk and reached underneath it, retrieving his bag and then turned back toward the door. "You two just … continue, okay?" He waved and walked out the door.

"You heard him," Adam murmured, leaning in and resuming the kiss.

Melena laughed, breathily, and kissed him back.

Finally, Melena pulled back, clapping her hand on his chest. "Okay," she breathed in deeply. "I doubt your superiors would approve of this while you're supposed to be working."

"Oh, no, it's encouraged." Adam put both of his arms around her waist and kissed her cheek.

"Maybe I do need my own chair." She peeled his arms off of her and went to Droven's desk. She wheeled his chair next to Adam's and sat in it.

Adam chuckled, quietly.

Melena cleared her throat and turned to face the desk. "So, you said you were searching. What are you searching for?"

Adam gestured with his hand to expand the images over his desktop.

"I'm looking for S.O.U. intrusions into Independence."

"Oh, yeah? How's it going so far?"

Adam narrowed his eyes, studying the data in front of him. "Well, I have one lead so far. Female, early twenties, arrived recently, strong ties to local S.O.U. leadership. I have a location on her now. I should just bring her in, but I'm trying to anticipate her next move."

"Hmm." Melena leaned forward, pretending to study the data as well. "She seems pretty smart."

"Yeah?"

"I mean, she's gained the trust of some pretty influential revolutionaries, she's deep under cover …"

Adam blew his breath through his mouth and shook his head. "Yeah, I have to agree. Plus, she's like … an eleven. That's dangerous."

Melena turned her face toward his and found his eyes. "That *is* dangerous. What are you going to do?"

Adam took Melena's face in his hands and leaned in close. "I'm not gonna take my eyes off of her. I'm gonna try and get close to her, see what she knows."

"That's good thinking," Melena whispered. "Does she know you're on to her?"

"She has no idea."

Melena's mouth formed into a smile.

"Tomorrow's Sunday," Adam mused. "I wonder if she'll be at church."

"Is she invited?"

"Oh, yeah." He nodded. "She has a standing invitation."

"Well, I wouldn't be surprised if you saw her there."

"Really?"

Melena's eyes fluttered as her memory was triggered. She looked down, smiling to herself this time. "Sorry, I know we're doing a little thing with the … anyway, did you know my mom met her husband at church? He was her, uh, church professor or spiritual-advisor-guy."

"He was?" Adam asked, tilting his head to the side. "Was he also her Sunday School teacher?"

"Yes, that's what he was." Melena frowned. "You already knew that?"

Adam winced. "Actually, I did know that, but it's still a great story."

"Are you going to be *my* Sunday School teacher, Adam?" Melena asked, batting her eyelashes.

"Even better. I will be sitting next to you as a fellow member of Heaven Gildrich's class."

"Heaven's the teacher?" Melena asked, amused. "That sounds fun."

Adam nodded. "So, things are going well with you and your mom?" he asked.

Melena's face lit up. "Yes! She is beyond great. I'm loving getting to know her."

"I'm really happy for you."

"Oh!" Melena gasped. "I almost forgot. I'm supposed to invite you over for dinner at the Luna's tomorrow afternoon."

"Okay …" Adam answered slowly. "Do you know if Jivvy's gonna be there?"

"Yes. My mom said she would be."

Adam smiled. "You like saying '*my mom*' don't you?"

She beamed. "I kind of do like saying that, yes."

"So, are Jivvy and your mom speaking now?"

"They've only talked a little bit, but I think Jivvy agreed to be at dinner as a favor to her dad."

Adam nodded, thoughtfully. "Okay. I guess I'll plan on being there."

Melena studied his face. He seemed uncomfortable. "Is that a problem for you?"

Adam shrugged and shook his head. "No. It sounds wonderful."

Chapter 41

"So, you believe that God actually influenced the authors of the U.S. Constitution?" Melena asked, looking up at Adam and squinting in the afternoon sunlight.

"I do," Adam confirmed. "I wouldn't necessarily consider it a revelation from God, but I believe he inspired the minds of the men who authored it to create a document that would protect the rights He, Himself granted to men and women."

"Is there a copy of the original in Independence?"

Adam grinned. "Actually, there are many copies here. The most impressive, though, is at City Hall. It's an aged replica that looks almost identical to the original."

Melena shielded her eyes from the sun with her hand so she could look up at him. "I heard a legend when I was at University that a group of patriots stole the original Constitution the night before the ceremony when the S.O.U. was to burn it, and that it was actually a replica that was burned in its place."

Adam raised his eyebrows and nodded to acknowledge his interest in Melena's story. At the same time, he smiled inwardly, not yet willing to reveal his insights into this "*legend*". "Huh," was the only response he elected to give her.

Melena wrinkled her nose and studied his face for a moment. "Well, do you think it's possible that there could be some truth to it?" she asked, pulling the lock of hair the breeze had blown into her face away.

"Yeah. I've heard the story as well. I think it's a possibility."

Adam looked down at his and Melena's intertwined fingers and smiled. It was a beautiful, muggy Sunday afternoon, and even though the heat was a little extreme to be walking back from church in, he was glad to be holding hands and spending time with Melena. She had been pleasant and affectionate and was anxious to learn about the things that were important to him. He admired her resiliency, considering what she had been through recently.

A pit began to form in Adam's stomach as the Luna home came into view. He hadn't seen Jivvy since her awkward visit to his apartment and wasn't sure what her reaction would be at seeing him and Melena together.

"My mom said she was making roast beef and mashed potatoes for dinner," Melena commented. "Do you think I'll like that?"

Adam laughed. "Oh, are you eating meat besides rabbit these days?"

She squeezed his hand. "I don't want to be rude! I've never eaten roast beef before. Do you like it?"

Adam inhaled through his nose and closed his eyes. "I can smell it from here, and it is exquisite."

Melena gasped and grabbed Adam's arm. "I didn't tell you, but I had a cheeseburger at lunch with Heaven yesterday." Her hand flew up to cover her mouth as if she were ashamed of her confession.

"Are you serious?" Adam muttered in a low voice, looking over his shoulder. "Who else knows about this?"

"Ha!" Melena laughed, yanking on his arm to pull him into a hip-check.

"And …" Adam encouraged, "what was the verdict?"

She bit her lip and looked up at him with squinty eyes. "Um, it was really, really good."

"If you liked that, you are about to become a true carnivore."

They reached the Luna's front porch, and Adam gave a quick rap on the door.

"Come on in, you two," a friendly male voice called out as the door swung open.

"Hi, Joseph." Melena smiled and hugged him.

"Hi, Melena. It's great to see you," Joseph Luna replied, returning her embrace.

The slender man with graying hair looked at Adam and then back into the house. "No one told me Adam was coming." A grin played on his lips. "How many roasts did you make, honey?" he called over his shoulder.

"Oh, you eat like a bird, Joseph," Adam countered. "I'll save you a few scraps."

Joseph offered Adam his hand. Adam shook it and slapped him on the shoulder.

Emaya emerged from the kitchen with a broad smile. "Hey!"

Melena hugged her. "Hello!"

"Adam, how are you?" Emaya asked, reaching out to him.

"I'm great, thanks. How are you?" He smiled and hugged her.

Adam scanned the house for Jivvy. She was nowhere in sight, but he detected her scent.

"Take a seat at the table, you two," Emaya offered. "I think we're just about ready."

Adam followed Melena to the dining room table and pulled a chair out for her. Once she was seated, he pushed her chair up to the table and stood behind the seat next to her.

"Is Jivvy joining us?" Melena asked in the direction of the kitchen where both Emaya and Joseph had retreated.

"Yeah," Joseph replied, poking his head out of the kitchen. "She's upstairs. She'll be down in a minute."

The table was set with formal china and silver and a center piece of fresh cut flowers that looked like some Adam had noticed in the yard earlier.

"So, Melena," Emaya called out from the kitchen, "what did you think of church today?"

Melena leaned back in her chair and raised her voice so that it would carry to the kitchen. "I thought it was really nice. Lots of friendly people."

"Oh, good," Emaya called back and then emerged from the kitchen carrying a large bowl filled with fluffy, white whipped potatoes. She set them down on the table and sat down across from Adam and Melena.

"Okay," Joseph breathed as he exited the kitchen carrying a silver platter full of steaming roast beef, "here we go."

He set the platter down in the center of the table and walked to the base of the stairs.

"Jivvy?" he called up the stairs. "We're ready when you are."

"I'm coming," Adam heard Jivvy reply in a pleasant tone.

Joseph returned to the table, a wide smile on his face. "It's nice to have a few more of these chairs occupied for Sunday dinner. I'm sure Jivvy's tired of being ganged up on by her mother and me every time she comes over."

"I am," Jivvy confirmed, descending the stair case looking like she had just walked off the set of an image shoot. Her corn silk hair was up in a stylish do on the top of her head. Her blood-red lipstick exactly matched the elegant, floor-length dress she wore. She reached the bottom of the stairs and paused to gaze at her audience in the dining room. She smiled and walked briskly to the table.

"Hi, Jivvy," Melena greeted, cheerfully.

"Hello," Jivvy replied, smiling and making brief eye contact with Melena and then Adam before making a downward gesture with her hand. "Sit, sit," she commanded, breezing past both of them on her way to the head of the long rectangular table. "No one needs to stand up for me."

"You look breathtaking," Melena complimented. "I didn't see you at church. Were you wearing that dress?"

"Thank you." Jivvy looked down, smoothing out the fabric on her abdomen. "I was, but I attended a different congregation today."

"Oh. Well, it's gorgeous. I doubt I could have missed you if you had been to the meeting we went to," Melena gushed.

"Thanks. You look nice, too."

Adam glanced at Emaya as he finally took his seat. She was staring at Melena, her eyes full of pride.

Joseph cleared his throat. "Adam, would you mind asking a blessing on the food before we get started?"

"Be happy to," Adam replied, bowing his head. "Father in Heaven," he began, "we're so grateful for this beautiful Sabbath day and for the many blessings we enjoy. We're grateful to be together as family and friends to share this meal. We're thankful for the wonderful food that we're about to partake of and ask that it be blessed to nourish our bodies. In Jesus Christ's name, amen."

"Amen," the others echoed.

"Adam's been here for dinner before, Melena," Emaya noted, "so he knows that there is no real system here. We kind of all just pass everything around until everyone gets what they want, okay?"

"That sounds great," Melena replied. "Everything looks delicious."

"I can't take much credit," Emaya admitted, glancing at her husband. "I married a pretty fantastic chef."

"Chef?" Joseph repeated. "I would say *artist* would be more appropriate, but I guess *chef* works too."

"Wow," Jivvy remarked, eyeing her father incredulously. "I think that's a bit of a stretch."

Joseph feigned deep offense, while Emaya's shoulders bounced lightly with quiet laughter.

Jivvy passed the large bowl filled with the white stuff in it to Melena, who held it with some degree of uncertainty. Adam took the serving spoon from inside the bowl and scooped up a large spoonful and plopped it onto Melena's plate. "Let me show you." He took the spoon and hollowed out a large crater in the center of the white blob. "That's for gravy."

Melena gave him a tight-lipped smile and nodded.

"This is probably a little strange for you, Melena," Jivvy observed. "The food's a little … *downhome* and there aren't any servants to bring it to you."

An awkward silence hung in the air for a moment before Melena broke it.

"Actually …" She looked around the table. "I would much prefer this. It's much more intimate than what I'm used to."

"Did you know, Melena," Joseph began, changing the subject, "that your mother grew these potatoes right outside here in her garden?"

Adam glanced at Jivvy. She cringed, ever so slightly, at the words "*your mother*". Something between resentment and annoyance flickered in her eyes.

"Really?" Melena looked impressed. "That's amazing."

"Yep." Joseph pointed to another dish. "The green beans there are also homegrown."

Melena looked at her mother with warm eyes. "You'll have to show me your garden."

Emaya smiled back. “Maybe after dinner we can go out and have a look.”

Melena nodded, her eyes wide, indicating her genuine interest.

“So, Melena,” Joseph swallowed his food before continuing, “how are Paul and Esther? I imagine they are enjoying having you stay with them.”

“Oh, they’re amazing,” Melena replied. “I’m sure I’m wearing out my welcome, though. I think it’s about time I started looking for my own place.”

Joseph glanced at Emaya and then back at Melena. “You’re always welcome here you know. We have a couple of empty bedrooms.”

Adam watched Jivvy out of the corner of his eye. Her eyes narrowed, and he could hear the speed of her breathing pick up.

“Right, Dad,” Jivvy began, sarcastically, “I’m sure she wants to live here like a teenager. Maybe Mom can make her pancakes each morning and do her laundry for her.”

“Jivvissa!” Emaya’s eyebrows pulled together in a scowl. “Take it easy.”

“No, it’s okay,” Melena broke in. “I don’t want to impose on anyone. I think I ought to have my own place.”

Joseph shot Jivvy a warning look and then turned to Melena. “Maybe you haven’t had time to really think things through yet, but how long do you think you’ll be staying in Independence?”

Melena smiled, cautiously. “I really like it here. I can’t imagine going back outside the walls at this point. I can’t go home, and I can’t imagine trying to live among the general populace.”

“Being starved, oppressed and controlled doesn’t sound too appealing does it?” Jivvy snapped at Melena. “Maybe your dad ought to get an apartment in downtown Rugby and try it out for a while, see how he fares."

"Hey!" Joseph glared at his daughter. He opened his mouth to say more, but Adam interrupted.

"You know," he began, calmly, "Jivvy's got her own place. Maybe it's time she got a roommate."

The room fell silent. Jivvy swallowed hard and stared at Adam, her face darkening a shade. Adam stared back, unapologetically.

Melena cleared her throat. "I'm sure Jivvy enjoys her privacy. I wouldn't want to impose on her. I'm sure I can find a place—"

"Well, that's an interesting idea," Joseph interrupted, his voice suddenly much lighter. "You've got an empty bedroom, Jivvy, and that great big kitchen …"

Jivvy worked up a tight, diplomatic smile. "My place is in the middle of the city. I think the hustle and bustle might be a little much for Melena. Plus, she doesn't have a vehicle to get around in. I doubt she has a driver's license anyway."

"Really, it's fine." Melena laughed nervously. "Jivvy, I don't want to get in your way. Don't worry about it."

Joseph folded his arms and leaned back in his chair. "That's a good point, Jivvy. How is she going to get around town without a vehicle?" He rubbed his chin with his fingers. "If only she knew someone who could help."

Jivvy stared down at her plate and sighed. She speared a piece of roast beef with her fork and raised it to the level of her mouth before pausing to speak. "Melena …" She glanced over, finally acknowledging her sister. "Would you like to move in with me?"

Melena's eyebrows shot up. "Are you sure? I really don't want to impose on you. I'll get a job as soon as I can—I don't expect you to carry all of the financial burden."

"I'm sure," Jivvy answered, flatly, before shoving the bite of roast beef into her mouth.

Emaya smiled warmly. "That's very generous of you, Jivvy."

Jivvy smiled, curtly at her mother, then turned her gaze on Adam. Her eyes narrowed, and her jaw tightened. Adam fought to suppress a huge grin. His mouth turned into more of a frown, but there was obvious amusement in his eyes. Jivvy's eyes became tiny slits for a moment, shooting waves of ice in Adam's direction.

"So, Melena," Joseph spoke up, "what did you study at University? We should see about getting you a job if you're going to stick around."

"Oh," Melena began, pausing to swallow what was in her mouth, "my undergraduate studies were in psychology, but I have a Master's in Public Administration."

Jivvy chuckled. "Looks like you've thrown a little wrench in your own career path."

"Not necessarily." Emaya's face was thoughtful. "Melena, what did you think of the speech I gave in Rugby?"

Melena hesitated for a moment, her eyes becoming moist. When she spoke, it was barely above a whisper. "I thought that seeing you standing up there in the face of hostility and ridicule was the bravest thing I'd ever seen, and I thought it was the most thought-provoking and insightful political speech I'd ever heard."

Emaya nodded intently.

"I have to be honest," Melena continued, "before meeting Adam, I was barely even aware that your ideals still existed. I thought he was crazy when he told me about Independence and the old American values that had been perpetuated here. But after seeing this city and meeting the people who are a part of it, I can't argue the success that self-government can have on a society. And having now seen the damage that the S.O.U.'s policies have done to the people and the oppression they are enduring, my entire perspective of the role of government has begun to evolve.

"I was taught to believe that citizens couldn't thrive without the assistance of the government, and that they should be grateful that someone was looking out for them. In reality, the government has made the citizenry slaves—serving the interests of their so-called leaders. To say these discoveries have been a wake-up call would be a huge understatement."

"In summary," Adam broke in, "she gives the speech a solid B-minus."

Everyone at the table chuckled, with the exception of Melena.

She turned to Adam with a confused smile on her face. "What's a B-minus?"

"They used to give out grades in school to measure success," he explained. "A, B, C, D, and F, with pluses and minuses in between—an A-plus being the most satisfactory grade. We still do it at our schools here."

Melena nodded and turned back to Emaya. "I give Adam's humor a D-minus and your speech an A-plus."

Emaya eyes twinkled as she smiled at her newly discovered daughter. "Thank you, sweetheart."

Joseph turned to his wife. "Perhaps Melena's political insights could be put to use in your organization, honey."

"I'd be lying if I said it hadn't crossed my mind," Emaya agreed. She looked back at Melena. "If you're interested, maybe public administration could still be in your future."

Melena nodded. "If you think I could help, I'd be very interested."

"Jivvy ..." Emaya turned to her younger daughter. "I think we need to take Melena shopping tomorrow before she comes into the office. Are you available?"

The annoyance on Jivvy's face was obvious to Adam. "I can't tomorrow. Sorry. You two have fun, though."

"All right …" Emaya ignored Jivvy's coolness. "I'll bring her to your place after work so I can help her settle in."

"Are you sure you're okay with this, Jivvy?" Melena asked.

"Of course." Jivvy tried to smile, hiding her obvious irritation.

Adam smiled to himself, deeply satisfied. He scooped up a large spoonful of mashed potatoes and plopped them into the spot on his plate where his first helping had been. "Can someone please pass the gravy?"

Chapter 42

Adam glanced at the clock on his desk. Nine twenty-seven. He chuckled silently to himself as he thought of Melena settling in at Jivvy's. They would likely be there together by now. He hadn't yet had an opportunity to talk to Melena about her first day on the job. He determined to give her another thirty minutes or so to have some awkward time with her sister before calling.

"Adam?" Droven's voice called from inside Adam's pants pocket.

Adam removed the tiny cylindrical projection device from his pocket and placed it on the desk in front of him, the projector side facing into his bedroom.

"Go ahead, Droven," Adam replied.

A life-size projection of Droven appeared a few feet from the device. "Hey, man, you need to come down to the security center as soon as you can." He was out of breath, his chest heaving in and out.

Adam straightened up in his chair. "What's going on?"

"I think I've identified our saboteur."

"Who is it?" Adam demanded.

"Someone posing as a member of the night cleaning staff. I caught him logged into the security settings trying to change the density of the grid. I tried to detain him, but he was *quick*." Droven emphasized the last word.

"He was quick?"

"Yeah, like really quick. Like, *you* quick."

"Really?"

"We think he's still in the building. You're probably the only one who can catch this guy."

"I'll be there in thirty seconds." Adam shoved the projector into his pocket and raced from the apartment. In the relative calm of the evening, few pedestrians were on the streets outside. He covered the five blocks to the security center in a matter of seconds, stopping at the security entrance.

"Hurry, guys, I need to get inside now!" he shouted to the two guards manning the booth.

One of the men tossed out a glowing blue orb that scanned his body, pausing at his eyes to scan them more completely.

"Thank you, Mr. Winter," one of the guards called after him as Adam rushed through the narrow passage and disappeared into the parking structure below the building.

Adam dug the projector out of his pocket and held it near his mouth. "Droven?" he called into it. "Droven, I'm here. Where do you think he is?"

"No idea."

"Do you have the exits and roof covered?"

"Yeah, I don't think he could have made it out before we got them covered."

Adam sighed. "All right, I'll start at the lower parking level and work my way up the building. Have everyone else stay right where they are, and let me know if anyone spots him."

"Will do."

Adam stood in the center of the bottom parking level and closed his eyes, allowing his ears to go to work. After fifteen seconds, he heard nothing but the consistent hum of the mechanical room. Cautiously, he walked around the perimeter of the garage, listening as he passed each parked vehicle. Satisfied that he hadn't missed anything on the first level, he sprinted up the ramp to the next parking level and repeated the exercise. Initially, there weren't any significant noises, just the sound of a vehicle passing by the building or voices carrying from across the street. As he circled around the perimeter, he detected a faint, airy sound. He cautiously moved toward its source. As he approached the far corner of the level, the sound grew louder. The closer proximity confirmed the source of the noise—definitely human breathing. Adam crouched down and scanned the various vehicles in the vicinity. The breathing sounded muffled, and Adam decided that whoever it was, he must be inside a vehicle. After a moment, he spotted it—a black sedan near the far corner of the parking level. The driver's seat was reclined slightly, and the person sitting in it was slumped down, but the top of a head was visible through the privacy glass to Adam's sharp eyes.

Adam crouched down even closer to the ground and stealthily approached the sedan from the side, ducking in between the few other parked vehicles as he went. Avoiding the sedan's cameras and mirrors, he crawled around to the driver's side of the vehicle and lay beneath the door for a moment. At this proximity, he could hear the steady heartbeat of the person inside. The heart rate was fairly slow, and the breathing sounded calm. Keeping a close eye on the vehicle's side mirror, Adam sat up with his back against the driver door. He took a deep breath and then snatched the door handle and pulled it open. He flung the door open wide, sending it crashing into the vehicle next to it with a loud thud. He reached into the driver's seat and grabbed the dark figure by the collar, dragging the person out of the vehicle and onto the ground. The older woman's eyes flew open with a look of shock and confusion as her body slammed against the concrete. She gasped loudly at the sight of Adam leaning over her. Startled, Adam scrambled to his feet and then reached down to help the woman up. She gaped at him, unable to speak.

"I'm so sorry. Are you okay?" Adam asked, grabbing onto her wrist and pulling her to her feet. "I'm really sorry. I thought you were someone else. Are you hurt?"

The woman's eyes were wide. She finally managed to speak. "No, I'm not hurt." She brushed off the back of her slacks. "Why would you do that? Why would you pull someone out of their car like that?"

Adam felt his cheeks getting warm. "I'm so sorry. There's a dangerous man somewhere in the building. That's who I'm looking for. I didn't expect anyone else to be here."

"Well," the woman continued dusting herself off, "I'm certainly not a dangerous man. I'm working the evening shift in the control room and was just taking a break."

"In your car?"

"It's really none of your business, but I was just having a little power nap." She looked at her watch and sighed. "It looks like I overslept a few minutes. If you'll excuse me, I need to get back." She reached for her car door, examining the edge for damage. Satisfied, she shut it and glanced over at the vehicle parked next to her. There was a quick intake of breath, then she looked up at Adam, her eyes disapproving. "You put a dent in that car, young man. You'd better find out who owns it and arrange for payment of a repair."

"I will, ma'am," Adam promised. "Actually, ma'am, it would help me if you would just stay in your vehicle. It may be the safest place for you right now. The building is on lock down."

"You want me to get back in my car?" the woman clarified.

"Yes, it'll be easier for me to find the man I'm looking for if people aren't moving around the building."

"I'll need to clear this with my supervisor," the woman protested.

"No, I promise it'll be fine. Please, just stay here."

"All right." The woman turned back to her vehicle. "I guess I'll just go back to my power nap."

Adam opened the door for her. "That sounds great. Again, I'm sorry for what happened."

The woman just nodded as she sat back down in the driver's seat.

Adam closed the door behind her, then pulled the projector from his pocket. "Droven, I need a little help here. I just threw a lady to the ground after pulling her out of her car."

"I know," Droven responded. "I'm watching security images. I saw the whole thing."

Adam shook his head. "Fantastic." He tried to refocus. "How many legitimate staff members are in the building right now?"

"Should be twenty-four, including me."

"How many are armed security?"

"Ten, including me. Four are from the Sherriff's office, five are building security. The rest are technicians, office staff and cleaning crew."

"Where are they? Can we gather the non-security people together?"

"Yeah, we tried. Eight of them are here on the fifth floor in the conference room. The others are scattered."

Adam quickly did the math in his head. "So, there's one office lady here in the garage … that leaves five others who aren't with you."

"Right. Three are cleaning staff, one woman and two men, and the other two are male technicians.

"All right, if you come across anyone else, keep them in the conference room and notify me, please."

"You got it."

Adam shoved the projector back into his pocket and headed for the entrance into the building. Vigilantly, he patrolled the hallway and offices, listening and searching. From somewhere on the other end of the floor, he heard the faint hum of a motor. He headed toward the sound, continuing to check the offices and lobbies as he moved through.

The hum grew louder as he drew nearer. He recognized the sound of a commercial vacuum cleaner motor coming from down a perpendicular hallway. A row of chairs sat outside the door of one of the offices at the end of the hall. Adam focused his eyes on the chrome finish of the frame of the chair on the end of the row. In the tiny reflection, he could see a man down the hall vacuuming the carpet. The man seemed oblivious to anything else going on around him. His head bobbed up and down in measured rhythm. Adam smiled to himself, guessing that the man must be listening to music as he worked.

Apprehensively, Adam turned the corner and began approaching the man's position. He darted across the hallway and opened an office door for a potential retreat should this man turn out to be a great actor instead of an actual cleaning staff member. He stepped out into the hallway and called out to the man. "Sir?" He crouched, ready to either chase should the man bolt or retreat should he attack. The man continued vacuuming without lifting his gaze. He continued moving to a beat Adam could only faintly hear. "Sir?" Adam called out much louder than before. Still, there was no response. Adam ducked back into the empty office and took the projector from his pocket, pointed the recording end at himself and projected his own image directly in the man's path. The vacuum nearly penetrated the shoes of Adam's projection before stopping abruptly.

"Whoa!" The man jumped backwards with startled eyes, nearly tripping on his own feet. He tapped on his ear to quiet the music. "Sorry, I didn't see you there," he blurted, louder than necessary.

"No problem," Adam's projection responded in a calm voice. "Sir, I need you to go up to the fifth floor conference room for me."

The man looked confused. "What?"

Adam kept his voice even. "The building is on lock down, and I need you to report to the fifth floor conference room for me right now. Can you do that?"

The man looked down at his vacuum and then back at Adam's projection.

"You can just leave the vacuum and head upstairs, okay?"

The man nodded, slowly. "Okay. Is everything all right?"

"It will be," Adam promised.

"I'll head up to the fifth floor then." The man turned and headed toward the elevator, glancing back at Adam periodically. When the elevator door opened, he peered down the hall at Adam one last time before entering.

No sooner did the elevator door slide shut than a set of double doors at the end of the hall flew open and another cleaning staff member entered the hallway, pushing a large trash bin in front of her. The young woman, a petite redhead in a baggy uniform, slowed as she approached Adam's projection. Her eyes were wide and darted from side to side, unsure of where to go.

Adam's projection held up his hands, palms out. "Miss, I need for you to head up to the fifth floor conference room, please. The building is on lock down."

She hesitated and then cleared her throat. "Um, okay, I just need to empty this trash bin and, and I'll, uh, go right up to the fourth floor," she stammered nervously, her broom-like hair brushing across her panic-stricken eyes.

Adam paused. He heard two heart beats and two sets of lungs inhaling and exhaling, one severely muffled. His projection stepped aside, making room for the trash bin to pass. "Okay," he relented, "but it's the *fifth* floor. Please head up there as soon as you finish emptying the bin."

"O … o … okay," she stuttered. "*Fifth* floor. Sorry." Hesitantly, she resumed pushing the bin down the hall.

Adam's projection dissipated. Silently, the real Adam stepped into the hallway, placing an index finger over his lips to shush the young woman as she approached. He made eye contact with her and then pointed at the trash bin. Her eyes followed his to the bin and then looked back at Adam. Adam pantomimed a gun with his thumb and index finger and raised his eyebrows as if to ask a question.

Fear flooded her face as the young woman nodded, vigorously. Adam nodded back at her and then waved her forward. As she caught up to him, he grabbed onto the bin handle with one hand and her shoulder with the other. He gestured toward the elevator with his head. She nodded again and transitioned the bin over to Adam. She pointed in the direction of the elevator and raised her eyebrows. Adam nodded and she tip-toed toward the elevator. Relief showed on her face as the door slid open. "Thank you," she mouthed before ducking safely inside.

Adam wheeled the bin down the hall in silence. He spotted the men's restroom and wheeled the bin inside, stopping in the middle of the room. He stepped to the front of the bin and crouched down, anticipating that the man inside would look behind the bin at the person pushing it whenever he decided to emerge. It only took five seconds for the infiltrator to become impatient. The bin's lid rose slowly, and the barrel of a hand gun stuck out, aimed toward the rear of the bin.

"Nyvia, why have you stopped?" the voice inside the bin growled.

The lid opened another two inches for the man to peer out. Like a coiled cobra, Adam struck at the gun in the man's hand with his open palm. The gun fell to the tiled floor and was quickly recovered by Adam. He pointed it at the bin with one hand and threw back the lid with the other. The man inside was poised to strike back until his surprised eyes spotted the barrel of the gun aimed at his face just a few feet away.

Adam took a step backward. “Does it stink in there?”

The man put his hands up and stood slowly to his full height, which looked minimal to Adam. His build was slight, but athletic. He appeared to be in his early forties. Prominent cheek bones jutted out below his eyes, making his cheeks appear hollow. His thinning light brown hair stood straight up from the static electricity off of the lid of the bin, except for a small patch on the top of his scalp that had been shaved. The line of stitches running the length of the shaved area seemed oddly familiar to Adam. The man’s grey eyes were set deep in their sockets, and they shifted back and forth as he tried to access the situation.

Adam shook his head. “It’s okay. That was a rhetorical question. I know it stinks in there. You’re a little ripe on your own, but there’s a funk from the trash as well, so don’t feel too self-conscious.”

“Who are you?” the man asked in a gruff voice.

Adam pointed his free thumb at his chest. “Me? Oh, I’m just the guy who’s taking you to jail.”

The corner of the man’s thin lips pulled up into a sly grin. “Really? I don’t think you’re that guy. I don’t think you’re going to take me anywhere.”

Adam frowned and shrugged his shoulders. “I guess you’re entitled to your own opinion.” He gestured at the bin with his hand. “Would you prefer to ride or walk? You’re already comfortably situated in the trash. Why don’t you just squat back down, and I’ll wheel you on over?”

The man smiled, confidently. “I think I would prefer to walk.”

Adam retrieved the projector from his pocket and held it near his mouth. “Droven, did you see the restroom I wheeled the trash bin into?”

"Yes, sir," Droven's voice responded. "Help is on the way."

"Thank you very much." Adam returned the device to his pocket.

"We can just hang out here for now," Adam offered, nonchalantly. "More guys with guns are coming, so …"

The man smiled and stared into Adam's eyes for a moment, then shifted his eyes to the restroom door. Adam's eyes left the man for a fraction of a second and followed his gaze. With Adam's attention averted, the man sprung from the bin like a jack-in-the-box. Still airborne, he struck Adam in the side of the head with the back of his fist, his other hand chopping Adam's right forearm. The gun crashed to the floor once again. The man bent down to recover it, but his face met Adam's knee moving in the opposite direction. A spray of dark red splattered against the mirror on the wall as the man's head snapped back. Adam kicked the weapon under a toilet stall and turned to face his staggering assailant. The man wiped at his tear-filled eyes with his sleeve. Adam flew to his side, grabbing him by the wrist and twisting his arm behind his back. The man kicked his foot backwards, connecting with Adam's shin. Adam cried out in pain and released the man's wrist. In one fluid movement, the man took a step and then leaped up, pushing off of the sink with one foot and striking Adam in the side of the head with a devastating roundhouse kick with the other.

A firework show played behind Adam's eyelids as he went to the floor. He heard footsteps racing toward the restroom exit and the door open and shut, and then all noises faded away. Adam blinked his eyes. Slowly, light began to return as Adam fought to keep them open. Gradually, shapes began to appear in his vision, though they seemed to be spinning around the room. With his teeth clenched tightly, he writhed on the floor, his head pounding in response to the vicious blow it had just received. After a few moments, he reached a hand up and found the sink. He pulled himself to his feet and peered at the three reflections of his face in the mirror.

Droven's voice bellowed from inside his pocket. "Adam! Adam, are you okay?"

Adam closed his eyes and shook his head. He fumbled in his pocket, finally retrieving the projector. "Yeah, Droven, I'm okay. Just got my bell rung a little bit. Did you see where he went?"

"Yeah, he's in the stairwell. He's heading up."

Adam's blinked his eyes until his vision began to return to normal. His head was still pounding, but he headed for the restroom exit, throwing the door open in frustration. "All right," he growled into the projector, "try and have security force him onto the seventh floor then kill the power. We'll see how he does blind."

"Truth and honor, man."

"Truth and honor." Adam spit the words out, but not with disdain. An intense emotion began to emit from his core. A fierce sense of indignation welled up inside of him, causing all of his faculties to focus. Independence was his home and his model of peace and freedom. This trespasser, this saboteur, was not worthy to set foot in his home, and Adam determined to see to it personally that this man was removed from it.

He sprinted down the hall to the stairwell, then began ascending the stairs, taking an entire half flight in two leaps.

"He went for it. He's on the seventh floor, Adam. Lights out," he heard Droven announce from inside his pocket.

"Good. Thanks. Let's go silent until I take this guy out."

Adam reached the seventh floor and paused at the door to catch his breath. Once his heart had slowed down enough so that it wasn't dominating his entire auditory input, he put his ear to the door to listen. The floor was silent. He opened the door a crack and peered inside. The space before him would have appeared nearly pitch black to normal eyes. The seventh floor was being remodeled, so the space was open and littered with scaffolding, tools and building materials. A very faint light from neighboring buildings and the stars shown through the plastic sheeting that hung over the windows. Adam viewed the room in front of him perfectly in green and grey hues. He quickly pushed the heavy metal door open and stepped inside the room, closing the door behind him and eliminating the shaft of light from the stairwell that momentarily penetrated the thick darkness.

He took in the cluttered room in front of him. The ceiling was about fifteen feet tall with scaffolding for the painters reaching nearly two-thirds of the way up. The man Adam was pursuing was nowhere in sight, but the scent of garbage and blood wafted across the room into his nostrils. Adam maneuvered silently around the various obstacles in the space until he came to the doorway leading into the next room. He scanned the scene before him. It looked much like the room he had just left, but the scent was stronger.

In the distance, he heard the tiny whine of metal rubbing against metal. He stopped to listen. He detected the faint sound of breathing and heard the metallic rubbing again. He covered the distance of the room in just a few seconds and peered around the doorway of the adjacent room. He paused again to listen. The breathing sounded much closer, accompanied by a rapid heartbeat. Adam followed the sounds with his eyes until he spotted the intruder perched on top of the scaffolding directly over the doorway leading into the next room. The man clutched a three-foot length of steel pipe in his hand. Adam assumed it had been removed from the scaffolding somewhere. It was now the man's weapon.

Adam thought of several different ways he might be able to apprehend the trespasser. First, he could race in undetected and pull the scaffolding out from under the man and send him crashing to the floor, or second, he could just keep an eye on him and call for back up. He deliberated for a few moments and decided on a third option—spring the trap. The man was obviously waiting for him. He was perched up high in order surprise Adam. There seemed to be enough light coming through the obscured windows so that the man would likely be able make out Adam's shape in the darkness.

Adam entered the room slowly. He stepped quietly, but deliberately bumped into a large bucket of paint, spilling its contents all over the floor to his right. In his periphery, Adam saw the man crouch down, preparing to drop onto his prey. In six steps, he would be directly under the scaffolding. Cautiously, he moved forward, keeping the man in sight for as long as possible. After five steps, he heard a sharp intake of breath and a quiet grunt. He stepped aside as the steel pipe hammered onto the concrete floor, followed by the man's feet. The vibration from the pipe hitting the floor made it impossible for the man to hold onto it, and it bounced away, crashing against the wall. Adam recalled the feeling of hitting a baseball too close to the grip of the bat and the pain it inflicted on one's hands. He imagined that hitting the floor with the pipe must have been like that … times ten. The man stumbled backwards, landing on his back. Adam pounced on top of him, straddling his midsection and landed a lightning-fast three-punch-combo to the man's face before he knew what was happening. As if powered by a spring, the man's foot flew up and kicked Adam in the back of the head. Adam toppled forward, and the man wriggled out from beneath him. The man scrambled to get to his feet, but Adam kicked his legs out from underneath him, sending him crashing onto the floor. Immediately, Adam disappeared, retreating into the shadows. The unwanted visitor got back on his feet, his head swiveling back and forth as he tried to locate Adam. Adam waited until the man straightened to his full height and then lunged forward and buried his shin into the man's stomach with an annihilating kick. The air immediately evacuated the man's lungs with a sharp hiss as he doubled over and fell to his knees. Reaching his hands out to catch himself, he went down on all fours, gasping for air.

Before he could catch his breath, Adam delivered a second kick, this time to the chest. The man went tumbling across the floor and crashed into the wall underneath the scaffolding. Propped up against the wall, he clutched at his chest, his eyes the size of golf balls. Finally, he wheezed in a small breath. Adam sprang forward to deliver what was to be the destructive blow to the head that would render the man unconscious. Before Adam could slow his pursuit, however, the man reached behind his body and wildly swung the steel pipe into the darkness in front of him. It connected with Adam's shoulder mid-swing, sending him staggering across the room. His feet met with the spilled paint on the smooth floor and came out from under him. He landed on his back and slid to a stop in the center of the room. He looked up in time to see the saboteur running in his direction, blindly swinging the pipe back and forth. Adam ducked and rolled twice. His attacker missed and then lost his grip on the pipe as he slid past Adam, the pipe bouncing off the hard floor in front of him. His feet ran in place without catching traction, and he fell forward into the paint.

Suddenly, the heat of indignation ignited inside of Adam once again. Gritting his teeth, he dove through the paint and onto the man's back. The intruder struggled to escape. The slick paint caused Adam to lose his grip on the man, but he locked his legs around the man's torso in a scissor hold. The man shifted onto his back and threw a backhand toward Adam's face. Adam reached out and caught his wrist before the man's fist could reach its mark. He then pulled the arm across his own torso and lifted his hips off of the floor—his body acting as a fulcrum under the man's outstretched arm. The intruder cried out in pain.

"I've got a pretty nasty arm-bar here, sir," Adam breathed out from behind clenched teeth. "Would you like to say '*uncle*'?" The man pounded on Adam's leg with his free hand and struggled to free his body. "No? Okay." Adam tightened the scissor hold he had with his legs and wrenched the other man's arm as tight as he could across his abdomen. With all of his might, Adam threw his hips up off of the floor. A gruesome crack and several pops rang in Adam's ears as the man's humerus bone snapped. A guttural scream tore from the intruder's throat as the pain of the break registered in his brain.

Adam released the broken man and let him writhe on the floor. He sat up and spoke into the projector. "Droven, the perpetrator is ready for the deputies to come and get him, and you can turn the lights back on."

"Surveillance is down on your floor because of the remodel. What happened? Are you okay?" Droven asked.

"I'm good," Adam replied, "but this joker here isn't. He wouldn't say '*uncle*', man."

Droven paused. "He wouldn't?" He tried to sound incredulous. "Someone should have told that guy that he should say '*uncle*' when you tell him to. Hey, guy, if you can hear me, you should have said '*uncle*'."

Adam sighed. "Hind sight is always twenty-twenty, isn't it?"

"Indeed," Droven chuckled.

Just then, the lights powered on and color returned to Adam's vision. The sky blue paint had gotten everywhere. Adam looked down at himself. He was covered in it. The man with the broken arm—who was also covered in paint—had gotten up on one knee, cradling his right arm with his left. He tried to stand. Adam was at his side in an instant. He placed his index finger on the man's right shoulder and looked over at him, eyebrows raised. “I think it would be best if you stayed still.”

“I’ll kill you,” the man panted, his face twisted in an expression of pain; his furious eyes boring into Adam’s. “I’ll kill you for this.”

The four Sherriff’s deputies burst through the door, weapons drawn and trained on the sky blue painted man kneeling on the floor.

“Hey, guys,” Adam greeted the deputies. “His right arm is broken, so only touch it if you’re ready to hear a really girly scream.”

One of the deputies holstered his weapon and grabbed the intruder by the left arm and pulled it behind his back. The man cried out in pain at the jolt. His right arm hung uselessly at his side.

“I’m sorry about the paint, guys. That was my fault,” Adam admitted. “Try not to get it on your uniforms. Oh, also, I dented the door of a red car on the second parking level. Send me the bill for the repair.”

The deputy smiled and nodded. “Let’s go,” he commanded, trying to be gentle as he helped the injured man to his feet.

The man grimaced as he rose to a standing position. He turned his head to glare one last time at Adam. “I *will* kill you,” he vowed.

“I know,” Adam replied, casually. “You already said that.”

Chapter 43

Melena plopped down on the light-pink, cloud-like sofa in Jivvy's living room. She sank at first, and then the velvety cushion buoyed her back up. "What are these cushions made of?" she called out in the direction of the kitchen.

"I don't know," Jivvy called back, "I just saw the sofa at the mall and thought it was comfy."

"It is." Melena confirmed.

Jivvy held out a glass filled with a white liquid. "Do you want some?"

Melena squinted. "What is it?"

Jivvy paused for a beat. "It's goat cream. We keep her tied up in the courtyard and all take turns milking her."

"Oh." Melena hesitated. "Uh, sure, I guess I could try some."

Jivvy snorted. "I'm kidding. It's just milk. Cow's milk. From the grocery store."

"Oh, that's too bad." Melena smiled, playfully. "Fresh goat's cream sounded good."

Jivvy laughed as she delivered the glass to Melena, then sat down in the small recliner next to the sofa and sipped at her own glass. "Actually, we need something else." She set her glass down on the coffee table and went back to the kitchen. Melena heard the rustle of plastic packaging, and then Jivvy returned with a small plate. On the plate were several stacks of what looked to Melena like some sort of wafers or biscuits. Each had two little black disks with something white sandwiched in between. "Have you ever had these before?" Jivvy asked.

Melena looked closely as Jivvy set the plate on the glass table. "I don't think so. Are they pig intestines?" She fought to keep a straight face.

Jivvy chuckled. "Yes, they're pig intestines." She picked one up, holding the edge of it between her thumb and index finger. "I'll show you." She hovered it over her glass and then looked over at Melena to make sure she was following along before plunging it into the milk. She held it there for four or five seconds and then popped it into her mouth. "Now, you try," she commanded through her mouthful.

Melena picked one of the black and white sandwiches up off the plate and followed Jivvy's protocols. She tried to lean over the glass as milk dripped off of her fingers. She smiled and nodded as she chewed the … *cookie?*, she guessed. "That's really good," she admitted.

"Yeah," Jivvy agreed, "now, have some more so I don't eat the whole plate."

"No problem." Melena picked up another and repeated the process.

The room fell silent for a while, aside from the crunching of cookies. Melena spotted an image book sitting on the end table. She held it up to Jivvy. "May I?"

"Sure," Jivvy answered through another mouthful of black and white cookies.

Melena opened the book and flipped through the first few pages of two-dimensional images. They were images of Jivvy and some other girls. They looked to be about fifteen. "Is this prep school?" Melena wondered.

Jivvy leaned forward to see what Melena was looking at. "High school," she corrected. "That's the sophomore dance team."

"Oh, so you're a dancer and an MMO—or whatever—fighter?"

"What?" Jivvy wrinkled her nose. "Are you trying to say *MMA fighter*?"

Melena nodded. "Yeah, like Adam."

"Well, I *was* a dancer," Jivvy clarified. "I haven't danced in a long time."

Melena pulled her eyebrows together and spoke in a gruff voice. "Hard to find time to dance when you're trying to save the world, right?"

"Yep." Jivvy half-smiled.

Melena flipped through a few more pages and stopped on an image of two young men standing on a grass field with white stripes painted on it. Melena swiped the surface of the image and sent it out into the room. The now three-dimensional image became life-sized. Melena let out a little giggle as recognition set in. The two young men wore pads on their shoulders with tight jerseys stretched over the top of them and each held a helmet by the facemask with their outside hand. Their inside arms were around each other's necks. The one on the left was tall and lean. The chocolate brown skin on his face glistened with sweat, but the dimples were unmistakable. The one on the right was about the same height, but more broad. His dark, wavy hair was matted down on his head and a few pieces of it slithered down around his eyes. A broad grin nearly split his face in two.

"Ha!" Melena exclaimed. "They are so cute!" She glanced at Jivvy. "This is American football, right?"

"Yep, *American* football," Jivvy repeated absently, focusing on dunking her cookie.

"Those are some tight pants," Melena observed, rotating the image around with her hand and pausing with the rear of the image facing her.

Jivvy looked up and nearly choked on a mouthful of cookie and milk as she burst out laughing. She put a hand up to her mouth, and white liquid with little black chunks spilled out between her fingers. Melena burst out laughing at Jivvy, who was still struggling to get the cookie down without spitting any more of it out.

"What?" Melena protested through her laughter. "I was just making an innocent observation."

Jivvy stood up and walked to the kitchen to clean herself up. Melena retracted the image back into the book.

"Jivvy?" Droven's voice called from inside the purse that sat on the small table close to the front door. "Jivvy, are you there?"

Jivvy wiped her mouth on a hand towel and crossed the room briskly to her purse. She retrieved the small, cylindrical device and set it on the glass coffee table in the center of the room before plopping back into her chair. "Go ahead, Droven."

Droven's life-sized image projected into the room. "Is Melena with you?"

"Right here," Melena sang, still feeling a little goofy.

"Good. Can the two of you come over to the security building right now?"

"No," Jivvy groaned. "We were just about to go to bed."

"I know," Droven sighed, "but we need to see if Melena can ID our saboteur."

Jivvy sat up straight. "You have someone in custody?"

"Yeah," Droven answered. "The guy's a professional. He is unusually quick also. We think he's got a stamp in his head like Adam. Adam had to come and take him down for us."

"Is Adam okay?" Melena asked, the levity suddenly absent from her voice.

"He's got a big, purple bruise on his shoulder and he's covered in blue paint, but other than that, he's good."

"He's covered in what?" Jivvy asked.

"How bad is his shoulder?" Melena asked at the same time.

"Just come over here, please." Droven sounded exasperated. "Adam's fine. The bruise is pretty gnarly, but will probably heal before you get here, so hurry up if you want to see it."

"Can we wear our pajamas?" Jivvy asked.

"Bye." Droven's image dissipated. He had apparently run out of patience with the two of them.

Chapter 44

Melena burst from the elevator as soon as the door opened. A stocky, middle-aged security guard smiled at her as she approached and gestured down the hall with his head. "Room 508."

Melena nodded and turned to her left, picking her pace up to a half-run.

"I'll just be back here, Melena," Jivvy called after her, "walking at a reasonable pace like a normal person."

Melena ignored her and hurried down the hall, mentally checking off room numbers as she went. Another guard stood outside room 508. This one was young and thin, with a cropped hair cut. He held up his hand to her. "One moment, please, miss." He released a small blue orb from his hand, which proceeded to scan her body from bottom to top, pausing in front of her eyes.

"I already did this before entering the building, sir," she protested.

"I know you did, miss, but we're just being a little extra cautious tonight."

Jivvy arrived just as the scan finished confirming Melena's identity. "Hey, Philip."

The guard's face colored, slightly. "Hello, Miss Luna."

Jivvy smiled at the young man's discomfort. "Sounds like you guys saw a little action tonight, huh?"

He looked everywhere except at Jivvy's face. "Yeah, it got a little lively there for a while."

"Nothing you couldn't handle, I'm sure." Jivvy patted his shoulder and shrugged past him to the door.

"Uh, Miss Luna?" The young guard caught her by the arm. "I need to scan you before you go in."

Jivvy took one giant step back out into the hallway and stood with her feet together and arms outstretched. "Okay, Philip, do what you gotta do." She put her chin up and looked straight ahead in total compliance as she waited for the blue orb to finish the scan.

"Can we go in now, please?" Melena asked.

"Yes, you're all clear."

Melena pulled the door open and held it for Jivvy.

"You're doing great, Phil." Jivvy smiled and touched the young guard's arm as she moved past him.

Melena rolled her eyes at Jivvy as the door shut behind her. "Wow."

"I'm just being nice," Jivvy defended. "He asked me to the Christmas dance our senior year of high school, and I had to say no because I already had a date."

Melena had already lost interest in the conversation and was heading toward the cluster of people in the center of the room.

Peter Gildrich spotted her and went to meet her. "Melena, thanks for coming so quickly. We need to move this man to the sheriff's office, but we wanted to see if you could ID him first."

"Yeah, of course." Melena fell into step beside him. "Where's Adam?"

Peter pointed at a nearby door. "He's there in the restroom getting cleaned up. I'm sure he'll be right out."

As they approached the group of security guards and sheriff's deputies, Melena caught a glimpse of the seated man they surrounded. His head was down, and his thinning hair was clumped and covered in what Melena assumed was the same light blue paint that Adam was reportedly covered in.

"She's here," Peter announced. The small crowd parted to allow Melena access. The man she was supposed to check out had his left wrist and both ankles cuffed to the chair he sat in. His right arm was in a sling.

Droven stood next to the man and tapped his left shoulder as Melena approached. "Hey, you have a visitor, man." There was no response from the paint-covered prisoner. Droven gave him a light tap on his right shoulder. "Hey, head up, please."

The man winced, sharply, and raised his head, his grey eyes meeting Melena's. Melena's breath caught and the man's eyes went wide as recognition of one another set in. Melena's heartbeat increased as the man's eyes narrowed and his jaw tightened.

Peter put a hand on Melena's shoulder. "Do you recognize this man?"

Melena nodded slowly, her eyes still locked on the paint-covered prisoner. "Colonel Helsen Winde," she reported in a quiet, but even voice. "He's over the Kansas City Police Battalion."

"You're a traitor, Jaxon," Colonel Winde growled. "You're going to prison. Do you know that? Do you know what they'll do to you in there?"

Droven placed two fingers on Colonel Winde's right shoulder and pressed down lightly, cutting the angry tirade short. The injured man howled. Droven patted him on the left shoulder. "We'll let you know when we wanna hear from you, Colonel."

Melena turned her head at the sound of a door opening. Adam emerged from the restroom. His dark, wavy hair was wet and there was blue paint on his ears. He looked up from wiping his hands on a towel, and his warm, smiling eyes found Melena's. His smile broadened. Melena went to him immediately, wrapping her arms around his waist before he could stop her.

"You're gonna ruin your clothes." He warned.

Melena didn't care. She tightened her hold on him. "You're okay, right?" she whispered in his light blue ear.

"I'm great," he whispered back. "Didn't you see the other guy?"

Melena laughed once. "Yeah, I saw. I'm just glad you're okay. How's your shoulder?"

"It's perfect. You don't need to worry about me. I'm pretty durable."

"I know you are. Sorry." Melena laid her face on Adam's shoulder and raised it back up as she felt something cold and sticky on her cheek. She pulled away from him, wiping her cheek with her fingers. They came back light blue. She looked down and noticed the same color all over the front of her clothes.

"Uh oh." Adam wiped her cheek with the paper towel. "Sorry about that. I did try to warn you, though."

Melena smiled. "It's fine."

Peter cleared his throat. "Are you two about done?"

"Sorry." Melena turned back to the group huddled around Colonel Winde. "I highly doubt this man is working alone. He's a Battalion leader, not an agent."

Peter nodded. "All right, let's get the Colonel secured. Deputies, will you escort him to a cell at the station? We'll resume our interviews in the morning."

Colonel Winde was helped to his feet by two Sheriff's deputies. They began leading him out of the room. The Colonel glared at Melena. "They're going to love you in prison, Jaxon."

"That's enough!" Peter barked. "Get him out of here."

"You're a traitor!" Winde shouted and spit in Melena's direction, missing her by a good meter.

"You're a slave to tyrants … and a terrible shot," Melena fired back.

"Hey, buddy, how's the arm?" Adam taunted with mock concern.

Winde's face hardened as his attention turned to Adam. "You're a walking corpse, kid," he growled through gritted teeth.

Adam nodded. "Yeah, I know."

Chapter 45

The evening sky burned amber, salmon and orange behind the leaves of the swaying, majestic white oaks that defined Paul and Esther Fransen's western property line. Adam slowed the vehicle to a stop in front of the house. Melena sighed and turned her head to face him. He smiled at her, the corners of his eyes narrowing the way they did when his smile was the most sincere. He reached out his large, strong hand and took hers. Melena returned the smile and squeezed his hand. She held his soft brown eyes for several seconds. There was no doubt in her mind now. She had completely fallen for him. He reached over with his free hand and gently touched her face before letting his fingers comb through her hair. When his hand reached the back of her neck, he pulled her closer to him. Melena finally let his eyes go as he leaned in to kiss her. Her heart fluttered as their lips met. The thrill was still very much intact.

"Okay," Adam murmured, pulling away, "have a good time tonight."

She sighed again and looked at him with an exaggerated frown. "Are you sure you can't stay with me?"

He smiled. "And spoil your first babysitting gig?"

Melena laughed and slapped his arm. "This was *your* gig."

"I know and appreciate you filling in. The kids will be much more excited to see you than they would me."

"Right." She wasn't buying that. "Is that supposed to give me confidence?"

"Yes." He nodded. "Did it work?"

"No."

"I honestly would love to stay, but it's Mr. Green asking for me this time. He said the data he needs is extremely urgent."

"Who's Mr. Green?" Melena asked.

"He's the Chairman of the Security Council—kind of a big-wig around here. I'll try and hurry."

"You'd better." She leaned over and gave him a quick peck on the lips. "Okay, here I go." She opened the door and stepped out onto the lawn. Unsure, she turned back to the vehicle and bent down to get one more reassurance from Adam. "I can do this, right? It's no big deal."

"Of course." Adam's smile and mild voice did ease her anxiety a bit. "You're going to be fantastic. Just don't let them push you around. They'll do what they're supposed to if you're firm."

"Yeah." She took a deep breath. "Okay, I'll see you soon."

"Relax," Adam soothed. "Have fun." He waved as she shut the door and turned back to the house.

Melena had only taken two steps toward the house when Joy and Elizabeth burst through the front door with Aaron hot on their heels.

"Melena!" Elizabeth squealed.

"Stop!" Aaron commanded his sisters. "Me first! I saw her first!"

Elizabeth ignored her brother's protests and ran to Melena, her arms outstretched.

"Hey guys!" Melena bent down to receive Elizabeth's hug. "How are you?"

Joy had allowed Aaron to pass her. He ran up and pulled at Elizabeth's arm until she took a step back and he was directly in front of Melena.

She tousled his thick blond hair. "Hi, Aaron."

He wasted no time with chit-chat. "Melena, do you want to see the egg I found? It's from a wild bird, and it probably has a wild baby bird inside. Come on. Come on." He snatched her hand and pulled her toward the house.

Melena lurched forward, slowing only a moment to give Joy a quick hug with her free arm. "Hi, Joy."

The little redhead beamed. "Hi, Melena. Thanks for coming."

Before she could respond, Aaron's mouth was going again. "Melena, Lizzy lost a tooth yesterday, and she put it under her pillow last night, and the tooth fairy forgot to come. It's still there. Her tooth is still there. She didn't take it."

"Oh, my goodness," Melena replied, looking shocked. "The tooth fairy must be really busy. Maybe she'll come tonight."

Aaron shoved a finger into his mouth and moved it back and forth over one of his bottom front teeth. "I 'ave a loof toof too."

"No you don't, Aaron," Elizabeth chided. "It's not loose at all."

"Yes it is!" Aaron insisted, scowling at his sister.

"You guys take care of Melena for me, okay?" Adam shouted through the open passenger window. "Don't let her get into any trouble."

Melena made a nervous face at the children and then smiled to reassure them that they would be able to manage.

"We will, Adam," Joy called back to him.

"She's a grown-up, Adam," Elizabeth yelled in the direction of the street, accompanied by an eye roll. "She doesn't get in trouble."

"Oh, you don't know her like I do, Lizzy." Adam matched her serious tone. "Trouble will find her."

"Adam, come and see the wild bird egg I found," Aaron commanded at the top of his lungs.

"I can't right now, buddy, but I'll see it tomorrow maybe, okay?" Adam shouted back.

"Okay, bye!" Aaron flashed a quick wave in Adam's direction and then sprinted for the house. "Come on!" he shouted over his shoulder.

Melena followed the children into the house as Adam pulled onto the street and sped away. Esther and Paul were milling around inside looking for Paul's shoes and Esther's purse as they prepared to leave. Esther smiled when she saw Melena. "Is this what we have to do to get you to come and visit once in a while?"

Melena smiled back. "I'm sorry. It's good to see you, though."

Esther hurried over to her and hugged her. "It's good to see you, too. Thanks for filling in for Adam. I hope it's okay. We have a neighbor girl who tends the kids sometimes. I can call her if you'd rather."

Melena waved her hand in front of her face. "No, no, no. I'm happy to spend some time with the kids. I was missing them."

Esther smiled. "If you're sure … Paul and I haven't been on a date for a long time, and it'll be good to get out together."

"Yes, it will," Melena agreed. "You two go have a good time."

John was watching the wall display in the family room, but looked over at Melena, trying to hide a smile. "Hey, Melena," he mumbled.

"Hi, John," Melena cooed back. "How are you?"

Embarrassed, he turned back to whatever he was watching. "Good."

"It's the homeless girl again," Paul's big baritone voice boomed from down the hall.

Melena smiled and waved to him. “Yep. You thought you were rid of me, didn’t you?”

His deep laugh rumbled in his chest as he approached her and nearly crushed her in a bear hug. “I thought you’d discovered that you’re way too pretty for Adam and moved on.”

“Hmm. I guess I haven’t made that discovery yet, but you never know.”

“Well, ignorance is bliss, right?” He patted her on the back and moved to his wife and took her by the arm. “It’s now or never, Esther. Let’s get out of here.”

Chapter 46

Melena helped the children put Aaron and Elizabeth's toys away. She had used them for a game. Random toys were put into a box, and the children took turns removing one at a time and placing them on the floor in the sequence they were drawn in. Once they had all been selected and put in order, the child whose turn it was had to tell a story using the toys as either characters or props. It had been a big hit with the children, especially Aaron who was an avid story teller anyway. John's participation was unenthusiastic in the beginning, but by his last turn, he was laughing and entertaining his siblings with tales of sword-wielding princess dolls and a spell-casting cowboy.

Aaron insisted that he wasn't tired, but his slow blinking was a giveaway. He was unconscious shortly after his head hit his pillow. Elizabeth too succumbed to her heavy eyelids and was asleep soon after being put to bed.

Joy got into bed and looked at Melena as though she wanted to say something.

She didn't, so Melena pulled the bedding over her. "Good night, Joy."

"So, do you like Adam?" she blurted out before Melena could leave the room.

Melena turned back and smiled. "Yeah, I like Adam a lot."

"Do you think you'll … maybe … get married or something?" she asked, her little rust-colored eyebrows raised in an inquisitive look.

"I don't know," Melena admitted. "We care about each other a lot, but we haven't known each other for very long. We'll just have to see what happens."

Joy nodded, slowly. "If you do get married, would you move away from Independence? My friend Avryn's aunt got married, and she moved to Dallas right after."

"Really? I think Independence is a pretty special place. I can't imagine Adam ever wanting to leave, and I really like it here too, especially since I found out that my mom and sister live here. I guess we'll just have to see how it goes, okay?"

Joy nodded again. "Okay. Good night, Melena. Thanks for playing with us tonight."

"It was my pleasure." Melena touched the pad on the wall near the doorway, and Joy's light turned off, and her window went dark. She began walking down the hall when she heard a high-pitched chime coming from the family room behind her. John's head poked out of the bathroom, white toothpaste bubbles clinging to the sides of his mouth.

"What's that?" Melena asked him.

"Security," John gargled through a mouthful of toothpaste lather. His head went back into the bathroom. She heard him spit into the sink, and then he reappeared in the hallway. He hurried past her to the family room and stood in front of the wall display. It had been the same pale yellow as the rest of the walls in the room, but now it was a vivid display of trees, grass and a patio.

"Is that the backyard?" Melena asked.

"Yeah," John answered, his eyes searching the image. "Thermographic," he commanded the display.

The trees and plants in the display instantly turned a deep violet color and two distinct yellow, orange and red shaded human forms appeared just inside the fence near the rear of the yard.

Melena gasped. "John, do you know who they are?"

John studied the moving figures for a moment before answering. "No, I don't think so."

One of the figures was manipulating some sort of handheld device. Suddenly, the display disappeared and the lights in the house went dark.

Melena's eyes scanned the house from left to right. "What happened?"

"I don't know," John replied, concern apparent in his voice.

Melena felt a wave of panic through her body. "We need to call the Sheriff." She groped through the darkness to the wall display in the kitchen and tapped it with her finger. The display remained dark. She tapped it again and again and then slapped her palm on it. Nothing. She dug the projector Adam had given her out of her pocket. "Adam?" She waited for a response—a voice, a projection. None came. She went to a window with a view of the backyard and tried to see outside, but the windows had all been darkened when they had left the living area. The controls were now unresponsive. A half-circle shaped window high above the front door allowed a combination of moonlight and a street light into the house, just enough to illuminate the shapes of the furniture. Melena's eyes began to adjust to the dark. She walked to front door and checked the deadbolt. She remembered electronically sealing the doors after Paul and Esther had left, but asked anyway. "We sealed the doors, didn't we, John?"

"I think so. Yes." He was trying to be brave, but his voice waivered. "But the power's out. Is someone trying to get in our house?"

Fear gnawed at Melena, increasing her heartbeat and heightening her senses. For John's sake she did her best to hide it. "I don't know, buddy, but it's going to be okay. Okay?"

John nodded, his eyes glistening beneath rapid blinks.

"Do your parents have a gun in the house?"

"Yeah."

"Where is it?"

"Locked up in the safe in their closet."

"Can we get it out?"

John looked at her, incredulously. "Do you think my parents would keep a gun where I could get it?"

Melena pressed her lips together as she considered this. "Probably not, huh?"

John shook his head slowly at her.

Melena's head snapped to her left to face the back door as she heard the knob rattle softly. Her heart pounded so hard in her chest that she could hear it in her ears. She looked at John. His eyes were wide, and his mouth hung open. They stared at each other for a long second. The wooden stairs leading up to the back door groaned under the weight of whoever was standing on them. Melena tip-toed over to John and took his arm, leading him down the hall toward the bedrooms, stopping in front of Aaron's door.

"Melena," John whispered, "let's say a prayer."

"Okay," she whispered back. "Do you want to say it?"

He shook his head. "Can you?"

Melena's breath caught. She had never prayed before. Seeing the desperate look on John's face made it impossible for her to refuse. She nodded. "All right." He knelt down and looked up at her. She knelt beside him. She tried to remember the prayers she had heard offered each night and morning while staying with John's family. She inhaled through her nose and exhaled through her mouth, trying to calm herself. She glanced over at John. His head was bowed and his eyes were closed. Melena closed her eyes. "Our Father in Heaven …" Hearing her own voice, the words sounded strange. She closed her eyes tighter, trying to imagine a father in her mind—a father unlike her earthly father—one who loved her completely. Her throat tightened as her mind grasped onto the thought of speaking to a father who knew her and who cared deeply for her. She cleared her throat. "Our Father in Heaven," she repeated, "please help us. We may be in danger, and we need help." She felt a faint heat begin to build in her chest. She continued in earnest. "Please help me know what to do to keep these children safe. I need to know what—" Suddenly, her head jerked up and her eyelids popped open. Thoughts and images flooded into her mind. She knew exactly what she needed to do.

Three minutes later, the rattling and clicking of the back door's lock stopped, and the hinges squealed as it slowly swung open.

"Hurry, kids. Down the ladder. Come on," Melena's panic-stricken voice commanded.

Two seconds later, footsteps hurried across the hardwood floor a short distance and stopped.

"It's okay, it's okay. Everybody quiet. Just sit still." Melena's voice was muffled and little more than a loud whisper, but it carried through the silent house.

After a moment, Melena heard the creak of the storm cellar's trap door as it opened and the thump of it falling flat on its back onto the floor. The aluminum ladder clanked as two sets of feet and hands descended it. Melena waited a beat and then scurried out from beneath the kitchen table and ran on her toes to the open trap door. She reached down and grabbed the ladder, pulling it up and out of the opening and tossing it onto the floor before slamming the trap door shut. The refrigerator was already pulled away from the wall. She got behind it and wheeled it over the trap door just as a hand pushed up on it. It only opened a few centimeters before hitting the bottom of the refrigerator and slamming back down.

"Okay, John," Melena called out as she began jamming pieces of furniture into the spaces around the refrigerator to secure it.

Muffled, angry voices from below began yelling threats. A gunshot blasted from below and shards of wood from the trap door scattered across the floor. Melena snatched the small box off of the kitchen counter and opened it up, calling her homing pigeon back to her. Immediately, the tiny blue particles seeped up through the floor and rematerialized into a tiny orb and returned to the box. She shoved the box back into her purse and threw the strap over her head and onto her shoulder. The little messenger had done its job – taking Melena's recorded voice into the storm cellar and leading the intruders after it.

Melena's hands flew to her head, covering her ears as more gunshots rang out. Just then, John turned the corner from the hallway, a wide-eyed Aaron in his arms. Elizabeth was right behind him, her little fingers clutching the bottom of his shirt. Joy poked her head around the corner just as Melena reached them.

"Okay, guys, we're going to run, okay?" She picked Elizabeth up and reached for Joy's hand. She considered that someone dangerous might be waiting for them at the front of the house, but something inside her told her to run. She unlocked the front door and pushed it open. She took Joy's hand again, and they ran across the front lawn. Melena scanned up and down the street. It was empty. They raced down the sidewalk, passing darkened homes until they came to one with lights on inside. "Right here, John." She turned into the driveway and ran up to the front porch. She beat her fist on the door, then turned to John. "Do you know who lives here?"

He nodded, his chest rising and falling rapidly. "The Delanys," he managed, between gasps for air.

A short, balding man in his mid-thirties opened the door and peered out.

"Can you help us?" Melena asked, trying to catch her own breath.

The man opened the door wider and noticed the children. He went up onto his toes trying to see behind Melena and the kids. “Of course. Come in.” They rushed past him as he held the door for them. He leaned out the doorway, looking up and down the street and then pushed the door shut behind him.

Chapter 47

It took Adam several minutes to realize that his teeth were in danger of being crushed by his jaw with how tightly he was clenching it. He made a conscious effort to relax, but his emotional state was beyond strained. Not only was he furious that someone had put Melena and his nieces and nephews in danger, but guilt ate at him for not doing a better job of protecting them. He asked himself how he could have let this happen. How could he have been so casual about leaving Melena and the children in such a vulnerable situation? He had been overconfident in the security of Independence and had underestimated those who wanted him and Melena to pay for what had happened over the past few weeks. He loathed himself for not having the foresight to see something like this coming. By bringing Melena to Independence, he had effectively put a target on her back as well as his own. Deep down, he knew that Senator Jaxon wasn't just going to forget that his daughter existed or let a rogue city and its outlaws get the better of him and make him look like a fool. Of course someone had come after her. The more he thought about it, the more surprised he was that this was the first attempt to take her. Encountering and capturing Colonel Winde just a few nights earlier should have clued him in that there would be more enemies who would breach the city's security. Melena had warned him as much.

Adam cringed as he listened to Melena and John recount the evening's events from outside the room where the sheriff was interviewing them. Esther and Paul must be sick with worry, he thought. He was ashamed to admit that he was relieved that he didn't have to be in the same room with them while they were being told about what had happened. He didn't want to see their anguished faces.

Finally, he heard Sheriff Tenby tell them to go home and get some sleep. He promised them that he would assign deputies to watch over both the Fransen home and Jivvy's apartment where Melena was staying. Adam wished he could be in two places at once. He too wanted to protect them all.

The door beeped and popped open. Paul pushed the door open with one hand and held it for his wife. He held a sleeping Aaron in the other arm, the little guy's head resting on his shoulder. His eyes met Adam's as Adam rose from his chair across the hall. Paul gave him a weak smile. Adam could only hold his gaze for a moment. Esther emerged from the room and saw Adam standing there. She walked to him with outstretched arms. He hugged her tightly, burying his face in her shoulder. "I'm so sorry," he muttered. "This is my fault."

"It wasn't your fault, Adam. It wasn't your fault," she soothed. "The Lord watched over us. Everyone is okay."

Adam blinked rapidly, trying to keep the moisture in his eyes from spilling over. He knew what she said was true, but it didn't take away the sting of the guilt he felt. He looked down and saw John looking down at the ground behind his mother. Adam took him by the arm and pulled him close. John wrapped his arms around Adam's waist and pressed his face against his abdomen. Adam pushed him back so he could look him in the face. "I couldn't be more proud of you, Johnny." His voice had gone husky. "You were a man tonight. Thanks for protecting your brother and sisters and Melena." John just nodded his head and looked away, embarrassed by the attention.

Joy and Elizabeth sauntered out of the room looking half asleep. "Hi, Adam," Joy greeted, mid-yawn. "Did you hear what happened?"

Adam tried to smile at her. "Yeah, I heard you were pretty brave, Joy-bug—Lizzy too."

"We were?" Joy asked, rubbing her eyes.

"That's what I heard."

"Well, I was mostly asleep."

"You look like you're about to go back to sleep right there on your feet," Adam teased.

She smiled and rubbed her eyes some more. "You were right about what you said to Lizzy before."

"What did I say?" Adam asked.

"That trouble would find Melena."

"Hmm," Adam grunted. "I guess I did say that, didn't I?"

Paul put his hand on Esther's back, urging her forward. "We'd better get these monkeys back in their cages."

"Yep," Esther agreed. "Let's go, guys."

Paul squeezed Adam's shoulder with his free hand as he walked past. "It's all right, bud."

Adam's throat tightened, and he gave Paul a wan smile. He could feel his eyes getting warm again. He turned to watch his family make their way out of the station. When he turned back, Melena stood in the doorway, watching him. For just a moment, he allowed his eyes to search hers. His mind flashed back to the first time he'd seen her eyes. He was being interrogated in his cell in Rugby and could barely stand to have his eyes open at all, but he couldn't forget hers. He looked at her now. His vision still allowed him to clearly make out every strand and spec of the blue hues that populated her irises. They were still beautiful and lustrous, but they were different now. They were a window into a soul with far more depth and character than before—a soul that Adam loved. Her mouth twitched and then formed into a warm smile. She tilted her head and gave him an almost imperceptible shrug of her shoulders.

"I'm sorry," Adam croaked, his voice breaking. "I should never have left you alone." He couldn't meet her eyes any longer, so he studied a black spot on the white and grey vinyl tile near her boot. “I’m such an idiot, Melena, and I’m sorry.”

In two steps, she was to him, her hands sliding from his waist up to his back. She pulled him close and laid her forehead on his chest. He breathed in the sweet scent of her hair as he pressed his nose into it and wrapped his arms around her shoulders.

She let out a short, breathy laugh. “Don’t be sorry, Adam. It wasn’t your fault.”

“Yeah, it—”

She cut him off. “No. No, it wasn’t. You can’t attach yourself to my hip and be with me all the time—though I’m not completely opposed to the idea.” She tightened her hold around his waist and looked up at him with a flirtatious grin. “Anyway, the kids and I weren’t left without protection.”

Adam narrowed his eyes. “Yes, you were. You didn’t have access to a weapon and all of the electronic security equipment failed. That is the definition of being left without protection.”

“No, Adam.” Her eyes gleamed with fervent intensity. She paused and then went on. “Do you think Esther and Paul asked God to protect their family at some point during the day today?”

Her question caught Adam by surprise. He thought of the morning and evening family prayers he had been a part of for years. “I’m sure they did.”

“Do you believe that God has the power to grant that request?”

Adam had to smile at the obvious role reversal. “You know I believe that.”

“Well, when those men were at the door, John asked me to pray so we would know what to do. So, I did. I didn’t just say words, either. I sort of … *channeled* God and tried to really speak to Him, and as I spoke, I knew He could hear me. He told me what to do, Adam. I saw in my mind what I needed to do. I don't know if I forgot that I had a homing pigeon in my purse or if I just assumed it wouldn't work because of the pulse that knocked out everything else that was electronic, but—"

"Well, the homing pigeon isn't really electronic," Adam began to explain, "it's part biological and—"

"Whatever." Melena interrupted him back. "Anyway, I knew it would work, and it saved us." She gave a slight shake of her head. "I mean, *it* didn't really save us." She paused and looked at him with complete sincerity. "God did." She searched his face, looking for some validation.

He reached up and took her face in his hands and smiled, tenderly. "I know He did." He leaned in and kissed her, gently. "I know He did."

Chapter 48

Adam's throat burned from the little bit of vomit his stomach had heaved into his mouth. The pungent body odor of the detainee—who was strapped to a chair at the opposite end of the small interrogation room inside the sheriff's office—wafted across the room and threatened to bring up Adam's entire dinner. It was times like these when Adam wished he could turn off the hyper-sensitivity of his senses.

Sheriff Tenby's bushy mustache looked like a caterpillar crawling across his lip as he spoke. "How long have you been in this city?" he drawled, sounding one-hundred percent like he had been born and raised in "*Missoura*".

"About a week," the gaunt-faced man in filthy clothes replied in a thick French accent.

The sheriff's voice was deep and even. "How did you get into the city?"

The man looked around the room at the other faces present. "I am not saying. Don't I get a lawyer?"

"No," Sheriff Tenby answered simply. "How did you get into the city?"

The man folded his arms and stared back defiantly at the sheriff.

"All right," the sheriff leaned back in his chair. "Have you retained the services of an attorney here in Independence or shall we provide you with one?"

"You will provide a lawyer for me, and I will consider answering your questions only in his presence," the French-accented man declared.

"Very well." Sheriff Tenby turned to Peter Gildrich, who was standing near the door. "Peter, would you be so kind as to invite Droven Harper to come in here and represent this man?"

"Certainly," Peter replied and let himself out the door.

The sheriff sat, silently, waiting for the man's appointed representation to join them before proceeding. Adam smiled to himself, knowing it wouldn't take long to find Droven since he was observing the interrogation from the next room. After thirty seconds, Peter pushed the door open and held it for Droven. Droven strolled in confidently, nodding formally at everyone in the room. Adam suppressed a grin as Droven tilted his head and offered an exaggerated nod in his direction. He sauntered over to face the detainee, reached for his fettered hand and shook it. "Droven Harper—a pleasure to meet you." The man nodded once back at him. "Sheriff, may I have a moment to confer with my client, please?"

Sheriff Tenby gestured with his hand for Droven to proceed. "By all means, sir."

Droven turned the detainee's chair around a hundred and eighty degrees, then took the empty chair next to it and dragged it across the white tiled floor until it faced the man. He slowly sank into it and sighed deeply, eyeing the man in front of him. "I took a moment to review your case before I came in, and it appears that you have only two options. First, you can choose to remain silent—stand your ground and hold out until formal charges are filed against you, and then you can stand trial." He paused to let what he had said sink in before continuing. "You will be incarcerated until a trial can be scheduled, and then you will have the opportunity to face the following charges: trespassing, tampering with city utilities, breaking and entering, vandalism, attempted kidnapping, attempted murder, discharging a weapon inside city limits, disturbing the peace and disregard for personal hygiene. If convicted, each charge carries a certain amount of jail time and substantial fines. There is an ample amount of evidence to convict you as well as several reliable witnesses, including law enforcement personnel. The likelihood of conviction for you and your accomplice is high, even considering my highly regarded talents as a defender."

Adam covered his mouth with his hand to conceal his smile. In a way, Droven was telling the truth. He was a talented defender. Perhaps not a credentialed lawyer, but he had been the leading tackler on their football team.

Droven paused for effect and then went on. "Your second option is to cooperate completely with the sheriff, telling him everything he wants to know and identifying the person or persons who hired you to perform this crime as well as their motives. As a consequence of choosing this option, you will likely be removed from the city of Independence and released." Droven lifted his chin and stared down at the man, awaiting his response. After a moment of silence, he went on in a matter-of-fact tone. "I wouldn't recommend staying in the jail here—well, it's really more of a dungeon than a jail. The cuisine consists mainly of the severed limbs of the prisoner who scores lowest in the weekly trivia game."

The detainee's eyes widened, his mouth falling open. A sly grin played on Droven's lips, stretching into a wide smile. "I'm joking, of course, about the food, but it is strictly British—mainly blood pudding."

The man's eyebrows shot up. "So, you are saying if I answer this man's questions and identify who sent me, I will go free?"

Droven nodded his head, one eyebrow raised as if considering the question. "I believe that is quite likely, although you would be forced to endure a severe reprimand for your actions, and if you ever returned to Independence, you would be immediately fed to the prisoners residing inside our dungeon. No questions asked."

The man looked confused for a moment, but opted not to clarify. He turned his head as far as he could over his shoulder to address the sheriff. "I will answer your questions if you will let me go."

Sheriff Tenby gestured with his head "Turn him back around, please, *counselor*."

"Yes, sir," Droven complied, twisting the man's chair around to face the sheriff again.

The sheriff looked down at the table and sighed, his bushy gray eyebrows concealing his tired gray eyes. "Let's start with your name this time. What is your name?"

The man inclined his head. "Je m'appelle Adrien Batiste."

"And you're from Montreal." The sheriff stated, matter-of-factly.

"Oui." Adrien Batiste pulled his eyebrows together. "I told you this?"

"Now you did. All right, how did you get into the city?"

"Through the tunnel from Kansas City."

The sheriff looked disgusted. "You posed as a refugee?"

"I did what?"

"You pretended to need help? Is that why you were brought here?"

A corner of Batiste's lips turned up in a half-grin, as if he had done something clever. "We didn't pretend. We were hungry. We were offered one year's worth of food credits each to bring back the Jaxon girl dead or alive."

"You and your friend came together?"

"Oui."

"Who offered you extra rations?"

Batiste hesitated then decided to continue. "It was a police man, but not one in a uniform. He was a … big-shot police man."

"Who was he? What was his name?"

"I don't know his name."

"What did he look like?"

"Uh, he was thin, brown hair, but going bald. His face looked like this:" He sucked in his cheeks and made a fish-face.

Sheriff Tenby turned to look at Adam. Adam nodded back at him—a silent communication that he recognized who Batiste was describing.

The sheriff turned back to Batiste. "Where did this police man recruit you for the job? In Montreal?"

"No, we moved from Montreal last year. We have been living in Kansas City now in an old warehouse. He just walked into the building one day and asked us if we are hungry."

The sheriff nodded, slowly. "Where were you to take Ms. Jaxon once you had her?"

"We were supposed to contact someone on the page he gave us when we had the Jaxon girl and then meet them tomorrow night in a parking lot near the west wall. He said there would be a truck that would take us out of here and back to Kansas City, and there we would receive our credits."

Adam pushed off of the wall he was leaning on and rushed to the table, leaning over it and getting right in Batiste's face. "Who are you meeting? Who are you to turn the girl over to?" He had to hold his breath once he had spoken as Batiste's stench threatened to knock him out.

Batiste leaned back in his chair, trying to create some space between himself and Adam. "I don't know." He shrugged his shoulders. "Maybe the police man, maybe someone else. He just put a code into the page and said to send an image of her when we had her."

Adam grabbed a handful of Batiste's shirt and pulled him halfway across the table. "An image? He wanted you to send an image of the girl?"

"Yes," Batiste answered, meekly. "So he would know we had the right girl."

"Were you going to kill her? Did he want an image of her dead body?" Adam shouted in the man's face. He looked at the hand that gripped Batiste's shirt and noticed he was shaking.

"Easy there, Adam." Sheriff Tenby patted Adam's arm. "Why don't you let go, and let's give him a chance to answer."

Adam released the horrified man and eased his elbows off of the table. He straightened back to his full height and took a step back.

Batiste leaned back in his chair again, keeping his eyes on Adam. "We didn't want to kill her. The police man said to bring her either way, but we didn't want to hurt her."

"When were you to deliver Ms. Jaxon? What time?" Sheriff Tenby demanded in a calm voice.

"Eight o'clock."

Adam took a deep breath to calm himself. An idea began to take shape in his mind. He turned to Peter Gildrich. "I'll bet whoever is expecting to meet these two would be disappointed if they don't show."

Peter looked puzzled for a moment and then nodded his understanding. "Well, then I think they ought to be there."

Adam leaned over the table again toward Batiste, his eyes ablaze. "You're going to send the image and let them know that you have the girl and you will deliver her as planned. *Comprendre*?"

Chapter 49

Melena craned her head in the direction of the cheering and applause, even though she knew her view would be no better than the last time there was an eruption. Anyway, they were a good 2 kilometers away from the gathering. Half of the city had come together to celebrate the victory of a Senatorial election in the Mountain Dominion. One of the party's candidates had won the seat, dethroning a three-term Senator. Melena knew that Senator Bills had been critical of the President and several other North American Senators over their decision to resurrect the space exploration program and locate the operation in the Mountain West. He didn't want the added burden of staffing and overseeing the program. It appeared that Senator Bills' punishment had been a fair election, in which he had been ousted.

The win was progress, but Melena knew the President and some of the more powerful Senators were still pulling all of the strings. It was likely that some of the other candidates associated with the Independence group would also have been elected if the voting had had any degree of integrity. Under different circumstances, Melena would be with her mother right now celebrating the victory. Melena and Jivvy had decided not to tell their mother or Jivvy's father about Melena's attempted abduction or their current operation. They would fill them in once it was all over.

Sitting next to Melena in an office building lobby, across the street from the meeting place appointed by Colonel Winde, Adam spoke into the palms of his hands as he rubbed his eyes in frustration. "I don't think I like this idea after all, Peter."

Peter looked just as flustered. "It's *your* plan, Adam, and I don't see another way to discover how these people plan to get out of the city. We have to sell the abduction to find out who is involved and how much they know."

Melena didn't like the idea either, but the alternative she had suggested had fallen flat. She shuddered now, remembering how it had felt posing as a corpse for an image to send to the people who wanted her. She wasn't sure if she could do it again, but was trying to be brave. "Please, just let me do it. I want to," she lied, giving it one last effort.

"Hey!" Jivvy nearly shouted. "There's no debate here. We're doing it the way we planned, and everyone just needs to get on board with it."

"Heaven and Droven are already in position," Peter argued. "If anything goes wrong, they will take out their targets. Now, Jivvy is plenty capable. Let's show a little bit of confidence in her."

Melena could feel the tension in Adam's body as she leaned her shoulder against his. He closed his eyes and pinched the bridge of his nose with his thumb and index finger, still trying to work out a solution in his mind. "What if we rigged up some sort of harness they could wear around their necks so I didn't look as heavy for them to carry?"

"We don't have time to engineer something like that, Adam," Peter countered.

Jivvy was exasperated and was nearly shouting again. "That's just stupid! You're like six inches taller than Melena! Now, let's go. We have ten minutes."

Adam blew out a long breath in defeat. "All right, Jiv. You're doing it, but if I smell so much as a hint of distrust from them, or if these morons try to alert them …" He gestured with his head toward the two ragged Canadians sitting behind the glass wall in the next room. "We abort. Got it?"

Jivvy snorted. "Who's to say what *you* might smell? Could be a cat pooping two blocks away."

Melena had to smile, despite the obvious tension among the team. Her little sister was one brave girl, and Melena knew Jivvy could handle herself in a dangerous situation much better than she could. Still, she hated the idea of having Jivvy in such a vulnerable position, in the hands of bad people.

Melena let her mind drift back to another plan she had suggested to Adam earlier in the day. She had asked him to escape the continent with her and draw all the government attention away from Independence. They could make it look like they were headed to Japan by jet, but they would actually travel by boat to Brazil and hide out there. Adam had friends there who could help them. Adam had dismissed the idea, of course, but not before rewarding her creativity with smile and a kiss. He told her that it sounded like fun, but running away wouldn't help the cause of restoring freedom here. He reminded her that he loved this country and would never abandon it. Melena had known what his response would be before she even asked, but figured she would throw it out to him anyway. Her heart fluttered at the idea of hiding out with Adam. She pictured the two of them nestled away in a little country cottage in some remote Brazilian town. She was forced out of her fantasy by the sound of her name being called.

"Melena?" Peter called to her again.

"Yes. Sorry," she replied.

Sweat was beading up on Peter's scalp and slowly dripping down onto his forehead. She wondered how much of it was caused by the muggy heat of the evening and how much was due to the stress of the situation. "You understand that you are to remain out of sight no matter what happens, right?"

Melena nodded. "Yeah. I'll be inside the shop on the corner with you until they secure the bad people."

He sighed. "I really don't like having you anywhere near these people, but I don't want you out of our sight either."

"It's okay. I'll just stick close to you and wait until it's all over."

She was confident in Jivvy and Adam and the others. They would catch whoever was coming to meet her would-be kidnappers, find out how they planned to escape the city and take them to a cell in the sheriff's office. Despite her confidence in the team, she remained concerned about her sister's safety. She took Jivvy by the arm and pulled her aside. "You've done stuff like this before, right? You know what you're doing?"

Jivvy rolled her eyes and inhaled deeply before blowing her breath out through her teeth. "Yes, Melena. Stop freaking out."

"I'm not freaking out," Melena insisted as calmly as she could, "I just don't like that you might be in danger because of me."

Jivvy shook her head. "I won't be in danger because of *you*, okay? It's my job to keep the people in this city safe from disgusting, murderous animals like the ones who broke into the Fransen's house to take you and like the ones who hired them to do it. We're going to end this tonight."

Melena looked into the fiery eyes of the little sister she was just getting to know. She wondered what Jivvy must have been like as a child. Had she always been so tough and determined? Had she preferred to play with guns and swords over dolls and dress-ups? There was so much about this confident, beautiful young woman that Melena didn't know. She wanted to know her. She respected her. She watched as Jivvy tucked her long, blond hair into the cap that Melena had worn the previous night when they had taken an image of her to send through the kidnapper's page to confirm her capture and death. Jivvy's face was heavily made up. The tone of her skin was sort of a bluish-white with a light purple shade under her eyes. Melena had been made up the same way the night before. She and Jivvy did not look a lot alike, but there was enough of a resemblance with the make-up for Jivvy to pass as Melena.

Peter's head snapped up suddenly, and he put his finger to his ear. "Sheriff says Colonel Winde's cell was found empty at last check. He's not sure how he got out, but a red delivery truck was seen leaving the area of the station. Same truck just passed his checkpoint a mile and a half from here. It's probably headed this way. Let's get the Canadians ready."

So, they had busted Colonel Winde out and were coming to collect her dead body before getting out of town, Melena thought. She reasoned that whoever was leading this group must be pretty confident in their ability to get outside the walls. *She* wasn't even sure how that was done. She had traveled through the Kansas City tunnel when she had left Independence, but a delivery truck wouldn't fit through it. It would be tight for a Vector. She gave Jivvy's forearm a squeeze before leaving her. "Be safe."

"I'm bulletproof. *You* be safe and stay out of sight, Melena. No matter what."

"I will," Melena promised, jogging down the sidewalk to the little flower shop where she and Peter would observe the operation.

Chapter 50

The last red-orange light of the setting sun was beginning to fade as Adam's eyes met Jivvy's for a brief moment before her face was covered with the black fleece blanket he was rolling her up in. He thought she looked ready. No fear, just anticipation and focus—typical Jivvy.

Adam turned to the two Canadians who had attempted to kidnap Melena the previous night. His voice was little more than a growl. "Understand that there are multiple snipers positioned in buildings all around this spot. If I even think that you're trying to give us away, I will give them the signal. They will not miss. Understand?" Both men nodded. Adam continued his warning. "Even after you're in the truck, I'll hear you. If you betray us at any point and put my friend here in danger …" He indicated Jivvy wrapped in the blanket next to them. "I will hunt you. And punish you. Is that clear?" They both nodded, vigorously. From their expressions, Adam decided to believe that he had scared them enough to ensure their cooperation. "Okay, there's a truck about thirty seconds away. It's probably them. Just act like you've fulfilled your assignment. For all they know, you have." He glanced down the street in the direction the truck would be coming from. He could hear the engine sounds and tires on pavement growing louder. "Here we go." He backed up and took his position in the office building lobby.

"Adam …" Droven's calm voice was in Adam's ear through the coms. "We got this."

Adam looked up at the ceiling as if he could see Droven in his position through three floors of office building. "Yeah," he sighed.

"You okay, Jivvy?" Peter's voice came over the shared coms.

"It's pretty warm in here," Jivvy complained. "It's putting me to sleep."

Adam smiled. He had just seen her face. She was calm, but there's no way she was sleepy. She was just trying to show off her steely nerves now.

The sounds of the approaching truck grew louder in Adam's ears. He glanced over at the flower shop where Melena was hiding with Peter. The street curved just enough that he could see into the shop's front window. Neither of them was visible. He breathed a little easier, but still felt the anxiety of being responsible for extracting Jivvy once the truck made its move to exit the city. He would have to stay close. He knew he was fast, but if the truck made it outside the walls and onto a highway, it was doubtful he could keep up with it. He determined not to give it a chance to leave the city at all.

The red box-truck slowed as it approached. Adam peered into the driver-side window, which was darkly tinted. In spite of the tint, his eyes could still make out the features of the driver. Unfortunately, Adam didn't recognize him. His head and shoulders blocked Adam's view of the person in the passenger seat.

The truck gradually pulled into the small parking lot and came to a stop. The Canadians picked up the black fleece blanket with Jivvy inside—one at her shoulders and one at her feet—and scrambled across the street. The rear door of the truck rolled up, and two men jumped out to meet them. One of the men was tall and thick with sandy blond hair. He gestured with his hand for the Canadians to hurry. The other man had one arm in a sling. Adam immediately recognized the deep-set grey eyes and receding hairline of Colonel Winde. The muscles in Adam's neck tightened at the sight of him. It took all of the discipline he could muster to keep himself from darting across the street and pounding the man. The large blond man helped the Canadians lift the black bundle up into the truck. A woman with dark brown hair leaned out of the truck to help pull the body inside. The dark hair hung over her profile, hiding her face from Adam's view. Once the body was inside, the four men climbed in, and the blond man reached up and pulled the door shut. The truck immediately began to roll forward. The pick-up had occurred much quicker than Adam had anticipated. No words were spoken, and no one had looked at the body before loading it.

"Okay, Adam." Peter's voice came through the coms. "Stay out of his mirrors and cameras, but keep as close as you can."

Adam crouched, preparing to move. He halted at the sound of screeching tires as the truck skidded to a stop. Five seconds passed, and then the truck's rear door rolled back up. The black bundle with Jivvy still inside rolled out of the truck and landed on the pavement with a thud. The blanket fell away from Jivvy's head and shoulders, but she remained on her back and kept still. The blond man shoved Batiste and his partner out of the truck. Both men fell, but quickly got to their feet. The dark-haired woman Adam had seen emerged from the back of the truck, jumping down to the pavement to stand next to Jivvy. The woman looked up and down the street and at the nearby buildings. Adam studied her face. Her dark eyes were droopy, and her nose was unusually long. She looked different to Adam, but it only took a few seconds for him to recognize her.

The woman pulled a handgun from the belt behind her back and pointed it at the black bundle at her feet. "It was a good try, Adam." The woman's low voice echoed off of the tall buildings surrounding her.

Adam heard Melena's gasp from inside the flower shop. Fortunately, it wasn't loud enough for anyone outside the shop to hear.

The woman continued searching the surrounding buildings with her eyes. "If only it had been someone besides me in the truck, right?"

Adam suppressed the string of curse words that nearly made it to his tongue.

"I have a shot." Heaven's voice came over the coms. "Just say the word."

"Hold on, Heaven," Peter's whispered voice answered. "Jivvy isn't clear of the others inside the truck."

Adam shook his head, realizing why he hadn't recognized her right away. The facial tattoos were gone, and the skin on her face was a light bronze.

Hava pointed her gun at the Canadians. "Kneel," she commanded. The two men complied. Hava turned with a grin as she continued speaking to the empty buildings. "I'll make you a deal, Adam. You come out here and get in the truck with me, and I won't shoot all of your friends here."

"No!" Melena exclaimed in a loud whisper.

"We'll start with this one." Hava cocked her weapon and pointed it back down at Jivvy's chest. "You've got five seconds to decide. One …"

"Hold your positions," Peter whispered over the coms. "Let this play out."

"Two."

Adam heard a voice inside the truck give the driver an order. "If she fires, wait for her to get back in the truck and then head for the gate as fast as you can." It was Colonel Winde's voice.

"Three."

Adam swallowed hard and looked down at his hands. They were trembling. He realized that his plan had been poorly thought out. He hadn't counted on someone who knew Melena being in the truck. Jivvy's face would have likely fooled Colonel Winde or the other men, who likely had only seen images of Melena.

The grin faded from Hava's face and was replaced with a scowl. "Four."

Heaven's voice was back in Adam's ear. "I'm going to take her out."

"Negative, Heaven. Stand down," Peter demanded.

"Five."

Without a moment's hesitation, Hava looked down at Jivvy and pulled the trigger three times. The gunshots were nearly deafening to Adam's ears. He saw Jivvy's legs flinch from the impact of the bullets as they hit her in the chest.

Almost instantly, Adam heard a horrified shriek come from the flower shop. "No! Jivvy!"

Adam turned to see the glass door swing open and Melena burst out of the shop. Peter was struggling, unsuccessfully, to grab onto her and pull her back. "Jivvy!" she screamed again, running into the street toward her sister.

Adam's heart stopped at the sight of Melena out in the open. He shoved the door of the office building open and burst out onto the sidewalk. "Melena, stop!" he yelled to her.

Adam saw Hava turn toward the sound of Melena's voice, a wicked grin reappearing on her face. She raised the gun and fixed it on the girl running toward her. Adam lunged forward, sprinting for all he was worth. Two shots fired simultaneously as Adam reached Melena, grabbing her and picking her up off of her feet. Melena grunted as the breath was forced from her lungs from the impact of his body slamming into hers. Adam felt a searing pain on the right side of his back, but kept moving. He carried Melena the rest of the way across the street, past the truck and stopped in an alley between two brick buildings. He set her down on the pavement next to the closest building and took her face in both of his hands. "Are you okay?"

She was breathless, but nodded, her eyes wide with fear. He peered out from around the edge of the building and could see Hava's still body lying next to Jivvy's. The Canadians were still on their knees, looking as terrified as they were confused.

"Adam!" Melena exclaimed.

He turned back to her, and she held her hand up to him, her fingers glistening red with blood. He gasped and turned to her, his eyes searching her body. "Where? Where is it?"

"Not me." She reached over and pulled his shirt up in the back. "It's you, Adam!"

Just then, Adam heard the truck's engine rev and turned to see it lurch forward. It only made it a few feet before Heaven's and Droven's bullets exploded the tires and a bright blue bolt from a lightning rod struck the hood, sending sparks showering down across the street.

Adam heard a voice inside the truck begin barking out orders. "Our priority is the bag. We're getting this bag out of the city. I'm going on foot. We got multiple snipers in the two buildings across the street. You three, get behind the truck and provide cover fire. Winde, I want you and Taylor to go after Winter and the Jaxon girl. Take them out and proceed to the gate. It'll be open when you arrive. Let's move!"

Adam grabbed Melena by the arm. "I need to get you out of here." He pulled her to her feet and headed deeper into the alley.

"Adam, stop," Melena protested. "You need a doctor! You're shot!"

Adam heard gunfire blasting into the windows of the office buildings behind them and footsteps on the pavement. The rhythm of the two sets of footsteps was unusually rapid—Winde and Taylor, he assumed. Winde had been implanted with a stamp, giving him extreme quickness. Adam figured that whoever Taylor was, he must have one too.

Adam quickly decided that there was no point in trying to outrun the two men while dragging Melena behind him. He noticed a doorway in the building to his right that appeared to be deep enough to conceal Melena. He pulled her into it and pressed her up against the metal door. “Don’t move from here until a member of our team comes for you,” he instructed.

“Adam, wait,” Melena began, but before she could finish, he was gone.

Chapter 51

Melena covered her ears as the sound of gun blasts rang through the alley. She peered around the corner of the doorway, silently praying that none of the shots had found their target. Two men stood in the opening of the alleyway firing hand guns in the direction of the blurry figure sprinting across the alley toward the adjacent building. Adam found a door and threw it open—bullets ricocheting off its metal surface—and disappeared inside. The gunmen pursued him. Melena drew herself back as close to the building as she could in order to stay out of sight. When she was certain that the running footsteps were headed to the building that Adam had entered and not toward her, she peeked around the corner again. She could see the men more clearly now. She recognized Colonel Winde, his arm still in a sling. She didn't recognize the other man, but he was tall and blond with a thick neck and chest.

The blond man made it to the door first and reached for the handle. Just as he was about to grip it, the door swung open, striking him in the forehead and sending him reeling backwards into Colonel Winde. The two men tripped over one another and fell to the pavement, tangled in each other's legs. Adam sprang out from behind the door. Moving with tremendous speed, he kicked the blond man's arm, sending his gun hurling into the alley. With his other foot, Adam stepped on Colonel Winde's wrist, causing him to cry out and drop his weapon. After that, it was difficult for Melena to determine exactly what was happening. All three men moved with blinding quickness. She saw fists and feet in motion, some being blocked and some connecting, accompanied by grunts and groans.

After a few seconds, she saw Adam's foot slam into Colonel Winde's chest, sending him sprawling into the alley. Adam spun and kicked the blond man's legs out from under him. Before the man even hit the ground, Adam was on top of him. The man raised his arms to try and shield his face as Adam's fists pummeled him.

Melena flinched at the sound of Colonel Winde's voice echoing off of the buildings' walls. "That's enough!" He was back on his feet, the blond man's gun in his hand and pointed at Adam's head. Adam froze.

"Get up," Winde commanded.

Adam raised his hands, palms forward and got to his feet. The blond man rolled onto his side, his hands still covering his face.

"Where is she?" Winde demanded.

"Where's who?" Adam asked between breaths, his chest rising and falling rapidly.

"Where's the Jaxon girl?" Winde barked, taking a step toward Adam.

"Oh," Adam breathed, "she's long gone—probably to the Sheriff's office by now. Good thing for you. Don't you think the Senator would have been a little upset if one of you had killed his little girl?"

Winde smiled. "Us? No, no, it won't be us. See, the story will be that your people wouldn't let her escape with all of the intel she has now. No, it'll be your people. We're just trying to bring her back safe to her daddy." He chuckled to himself.

"You don't really think he would go for that," Adam argued. "She's already been here and left once before."

Winde shrugged. "Maybe so, but we have all of these eye witnesses now."

Adam didn't respond. Melena watched the blond man raise himself to a crouch behind Adam.

"Weeell," Winde drawled, "if you're not going to tell us where she is, I don't think you're of any further use to us. We'll just have to find her on our own." He grinned, wickedly. "Anyway, I seem to remember making you a promise."

Melena's heart stopped, and a desperate scream ripped from her throat. "Adam!"

Melena watched as a distinct movement from each man seemed to happen simultaneously; at the sound of her voice, the blond man stood up straight glancing in her direction; Adam dropped to the ground; and Colonel Winde's arm recoiled behind the force of the weapon he had fired. Then, from flat on his stomach, Adam retrieved the gun Colonel Winde had lost earlier and fired twice, just as the man behind him crumpled to the ground. The echo of the gunshots faded into silence. As if in slow motion, Colonel Winde's good arm dropped to his side, the gun in his hand falling to the pavement. His knees buckled, and his limp body fell forward.

Melena gasped at the sight of all three men lying motionless on the ground. After a second or two, Adam groaned and pushed himself up onto his knees. Melena exhaled in relief and ran across the alley to him. "Adam! Are you okay?"

Adam looked dazed as she reached him. He was kneeling up staring at Colonel Winde's body in front of him. His eyes and cheeks were red and swollen and blood was running out of his nose.

Melena knelt beside him. "Hey, are you okay?" She gently took his chin in her hand and turned his face toward hers.

He stared at her blankly for a moment. "I shot him," he whispered.

Melena glanced over at Colonel Winde and then back at Adam. "I know. It's okay."

"I think he's dead."

"I think so, too." She pushed his hair back from off of his forehead. "What about you? How are you?"

Adam looked down at himself, his hands absently searching his chest and abdomen. "I'm good."

Melena remembered the bullet wound she had discovered earlier on Adam's back and leaned back to examine it. She was amazed to see the skin already closing in around clumps of dried blood.

"I think it just grazed me," Adam muttered. "It's fine."

Melena noticed the blond man's still body lying in a heap behind Adam.

Adam looked over at him as well. "I saw the tendons in Winde's wrist tighten as he was pulling the trigger, so I hit the deck. I didn't even think about the other guy being behind me."

Melena put her hand on his cheek and turned his head to face her. "It's okay, Adam. They were both trying to kill you. They would have killed me too. They were bad guys."

Adam nodded, slowly. "I know."

She traced the lines on his face with her fingers, trying to read the faraway look in his eyes.

Abruptly, his head snapped up, and his eyes glanced up the alley. It almost looked to Melena like a switch had turned on in his head. He jumped to his feet and pulled her up by the arm. "Yeah, I'm okay. What's going on over there? I don't hear any more shooting."

"What?" Melena asked with a confused expression.

Adam pointed to his ear and mouthed "*Droven.*"

She nodded, comprehending that there was a voice in his ear over the coms.

"Were they all contained?" After a beat, he turned to look at Melena with panic-stricken eyes. "I have to get that runner."

"Who? Adam, what runner? What do you mean?"

"Inside the truck, I heard whoever was in charge giving orders to the others, and he said he was going to get out of the city with a bag. He said the bag was their priority."

"A bag?" Melena asked. "What's in it?"

"I don't know, but it was important to them, and that can't be good for us." He took her hand and urged her forward. "Come on. We need to go."

Melena tried to keep up with Adam as he pulled her along. Her heart suddenly sank as a realization of the previous scene returned to her. "Jivvy!" she cried out, blinking quickly as tears began to blur her vision. She felt Adam's pace quicken. Her legs were moving so fast that she worried she might fall.

Adam was having a conversation with someone over the coms. "How could this happen?" she heard him asking. "That would compromise the entire city!" He looked back at Melena with a look of overwhelming concern. "Yes, sir. I won't, sir."

As they emerged from the alleyway, Melena had to dodge the pieces of glass and other debris that littered the street. The smoldering truck, riddled with bullet holes, was at the center of activity as sheriff's deputies shouted to each other and rushed about.

"Peter!" Adam shouted. Melena spotted Peter in the middle of the street barking out orders. He turned his head at the sound of Adam's voice. Abruptly, Adam stopped and pulled Melena around to face him. "I have to go. Peter can tell you what's going on. Stay close to him."

"Adam, wait." Melena tightened her grip on his arm. "You need to get to a doctor. Where are you going?"

He shook his head, intensely. "There's no time." Without another word, he took her face in his hands and pressed his lips hard against hers. He wrapped his arms around her waist like a vise. Breathlessly, he pulled away from her. "I love you," he choked out, touching her face with his fingers.

Without waiting for a response, he spun out of her arms and catapulted himself into a full sprint down the street. After a second, he disappeared into darkness.

Chapter 52

"I love you, too." Melena stared at the spot where Adam was last visible for a few seconds before turning and running to Peter. "Peter!" she called out. He was in the midst of an intense conversation with a man in a suit that Melena didn't recognize when she reached him. She grabbed his arm. "Peter, where did Adam go?" she asked between labored intakes of breath.

He turned to her, taking hold of both of her arms. "One of their men broke our containment. He has stolen technology and artifacts that we can't afford to lose. He's on foot. Adam went after him."

Melena scanned the area around the truck. The two female bodies that had been lying behind it were gone. "Where's Jivvy?"

Peter pointed to the office building where they had gathered earlier in the evening. "She's in there."

"Is she …?" Melena asked, her voice breaking.

Peter opened his mouth to answer and then reached his hand up to cup over his ear. "Droven, back him up! All personnel, head west. Keep that wall sealed!" he shouted.

Melena didn't wait for an answer. She turned toward the office building and ran up to the tall glass door, throwing it open and scurrying inside. She pulled up quickly, nearly stepping on a figure covered by a gray wool blanket. There were two more blankets next to it covering human forms. Melena's throat became so tight she could hardly breathe. "Jivvy?" she whispered. Warm tears streaked her cheeks as she reached for a corner of the blanket near the head of the closest body and began to pull it back, slowly.

"You don't want to see that."

Melena flinched at the sound of the voice behind her and then whirled around to face its owner. For a long moment, she wondered if she could possibly be seeing a spirit. Heaven Goodrich had taught her that at death the spirit leaves the physical body behind, but despite the pale white make-up, the face before her looked far too smug to belong to a dead girl. "Jivvy?"

"What were you thinking running out of that shop?" Jivvy asked. Melena gaped at her. Jivvy grinned. "Close your mouth, Melena. You look ridiculous."

Melena slowly closed her mouth, her eyebrows pulling together. "I saw her shoot you … like, three times." Jivvy just shrugged. Melena took a step toward her and threw her arms around her little sister's neck and held her.

After a few moments, Jivvy pulled back from her. "You need to pay attention. I told you I was bulletproof." Jivvy pulled her shirt up, revealing a black mesh body suit. She patted her head with her palm. "Even this stylish cap could have repelled a bullet."

Melena reached out to touch the mesh material covering Jivvy's abdomen. It was scaly and cold and reminded Melena of snakeskin. "I thought you were just trying to sound tough when you said that."

"I was." Jivvy smiled. "I *am* tough—getting shot at close range feels like getting kicked in the chest by a horse."

"How do you know that?" Melena asked, innocently. "Have you been kicked by a horse before?"

"What?" Jivvy looked incredulous. "No, I just have an imagination."

Melena looked back at the blanket-covered bodies. "Is she one of these?"

"Who?" Jivvy asked.

"The woman who shot you."

"Oh. No. I think she's lying out on the sidewalk." Jivvy pointed out the front window. "Those three deputies are watching her."

"Why don't they just bring her in here with the others?" Melena asked

"'Cuz she's not dead," Jivvy answered matter-of-factly. "She's not even hurt all that bad. The bullet passed through right under her collarbone."

Melena inhaled deeply through her nose. Anger began to boil in her chest. Her neck tensed, and her fists clenched and unclenched. "Excuse me." Melena turned and stormed out the door and onto the sidewalk. One of the deputies was kneeling at Hava's side, applying handcuffs, while the other two guarded her with weapons drawn. Melena stood over Hava, looking down at her as she squirmed and threatened the deputy. She went still at the sight of Melena. A look of surprise flashed across her face, but it was soon replaced with a smirk. Melena reached down and smudged the bronze make-up from Hava's face, revealing the dark ink beneath it.

Melena exhaled through her teeth. "You know what, Hava? It would be really easy for me to just kick you right in the face right now."

"Go ahead," Hava growled. "Take your best shot."

"Part of me thinks it would make me feel better. You're willing to murder, just to create a higher probability of your gaining power. I think that's genuinely pathetic. The other part of me—the part that's winning—pities you. I look at you and the choices you've made and I know now that you're going to have to account for those choices either in this life or the next, and that's sad for you."

The breath burst from Hava's mouth, her pursed lips spraying saliva over her face. She closed her eyes and let out a laugh from deep down in her belly. "Oh, Melena, you must have been so easy for these freaks to brainwash. The fact that you are that gullible is what's sad." She laughed again. "Is God going to strike me down for my wickedness, Melena? Am I going to hell?"

Melena had heard enough. She shook her head and turned her back on Hava, who continued shouting at her as she walked away.

"You think you've won? You're nothing! These people and this city are nothing! You're all going to be leveled in a few minutes anyway." She belly laughed again.

Melena took a deep breath to clear her mind and suddenly remembered the wild intensity in Adam's eyes, the finality of his kiss before he had rushed away. In the moment, her concern for Jivvy had pushed the anxiety she felt for Adam aside. It returned now like a heavy weight, pressing down on her heart.

Jivvy was outside standing on the sidewalk when Melena returned. "What's going on with Adam?" Melena asked. "Is he okay?"

Jivvy shook her head. "I'm not sure. I just found out that the man he's pursuing is carrying a device that he stole from us that's capable of overriding our security measures. He could use it to disarm the wall and shut down the canopy grid above us."

Melena gasped. "With the canopy down, they could just send Hummingbirds into the city."

Jivvy nodded. "The wall has gates in various locations too. We shoot projections in front of them when we open them, so no one on the outside can see in. It just looks like our vehicles disappear into the wall. If he shuts those down, he could expose the gates to ground vehicles as well. We could be invaded by air and land."

Melena closed her eyes and prayed silently that Adam would catch the man with the bag and return to her in one piece.

Chapter 53

The man Adam had been chasing placed the security override device back into the large black leather duffle bag and got to his feet. Overhead, the lasers in the grid flashed blue one by one, as if in a wave, beginning at the west gate, as they began to deactivate. Light flooded through the space in the wall where the gate stood open. From two hundred yards away, Adam could see a unit of Federal Police agents making their way toward the opening on foot. Behind them, a long row of armored vehicles waited in a single file line.

"Droven," Adam whispered, "are you close?"

"About sixty more seconds," came the reply through the coms.

"The gate's open. A unit of foot soldiers is close and it looks like around fifty armored vehicles behind them. I've gotta take our man out now and get that gate shut."

Without wasting another second, Adam bolted as fast as he could toward the man who was making his way toward the gate's entrance. He could hear the crunch of tiny stones under his feet as they flew down the gravel road. Despite the slight noise, the man had not detected him. Three more seconds and Adam would reach him. He prepared for impact. A fraction of a second before Adam barreled into the man, he turned, and Adam saw a bright yellow-orange flash. A deafening *bang* ripped through the silent night air. Adam hit the man at full speed and sent them both sailing through the air and skidding across the gravel road.

When Adam came to a stop, he couldn't ignore the scalding pain in his left forearm. He looked down at it. Blood gushed from a jagged bullet wound. To Adam, it felt like a white-hot spike had been driven through the center of his forearm. He turned his arm over to see the exit wound. It looked fairly clean, but the pain was debilitating. He closed his eyes tightly and laid his head down on the gravel, wincing at the excruciating burning.

Pulling his focus back, he suddenly realized that he had to get up or the man who had shot him would either finish the job or get away. Adam rolled onto his left side and was about to stand up when a large boot pressed down firmly over the wound, pinning his arm to the ground. Adam cried out as the intensity of the scorching pain doubled with the pressure of the boot.

"This seems eerily familiar, Winter …" The hoarse voice was familiar to Adam. "Me standing over you with you at my mercy. Oh, it was in the tunnel. I was about to put a bullet in your leg. Boy, I wish I had done that. It's really quite rare that we get second chances like this."

Adam didn't need to look at the man standing above him to know who he was. "Marshal Marbury?" He looked up to see the gun that had shot him in the forearm now pointed at his right thigh. "Get off my arm!" Adam's right fist was a blur as it flew through the air and connected with the side of the Marshal's right knee. The crack of another gunshot rang in Adam's ears, but he felt nothing. Marbury had missed. The Marshal howled in pain as he dropped to the ground. Still on the ground himself, Adam searched for the bag. He spotted it about fifteen feet away. Some of its contents had spilled out onto the ground, including a white plastic tube about three inches in diameter and two feet long.

Adam heard the whir of a solo-rider coming toward him quickly. He glanced over at Marshal Marbury who was clutching his knee with both hands, his gun on the ground beside him. Adam rolled toward him and snatched up the gun with his right hand. As he raised it, the Marshal swatted it away, sending the weapon flying across the road into the tall grass at its edge. In almost the same motion, his elbow crashed into Adam's cheek, whipping his head backward. The Marshal was on top of him in an instant, his fist cocked back to deliver a blow.

"All right! We can do this one of two ways …"

Marshal Marbury swung his head around to see who was there. No sooner did he take his eyes off Adam than Adam's fist slammed into the side of his head. The Marshal's body went limp, and he fell onto his face in the gravel.

"Okay, I guess there are *three* ways we can do it." Droven lowered his sniper rifle and smiled at Adam.

Adam turned his head toward the open gate. "Get the gate shut!" he commanded, pointing at the bag.

Droven raced to the bag and dug through its contents until he found the security override device. The light from its screen illuminated his face as he began entering the series of required codes. Before he could finish, several small puffs of dust erupted from the ground in front of him, followed immediately by the crackle of automatic weapon fire in the distance.

"Droven, get outta here with that!" Adam shouted. "Get out of range! Now!" Droven shot Adam a conflicted look. Adam met his gaze with one of intense desperation. "Go now or Independence falls tonight!"

Nodding his head, Droven leaped to his feet and scurried back toward his solo-rider. Bullets pulverized the piece of ground he had vacated. He jumped onto the machine, and it sped away, spraying loose gravel behind it. Adam turned back toward the gate to see that a few of the men had reached the entrance and had penetrated the wall. Just then, Adam felt a cold, shocking sensation in his left side just above the hip. The cold turned viciously hot as he looked down to see Marshal

Marbury's outstretched hand retracting a now dark-red steel blade.

Adam's body seized up as the new wound throbbed. He retched, and a foul taste of bile mixed with warm, salty blood filled his mouth. He rolled onto his side, writhing in agony. After a moment, he became still. The intensity of the pain began to subside. It was replaced with an icy chill that swept like a wave over his entire body. He lay still, his face toward the open gate. He began blinking rapidly to clear his vision as something near the gate caught his attention. He struggled to focus. A moment before his eyes closed, his mind registered what he was seeing—two familiar men, both in business suits, walking side by side behind the armed unit of police agents.

Adam closed his eyes and a hundred different images flooded into his mind all at once—his mother's face, Droven in a helmet and shoulder pads, his Aunt Esther and Uncle Paul laughing together, Melena's deep blue eyes closing as she leaned in to kiss him. Suddenly, it all went black, and everything was silent. Then, from a distance, a man dressed all in white moved slowly toward him through the blackness. As he approached, his face came into focus.

"Dad?" Adam called to the man.

"Son," Adam's father answered.

"What is this? Have I passed through the veil?" Adam wondered.

"No, Son; your time is not yet."

The sound of his father's voice filled Adam with warmth and comfort. His face was that of a young man's, and it radiated with a glorious light.

Adam tried to see beyond where his father stood. "Where are Mom and Anna and Jacob and Joseph? Are they with you?"

"They are here. They are happy."

"Can I stay with you, Dad?"

His father smiled. “Adam, you have work to do, Son.”

Adam’s heart ached. “I miss you, Dad. All of you.”

“I know, Son. We will be together soon enough. For now, your place is in mortality. You will live to serve mankind. Be diligent, be faithful, and your life will be a great blessing to many.”

Adam paused to let his father’s words sink in. “I’ll do whatever is required of me. Just let me be with you a while longer.”

His father smiled again as he began to fade back. “Open your eyes, Adam.”

“But, Dad …”

“Son, open your eyes.”

Obediently, Adam’s eyes fluttered open. As they came into focus, he saw the gate. It was closed. He rolled onto his back and turned his face skyward. Above him, one bright flash of a blue strand was followed by another. The flashes were slowly rippling back in the direction of the wall. Adam propped himself up onto his right elbow as his hearing returned in crescendo. Pops from gunfire sounded in the distance. His eyes followed a loud buzzing sound to a Hummingbird hovering just inside the wall. A dozen rope ladders dangled from it as it descended toward fifteen or sixteen Federal Police agents below. The agents were engaged in a firefight with Independence Sheriff’s Deputies and security forces.

A limping figure with a white tube in his hand was making his way toward one of the dangling ladders. Adam pushed himself up onto his knees, focusing on the tube in the hand of the retreating Marshal. Stumbling to his feet, he staggered forward, nearly falling. As if injected into him, the familiar fire of indignation he had drawn on before returned and washed from his chest out to his extremities, penetrating his bones. Jaw set and eyes locked on his target, his steps steadied, and he began picking up speed. The Marshal was only a few yards away from a rope ladder. Adam glanced upward. The grid was closing in. The Hummingbird pilot must have detected it as well because the craft began to lift with the remaining police agents clinging to the ladders below it. Marshal Marbury reached the ladder and jumped up, grabbing hold of the lowest rung with his right hand, the white tube still clutched in his left. He swung back and forth as the craft gradually gained altitude.

Adam lowered his head and surged forward, barely feeling his feet hit the ground as he covered the remaining forty yards in less than a second. The velocity nearly propelled him into flight as he planted his left foot and vaulted himself toward the Marshal's boots dangling nearly twelve feet off of the ground. The fingers of Adam's right hand found the toe of Marbury's left boot and clamped down. The Marshal, alarmed by the sudden increase in weight, nearly lost his grip on the ladder. He dropped the plastic tube and grabbed onto the rung with both hands. Adam snatched the tube with his left hand as it was falling past him. Marshal Marbury looked down at Adam and then beyond him at the diminishing space between the grid and the city wall. He began thrashing, trying to shake Adam off. Adam held on, trying desperately not to fall onto the grid closing in below him. The Hummingbird hovered directly over the wall as the Marshal pressed the tread of his free boot down onto Adam's fingers. Adam gripped the tube tightly with his left hand as the fingertips of his right hand slid off of the toe of the Marshal's boot.

It felt utterly surreal as Adam free-fell in what seemed like slow motion. He saw a blue strand flash just inches above his face as the grid reactivated above him. The sudden reduction in weight from Adam's fall caused Marbury to lose his grip on the ladder. Adam watched as the Marshal's body hit the grid and was thrown over the wall. It was the last thing he saw before everything went dark.

Chapter 54

Melena peered through the small window of the armored vehicle she and Jivvy were riding in and marveled at the wave of blue strands moving across the sky over the city. In the distance, she could see a Hummingbird hovering over an open field just inside the wall. Below it, tiny flashes of light broke through the darkness, accompanied, after a short delay, by sharp pops. A firefight had erupted between the Federal Police Agents who had made it through the gate before Adam and Droven had gotten it closed and the Independence Sheriff's Department.

As the vehicle approached the scene, Melena could see that the police agents were suspended off of the ground somehow. The flashing blue strands were closing in on the Hummingbird's location. The hovering aircraft began to lift in order to avoid coming in contact with the approaching grid. The flood lights from the three armored vehicles that had come to assist the deputies, including the one carrying Melena and Jivvy, illuminated the fight. Melena could see that the police agents were hanging from rope ladders that had been lowered from the bottom of the Hummingbird. As the Hummingbird ascended above the grid, Melena noticed that the popping noises from the weapons became infrequent and then stopped. She supposed it was because there was no point in trying to fire through the grid from above.

Jivvy leaned over Melena and pointed out the window. "Look at that. There's a guy hanging from another guy's foot."

Melena strained to see what Jivvy was pointing at, and then she saw it. Two men dangled at the bottom of one of the ladders, with one of the men holding onto the other's foot with one hand. The man holding onto the ladder was desperately trying to shake the other man off. The Hummingbird rose above the retracting grid, but just before it reached the wall, the two men fell. The one who had been holding onto the other's foot fell through the small space next to the wall where the grid had not yet reached and landed on the ground on his back. The other man fell onto the grid and appeared to bounce off it and was sent, flailing, over the edge of the wall. A huge blue ring flashed all along the perimeter of the wall, signaling that the grid had sealed itself safely back over Independence.

Melena watched the deputies emerge from their places of cover and rush to the bodies of the fallen police agents, including the one who had fallen from the Hummingbird's rope ladder. Melena squinted as she sifted through the deputies with her eyes, searching for a familiar form.

"Droven, do you have a visual on Adam?" Jivvy asked through her coms. Melena turned to watch Jivvy's face for a response. After a few seconds, she shook her head. "The last Droven saw of him, he was near the gate, but he's not there now. Droven's looking."

"He's not answering on his coms?" Melena asked.

Jivvy just shook her head, a look of deep concern in her eyes.

The vehicle reached the scene of the fire fight and skidded to a stop. Melena stepped out as two medics rushed past her. One of them carried a long, flat board with handles around the edges. "He's one of ours," Melena heard one medic tell the other. Jivvy turned to look at them. She had obviously overheard the same phrase. Melena fell in step behind the two medics. Her heart raced as she considered the possible implications.

A small group had formed around a still figure lying on the ground next to the wall. Melena pushed her way to the front of the group. Her hand flew to her mouth as she recognized the blood-smeared and dirt-stained face of the man on the ground. She instantly fell to her knees beside him. "Adam!" she cried out. His face went out of focus as her eyes clouded with tears.

She reached out to touch his face, but one of the medics caught her by the wrist. "Don't touch him. His neck is broken."

Melena turned to the medic, surprise registering on her face. "He's alive?"

The medic nodded. "Yeah, he's alive, but he's in pretty bad shape."

"Adam!" Melena cried again. She wanted so much to hold him. He looked lifeless lying there in the dirt, and she felt completely helpless kneeling beside him.

One of the medics gently took her by the shoulders. "We need you to move back, miss." He helped her to her feet, but Melena's eyes never left Adam. For the first time, she noticed a cylinder tucked tightly to his body with his left hand over it. His left forearm was mangled and bloody. The plastic cylinder was covered in dark red smears, and a jagged crack ran down the length of it. The medic pulled Melena a few steps back and then knelt down next to Adam. He carefully pried Adam's fingers one by one off the cylinder until it came loose. He held it out to Melena. She absently took it from his hands and watched him attend to Adam.

Only when the other medics had closed in around Adam, blocking Melena's view of him, did she look down at the object in her hand. One of the end caps had come off and the large crack in the plastic partially revealed its contents. The yellowed documents inside piqued her curiosity. She gently slid the documents out of the cylinder. The upper left corner of the document on the top was stained with Adam's fresh blood. Her eyes moved down to the large hand-written calligraphy—"*We The People*", she read. The size of the characters became smaller and the ink had faded to the point that she could barely make out the cursive text. She squinted and brought the document closer to her face. "*... of the United States, in Order to form a more perfect Union, establish Justice, insure domestic Tranquility, provide for the common defense, promote the general Welfare, and secure the Blessings of Liberty to ourselves and our Posterity, do ordain and establish this Constitution for the United States of America.*"

She skimmed over the rest of the page and the next three pages behind it, which appeared to belong together. The fourth page had another large, hand-written heading—"*Congress of the United States*", again followed by smaller print, "*begun and held at the city of New-York, on Wednesday the fourth of March, one thousand seven hundred and eighty nine.*" The final document in the stack also had a pronounced heading—"*In CONGRESS, July 4th, 1776. The Unanimous Declaration of the thirteen united States of America.*" She skimmed this page as well until her eye caught one distinct, beautifully penned signature below the contents of the document that was slightly larger than the others—*John Hancock.*

Melena became aware of someone looking over her shoulder. She turned to see Peter Gildrich staring at the documents in her hands with an awed look on his face. He moved to stand in front of her. "Can I take those from you, please, Melena?"

Melena felt dazed. "Yeah, of course," she almost whispered. She held the ancient documents out to Peter. He looked as if he were taking a newborn infant from her arms. He gently lifted the stack of curled documents out of Melena's hands with the tips of his fingers and held them out in front of him.

Peter looked up at her, thoughtfully. "Adam very nearly gave his life to preserve these." His lip quivered. "And I'm sure he knew that it was likely that he would when he decided to go after them."

Melena looked down at the documents and then up at Peter. “Originals?” she asked.

Peter smiled and nodded once before turning and walking carefully toward one of the armored vehicles.

Melena became confused when she turned to see Jivvy standing a few paces away, her face a combination of fury and agony. “What an idiot!” she blurted out through gritted teeth. Melena just looked at her, but Jivvy wouldn’t make eye contact. She fought to mask her emotions, but it was obvious to Melena that the dam was about to burst. “We have replicas and transcripts.” Her green eyes glistened in the artificial light coming from every direction. Despite her best efforts to hold them back, the tears spilled over and streamed down her cheeks. She pounded her clenched fists together and glanced back in Adam’s direction. “You should’ve just let them go!”

Without saying a word, Melena stepped forward and wrapped her arms around her little sister’s neck. Jivvy’s sobs racked her body as Melena held her close. Eventually, Jivvy lifted her arms and returned the embrace. Melena cried too, but hers were not tears of sorrow, but of gratitude. She closed her eyes and offered a silent prayer—thanking God for sparing Adam’s life. She felt a quiet peace and somehow knew that everything would be all right.

Epilogue

Adam felt as though he were in some sort of tunnel. Bright gold light seemed to swirl before him in a sort of conduit. The light began opening up around him and increased in intensity. Simultaneously, Adam's auditory faculties began to escalate beyond a comfortable level. He cringed at the deep thud of a heart beating. An annoying electronic beep seemed to echo inside of his skull. He heard the muted sounds of voices and general commotion somewhere in the distance. Slowly, his eyelids lifted slightly and then shut tightly. The light was so blinding, his eyes couldn't possibly shut tightly enough to block it out.

"Hey, there he is," a deep voice boomed in Adam's ears. He wanted to reach up and cover them with his hands. His brain commanded his hands to rise, but for some reason they did not comply. Once the pain of the loud noise subsided, Adam realized that he recognized the voice. It was Droven.

"Droven?" Adam tried to whisper. It came out as little more than a croak. His throat felt as though he had swallowed sand paper.

"Yeah, man, it's me."

Adam cringed at the booming sound of Droven's voice. "Whisper, please."

"Yeah. Sorry," Droven whispered, not seeming to need an explanation. Adam heard him stand up and walk across the floor. Suddenly the light on the other side of Adam's eyelids diminished in brightness. "Is that better for your eyes?" Droven whispered. Adam heard a click, and the light subsided even further. Droven must have darkened the window, he decided. Adam let his eyelids pull open. It took a moment to focus. The objects in the room had a green tint to them because of the darkness. He made out a door across the room with a sliver of light spilling out from underneath it. His eyes moved across the room until they reached the face of his friend. Droven smiled.

"That's better. Thanks." Adam tried to clear his throat. It sounded more like a cough. "Where are we, man?"

"Medical Center in Independence."

"Why?" Adam asked, puzzled.

"Cause you can't fly."

"What?"

"You must have thought you could fly. You held onto Marbury's boot until you were higher than the wall. I fully expected you to take flight when you let go, but I guess there are some limitations to your superpowers."

Adam was thoroughly confused. Something Droven had said sounded familiar, but he didn't know why. It seemed like he had been dreaming about falling. He thought he had dreamed about blue strands of light shooting across the sky as well.

"Do you remember, Adam?" Droven whispered. "Do you remember what happened?"

Adam tried to focus on the garbled images that swam through his mind, but he was distracted by the strange sensation of not being able to control his arms or legs. It reminded him of being in the lab with Melena and Hava and having the collar that they put around his neck activated. He felt his chin resting on something. "What's around my neck?" he asked.

Droven leaned in and examined Adam's neck. "It's a brace to keep your head stationary."

Adam's eyebrows pulled together. "Oh, good. I thought maybe I was wearing one of the collars they put on me at the lab."

Droven looked confused.

"I can't move," Adam whispered.

Droven pressed his lips together tightly, his face growing somber. "Yeah, I know, man." He looked away and then down at the floor.

"What is it?" Adam asked.

Droven hesitated before answering. "Do you remember chasing after Marshal Marbury?"

Adam considered that for a moment. Like a puzzle, images and events began to come together in his mind. He remembered a white plastic tube. His heart jumped. "The tube! Marbury had a tube! It was the Constitution and the Bill of Rights and the Declaration of Independence!"

Droven put his hand on Adam's arm, but Adam couldn't feel it. "I know, I know. You got them. You got them back. We have them. They're safe now."

Adam was having trouble getting his memories into sequence, but they were starting to come back. "Yeah … yeah, he dropped them, and I caught them. They're safe now?"

"Yeah." Droven nodded. "You were amazing. You ran him down and got them back."

Adam felt himself relax, though he was still confused.

"Marbury was hanging on a rope ladder from a Hummingbird, and you jumped up and caught his foot. Do you remember that?" He went on without waiting for a response. "The Hummingbird got pretty high, and Marbury dropped the tube, and you caught it, but then you fell. Do you remember that?"

Adam smiled. "I thought I dreamed that. I guess I kinda remember the feeling of falling."

Droven lowered his voice as much as he could and spoke slowly. "Yeah, you were up there pretty high, and you couldn't hold onto Marbury's boot anymore and, uh … you fell."

"I did?"

"Yeah, you did." Droven looked back down at the floor. "You fell a long way, man … and when you hit the ground … uh, you, uh …" He exhaled loudly through his nose. "You broke your neck." His glistening eyes finally looked up and met Adam's. "That's why you can't move, Adam."

Adam's heart instantly sank in his chest. He tried to swallow, but his throat was too tight. He just stared at his friend in disbelief.

"I'm so sorry," Droven whispered, his own agony evident in his expression.

"Right here, sir," a female voice directed from outside the door. Abruptly, light from the hallway poured into the room as the door swung open. Adam instinctively closed his eyes, but found that the sensitivity was wearing off. He was starting to control his senses, the way he had learned to do before.

Two figures strode into the room. "There's our man," a man's voice thundered.

"Sir, if you could keep your voice down—Adam's ears are a little sensitive," Droven explained.

"Of course," Mr. Kent complied. "Sorry about that. We just wanted to drop in and see how you were doing, Adam."

Adam looked at Mr. Kent, then at the slender, older man next to him, but didn't respond. Something about Louis Green troubled him.

"He just woke up a few minutes before you got here, sir," Droven explained. "We were just discussing his condition."

Mr. Kent nodded, slowly. "I see. I'm very sorry, Adam. I'm sure this is quite a shock to you."

Mr. Green turned to address Droven. "Does he remember what happened the night of the … accident?"

"Not clearly right now, but it's starting to come back in pieces."

Adam didn't take his eyes off Mr. Green. An image flashed through his mind. A gate in the wall of Independence stood open. Senator Cai Jaxon and another man—this man—were walking toward the opening. Adam flinched. Mr. Green was with Senator Jaxon and an advancing police force coming to invade the city, he recalled. Louis Green was a traitor! Adam felt his face turn cold. Still, he said nothing.

"Well, son, your service to our people is commendable, and we thank you for your sacrifice," Mr. Kent offered in a low voice. He nodded at Adam, then at Droven, then both men turned and left the room.

"Can you shut the door?" Adam asked. Droven rose and pushed the door shut. "It was him, Droven. Green is responsible for the invasion."

"What?" Droven asked, incredulous.

"I saw him. Coming through the gate from the outside with Cai Jaxon, right after you went to close the gate."

"Are you sure, man? Maybe you need some time to clear your head a little and—"

"I'm sure," Adam interrupted. "As sure as I am of anything. That's why he wanted to know what I remembered. He's not sure if he was seen."

Droven's eyes narrowed. "If you're right, that would explain how Marbury got access to the founding documents and to the city's security."

"I'm right," Adam assured him. "We need to be careful with what we do with this information. We can't just …"

Adam heard two sets of footsteps outside the door, and then it swung open again. Jivvy and Melena were chatting back and forth, unaware of Adam's consciousness. Jivvy tapped the light control on the wall. "Why is it so dark in here?"

Droven got up from his chair and headed toward the door. "Turn it off. Adam's eyes need it dark," he whispered as urgently as he could.

"It's okay, Droven; they're getting better. Just leave it so they can adjust." Adam blinked his eyes rapidly as he tried to open them and focus his vision.

"Adam!" Melena exclaimed. Adam heard the soles of her boots click against the tile floor as she ran toward him.

"He's awake?" Jivvy asked.

Adam felt a warm hand on his forehead, brushing his hair back. He squinted and tried to focus his eyes. After a moment, he could make out each wrinkle and sparkle on a pair of full, lavender-shaded lips. His eyes moved north and found two wide, deep-ocean-blue eyes. The lips weren't smiling, but the eyes were.

"Hey," Melena's gentle voice sounded like silk.

Adam smiled. "Hey."

"How are you?"

"Good now."

Melena chuckled. "Me too."

"So, Adam," Jivvy interrupted, stepping to Melena's side. "I have some good news."

"Well, I would certainly welcome that, Jivvissa."

"I have engineering working on a modified Chameleon that can be controlled by facial muscles," Jivvy reported. "Don't think you're retiring, okay."

Adam smiled, but couldn't quite get himself to laugh. "Okay."

Jivvy went on talking about other things Adam would still be able to do, but Adam stopped listening. Unexpectedly, he made an interesting discovery. His heart skipped a beat with excitement. He interrupted Jivvy's scheming. "Would you guys excuse Melena and me for a few minutes?"

"Sure." Droven put his hand on Jivvy's back and urged her toward the door. "Come on, Jivvy."

"Okay. We'll talk about this later." Jivvy waved over her shoulder.

When the door shut behind them, Melena resumed stroking Adam's cheeks and head. "My mom told me about an apartment two buildings down from the rehab center where they're going to take you. I want to get moved in as soon as possible." A slight movement and rustle of the sheet near the foot of the bed seemed to catch her attention, briefly, but she dismissed it and continued. "I'm taking some time off of work so I can come and be with you during the day …" she trailed off, and Adam smiled as another movement caught her attention and caused her to gape at the sheet covering his feet. "What was that?"

Adam's smile grew as his fingers slowly travelled across the six inches that separated their hands. "Melena," he whispered. Her eyes widened in disbelief as she felt him grip her fingers and squeeze, ever so slightly.

Acknowledgements

No person deserves more of my thanks than my beautiful wife, Megan, for enduring my late night writing, and constant rambling. Thanks also to my four sweet children, Leah, Haylie, Caden and Layla, for their love of reading, and for cheering me on. Thanks to Mom, Dad, and Ashley for reading my manuscript, and helping me to shape this story.

My sincerest thanks to Melinda Frederickson for the many hours spent editing, proofreading, and ensuring consistency and continuity. Thanks to Lee Guile for the spectacular cover design and artwork.

Lastly—and most significantly—thanks to my Heavenly Father and to my Savior, Jesus Christ, for allowing me to experience mortality with the hope of eternal life.

Made in the USA
San Bernardino, CA
25 March 2020

66359062R00197